RESUЯЯECTION

BORIS JOHNSON

For, and forever, the boss.

RESUЯЯECTION

Monday July 6th 2020

I can't remember the nurses' names, but they are without a shadow of doubt the most important people in my life. I wouldn't have my world without them. And this is where the story starts - three months after them immigrants saved my good old British bacon.

It's been a gruelling 90 days. Covid-19 is indeed a bugger. It's like an awful partner, you think she's gone and then suddenly you end up back in bed with it. I haven't shown my face much for the last few months, I have a baby of course as an excuse, but that's what it is and will always be, an excuse. The real reason is I'm tired, or as Dominic says to me sometimes, 'Boss, you're knackered'. He doesn't call me 'boss' of course, he'd never do that, he's talking to himself. Dominic Cummings refers to himself in the third person and calls himself 'boss'. And he tells himself he's knackered, constantly, but the great thing about Dommers is he keeps going. As George Galloway MP once said to Saddam Hussein, 'mate, you're indefatigable'. And Dominic, if he's anything, is exactly the same as Saddam Hussein. I'm a different beast entirely to Cummings/Hussein, I get tired easily. My wife, rather uncharitably, has a pet name for me – she calls me 'fatty', and she's got a point, I haven't got the strength to go on sometimes, so instead of fighting back I just eat another raisin and biscuit Yorkie. But even if I wasn't lazy, I reckon Covid-19 would have sent me packing. It really is a big piece of shit.

And straight off the bat I want to apologise for the 100,000 deaths in the UK (I'm estimating this of course in advance for the time of reading) - each and every one is a tragedy. I think what we can all agree though is not a single death is my fault. If I had died, sure, that would have been my fault. I admit it now, going around in early March shaking people's hands in hospitals at the very time when community transmissions were probably at their highest was in retrospect a huge gaff. But, as the saying goes, if your auntie had bollocks she'd be your uncle. It's very easy to say something and for it to appear true. If your auntie had bollocks she wouldn't be your uncle, I bow to JK Rowling on this point, she'd still very much be your auntie. Just because something appears definitely to be the case, it often sometimes isn't. To some it appeared absolutely nuts to be going around hospitals shaking hands with all the coughing and critically ill patients, but to me, certainly at the time, I couldn't see anything wrong with it, and that's why I did it. It's so easy isn't it after you've done something to not do it, but that's sadly impossible. For example, the last time I appeared on *Have I Got News For You* and I was getting a particularly savage grilling from Ian Hislop; it was days later that I thought I should have just told him to 'shut the fuck up'. It would have got a huge laugh, and would have had the added bonus of getting Ian Hislop to shut the fuck up.

But you can't go back in time, as Michael J Fox will tell you, and so here I am in early July 2020 convalescing in Number 10, still full of Covid regret and a house full of a crying baby. My father Stanley has gone to Greece the lucky bastard, and I'm sitting here, half watching the telly while writing this, trying to work out where we go next. Nobody seems to know. Not even Matty Hancock. 'The Cock' has I call him (with lashings of affection) has been an absolute superstar during this whole thing. He did probably one in two of the Daily Government Briefings and some mornings when I told him he was up again, he'd sometimes look at me and you could tell he was thinking 'You're taking the piss Boris', because he'd often say those very words. But he would never complain when he was on television, he just got on with it. And not even The Cock knows where we go from here. So where do we go from here? Greece!! Let's hope to God it's Greece. I love Greece. I wanted to become Prime Minister because I thought it would make me happy, but I now know what makes me happy is eating pineapple handed to me by an immigrant on a beach in Zante. Shit – A - Brick. Where's that bloody Delorean when you need it?

This is a mess, and when things are a mess I know I just make things worse. I never used to tidy my room as a kid, one reason for that is we had literally an army of cleaners, but the other reason was when things are in a real mess, making them even more of a mess doesn't actually seem that bad. I was in such a state the other day that I said, actually out loud on television 'The care homes didn't really follow procedures and that's why so many old people died'. I would say I regret that now, I can hear those two nurses who saved my life now… 'You're blaming the nurses for people dying Boris!!' But the truth be told, I was knackered, they'd sent me out to the arse end of nowhere at 6am, stuck a silly high-viz jacket on me and slapped me in front of a fork-lift and the whole thing is a mess and I thought well I'll just say anything it won't be any more of a mess. As Priti might say, I'm sorry if you felt that was wrong, I'm sorry if you think I'm the bad guy, but more than anything I'm sorry I have to get up so early. That's what killed dear old Margaret Thatcher of course, lack of sleep. She bragged for years about getting away with only having 4 hours sleep and then one day her body crumbled like Imhotep. I'd function a lot better and there would be far fewer gig-gaffs from me if I was just allowed to stay in bed. That's the first thing Dominic said when he came to visit me in hospital actually, he said 'well at least you won't be able to fuck anything up right now boss'. He was of course talking to himself but you know what I mean.

Tuesday July 7th 2020

The whole apology thing is a funny one isn't it, when you screw up as a Government people are obsessed with you saying 'sorry'. Good old Sir Elton John once sung 'sorry seems to be the hardest word' but I've never heard him apologise for all the drugs he took in the 70s or the Made in England album which was shite. 'Are you going to say sorry Prime Minister?' 'Will you say sorry Prime Minister?' 'Say sorry Boris or I'm leaving you and taking the kid'. Well, news-flash ok, news-flash. I'll tell you what saying sorry does – fuck all. Think about it, how many lives would saying sorry have saved? Fuck all. How many jobs would saying sorry have saved, jack shit. It would have probably cost jobs more than anything, as once you've said sorry then people think you're admitting culpability and then people have to resign. And the last thing the country needs with everyone losing their jobs is those people clever enough to have jobs resigning. Of course I'm sorry when things go wrong, of course I'm sorry when things go South, when care homes don't follow procedures and so on and so forth but what good does saying 'sorry' do really? If I had to say sorry every time something fucked up, I'd be saying 'sorry' about a thousand times a day, and where would that get us? Exactly the same place but with a slightly different headline. Instead of '30,000 care home deaths' it would say 'PM says sorry for 30,000 care home deaths'. Spot the difference between those two headlines? There isn't one – 30,000 people still died in care homes, and me saying 'sorry' saves not one of those lives, I'm sorry. I mean I'm not sorry but you know what I mean.

This isn't about looking back, it's about looking forward. The time for looking back is not now. It's in 100 years' time when we're all dead. We'll all be dead before long so let's all look forward to a brighter future. Summer's round the corner and the weather this weekend is looking top notch. Not as hot as Greece perhaps but still fab. The pubs are open for Christ's sake. And I know what you're thinking, 'You're the Prime Minister there's no way you can just go to the pub!' Well my friends, you couldn't be more wrong, I spent virtually the whole day in the pub yesterday in fact. That's probably why I'm feeling so knackered! Beautiful old pub round the corner from Downing Street, The Red Lion. Historical, gorgeous, lashings of lovely cold beer and delicious gin. I know the landlord there and I bung him a few quid (don't say I do nothing for small businesses!) to save me my favourite table, downstairs right in the corner away from prying eyes. It often gets a bit claustrophobic down there actually in the Summer so on my way to the toilets (which are upstairs) I often nip outside to the few outside tables and say 'hello' to everyone. And you know the funny thing, no one believes I'm me, they say 'you look nothing like him'. Ha ha! And most times I don't, I'll have just woken up, hair everywhere and when I'm half-cut my face has more of a rouge so they literally look at me like I'm just some nutcase pretending to be the Prime Minister. It's what I say to everyone, it's perhaps my biggest and best piece of advice to anyone who is in the public eye or maybe has committed a serious crime – hide in plain sight. It's what dear old Osama Bin Laden did of course and he got away with it for years, and I swear to Allah, if OBL instead of hiding in that house had just wandered the street of Pakistan going in all the pubs and shouting 'Hey everyone I'm only Osama Bin Bloody Laden' he'd still be alive today, the whole community would have just thought he was the local crack-head or maybe Russell Brand pulling one of his infamously shit pranks.

I'm often at my most lucid when I'm rat-arsed, I guess like dear old Sir Elton John wrote all his best stuff when he was off his tits, and then wrote Made in England when he was sober, it's really no surprise it was toss. No one makes a good decision sober, well it might be a good decision but will be a safe, boring decision. All my best ideas come when I'm pissed. I wouldn't be where I am today unless I got roaring drunk once in a while every couple of days, I'd be knocking on the door rather than feet up in Number 10, sipping on all the alcohol they can send me. And I had a great decision late last night, start writing a book, a diary. Prime Ministers' diaries sell for millions once they've fucked up one too many times. Start a diary and chart my and this country's resurrection post Covid-19. And there will be no hiding places in this book, no bullshit, that's what I decided yesterday. If you read Tony Blair's diaries (which I haven't) they will be full of 'oh new Labour was brilliant', 'oh Britpop, Noel Gallagher and me used to do pot', and it's all bullshit to cover up for the fact that he killed millions of Iraqis looking for weapons or gold that was never there. Here, you're getting warts and all, the whole truth. And the truth is I wrote the first entry when I pissed last night and I'm writing the second entry when I'm hungover this morning. But my roaring headache doesn't drown out the angels that visited me last night and gave me this wonderful idea – to record our collective come-back, our way out of this monumental shit-show. Welcome to your resurrection! My plan is to chart every day of a glorious resurrection until the deal is signed with the EU on or before October 15th. That's three and half months of writing; if nothing else it will give me an incentive to get the deal done sooner with the dear old EU (or of course fuck them off before then) as I completely hate writing. Such a bloody effort. I prefer consuming than producing. If only the UK could do a trade deal with me - I'd just buy the lot! Anyway, so this is the plan - every day you'll get a juicy update from me until or around October 15th when this country's perfect, oven-ready

Resurrection will be complete. And on that note, I shall see you tomorrow, I'm back off to bed and then down the pub again. 'Oh that idiot is dancing around saying he's Boris Johnson! What a pissed idiot.' You're the idiot mate, you're the prick who just missed out on a selfie with the Big Cahuna.

Wednesday July 8th 2020

I was slightly tanked up at PMQ's today. I don't really like drinking before work but since my resurrection I'll always have one or two just to give me that extra bounce of energy. I pay for it later of course, by about 3pm I'm about as useful as a chocolate toilet, but at around midday I'm feeling that buzz of the 'gin high' and I was ready to attack PMQ's today with renewed gusto. And although I say so myself, I'm back on form. Kier is hardly the most dangerous opponent bless him, he looks like Le Chiffre from that Bond Film but acts like Hannibal Lecter has injected him with opioids and sliced half his brain away. It was, if I may be so bold, a crackling performance from me, only marred slightly when I groped around for a slogan to finish things off and ended up blurting out 'Build build build, jobs jobs jobs' – that one's not going to trouble the greatest slogan writers of all time, but as soon as I said it I thought 'oh shit, we're going to have to keep it otherwise I look like a prick'. It's almost as bad as that Boots the Chemist one, 'Who cares?'. We laughed our heads off at that. Who cares?! Brilliant. I should have said that to my father today when he phoned up to tell me what a great time he's having in Greece. Who cares?! Honestly, the last thing you want to be told about is someone having a good time, particularly when it's family – he literally called me from a beach, what a tosser. Anyway, talking about slogans, dear old Rishi announced the 'build build build, jobs jobs jobs' thing and it shut the opposition up for a bit, 'ooh you should have done something before now' they wailed. Yeah I don't know if you noticed love but a few weeks ago I was dead, and whilst I was not on a ventilator and anywhere near death I could have died, and despite that, not two months later here I am, back at the dispatch box making Le Chiffre look like politics answer to Mr Ben, and then

9

dear old Rishi drills them against the wall with the 'eat out to help out voucher'. Take that you shits.

It was Dominic of course that came up with the 'eat out to help out voucher'. I mean he is good, he's bloody annoying but he's bloody good, I of course wouldn't keep him on if he wasn't good. I'm never letting him in front of the cameras again though – 'ooh I drove to Durham to test my eye-sight'. I don't say this without great thought but what a twat, I mean goodness talking about sending us a hospital pass. And for weeks all that Kuntsberg could go on about was 'driving to Durham to test your eyes would you advise that Prime Minister?'. Alright sarcy, Jesus, we all know it was bullshit can we just move on please? And they didn't move on, until a few weeks later when Dominic came up with the slogan 'Time to move on'. Fuck he's good. I reckon if I killed a prostitute he'd get me out of it with a slogan, something like 'Let's all forget about the Prime Minister murdering that prostitute.' Oh I don't know, not that but something like it, Dominic is the genius in such affairs, I'm shit at slogans. And yet still I wouldn't have come up with 'Who cares?' We really did laugh about that – 'Boots, who gives a fuck?'

So the devil's in the detail of course, and I came up with the detail on the 'eat out to help out' thing. It's basically half price nosh on Mondays, Tuesdays and Wednesdays during August. The genius of it is that no one goes out for dinner on Mondays, Tuesdays and Wednesdays apart from the wealthy and the scum, and the wealthy don't use vouchers as it's beneath us and for the scum their meals are like 99p or something so it really won't cost us much. Maximum publicity for minimum spend is really the secret of politics or just about anything. And I use the word 'scum' affectionately of course, don't get the cancel police on me! I mean scum in the sweetest possible way. People in my constituency, the great and the good of the glorious London Borough of Hillingdon pride themselves on being scum. Many of them have never even been to central London even though they are technically on a tube line. They delight in the fact they are different, they appreciate having nothing because wealthy people are, to them, scum. That's right, we think they are scum and they think we're scum, so it really does level out. The problem with their kind of scum though is there is a lot of drinking on street corners, drug-taking, low-level prostitution and the like (I could bloody kill them!!) and so it's no surprise that in Hillingdon today there was a spike in Corona cases and we had to close the emergency section of our beautiful local hospital. Not a huge problem of course – the local crack heads will just have to treat their own chlamydia for a few days.

Now I rarely go to Hillingdon of course, but I'm told the hospital really is the crown jewels in the Tower of Shite that is Hillingdon so this is very sad, but not wholly unexpected, scum have never been able to follow simple instructions, they can't even spell social distancing without being stuffed full of cocaine. And some people will say it's a poverty thing but really it's a brain thing – is it any coincidence that the two areas of the UK to have Corona spikes so far, Leicester and Hillingdon, are inhabited, to a great degree, with scum? There hasn't been a spike in cases in Chelsea has there? (Apart from Chelsea hospital of course when apart from me some people really haven't been strong enough bless them). Well the bottom line is now we are there for those people (not the dead ones but everyone else). We are here for the poor and the vulnerable but more than anything else we are here to take 50% off of your £9.99 spicy chicken trough-meal at Nando's. Because we care. Our resurrection won't happen in isolation. It will happen because we the Government work hard and you the people have half price peri peri chicken wings and shut the fuck up. And if you don't shut up, remember these two wisest of words – 'Who cares?' Ha ha ha, I really do fucking love that. Big fat LOL.

Thursday July 9th 2020

So we updated the 'build, build, build, jobs, jobs, jobs' shite to #PlanForJobs. I say we, you know who did. He loves the rule of three does Dominic, everything has to be in threes, but that's enough about his sex life! It's like Brexit means Brexit, that's the classic. So powerful, but at the same time so utterly meaningless. And the particular genius of #PlanForJobs is that we can all plan for everything and not have to actually do anything. It's like when we all planned our revision timetable as kids and didn't actually do any revision, because we didn't have to, the exam results were rigged in my school anyway. #PlanForJobs – I love it! What did you do Prime Minister? We 'planned for jobs'. Did you deliver any new jobs? Read the small print Columbo, I didn't actually say we were gonna. Genius. I do love a good three word slogan, the rule of three has been used throughout history. Dear old Angus Deayton once talked to me about it when I was on *Have I Got News For You* ages back. He said it was an old comedy trope, you know, give the dumb audience a list of three things and make the third thing the funny thing and they all go mental. Like for example ladies and gentlemen please welcome to the stage - Ian Hislop, Paul Merton and Boris Johnson! I've never understood comedy really, I mean I understand it but I don't think it's particularly good. Being funny isn't really a job is it? I have a job, and I'm funny, they are separate things. Being funny can't really be called a job. It's like darts isn't really a sport, Hillingdon isn't really a place. Don't get me wrong I love the great entertainers, Sinatra, Jimmy Saville, Benny Hill but they were more than just comedians, there were sketches and songs and I know it's not PC to say it now, but godamit there were titties! What I'm saying is there was more than one jumped-up prick like Ian Hislop churning out verbal sick on an audience that they lap up because they're morons, but actually what he's saying would at best only just pass for mildly amusing conversation down some very backward private members club. Dear old Rishi showed me something this morning, there's something trending on twitter, not #PlanForJobs sadly but #SaveLiveComedy, the old rule of three in work yet again I see, but other than that, this, my friends, is bullshit. Save Live Comedy? Don't make me laugh! We are saving lives over here mate not live comedy. I mean they say laughter is the best medicine but how many of those dying of Corona would have appreciated me taking them off of their ventilators and wheeling in Ian Hislop to spout some lefty bollocks at them? They'd have been dying before he reached his first shitty 'punch-line'.

RESUЯЯECTION

I'm sorry, but I'm not sorry. In an ideal world of course we'd save all jobs, apart from Ian Hislop's. But I think we're all in agreement that stand-up comedians are at the very bottom of the list of jobs we need to save right now. We need doctors, nurses, food on our tables, cleaners in our houses, I could go on for hours before I said… and then we need someone prancing around the stage telling us how funny garlic bread is. If people need a laugh, and of course they do, just turn on the television and watch *Family Fortunes*. I'd have to live until I was 103 before I could watch all the old episodes of *Family Fortunes*. One time Les Dennis asked 'Name a dangerous race' and they said 'Arabs'. I'm sorry nothing is going to be funnier than that. And that one where they said 'Name something black' and they said 'criminals'. I could have laughed for years at that. So we absolutely do not need to save the jobs of Jeff Unfunny or whatever his name is who is playing to 17 people down at the Laughing Hell-Hole or whatever. That's literally the last thing we need. When Rishi showed me that hashtag #SaveLiveComedy, well good Christ I had a massive laugh, so maybe in a way it achieved its goals.

So what are my goals? Well today I stopped to have a little think and my goodness I shouldn't do that. I usually like flicking from thing to thing, from pub to pub, drink to drink, woman to woman without stopping to think. Because thinking is a dangerous thing. Particularly right now for someone in my position. Because unlike Jeff Twat trying to work out what's hilarious about aeroplane food, I have to work out how to rescue the entire country. And forgive the language but it's fucking daunting. Where on earth do you start? Because I realise I can't spend the next four years hiding behind Dominic's slogans, I mean maybe the next few months but not years. And I just remembered this morning, we've got to do Brexit by the end of the year. Shit a brick. Does anyone have any idea how hard it will be to achieve Brexit? I mean Brexit doesn't actually mean Brexit any more but it's still going to be tricky. And Jeff Dickhead you still want your shitty job back do you? Well Jeff, I've got some advice for you, stick your microphone back in your bottom drawer and start learning some actual skills you prick, like cleaning or slogan writing. And I hear you cry, 'but Prime Minister, there are no jobs!' Bollocks. That's just an excuse that the lazy and the feckless will use. Yes there are no jobs, but my friends, that doesn't stop you planning. #PlanForJobs.

Well forgive me, but the enormity of my task has suddenly got too much for me, so although it's only midday I'm going to pour myself another drink and stick on another episode of *Family Fortunes*! Arabs!! Priceless. And if Jeff Shit-for-brains can beat that punchline, I'll give him the money myself! Ooh PS – just heard Boots has cut 4,000 jobs. Who cares?! (you see, being funny is EASY, and it ain't a job!)

Friday July 10th 2020

So before I get on with saving the country, let me cover quickly the spiky issue of Mark Sedwill and his £250,000 pay off. If you're not aware, and why should you be, these things are pretty boring, Mark was my Cabinet Secretary, and by that I don't mean he was the dolly-bird that typed up my letters and made me tea, I mean he was very important and advised me on, for want of a better word, stuff. Now, some have said that this is a massive amount of money to pay someone who is leaving a job that they have done for less than two years, with some more scurrilous reports suggesting that this is in some ways 'hush money' and 'surely he must have loads of dirt and this is to shut him up'. And I want to answer those allegations in the clearest, unequivocal way – there are simply things that you don't need to know. Really, this kind of stuff does not concern you.

Any old way, looking like a lovely weekend of weather ahead and the important news of yesterday of course was delivered by dear old Oliver Dowden announcing the opening of open-air theatre this weekend (again that's not for me, please see my comments about live comedy above), pools and gyms by the end of the month (I wouldn't be seen dead in either) along with nail bars and tattoo parlours (that's one for you Hillingdon!) and what I'm personally most excited about – orchestras. I love a good orch, and there will be some that say 'oh God that's so elitist', and those people are right, not everyone understands classical music, and that's why along with pressing ahead with plans (#PlanForJobs) for an indoor London Symphony

Orchestra later this year, I also made sure that we added plans for entertainment at the complete other end of the scale - at a Butlins Holiday Camp later this year too. So whilst I and my chums can enjoy the beautiful orchestra at St Luke's Church in the Autumn, the 'scum' (again affectionate) can look forward to seeing the bingo, the egg and spoon and Yogi Clemenbore the contortionist in a caravan park in Rhyl or whatever shit-hole we choose. Something for everyone.

I love Oliver Dowden. He looks like someone that maybe shouldn't exist, but I like him because he's excitable, just like me. I loved his little face as he came through the doors at the Government briefing yesterday, it was like 'Surprise!! Have I got news for you!!' And thank God it wasn't Ian Hislop, a man that constantly looks like Spitting Image has returned, but dear old Oliver, who looks like a beautiful extra in a period drama. He had a lovely tie on yesterday, I chose that for him. It's a little known fact that although I don't do the briefings really at all (why have a monkey and eat monkey shit yourself?) I am however right there, on the other side of the doorway, listening in and sometimes whispering words of encouragement, or if I have to, abuse. But with Oliver it's really just 'hooray' all the way. You enjoy your piss-filled pools and your tattoos of some girl's name that you will despise in three years, I'll enjoy my Mozart and Bach and Russell Watson. I guess I love classical music because I never have to pay to see it and now I'm Prime Minster I'd say it's one of the main perks, that you get to watch a load of people, some of whom have trained for 20 years, to perform for you for nothing. I'd imagine this is what Caesar felt like in the Coliseum when the Gladiators emerged in front of them to kill each other and wrestle the tigers. And whilst we can't do that any more (thank you fucking PC Brigade) what I can do is enjoy Mozart's 5th or whatever and have a good natter and a beer or three with like-minded people. And that's the other thing about Mark Sedwill, he wasn't a like-minded person. And I'm all for a broad church but, and again, there are things you don't need to know, but if you're going to have to work closely with someone all I'll say is you don't want your right hand man to be a Machiavellian sod. Surround yourself with people you like. That's what they taught me at school and it still stands true today, surround yourself with like-minded people and kill everyone else, and if you can't kill them give them £250,000 and shut them up.

I mean look, my final word on this, £250,000 sounds like a lot of money if you're saving up for your latest tattoo or Butlins holiday, but it's all relative isn't it and to me and Mark £250,000 is what is called in my circles 'chump change'. This big dog used to earn £2,300 per day! That's why people don't really need to know about the ins and outs, the machinations of the Government because what goes on, what we have to deal with day to day is really on a totally different level to how the layman operates. The layman was busy this week wasn't he and she, and gender-fluid 'they' my moaning wife keeps asking me to mention (no thank you) - filling in 5 numbers and 2 lucky stars on Euromillions because the jackpot was £127 million pounds. 'Oh Mick, get off the Universal Credit hotline and come and look at this, Euromillions Jackpot is £127 million pounds, let's spend 50 quid of money we don't have on this fucking pipe dream… Right then, ages and birthdays of our seven horrible kids – go!' Palpably ludicrous – I've got an idea Mick, the whole of Europe sticks ten pounds in a big bucket and then some greasy twat in Spain comes along and scoops it all up and spends it on cocaine and hookers til the end of time – ok amigo, here you go Pedro, have my kids' dinner money for the year. But I get it Mick, it makes you feel better for a few minutes, dare to dream.

And that is precisely why we've opened up the theatres and the pools and the gyms this week because we all need to dream don't we, we all need to go and see a play or do a bench press or take a piss in the shallow end because it allows us to dream, and takes us away for a moment from the utter futility of our existence and the certainty of imminent death. But as I say, while you lot are dreaming about Butlins and sucking off Terry to pay for your latest inking, I have to deal with the very real nightmare which is our country's resurrection. "Sorry" but we are operating on completely different levels. And that is why, and forgive me if this appears rude, but if you want to know exactly why I sacked the traitor Mark Sedwill, you can shove it up your arse.

Saturday July 11th 2020

So perhaps the greatest problem facing our resurrection is that, unlike Jesus who I assume wanted to come back to life, it seems like the UK as a whole isn't so sure. Scotland and Wales are off doing their own thing, and by that I mean they are doing our exact thing two weeks later to be deliberately shitty, and the people of our great nation can't agree their arse from their elbow. I was out for a photo opp in dear old Uxbridge yesterday, which often makes Hillingdon look like the first world, and I just chose a shop at random, stuck my face mask on and on I went in with a socially distanced cameraman. I mean bless them, when they saw me they shat themselves. I think they thought they were dreaming - a chap and his two daughters and one of them screamed 'this is a nightmare'. And by the end of my interaction with them all I could only agree, the general public are so dumb. These two girlies behind the counter I mean they weren't young or anything they were like 17 – neither of them was wearing a mask. I said to my cameraman Joe I said 'they're not wearing masks Joe let's go somewhere else' and he said 'can you ask them to wear a mask?' and I said 'well I don't particularly want to come in calling the shots like that.' Anyway to cut a long story short the shop owner (the dad of the two girlies) said 'What are you doing here?' and I explained it was for a photo opp for wearing masks in shops and his eyes lit up, I mean the shop was one of these shitty run down phone accessory shops - 'We will unlock your stolen phone no questions asked' kind of gaffs. The guy was clearly a petty criminal but we weren't here to arrest him, not yet anyway. There was sweets and pop and other shit. So I said to this geezer I said, 'can your daughters please wear a mask for this photo opportunity', and that's when it really kicked off.

Now to put what happened in context, I am not a racist. Some of my closest cabinet ministers are BAME. I do not and never have and never will negatively discriminate against any person of colour now or in the foreseeable future, and I also refuse to positively discriminate against those people either. When dear old Priti totally botched that Government Corona briefing and couldn't read out a simple number I gave her a bell the next day and very firmly told her that her performance was, and I quote, 'fucking shit'. I do not see colour, but I do see if you cannot read a number aloud. Anyway, back to the little shop of horrors. I was chatting to this dad, lovely fella, a Muslim or Hindu I didn't ask, and I said 'can your daughters wear a mask please that's the point of all this, we'll get a quick snap and then we'll be out of your hair.' He said something and I couldn't work out what he was saying, because he had a mask on, a lovely black one. He repeated it and it was just as muffled so I gestured for him to take the mask off and that did the trick and he scrunched it up below his chin. I then asked him to repeat what he was saying and he said 'I was saying that I can't hear you through your mask.' Jesus. Right old mess. I was wearing a lovely cobalt blue number that my seamstress knocked up for me. Lovely silky dream-like thing, I put it on and I commented that I looked like 'Hannibal Lecter at Pride.' She laughed at that, although to be honest thinking back I'm not sure she heard what I said. That is the problem with these masks isn't it, they are really fucking annoying. And the science is at best sketchy on the whole affair, but obviously I have dear old Chris Whitty in my ear 24/7 or as I call him 'The voice of doom' telling me that everyone should be wearing one of these things or we're all going to die so I'm stuck between a rock and a hard place. And I was certainly in a hard place now, Uxbridge, trying to make this geezer understand what I was saying through my silky distractor. So I started shouting but that seemed aggressive so I just lowered my mask slightly and repeated for the fifth time what I was asking him to do. By then I'm sure all the bits of spit that I'd chucked out shouting at this geezer probably went everywhere, we were stood right by the penny sweets so I hate to think what kind of local spike shit show that's gonna create. Anyway, I finally got my point across that I was requesting that his two daughters wear masks and he said, semi-aggressively I thought although that could have been his foreign accent, 'I'm sorry sir but we don't have any more masks, my girls don't believe in them.'

RESUЯЯECTION

That was a new one on me, I don't believe in masks, I'm a mask non-believer! I mean I get it as I say, we're not constantly predicting pile-ups like Chris Un-Whitty but, you know, I thought that was a little neggy. And that's when his missus comes out of the backroom toilet, pretty little lady and saw me with my mask pulled down and she shrieked 'Oh my God!' which in itself was slightly surprising and she very excitedly shunted her daughters out from behind the counter and asked my cameraman to take a photo of her behind the counter with me in front. I was obviously trying at this stage to get on their good side so I say 'Oh for fuck's sake why not' and so suddenly I'm standing their like a prize nana and they are behind me, and then behind me (I see later as there's a twist in all this) the dad only stands there taking a picture of his wife behind the counter! All a complete mess, but as I say there would be a horrible twist as it suddenly got a lot messier. Now, I repeat, I am not racist and can't think of any reason I ever would be. I was angry that's all it was. So the mom was all very excited as I say and asking me for more pictures so I had to put an end to all this, we had a car parked outside with my security on a double yellow and, on these occasions, I need to be in and out in 5 minutes or word gets about that Boris is in a shop and then all of a sudden I've got the whole of Uxbridge raiding Londis for eggs to come down and chuck at my face. And that is something I do not want, mask or no mask. So I say to this woman, again very politely 'Well no actually we don't have time for any more monkey business, the point of this whole shebang was get a photograph of me in a shop with people that worked there in masks'. I said I couldn't quite believe that they didn't have more masks as I thought that was the rules but to be honest I couldn't remember the rules and neither could Joe, my cameraman, so I said, again very politely, 'Could you and your daughters please clear off out of the picture and I'll get a picture with your dad and I'll be out of your hair.' That's all it was and they completely kicked off. I said something like it's shame you're not all wearing your burkas and as I say they just completely lost it. They were effing and jeff-ing half in their own language, half in mine but clearly I'd said the wrong thing or someone had and the dad started shoving me out the door screaming 'Get out Mr Johnson, kindly get out of my shop.' He was polite but his missus and daughters suddenly turned into a pack of wild dogs, shouting at me at the top of their voices all manner of curse words and anti-Conservative clap-trap, spit flying everywhere, Chris Whitty would have lost his shit. I told Joe to stop recording and thank goodness he'd forgotten to press record anyway, so we got to the doorway unscathed and then, out of nowhere, one of those shitty daughters chucked a bag of Doritos at me, and not the normal bags, those massive 'Grab-bags'. And it struck me right in the back of the head. I thought I'd been shot. I honestly thought at that split-second 'I'm JFK'. But then I turned round at realised it was a bag of Doritos, chucked from one of the daughters on the grassy knoll, but maybe it was actually the mom from the Book Depository – anyway at that split-second I looked at them all and I knew just like Lee Harvey Oswald I would organise the Government to shoot them down too, and as we bungled into the car and screamed away out of Dodge, I said to my cameraman Joe and my security, 'That's it fellas, I've decided, masks will be compulsory in shops forever.' There was a stunned silence for at least 5 seconds, and then I realised because I'd put my mask back on they hadn't heard me.

The twist by the way was that that the one photo we'd taken of me in my mask with Lee Harvey Oswald and her husband behind me, that's the one we had to use for the photo opp. Kind of nice in a way, if ever I question my decision (because I don't really believe in wearing masks it's a load of bollocks), I'll look back at that photo and I'll say 'I'm doing this to spite you'. And they will hear me because I'll be standing outside their shop, shouting, and I won't be wearing a mask. And neither will they probably, so I'll finally get them arrested. You can unlock phones but you can't unlock Broadmoor you cunts.

Sunday July 12th 2020

No entry today I've been out all day at the Red Lion getting shit-faced. Joe bought me a bag of Doritos! What a prick!

RESUЯЯECTION

Monday July 13th 2020

I always have my best ideas when I'm pissed, and last night I made a note on my phone before kissing my gorgeous son and going to bed in a separate room so the little sod didn't wake me up hanging out of my arse. And the note I woke up to this morning sums up the way out of this – three words – make shit up. I learned all I need to know in politics from the late great Paul Daniels – distraction is the key, don't look at what I'm doing, look over there, and while you weren't looking I've bagged a much younger, smoking-hot wife. And that's magic!! And on the subject of banging, I was banging the new ideas around with Dominic this morning and the only rule I made for our session – make shit up. The press will be all over it, the 45,000 death toll will be moved to page 11 along with the latest shitty drive-in gig to be cancelled and Bob's your uncle, old twinkle-toes is off the hook. Dommers and I came up with a few little beauties today I have to say – he did most of the donkey work as per but credit goes to me for THE greatest ever bullshit I think and there's stiff competition I know – 'let's move Parliament to York'. Yeah you heard. Love it. Bloody love it. Second only to the star-signs shifting around in this week's meaningless bollocks bingo chart – full house! Pay your fucking Poll Tax Full House!! I suggested that Parliament moves to York during refurbishments and tomorrow I bet you anything it's all over the front pages before you can say 'second spike'! I hate virtually all the press obviously but their never-ending gullibility is a constant delight.

What I like about the press is you think they report on stuff that's happened, that's literally 5% of the news. 95% is just making shit up, speculating about stuff that might happen. This will fill a whole day's news cycle, there will be maps of York drawn up wondering where on earth we'd put a temporary Parliament – news-flash you buzzards, it ain't gonna happen! MP's voting for a move to York would be like turkeys voting for Bernard Matthews. Pro knowledge here actually – Bernard Matthews died on Thanksgiving Day, which I think is rather fitting don't you? He fucked millions of turkeys and the day that they were fucked the most he carps it too. I'm not sure by those rules when would be the best day for me to die then? Maybe Mother's Day. Anyway, just like Bernard Matthews going vegan (he won't because he's dead), MP's will not vote for Parliament to move to York so it's a total non-story and just buys us a day. That takes us to Tuesday when I'll announce the masks in shop thing and Friday I'll fire out some bullshit about getting back to normal by Christmas, and Bob's your Auntie with bollocks it's the weekend again. Jesus the school holidays are really upon us aren't they, if you know what I mean they've been closed for normal kids for months, but doesn't the week drag when you have to work in the Summer? I have a rule that I don't drink before 4pm on a 'work day' so that's extra specially difficile. Most of the country is getting hammered now the pubs are open and poor old Boris has to work or at the very least pretend to work. Crushingly dull.

Dear old Dominic said something to me this morning actually and it's really stuck with me, he said 'boss, you're very powerful.' I said 'Jesus man can we stop talking about you for a second?' And he said 'Boss, I am talking about you.' After an age of confusion it turned out he was talking about me, and after a modicum of convincing I'm inclined to believe him. I've got a massive majority (ooh err!), now we've had this pandemic I can basically say anything and the whole country will comply – 'Wear a mask in shops' – Yes sir! 'Stay in your grubby homes Leicester scum' – 'Yes sir!' 'Let's move Parliament to York' – 'Fuck off Boris!'. Alright there are limits but I know what he's saying, pretty much anything I say goes. And I suddenly felt very powerful. And then dear old Dominic said something a little odd, and he said straight afterwards that he was only joking, but he leaned into me (we don't social distance as we are bubbling) and he said 'Boss, you can get away with murder.' I felt his meaty breath on my ear as he doubled down. 'I mean literally boss, you can literally get away with murder.' As I say he said he was only joking, but only after about five minutes of detailed explanation as to why he was absolutely serious. As we know now, it's almost impossible to get away with murder these days, and not just murder, GBH, or any petty crime. And Dominic reminded me of that Stuart Collier debacle, which annoyed me to start with, but straight after reminding me he said 'times have changed, and you could get away with beating someone up or killing someone now', before as I say totally confirming he was fully joking.

If I must remind you for context, 30 years ago (and didn't we all do something we regret 30 years ago) I may or may not or may have agreed to provide the address of News of The World 'journalist' Stuart Collier to dear old Darius Guppy who HE wanted to beat up. HE. It wasn't ME who wanted to break his ribs (although come on he was a News of the World hack - there's not a man, woman, or child on this Earth who wouldn't want to beat the living shit out of that scum) it was Guppy. I thought I was going to be in real shit for that until Guppy was banged up on separate charges, just in the nick of time. Anyway, the official line is that conversation was a joke, but I think we all know the truth. Stuart Collier was the scum of the earth, journalist scum, and I should know, I was a Daily Telegraph reporter at the time and so best placed to know how horrific journalists can be. Was me joining in with a plot to beat the crap out of the guy a joke? Well that's for history to judge, and for my next sentence to confirm. It wasn't. Did I think that if I helped to beat ten bells out of someone that I'd get away with it? No I didn't, categorically. And that was part of the thrill I guess. And then every year that has gone past, it has got, in my mind at least, harder and harder to conspire to carry out GBH or murder or indeed carry out dear old GBH or murder. DNA – it stands for Do Not Attempt round my manor. But Dominic had other ideas, he said to me, again really close in, I could differentiate the meat in his breath. It was lamb, cooked blue of course. He whispered, 'Who is the one man they would not suspect of committing murder today? The answer is you sir.' Chilling. 'You could kill, and then kill again.' As he said 'kill again' he slithered around in front of me and made a slashing motion across his throat. He then looked me straight in the eye and said 'I'm absolutely serious, I'm not joking'. So there we go. As I say, five minutes later after he had explained in detail all the people he'd like me to kill and how, I started to get a little freaked out, and then he absolutely assured me he was joking. And that was the end of that.

That's the thing with Dominic, even in the middle of a global pandemic, we can have a right old laugh.

Tuesday July 14th 2020

So there you have it, you over-sensitive shits from 'We will Unlock your stolen phones for U', the announcement has been made and I hope you're choking on your morning Doritos you dicks. Face-masks in shops from the 25th. But this isn't a time to gloat, this is a time to reflect on what we have done well as a Government, and done not so well, and the things we have done not so well we will do them well now so people will forget about us doing them not so well. From the 25th, everyone should wear a mask in all shops. 'Oh Boris why do that now and not when people actually had the virus?' they cry. For God's sake, they're never happy are they, whoever THEY are. The trouble with my job of course is I'm damned if I don't, damned if I don't. I got a a bit down this morning actually, I went 'into my cave' as I say, and as always dear old Dominic got me out of it. There's no ledge on this Earth that a little massage and pep talk from dear old Dommers wouldn't talk me down from – I say to him sometimes – when I'm on the ledge, I need the ledge. He always laughs when I say that, and he told me once he laughs because he thinks it's the world's shittest slogan. And that made me laugh. We laugh together.

I love Dominic Cummings, there you go I've said it. And not in that way, obviously. I'm fiercely heterosexual and have famously made love to more women than Jeff Leach (a comedian who did a wonderful BBC documentary about seven years ago about having banged 360 women). Ledge. I just love the way he makes me feel – not Jeff Leach, Dominic, and he has the right words for every occasion. I was feeling down this morning as I say, and you can't help feeling sometimes that maybe your critics are right, maybe you have made a mistake along the way, maybe you do care more about the kicks than the politics, the laughs more than the deaths, the Maxines more than the vaccines. And again as the sun rose and I retreated into my deep, dark cave, Dommers had the right words. He turned to me, coquettishly and purred, 'darling, even Jesus made mistakes'. And he's right. I mean I'm told he's right by himself, I've never read the Bible myself. This is my resurrection, and why did Jesus need his resurrection? Because he made the mistake, he made the mistake of bragging. He claimed to be 'The King of the Jews'. And in so doing, he was perceived as a political threat by some, and needed to be taken down. Or in his case, nailed up. As Dominic explained so beautifully, I may have the power of Jesus right now, but if I scream about it too much the crowds will gather to enforce my demise. If I secretly get on with being the son of God without too many people noticing, I can carry on performing miracles and get this country back on its feet. Soon enough, all the water will be turned to wine and this whole glorious country will drink that sweet nectar of alcoholic freedom!

Wednesday July 15th 2020

Kier Starmer is the kind of political opponent that makes you wish duels would make a comeback. I fear he's never going to go away until I shoot him from ten paces with a pistol. On that note I've always thought just turn on nine and a half, the other fucker will have no chance. Those thoughts were going through my head today as, yet again, Le Chiffre was bleating on about a public enquiry. 'When's the public enquiry, Boris?' Really Keir? The country is on free-fall, the parachute has failed and you really think this is the time for me to get on the blower to the parachute manufacturer and ask them to investigate wear and tear? Keir made it on to my top ten people I'd like to kill today, I know it's naughty and if anyone finds the list I'm in serious shit, but Keir just made it in at number ten (and there's a first!). It's unfair really by all accounts, I don't really know the man, but I guess anyone standing across from me at the Dispatch Box I want to box and dispatch. In no other job in the world would you have an enemy standing across from you whose sole purpose is to criticise everything you do, do you understand how wearing that would be? Next time you're packing boxes or filling the shelves with cans of tuna, imagine just for a second 'Sir' Keir Starmer popping up and bleating 'Sally, can you explain why every single can of tuna wasn't facing the same way and why you waited until 4pm to stack the tuna when you could have done it at 10am so there would have been more tuna for the unemployed? And what about the homeless Sally, tuna for the homeless? And we think Sally's wage should go up from £7.21 to £7.22 because her and her husband can't afford their Sky package any more.' Well fuck you Sir Kier, and fuck you Sally – we were all very grateful for you during lockdown as a key worker but now that's all over, you're back to what you were, the lowest of the low, stacking shelves of tuna, and by all accounts, doing it pretty badly.

So that death list in full, just for a bit of a fun. At number 10, Sir Tuna. In at 9, Michael Gove. Keep your friends close, and make your enemies Minister for the Cabinet Office. Number 8, Ian Hislop – cunt. Number 7, Ghislaine Maxwell – I can't go into detail on that one and when she finds herself dead soon don't go blaming me. Number 6, Wilfred Johnson. Oh but that's your new-born baby Boris! I know right, this proves the list is just a joke, but if you were up half the night like I was last night, trying to find a room in this gaff where you couldn't hear a screaming baby, you'd want it dead too. This is the first time a partner has expected me to be in the vicinity of the baby when it's in its screaming years and I have to be honest it's started to get to me. I thought my job in the first few years was just to give it a silly name and pay for its private tuition, and that has all gone fine and dandy for Lara Lettice, Theodore Apollo, Cassia Peaches and the other one or two. I hope it's not coming across as cold-hearted but I'm trying to clear up the mess of successive Governments (yes, including my own) and a global pandemic, please don't ask me to clear up the mess of a screaming nought year old too. I've lost track of this list now, let's just say for now anyway that the list exists, it's in my top drawer and every time one of my enemies dies I'm going to stick a red cross against their name and have a celebratory shot of Scotch. Particularly if Hislop dies, if that squidgy faced prick croaks I'll have the whole bloody bottle. Imagine his funeral, when even the biggest cunts gets nice words said about them. What's Hislop gonna get? At best he'll have Paul Merton standing up and telling everyone 'as a joke' what a little snivelling cock he was, and the gathered D-List celebs and hacks will laugh thinking Paul was joking but he wouldn't be joking because I know Paul hates him too, everyone hates him, and to be honest I think he hates himself. Number 5 is Mark Sedwill. You get the idea. I'm a bad man.

Thursday July 16th 2020

So there's a suggestion flying around today that I delayed lockdown by a week because Carrie would have had to cancel her baby shower at Chequers. I say suggestion, old 'he who must be ignored' Government's chief scientific adviser and nuisance Patrick Vallance tried to dob me in at the Select Committee, saying he'd advised me to recommend an immediate lockdown on 16th March and I sat on it for a week. Bullshit. Next accusation Pat Vallance, next fabrication please Pat Val. The delay cost 20,000 lives did it? Yeah, as if, itchy chin. Like a week's delay would cost 20,000 lives, have a word with yourself you worst case scenario prick. Yes, I'm tetchy today, I know it's because it's Thursday and I see the drinking oblivion of the weekend just out of reach over the horizon but really, all these little medical advisers like Pat Val need to do one. 'Ooh Boris remember I told you to do that thing three months ago and you sat on it for a week you bad boy, is that because Carrie was having her baby shower at Chequers?' As if I give a fuck about that baby. Jesus. Have you seen that film 'Sully'? It's about that plane in New York, bird strike takes out both engines and he has to land it on the Hudson, really terrific film with dear old Tom Hanks from Turner and Hooch. Anyway why I like that film so much, it's pretty boring but there's an enormously good scene where every single bastard nit-picking authority is saying that Tom Hanks could have reacted earlier and got the plane back to the airport safely and then by the end of the film Tom Hanks convinces them that they don't know what they're talking about and he's the only person who knows stuff. Well that's me all over! That's my life! These little fucking shits keep popping up every day saying 'Oh you could have done that then.' Yeah, cool, and you try being the man in the trenches pal, you trying being Sully behind those controls, half-cut, various mothers of my children not pulling their weight (bird strike!) and then ask him to make a split-second decision. I'm sorry I'm not sorry if it takes me a few days to get my head around a life-saving choice. And like Sully, if I bring this country back to Earth safely or crash-landed on the water with everyone suffering PTSD for years, the outcome is the same in my book, Sully rescued everyone and Sully (me) is a fucking hero. And there should be a film about him (me).

Pat Val's now on my death list by the way. I took off Nihal Arthanayake off of BBC Radio 5 Live. I need to make the list more focussed as to my enemies rather than just people I don't like for no reason. And I listened to Nihal on the radio earlier today and I actually quite liked him. And I'm not arguing that there's not going to be advantages down the line in making this particular list less diverse. It's treachery with Pat Val, just like it was for Mark Sedwill and Gove – what links most of the list now I've deleted DJ Nihal Arthanayake is that they are treacherous, and while I'm not King (as I say we know what happened to poor old Jesus when he claimed that) anyone that stands in the way of the King is a traitor and deserves to die. And one of these people will die very soon I guarantee. It's called creative visualisation according to Dommers. See in your mind's eye who you want dead and they will for sure die very, very soon. You will have wished death upon them, and they will have died, and you get off scot-free. Wishing someone to death is not a crime, and nor will it ever be under my leadership.

Anyway, let's never look back, let us now look forward, together. It's nearly 4pm and time for a drink. But just as importantly, we are a great nation and we will come back bigger, if not larger, and we will come back stronger, albeit with depleted resources and strength, all too soon my friends. But only if we stick together, if we kill our enemies and then stick together.

Friday July 17th 2020

'Things will be back to approaching normal by Christmas'. You cannot underestimate the importance of hope. But importantly, make it totally non-specific hope so when it's not that much better at Christmas, people can't quote me on something that didn't happen.

That's what people need right now, non-traceable hope. Princess Beatrice got married today – non traceable hope. Theatres will open on August 1ˢᵗ depending on certain unspecified measures being taken and they will open according to unspecified rules. It's like blancmange dripping through your hands isn't it? It looks bloody tasty doesn't it, but shit, where did it go? Another great speech by me this morning and now I have my feet up writing this before I let my lockdown hair down for real this weekend and get totally obliterated. It's been a hard week but a good week. The benchmark of a successful week for me is that I've done absolutely nothing but the country and Carrie and whoever think I've done loads. That's when I feel most like Paul Daniels and my loins are full of beans and I feel ready to bag another younger, hot wife. Not literally obviously now for the time being. There's hope my pretties, for the first time in months there is hope. Theatres are opening and goddamit even Jeff Twat and his unfunny mates can get up in front of 20 people at a so-called 'comedy club' on August 1ˢᵗ and make some lame jokes about Boris Johnson, someone they will never be. But more than anything, there's the hope of Christmas, and if not normality by then, then something approaching normality. In other words, abnormality.

I love Christmas – it's full of my favourite things – drinking, good Scotch, chocolate, food, receiving presents and television. But what people sometimes forget, Christmas is also about love. And if I can get serious for a second, I'm a nice guy. Yes I had a very privileged childhood, yes I went to Eton and yes I went to Oxford and yes I was in the Bullingdon Club and yes David Cameron stuck his dick in a dead pig's head. Well solidarity Mr Cameron, as you know I made love to that pig's head too. But just because I put my penis in a pig's head does not make me a bad guy. I'm a good guy that has made the best of a very difficult situation. I'm serious, and I realise you might not get this, but sometimes it's just as difficult to be ridiculously rich and privileged than it is to be poor. You imagine, and I imagine you have to imagine, you imagine for a moment having everything. Where does one go from there? Usually downwards. You will spiral downwards from having everything to a life bumming around the South of France spending daddy's money and snorting cocaine off a prostitute's arsehole. Well I'm not doing any of that any more. Ironically that's what daddy is doing in Greece now, allegedly! Oh good Christ I said 'allegedly' there as a substitute for real humour, I'm sounding just like that prick Hislop. And that's a case in point, Hislop paints himself as the man of the people, but my goodness he is just as privileged as me, and what has he done with his life? Fuck all. Stupid little jokes in Private Eye and reading out jokes on *Have I Got News For You* that have been written down for him by Shaun Pye. Which ironically is what his face looks like. A shorn pie. He's a shorn pie and I'm a nice guy. I'm a nice guy just trying to my best for this country. That was genuinely the vision at the start of all this. Look at my record as London Mayor for heaven's sake, I turned London into a world beater, I am responsible for the Olympics for fuck's sake. But as you rise higher and higher well the bastards just line up to tear you down or make you want to kill someone.

I need to get rid of Dominic I feel. I love him so very dearly and he's the reason I'm where I am right now. (I don't mean on the toilet I mean in number 10). But he's not like me. He pretends to be like me but he really isn't. And I don't mean he went to a State School and I went to Eton, whilst that is of course true. It comes down to this really. I'm Prime Minister, which to many would be a tremendous achievement, but to me, and the chances I was given, truthfully I consider it just as par for the course. This was the life I was expected to lead. But for Dominic, I know still today, the position he's in, it blows him away. I know he masturbates about it. I've heard him. When he cums he shouts 'I'm the King of the world'. But he's not the King of the world, I'm the King of the world. I'm the King of the Jews, and the Christians, and every single religion in this great country, even the ones I don't agree at all with. And so dear old Dommers is dangerous – he's fantastic, but he's dangerous. If I was to compare him to one man from history it would be Dr Harold Shipman. Undoubtedly a great doctor, an even better deceptionist, but with a God complex. That's Dominic Cummings all over – he thinks he's God. And that's why he was trying to convince me I am Jesus. He likes to think he created me, but the only person that created me is currently sunning his bollocks right now on a beach in

Pathos. So I end the week on a bit of a dilemma really, how do I rid myself of the one that created me? He keeps telling me I can kill. And I need to kill God. Number one on my kill list – it's Dominic Cummings. And I fear, just like Rasputin, or Raoul Moat, he's going to be an absolute fucker to finish off.

Saturday July 18th 2020

Jesus, my last entry was a little over the top reading it back. But I'm not editing anything here. Even the word 'deceptionist' when I was describing dear old Harold Shipman. I realise glancing again that deceptionist isn't a word, I think I was thinking 'receptionist', which Harold Shipman definitely wasn't. He was a doctor, a terrible doctor, so terrible that I thought of him every time I applauded the NHS during lockdown. Every time I applauded, he was the only doctor in my thoughts. A terrible human being, and I would hazard a guess, so was his receptionist. Come off it, she must have known something. 'Oh goodness Harry terrible luck, isn't it that's 200 dead now?' Have a word with yourself love, hello!!

And talking of Harold Shipman, well we turn to the Doctor Harold Shipman of world politics, no not dear old Donald Trump, he's more the Doctor Dolittle of world politics, I'm talking of course of Vlad the Bad, Vladimir Putin. And specifically, his ambassador to the UK, Andrei Kelin. The Russians are terrifying aren't they? The accent, the names, the cuisine. Vladimir! Kelin! And Andrei was Kelin me softly with his eyes today as we had a little private face to face and he tried to convince me that the Russians weren't trying to steal our vaccine research and didn't try to meddle in the last election. What, I wonder, is Russian for 'bullshit?'. Maybe not the most diplomatic way of starting our meeting, but I thought it was time to show him who's boss. And by that I don't mean I showed him Dominic Cummings, although he did end up getting on much better with him. I didn't think they knew each other but they really hit it off. And I'm not sorry, strike me down with plutonium from an umbrella's metal tip if I'm talking out of turnski, but the Russians are not to be trusted. Our National Cyber Security Centre (NCSC) have told me that they are

31

95% sure that a group called APT29 – also known as Cozy Bear – was part of Russian Intelligence Services and hell bent on stealing our vaccine research. They are NOT to be truski. I'm of course old enough to remember Gorbachov, Yeltsin, the real baddies of Russian politics. Just because Putin rides gayly around naked on a horse doesn't mean his finger isn't constantly tweaking the nuclear button like the left nipple of a Moscovian prostitute. USSR has always stood for U Should Suspect Russia. I've thought that for so long that I genuinely don't know what it really stands for. But I make no apology, the Russians are not my friends and Andrei Kelin will never be on my Christmas card list, unless that's the way we'd chosen to kill him.

What makes me laugh most about Russia's definite plot to steal our coronavirus vaccine research is that, as far as I know, right now we're about as close to finding a cure for coronavirus as we are the cure for my screaming fucking baby. It ain't gonna happen mate, so hack away dear Ruski, all you'll find if you're hacking my computer is my top ten wish list for death. And that's why I put that in my computer's trash and wrote it down on a bit of paper, you really can't trust anyone these days. I mean if you could trust folk not to hack your computer, imagine the amount of dodgy porn I'd be watching! And there is no doubt that they meddled in the election here just as they did in the US. And people say, why would they interfere in foreign elections? Jesus guys, wake up and smell the 'kwofee', of course Russia wanted Trump in because he is a weak leader who stood no chance on the global stage against Putin. A weak, moronic imbecile who would let hundreds of thousands die because, and it warrants repeating, this is a President who considered that injecting bleach could be a potential cure for the virus! He's a moron, and that is the why the Russians wanted Trump in and there must have been a similar but completely different reason why they wanted me in. I mean to be honest the injecting bleach thing was a bit overblown by the media I feel, I believe he was talking about injecting bleach in very diluted amounts, which I'd guess wouldn't be that dangerous.

The Russians deny everything, they deny this, they deny involvement in the 2018 nerve agent attack on Salisbury, give them half a chance they'd deny vodka. Well I can't deny vodka, and that's exactly where I'm heading right now, to Saturday night oblivion. I'm heading round to Dominic's tonight under the cover of darkness (I black-up slightly as a disguise) and we're planning a lads night in boozing til dawn and maybe catching that *Eurovision* film with dear old Will Ferrell. Now there's a comedian Hislop, and not even allegedly! Spokoynoy nochi comrades! And as frightening as that sounds, I'm just wishing you good night. Sleep tight, and dear friends, don't let the Novichok nerve agent bite!

Sunday July 19th 2020

Well, that *Eurovision* film was shite. But that was just the start of the weirdest night of my life last night. Dominic's wife and kids were with their family up North, and before you say it, they're bubbling, totally with the rules, and as far as all trusted reports go, dear old Mary's eyesight was perfect by all accounts as they shot up the motorway to her parents for the weekend. You know her parents are toffs don't you, her dad owns a castle ironically, Chillingham Castle in Northumberland, Dominic tells me it's haunted. Anyway that's neither here nor there, I think it's Dominic's Islington abode that is haunted. So we got to the end of the film, I was kind of slipping away from consciousness and Dominic was saying something about how he fancied Rachel McAdams loads, and there was a knock on the door. You'll never guess who it was – that's right, Mark 'The Traitor' Sedwill.

I know right, the plot thickens. What is that duplicitous shit Sedwill doing at Dominic Cummings House at midnight? Well, I sobered up like Princess Diana had died again. Here's the breakdown - Mark Sedwill when he's not being a treacherous little shit, is President of the Special Forces Club, a private members club in Knightsbridge full of ex SAS and current SAS figures, along with members of the intelligence community. And here it comes… he had heard rumblings of a Russian plot on my life. Now, it will come as no surprise to you that I get death threats every single day, and that's just from Twitter and Carrie! But there was something more chilling about Mark's words, however much he can't be trusted. Look, I said I wasn't going to tell you but I may as well tell you what he did. People know, my old friends in The Telegraph certainly know but thankfully agreed to keep it out of the paper, Mark Sedwill was apparently in contact with Vladimir Putin over Christmas and he had apparently said that he thought I was a pizda, which translates as Vladimir Putin thinks I, Boris Johnson, am a 'cunt'. I know right? And Sedwill sat on this for months, didn't tell me, while I continued to have the odd conversation with Putin acting like his best friend. Sedwill tried to tell me there are things I don't need to know, and I said, 'Yes Mark, and those things include who is lined up to appear on the next series of *Strictly Come Dancing*, but what it doesn't include is information that Vladimir Putin thinks I'm a cunt. Because if Putin thinks I'm a cunt then I'll think he's a cunt back thank you, and so a new Cold War begins.

Anyway, so I don't trust Sedwill one bit, but to his credit, he seemed to be being quite honest about this, he had heard the right whispers from the right places that I should be very, very careful from now on. Maybe for example, I shouldn't have just popped round Dominic's house to get pissed and watch a Will Ferrell film. He said maybe I should be home with my new baby. I know right, guilt trip, I'm allowed a night off for fuck's sake. Sedwill said he meant I would be safer in Downing Street, but I know what he meant the sarcy twat, I know what he meant all too well. If I can't go round and get pissed with one of my best mates then what's the point in living? I'm rescuing the country here, I need to let off a little steam. But whatever the reason, and I recognise the double standards in being in a room with two people who are on my own personal death list, but I am now worried, and I will double or even triple down on my security from now on, which is an awful inconvenience. No more trips to the Red Lion for moi, after today of course, I promised Joe I'd be his wing man later.

So I'm just home after spending the night on Dominic's sofa, and getting an Uber home in the morning. Yes you heard right, an Uber.

I'm not getting my official transport no more, I don't trust anyone. Those Uber drivers don't know who I am, most of them are bloody Russians! I joke, but for the first time in my life, I'm scared.

Monday July 20th 2020

I don't want to die! I've got a new baby that I'm legally obliged to support, I've got friends and parties and drinking and food and a wife. I don't want to die. And while everyone's still moaning about the virus I'm basically Salman Rushdie without the publicity. So unfair. I spoke with Dominic this morning and we chatted about potentially going public, but dear old Dommers had some calming words and said 'What? We go public on hearsay from some dick in a private members club, don't be a prick.' He always finds the right thing to say, and told me again that I'm the chosen one, I'm Jesus, and no one kills Jesus. Well they do, but he comes back to life by magic. And talking about magic, scrap what I said about the vaccine, news in from Oxford today that they are confident of their latest trials so I said, fuck it, let's buy 90 million of them. We did the payment before somebody reminded me there only 67 million people in the country, and I'm already immune, but fuck it it's like milk isn't it, it's always good to have extra that you can just throw away. But exciting right, if I didn't have this death threat hanging over me I'd be getting slaughtered tonight, it's really fantastic news, and of course it's Oxford University where this progress has been made, of course it is. Double helping of proud.

I wish I could have stayed at Oxford University my whole life really, that's where I was at my happiest. I became President of course, I loved my Degree and I should have got a first, of course I regret all that Bullingdon Club vandalism and debauchery but I can't deny it was rollicking good fun at the time. But more than anything else, I was liked. I did some self-reflection a few years ago after bowing out as London Mayor and while the vast majority of Londoners thought I did a good job, 36% of Londoners thought I did a 'bad job' and although vast swathes of that 36% will be dumb-nuts who just vote 'bad job' whoever it is, it's still someone saying they don't like you, and that burns. And it's never got easier. I thought after my huge success as London Mayor that I should bow out of a career that divides and do something where you're universally loved, but where are those jobs? There's only a few people on the planet that are universally loved – David Attenborough, Sir Tom Moore, Dame Judy, Dame Vera Lynn – and what links them all? Dead or nearly dead. There's very few people at my age who are loved by all, it just doesn't happen, maybe Gary Lineker but I've read his twitter and everyone keeps affectionately reminding him that he shat himself during the World Cup. And I really was the Gary Lineker of Oxford University, I never shat myself (apart from for a prank) and I was loved by everyone, I miss those days. I think people forget that I'm a human being, not a psychopath or as Putin thinks of me, a 'cunt'. I'm a human being with feelings. When I decided to stay in front-line politics in 2016 I had to make a conscious decision to ignore the criticism, to block it out… to, as Dominic keeps telling me to do, 'embrace my inner psychopath'. But it's a constant battle, because I'm not a psychopath, I'm a lovely guy.

So anyway the vaccine – great news right? I did an interview today and my direct quote about the vaccine is "Obviously I'm hopeful, I've got my fingers crossed, but to say I'm 100% confident we'll get a vaccine this year, or indeed next year, is alas just an exaggeration. We're not there yet." Dominic of course wrote that for me word for word. It's frighteningly clever. It contains the words 'hopeful', '100% confident', 'vaccine this year'. And still if you read it back it says absolutely fuck all, and actually errs on the side of us never finding anything ever. Clever man. Psychopath. As I said a few days ago, he really does leave me in a constant dilemma. Here I am held up in Downing Street, writing this and watching the cricket, and I'm scared. And why am I scared? Is it because the West Indies look like taking an unassailable 2-0 lead in the series? Not a bit of it. Those West Indians are currently clinging on and smiling their smiles but their smiles are soon gonna be batted off their faces by our brave boys. I'm scared because Putin think I'm a cunt, yes, but more than that I feel a little controlled by Dominic. It's him that told me about Sedwill, it's him that persuaded me to get rid of Sedwill, it's him that told me to take a hard line on Russian diplomats and it's at his house where I'm now told there is a credible plot to kill me. I can't help thinking I should have got rid of Dominic the day he told the press 'I drove to Durham to test my eyesight'. Fucking hell, in my fucking garden as well! Am I that much of a walkover?

Why don't I just sack Dominic? I won't be nearly as effective but I'll be liked more, maybe that death threat will be lifted. What's the point in anything if you're not liked? I bet if we did a poll about who likes Dominic Cummings, 100% of people would say he was 'bad', and while he'd put a positive spin on that I'm sure, that means something right? I'm associating myself with an essentially bad man, and I'm a good man. If I am Jesus, and who's to say I'm not, well right now I'm taking advice from the Devil, and that surely can't be the right approach. But I can't sack him. So maybe I should kill him, or get others to. If they can kill Jeffrey Epstein then they can kill Cummings. I need to talk to Sedwill again, maybe I can feed back up the Russian chain of command that I'm not a cunt, it's Dominic that's the cunt and he should be killed not me. Oh I don't know, I'll be alright. Owzaaat!

Not out. I'm getting worried now about the cricket. That's a good sign. I'll have a drink and calm down. The Russians won't really kill me will they? Obviously I'm hopeful, I've got my fingers crossed, but to say I'm 100% confident I'll get a reprieve this year, or indeed next year, is alas just an exaggeration. We're not there yet. Oh God, this stuff isn't strong enough for my mood tonight. I need something stronger. Maybe I'll down those extra 23 million vaccines we bought like the big, bloated incompetent twerps we are today. Dear God, what a fucking day!

Tuesday July 21st 2020

My head is spinning right now, I'm not thinking straight. I keep blaming Cummings for everything when of course everything is the fault of the Russians. Dominic isn't that bad, I guess his reputation proceeds him. He's affectionately known around Parliament as

'Hitler' because he wipes out anyone that disagrees with him, and for some today, Dommers is worse than Hitler as it was confirmed he kills off blonde, blue eyed nurses who disagree with him. Of course this is old news to me, and not really news. The complete non-story is that Ruth May the Chief Nurse was taken off the briefings as she refused to back Cummings over his trip to Durham. Jesus that fucking trip to Durham! Can we move on now please? Well apparently not it seems, as Keir Starmer's wank-rags keep prising off the last flecks of shit off the fan and pulling out one more turd from the U-bend. Oh have you heard the big news everyone? Ruth May the Chief Nurse (whatever the fuck that is) was dropped for refusing to back Cummings? Jesus Christ, obviously! Like we could really be having those briefings with Chris Whitty saying 'oh yeah well truth be told Boris is a bit of a prick' and me retorting 'coming from you, you sour-faced cunt.' Obviously the only way for anything to work in Government but particularly crisis briefings to the Nation is for everyone to be on the same page, even if that page is 'We agree that a sane man drove to Durham to test his eyesight.' As I've said, yes, obviously it was bullshit. They had a lovely day at Barnard Castle as it was dear old Mary's birthday and they were caught with their fingers in the drawbridge. I think we've all done this story to death now haven't we, well apparently not as poor old Chief Nurse is having a bit of a weep nearly two months after the event. With all due respect and weekly applause Ruth, it's no good coming out now and moaning because you couldn't have your 15 minutes of fame, you were asked a simple question in the run-through 'Do you back Dominic Cummings?' and you said something like 'Obviously not it's clearly bullshit' when what you should have said is 'Haven't we all got behind the wheel of a car to test our eyesight lads? Time to move on, let's eat out to help out.' Is that too hard for you Ruth? Clearly it was sweet-cheese, see you later. As I say, I don't agree with everything Dominic does, but in this instance, old Nursey Truthy-pants had to go. I repeat though I have undying respect for the two nurses that saved my life, and their names will come back to me soon.

Jesus Christ it's hard to focus with a Russian fatwa hanging over you, I hate it. But events today have obviously focussed my fatwigued mind with the publishing of the Parliament's Intelligence and Security Committee (PIS), sorry ISC's report detailing Russian interference in British politics. Now, ask me last week 'are you worried Boris?', as some did, when we knew this was coming, I'd have said 'don't give a shit mate'. Just another load of bollockski to brush under the Persian rug. But now I'm a target, and I'm sitting in my personal crisis room (the number 10 toilet) trying to get my head around this once and for all, with the sole purpose of working out why the Russian State want me dead and why Putin thinks I'm a cunt. So we know that Russia wants to destabilise the West because it makes them stronger, hence getting the wig-wearing buffoon into the White House and influencing the British Public to vote out in the EU referendum and for some reason I can't work out wanting to get me into Downing Street. That's all clear, and the problem was up until this point I've of course agreed with everything Russia has wanted to do, right up until the moment I found out they want me dead. It makes little sense. I am Russia's friend, or at least I was until I found out what Putin was saying behind my back, but I cannot begin to comprehend this complete sea change in a matter of weeks. A few weeks ago I was Russia's play-thing and that's the way I liked it. I made sure very little happened about the Salisbury poisonings (someone died because they picked up perfume from a bin and tried it out – what gimp does that?!) and I've of course welcomed all the fantastic Russian billionaires and Oligarchs into London or as they now call it 'London-grad'. I'm proud of that moniker. London-grad. Did you know that over half, 51% of all Russia's money now exists overseas, and I for one am proud that much of that has been spent in the fair (if not fair!) city of London. The profits of Harrods outstrips the profits of the UK's fishing industries and do you think that's because your grandma has taken you into Harrods to buy you a few marbles and get you a plastic bag? No, it's because Andrei RichFuckski has just bought another big old British yacht. It works for them and it works for us. And now I'm facing criticism that we 'actively avoided' Russia's threat. Well of course we 'actively avoided it' because it simply wasn't a threat to us, they were doing exactly what we wanted. Securing Brexit, securing a Conservative majority and securing the place in the priority queue at Harrods of brilliant Russian billionaires. You don't bite the hand that feeds you, even if it is feeding you nasty Russian death-shit.

Until now of course. They are trying to kill me. But why? I can't work anything out. So I'm calling up Dominic right now to come over and sort this out. And as I sit here on this toilet and wait, the stench of corruption gathering around me, I can't help but think of my father still in Greece and wonder, why am I here? Why am I doing this? I was happy as London mayor, everyone liked me (apart from those 36% of people that didn't like me) but I definitely got the sense that no one wanted me dead. And now look at me, pants around my ankles and fearing the bullet. This is how they got Elvis, and Marilyn and John Travolta in *Pulp Fiction*. I just want to be happy again. My father is 80 next month and he's so much happier than me. He travels, he goes on *I'm a Celebrity…Get me Out of Here!* I'd fucking love to do that, as my sex life proves I'll eat anything! And he's friends with that Toff off of *The Only Way is Essex*. Crikey she's so fit, and she's stupid enough not to know that's why my dad wants to hang round with her. But more than anything, he can do what he wants. I can't do anything now. I'm terrified on the toilet in one of the most guarded houses in the world. But I'm imprisoned, imprisoned by my success. Don't forget my father travelled to Greece before they lifted the ban on travel from the United Kingdom, he simply doesn't give a fuck. I long for those days, I yearn for that glorious day cometh when I can never give a fuck again.

Wednesday July 22nd 2020

I'm writing this in the early hours. Dominic has just gone. It's 1am and I'm already hungover, I haven't been able to drink since Dominic came in last night. Carrie is away and thank goodness as I've been buzzing around the place tonight like a headless chicken on Christmas Eve. I envy Dommers so much about so many things, but what I've always envied most about him apart from his money is his calmness under pressure, he never flinches. I'm reminded of that Prince Charles clip, you can get it on YouTube, and he's doing a speech in

Australia I think and someone starts shooting at him from the crowd.
He doesn't flinch and just starts fiddling with his cufflinks as if
nothing is happening before being rugby tackled to the floor by his
five slow-as-fuck security guards. Turns out they were just blanks but
he wasn't to know that, Prince Charles is the coolest fucker on the
planet, and if he did order his ex-wife's death in 1997, he wouldn't
have dripped a bead of sweat. Class act.

Anyway, as I say I was all over the place and Dominic, well he
grabbed me, he grabbed me at the top of the arm and he said 'Boss,
it's time to sort this out'. And I said 'I don't know how to sort this
out.' And he said 'No, I was talking to myself, it's time I sorted this
out.' He's not very manly of course Dommers, if he had gone to
public school he would have certainly been the post-box not the
package, but at that moment he looked every inch the man in my life,
the flared nostrils, the steely psychopathic gaze. I've never thought of
him as attractive really, obviously an attractive and charismatic
personality but aesthetically even at his best he looks like a starving
rodent, and in the last few years, bless him, he's aged like he's got
terminal cancer. But right then, at that moment, I could have been
looking at Clarke Gabel. He even had the little moustache, which is
why more people have been calling him Hitler.

Dominic believes this is a power struggle, after Theresa May, bless her
wooden heart, banished 23 diplomats and their families following the
poisoning of Sergei Skripal and his daughter and the subsequent
nonsense with that idiot and the perfume bottle. Tosser. Now dear
old Theresa, with the best in the world, was rightly regarded as the
worst leader this country has had since Sam Allardyce. Worse than
Big Sam really, at least he could grind out a few results by deploying
the long ball, poor old Theresa would find a way to lose a match from
20-nil up. 'Ooh let's replay the game shall we, I'm sure we can win
this by even more.' Good heavens she was shit. And chucking out
the diplomats was a huge mistake, I thought that at the time of
course, although I said the opposite. The reason for that is I was
Foreign Secretary, and unlike Sedwill I'm not a traitor, at least not
overtly. The stuff they used in that attack was Novichok, nasty shit

that can fuck you up within minutes. And I was strong in my condemnation of the Kremlin if you remember. I was unwavering in my support for Theresa May. Of course, behind the scenes, I was more guarded, and was saying the opposite in parties and stuff. Russia is a great country, my name Boris (not my real first name of course) is a Russian name and some of my best friends are Russian. Dear old Alexander Lebedev for example is a very close chum, from a very successful family - they own the London institution The Evening Standard newspaper and Alexander (my real name of course) is an ex-KGB agent so he's done really well for himself in his own right.

Alexander and I used to really rip a night a new arsehole, he being one of the few people who could drink me under a table. I joked at a lovely party in Italy at his son Evgeny's gaff, just after the Salisbury attacks, that's he'd spiked my drinks with Novochok. He laughed at that, but didn't deny he had done it. And he must have been well pissed that night because when asked about it afterwards by the press he denied meeting me. At least I can remember the night, it really was great fun. Anyway the Russians - they're great people, they like a drink and a giggle and if a few bad apples want to kill someone that they don't like well, it's not like everyone's not doing that is it now? I refer you to my kill list your honour, which is obviously a joke but if I could get away with it, I would. Anyway, many a time I arranged to suppress intelligence reports on the threats posed to UK democracy by Russia because, well, I just had an instinct off the back of being treated so well by them. Call me naïve but my instincts are rarely if sometimes wrong. Some of the stuff said in that report was clearly ludicrous, stuff about British MPs being in the Russian's pockets. That's completely ludicrous, I know of no MP who has any links at all with Russian oligarchs, and I know all the oligarchs and hang out with a lot of them all the time. And what's more Alexander hates Putin so there can't be a link there. Maybe that's why Putin thinks I'm a cunt.

This is what makes it all so harrowing – up until I found out what Putin thought of me I was all over Russia like shit beetroot soup. One of the first things I did when I became London Mayor in 2008 was create a new Russian Festival and whilst I had no direct dealing with Putin I had a great relationship with his chief of staff Sergei Ivanov who supported the Festival hugely, and I very much doubt he had anything to do with interference in the 2016 US Presidential Election which everyone else thinks he did, but I really don't think so because he supported this Festival as I say and was just an all-round nice guy. I sorted so many Russian Festivals during my hugely successful tenure as London Mayor that I lost count. And the women are so fit. They make Toff look like my father. Olga Balakleets I dealt with a lot, absolute stunner, and my goodness Stefani Gorbounva, although she's Swedish I think, but dear me she looks Russian. Anyway, loads of 'em. I know them all, have drunk with them all, and the rest, and they're generally just up for a massive party to be honest. Anyway I've lost my thread. Oh yes, Dominic Cummings, he said we need to bring Russia back on side. He said that's why Russia is angry with me and to be honest I'm sure he's right, recently I've been so busy with the baby and Covid and what have you, I've neglected my Russian friends hugely. This is my mistake and I'll put it right from the morning. No coincidence there's a red sky tonight.

Dominic was right, he's always right. And I said I was going to be honest in this diary. And here comes a massive slice of honesty. Because although Dominic remains top of my jokey kill list because I pride myself in never changing my mind, when he calmed me down tonight, talked me off that metaphorical edge of panic that I've been dangling precariously over for days now, and when he looked at me with those piercing, dead, red eyes like Terminator, I kind of wanted to kiss him. There you go, I've said it. And if that doesn't sell column inches when this diary is published in The Evening Standard, then nothing will! I didn't kiss him of course, but I wonder now if I had what he would have done. Oh deary deary me, this has just got fucking weird.

Thursday July 23rd 2020

One year as Prime Minister tomorrow. This should have been a night of celebration, a moment of triumph, a moment to get pissed. Sadly not to be, I'm knackered and alone once more, well the baby and the wife are here but very much alone. Dominic had suggested a week or so ago that I nip up to Scotland of all places today to take the news in a different direction. I told him to eat shit at the time but I was glad in a way for a day away, a day away from number 10, from Russia, from death threats, and from him. It forced me to do what I've always done, and put on a show. I'm a showman, if not The Greatest Showman, then I'm up there. And thank goodness for my cameraman Joe too, just the right side-kick for a day like today, no nonsense, likes a joke, and I'm not one to confide in him about death threats or homosexual fantasies. He bought another bag of Doritos on the plane up, he chucked them at me and smirked. I had to confess I didn't know what on Earth he was doing – I can't remember last night let alone last week at the moment. Oh no, actually I can remember last night all too well. Ironic with dear old Dommers heralding from Durham, today was all about a Union with a Northern friend. But should that friend be a foe? Should we push for independence, or ever close bonds? Should I crave the touch of Scotland's dick?

If Scotland had a dick it would be thick and surrounded with ginger hair. And Nicola Sturgeon wouldn't come anywhere near it, like she didn't come anywhere near me today. 'Ooh I don't think Boris should be travelling up to Scotland when we're in the midst of a global pandemic'… Alright love, I've actually had Coronavirus, what have you done? I'll tell you what you've done deary, done exactly what I've done a week later like a petulant little twat. Apart from caught Corona. I've been in the trenches my dear, where's your war wound you freak? I didn't want to be in Scotland either. Why would anyone want to come to Scotland apart from for a fight? And I don't want to fight, not with you anyway Sturgeon, I've got bigger fish to be scared shitless of. Oh the Union, the precious Union, Scottish Independence, oh Brexit, newsflash guys, I don't give a toss about any of this stuff. I love the way I was criticised for not having a fixed viewpoint early doors on Brexit, 'oh he wrote two articles one supporting and one rejecting Brexit.' 'Oh yeah I heard that too because I'm a gossipy moron'. Well whoopy-doo, I'm happy for you, because breaking news my friends, I am allowed not to give a shit. Are you OK? Is that too much of a shock for your precious snowflake little heads? I am allowed not to give a shit. Just like 15% of the Scottish who didn't bother to vote in the last Independence Referendum, just like nearly 30% who didn't vote in the Brexit Referendum. That's a statistic you rarely hear isn't it – 33.6 million people voted, there are what 66 million people in the country? (I still can't quite believe we bought 90 million vaccines, we are idiots) and while many of those 66 million are babies, the real babies are the ones who cry constantly for everyone to have an opinion. I am allowed not to have an opinion, I am allowed not to give a shit. Sometimes you have to pretend. So today, just like I had to pretend to give a shit about crab fishing in Orkney, 'Oh how interesting, you fish for crabs do you? Great! Has one ever pierced your bollocks with its claws?' And just like I had to pretend about the RAF 'What's it like killing a man, does it feel good?' What would happen if I killed a man? What would it feel like? What would it feel like if, as in that classic fuck/kill scene in Basic Instinct I made furious love with Dominic and just as it was time for, if you'll pardon the pun, 'Cummings', I reached under the bed for an ice pick I had prepared earlier and had kept rock hard cold through an under-the-bed cooling system and stabbed him through his heart, only to realise that his heart was colder than the ice? I fell asleep on the plane home, what a fucking dream that was.

And now I'm back at number 10, looking out of the window, and terrified to sleep. Yes I'm safe here, but who is waiting from 'neath the Iron Curtain? And so I'm sat here staring at a list, a list of Dominic's preparation that I need to sign off. 23 Russians that I need to absolve and let back in this country, off the record obviously. He says this makes me safer, but letting pissed-off Russians back into this country, surely this makes my position more precarious. I have to trust Dominic, but do I? Maybe I should tell him how I feel. Because that's all that matters isn't it? That's why I don't care about Scottish Independence for fuck's sake, who cares? Really, ask yourself, why do you care? Why do you really care one way or the other about Brexit? I would hazard a guess you care because you can pretend for those moments that it matters, that it will affect you or your children's lives to any great extent. Well it doesn't. Look back on your life just for a second, what are the top ten moments that have affected you? I can guarantee you that unless you're some politics prick like Gove, no Referenda will come anywhere near that list. That list is full of who you fell in love with, who you broke up with, who you inseminated, who you pissed off. It's full of those moments in our life where we share human emotion, human contact. I only have what 30 years left in this world, 30 years? That's 1990 for crying out loud, that's gone in a flash, it only seems like yesterday where we were all cheering Blair and wondering what was the best out of Blue or Oasis. And in another 30 years that's it. If I'm lucky of course. And forgive me but I want to spend the next 30 years worrying about emotions, and human beings, and fun, and big yachts and parties with wealthy Russians. My wealthy Russian friends. So I've just texted Dominic, and signed off all 23. I ended the text with a smiley face. And then I asked him what he's up to. It's been 48 minutes now and no reply. I hate that cunt more than Scotland.

Friday July 24ᵗʰ 2020

Carrie woke me up early with a card bless her. It said 'Happy First Birthday!' And there was a picture of a little pink teddy – she had put quotation marks around the word "happy". I would have laughed but it was like 6am and I was hanging out of my arse. But bless her, she's a good stick. I have very few regrets about the marriage and the baby so am hoping for the best. I hardly slept. Dominic texted me back in the middle of the night at about 3am, it woke me up but I'd turned my phone right up to make sure it did, I was worried he was dead. It just said one word 'Sleeping!'. The exclamation mark was great to receive, we do have a laugh. No time for laughs this morning though as we did a final briefing on my chat with dear old Laura Kuenssberg at Downing Street today marking my first year in office. And Dommers was full of surprises again – what I thought was going to be the usual 'We've done our best in trying circumstances', 'now is not the time to judge us, how about judging us in 30 years when we're all dead mate' kind of bollocks, Dominic dished up the mother of all curve balls and said that I should tell the truth. I know right. The truth is a powerful weapon in politics, he said, and must be used very sparingly but with laser-light precision. What a way with words that man has. And now was one of those rare moments where the truth would be amplified, the truth would be heard far and wide, and most importantly, the truth would hide the truth of those 23 Russian diplomats coming back. 'It's time,' offered up Dommers with his usual silky smoothness, 'to admit we fucked up.'

So there we were, back in the Rose Garden at Downing Street, lovely sunny day, and thankfully less tricky circumstances than when Dominic turned up half an hour late to vomit out the biggest load of bullshit for several political centuries and cry 'blindness' as a reason for driving. I will have a laugh about that with him one day but I'm not ready just yet. However it really was surprisingly tricky to tell the truth. It's far easier to lie, I have years of practice. My parents used to teach us to lie regularly, on Sunday afternoons as I remember just before *Songs of Praise*, and said it was the most important lessons we would learn. We had actual lying lessons at Eton as well. They brought in poker players and top psychologists to take us through step by step the art of the perfect bullshit. Very clever stuff. It's all about body language, intonation, what you say, the whole package, really frighteningly clever. They say you can tell when a politician is lying because they 'move their mouth'. Well yes, that's true, but only if you're someone like me, in the know. The beauty of it is that the aching majority of the British population are monumentally stupid, and couldn't spot a lie if it bounced off their Sky dish and landed in their Pot Noodle. So telling the truth was going to be hard indeed, but dear old Dominic took the edge off the difficulty rating by agreeing that we should blame the scientists. So, so incredibly fucking clever. It means we look like we're apologising for the biggest death toll in Europe by a country mile, but we're not really we're blaming the scientists, and it has the added bonus of framing that cunt Pat Val and shoving a big long hard one up the arse of the Prince of Darkness himself Chris 'Never been kissed' UnWhitty.

So it was 'Yes Laura we fucked up' and by 'we fucked up' I mean we listened to Pat Val and Chris Shitty and they were WRONG. Sozmo, but those twats were wrong and we all believed them. There was nothing dear old Laura could do with that, sitting there squirming in her little pencil skirt and high heels. I had a maths teacher like her at Eton, scared the living shit out of me. Laura doesn't bother me though, I tell her to cleanse her hands as soon as she comes into Downing Street and I feel that gives me, literally, the upper hand, as I point with my manly hand at the cleansing station and she has to cup her feminine hands submissively under the anti-bac drip. I like that. Little does shew know that as soon as she does that, she ain't got shit on me. So we very quickly moved on to Dominic's clever new mantra 'double-down on levelling up'. Double-down is a great expression, one we got from those poker players and shrinks at Eton. When there's even the slightest hint that people are buying the bullshit, double-down with an extra lie and hammer their mistaken beliefs to the bollocks mast. Really clever stuff again. And here we want to, apparently, 'double-down on levelling up'. So clever. As soon as people read or hear the words 'double-down' they think we are doing double what we should have done in the first place. And what we're talking about doing in this instance is to level up the UK to make the North as wealthy and prosperous as the South. Now, of course, those in-the-know again will realise that is utterly preposterous – oh yeah let's make Hull as good as London. Never going to happen. If London is the heart of the UK then Hull is the arse. Not even the arse as people sometimes admire an arse. It's the UK's duodenum, literally the sewage pipe of the country. I mean it really is, Hull is where we pump out a lot of sewage into the sea. And if I could buy a big chain saw and chop off Hull into the sea I would. Never going to be London, not in a bajilion years. Hull is built by scum for scum. Anyway where was I? 'Doubling down on levelling up'. Brilliant, because we were really going to do nothing with regards to the levelling up, so doubling nothing of course, as my scary but in hindsight freakishly sexy maths teacher at Eton would tell you, two times nothing is nothing. So a whole lot of press today generated by a whole load of nothing, beautiful.

And this evening, Dominic arranged something really quite lovely for me – another private performance from the bonny Olga D, the

48

electric (in all senses of the word) violinist who played for me when I became Prime Minister a year ago. Dommers knew that I fancied her – I know you'll say I shouldn't – ooh Boris she's thirty years younger than you – but of course bingo, that is the reason I fancy her. Anyway I thought there was a spark last year and I really do think there's a spark this year. We had a little cuddle at the end of the night (don't tell the Covid police!) and she gave me her number so I'll call in her in a few days maybe, I don't know, I am trying to be good right now with the baby and Carrie hanging around like a bad smell (although I'm sure that the baby's arsehole!). But it really does feel like the start of something special.

Anyway, talking about a beautiful relationship with Russia, Dommers called me afterwards to check whether I'd fucked Olga but also to tell me that my plan was working. Not my plan of course, his plan. Not a Russian sausage had been spoken about me opening the doors to the 23 Russian diplomats and their families back to these shores, under different names of course so they would be totally untraceable, usual shit. In short, my plan is working. And by my plan you know what I mean, what is mine is his. We are one. And if I could double down on the one to make two then I would. Yes, I guess if I'm being honest with myself (which is a weakness) that is why I didn't take things even further with Olga D tonight. My mind is elsewhere. Dommers also told me that my plan (his plan) was bearing immediate fruit, and Sedwill had suggested that the death threat had dissipated slightly. I don't know how he would know this and I don't want to know quite frankly. The whole thing terrifies me, and if I'm slightly less terrified tonight then that's next level unlocked in my book. Level up. Double down on level up. I've gone 2 levels up. I'm high as a kite. Literally, the baby is in bed and I'm finally celebrating one year in charge with a toke of beautiful South American wacky-backy, and, a little later between me and thee, I've been promised, I have you know, my first post-baby blowy! By Carrie of course, not Olga or Dommers (you can't have everything). Fuck you Corona!!

RESUЯЯECTION

Saturday July 25th 2020

Oh fuck. We have a problem. And her name is Carole Cadwalladr. Yeah I know, that's not a typo. And people call me, Alexander Boris de Pfeffel Johnson, privileged. Safe to assume Carole Cadwalladr didn't have to fight too hard for her job as a journalist. Seeing as though her family couldn't be arsed to ever fight for a sensible fucking name. Anyway news is that Carole Codswallop is on to me. Dominic called me in to a crisis briefing today to tell me, totally fucking up a day off watching the Test match. England are walloping the West Indies by the way, order rightly resumed. Dominic has sworn me to secrecy, he put his finger to his thin red-blue lips and made me promise. All that I am telling is this journal, and at this rate no one is reading this scorching scandal-filled page-turner so I can say what I like. Will.I.am isn't a very good singer and invariably dresses like a prick. There you go, no one will read it so I said it. And I'm saying this so if it's ever found after my imminent death you'll know who pulled the trigger. And she goes by the code name Cadwalladr, which bizarrely is her real name too.

Carole Cuntwaller is the bitch that reported in that shit-rag The Guardian of my friendship with Alexander Temerko. Jesus - unlike you Carole, I'm allowed to have friends. And the story she shat out back then; the ground breaking, earth-shattering journalism of the year? Alexander Temerko, a Russian Oligarch, gives the Conservative party money to try to influence policy. Jesus Carole, the Pulitzer Prize is on its way in the second-hand post. A rich man gives several million to me and wants a few favours in return, haven't you heard sweetheart, there's a thing called 'life' and that's how it fucking works? Anyway, now she's apparently had whispers of me opening the back doors for those dear old Russian diplomats, and she's digging. And while she's digging, she's writing some bullshit in tomorrow's paper, and then there will be questions, and more questions about calling out Russia's meddling and all the while this big fat Russian fatwa hangs over me and I'm not allowed to tell a soul. That's what you've done Carol Claptrap, you've reignited Russian's mafia against your Prime Minister. I hope you're proud of yourself you meddling old cow. If

Putin stopped thinking I was a cunt for a day and now thinks I'm a
cunt again Carole, I will never ever forgive you.

Sunday July 26th 2020

'If it walks like a duck and talks like a duck, it is a duck. Britain has a
national security problem. And his name is Boris Johnson'. She's
stuffed me. Carole Cadwalladr has stuffed me. Cow. If it walks like a
cow and talks like a cow, it's Carole Cadwalladr. Cowrol. The human
anagram. So yet again today Dominic isn't even allowing me to go to
the pub telling me 'Darling, if you order a single shot that's exactly
what you might get'. He called me darling. But he didn't stick around
for lunch and the footy. Carole has fucked up everything. I swear
right, I'd get Covid again if it meant I could pass it on to Cowrol. To
paraphrase dear old Kevin Keegan, I'd love it if she got Covid, I'd
love it. That's it for today, I may not be Covid sadly but right now
I'm fucking livid. I wish Dommers would let me give Alexander
Lebedev a bell, a few nods and winks in the right direction I swear
he'd dust off that KGB Novichok and send Carole some new
perfume that would blow her fucking skin off.

Monday July 27th 2020

I'm rather proud of myself today. Despite everything that's going on
I had a very normal day. What people know about me is I'm a
showman, what people don't know about me is I can flick a switch,
always have been able to, and for a 24 hour period I can pretend
everything is ok. It's a remarkable skill and just like Dommers and
the truth, I'll use this special skill sparingly as I fear if I do it too often
my magic powers will dissipate. But for today, it worked yet again.
Despite the fading but still very present Russian fatwa, despite 46,000
and whisper it with a big old cough actually 60,000 Covid deaths,
despite my really quite baffling feeling towards The Talented Mr
Cummings, despite Brexit, despite the whole shit show that has been
and the even bigger one looming into view, you can always trust in
dear old Boris and his very special superpower of burying his head in
the sand and pretending everything is ok. I really am like Superman,

or Batman, but whereas they fly and do whatever Batman does (drives around in the big car and what have you), I can pretend. I bury my head in the sand. I am Ostrich Man. Call me The Ostrich.

Talking about ridiculous creatures, I was out with Dilyn this morning (no relation to Cadwalladr), my little Jack Russell cross that I rescued from the rescue centre and rescued from certain put-down death because I am, as I have stated humbly previously in this journal, an undoubted great guy. A good egg. Never give a dog an egg by the way, good or bad. I love dogs, and I'm very proud to have given this little doggy life. I just fucking love dogs. The thing I love most about dogs is that the life expectancy is 15 years. That's perfect isn't it? No love lasts longer than 15 years. Dogs just have an instinct don't they – they know how many bones they're gonna get thrown before the marrow wears thin. I also love dogs because when anyone sees me with a dog, I get no criticism. Everything else I've ever done – moaning bastards everywhere, as soon as Dilyn is by my side, even Ian Hislop might have a kind word to say about me, in private of course, before he ripped into me with his team of writers the snivelling little cock. I'm sure he'd say actually I was being typical old Etonian by choosing a white, male dog. Well go fuck yourself Mr Hislop, Dilyn had a fucked up jaw when we rescued him and the powers that be were gonna inject him with death serum before I (and Carrie) saved him from doggy heaven, or doggy hell probably coming from the scum background that little Dyl had been born into. Anyway, I took Dylly out for our morning little jog this morning and seriously, everything seems better. The way I termed it in my telly interview this morning is that the run is so horrible that it makes the rest of the day seem better, but really it's looking at the dog first thing running around that makes everything seem better. Because I love him so much, but I also recognise how lucky I am to be me and not him. How awful to be a dog – all you do is shit, run and eat – it would be like every day being Paula fucking Radcliff. I'm so happy I'm not a dog, and that happiness just gets me through the rest of the day.

RESURЯECTION

I mentioned the interview just then, that's a funny one. That cheered me up as well. Get this right (if you haven't heard) this latest initiative is called (and again obviously thank Dommers with a splashing of Matty Hancock) 'Better Health Strategy'. Genius right? BHS. In one foul-smelling 'do I smell bullshit?' swoop it sounds a bit like the NHS for the young woke people who want to save that creaking dinosaur of the past, and it's a lot like BHS as in British Home Stores, which the older generation will cling on to as a glory time for this country, but of course it was only a glory time because they were 30 years younger, and at 40 they were happy and now they're 70 and they're depressed and diabetic. And that's what the Better Health Strategy is going to fix. And look, let me be quite clear, I can talk about fat people because I am one, or I certainly was one a few months ago. And just like black people can talk about black issues or gays can chat shit about homos, I can certainly comment about fat people from a perspective of being one or having been one in the recent past. And with that in mind fat people are an absolute drain on this society. The amount we make as a country from an extra pasty or ten guzzled by the fatties just pails into insignificance against the drain they cause on our wonderful NHS. I often laughed when I saw fat people applauding the NHS during lockdown (and again I'm allowed to make this comment because I too was a fat person), I just found that absolutely bat-shit mental. It would be like dogs applauding people picking up shit from the parks. Stop applauding bitches and stop crapping all over the lawn. And again, I know from first-hand experience, it's nothing to do with genetics or having 'big bones', it's about being lazy and feckless and eating three too many pies, just like I used to do, and now I've stopped. Jesus, the number of people I see moaning online about lockdown having piled on the pounds. Lockdown hasn't piled on the pounds you cunt, you have by shoving McDonalds down your gob. Fuck the NHS applause, when McDonalds started delivering one could actually hear the applause and cheering in all corners of this bloated Isle. So come on guys, let's not end up like our dear old friends in America who all look like they are permanently auditioning for some Channel 5 freak show, let's have Better Health, let's BHS to save our NHS. Jeez you can tell I'm in a better mood, why am I writing this here, I don't actually believe this shit and if I do I don't really care. I just care about getting a red bullet through my noggin. Irony is if I am gunned down, losing all this weight probably makes me more likely to die as there will be far less flab for the bullet to ping through. You know what I mean, some of these fatties you could pump full of lead and they'd just carry on eating their McHeartAttack.

I saw dear old Rishi this morning while walking Dyl. It's weird living here. I sometimes think – Christ what the fuck is the Chancellor of the Exchequer doing in my garden? And I suddenly remember it's his garden as well. We share a garden, a bit like an upmarket council estate. And he actually lives in number 10. I don't mean I live with him, I don't like him like that. Although he is lovely. I wish I was him. Tall, dark and handsome, a billionaire, and everyone loves him. Why does everyone love him and hate me? We're delivering exactly the same policies. So unfair. But I don't begrudge him anything, he really is a lovely, smooth man, in all senses of the word. G od, that's got me thinking about Dominic again. I dread tomorrow, I know this good mood only lasts 24 hours, but I'm so happy right now thinking about Dominic and wondering what if anything might happen between us. I'm coming over all school-girly diary now, but boy I'd love to suck his big, smooth cock. N-night.

Tuesday July 28th 2020

I told you my bonny demeanour would only last 24 hours didn't I, my Super-powers have deserted me once more, and I'm fucking depressed. I'm sitting in the back of the car on my way back from Nottinghamshire. Wasn't it the Sherriff of Nottingham that robbed from the rich to give to the poor?! Ha ha, wasn't that Jeremy Corbyn's election manifesto?! Remember him? Ha ha ha. My life is just nonsense though sometimes, all the way up here just to spout some bullshit about cycle lanes. I know it's important but it's not important to me. I mean I loved it when they called the bikes in London 'Boris bikes' - that was awesome, but like I really give a shit if some prick in Nottinghamshire takes a bike to work or not, even in the best of times why would I give a flying fuck? And these are very much not the best of times. I talked with Dominic at length this morning, we kept it very business-like as he seemed even more pensive than usual, as he just talked me through the big issues, none of which surprisingly was a poxy little cycle lane in Trent fucking bridge. But I get it, it's a distraction for the news agenda, I get it, it's important to do this, but right now it's doesn't seem important to me. Not after my Russia briefing from Dominic this morning.

Apparently the whispers continue to come in from Russia that my gesture the other day has been welcomed, but Dommy has a fear that it isn't enough. I asked him where he got this fear from and he just said a combination of factors, along with a sixth sense. Do you remember the film *The Sixth Sense*? Was great wasn't it, I won't ruin the twist if you haven't seen it. I wonder whether that will be the twist in this book? Sometimes I feel like I'm in a fucking apparition from some weirdo kid. The twists and turns of life at the moment can't be reality can they? But apparently they are. I didn't tell Dominic this as he's already said he wouldn't allow it but I'm cooking up a bit of a plan – when I get back to London tonight I am going to call Alexander Lebedev, I've had enough of this Russian cloud over my noggin. I thought about this long and hard in the train toilet just now and I can't live every day like this. Have you seen the film *Groundhog Day*? In this film Bill Murray must live the same day over and over again until he fucks Andi McDowell. That would be fun. That would be a fun day to live over and over again. My Groundhog Day is living permanently with the threat of death while I'm set different complex daily challenges, or in today's case, pointless trips to the arse end of nowhere to eulogise about a fucking cycle path. Well I've had enough quite frankly. Someone wants me dead, Putin thinks I'm a cunt and dear old Alexander will help me I'm sure. He's got 3 billion dollars for Christ's sake, or he did the last time we spoke about cash, that's more than Rishi Sunak. I do love it when everyone says they have no money but love Rishi Sunak. Rishi has a billion pounds, a thousand million pounds. He could give everyone in the country fifteen quid and he's still have plenty left over. And instead he offers everyone a free Nando's and people think he's Mother fucking Theresa. A notorious cunt by the way. Mother not Rishi. Rishi's lovely.

Anyway I'm not sure what my plan is but I'm hoping Alexander will have something up his gold-lined sleeve. He could at least ensure that some subtle but favourable stuff is put out in the Evening Standard and The Independent. Ha ha, 'Independent', I love that. And next I shall call my newspaper 'The Daily Definitely Not Corrupt'. Ha ha. God I used to love his parties, they were the good old days weren't they when I could do exactly what I wanted as London Mayor. Nothing was off the menu, especially sexual intercourse - that was on the menu. Alexander's parties were off the hook. At one jambo in Umbria in Italy I went to (I was there all the time back in the day), there was me, Mick Jagger, Eddie Izzard (the comedian), Joan Collins and Princess Eugenie, Prince Andrew's daughter. And not just someone that could be his daughter! No no, terrible business. Eugenie forced to marry that chap just to get her father off the front pages. Awful business, that's when I despair about the world. Look, God, it's a tricky one isn't it? I can tell you what happened but you won't want to hear it. Prince Andrew fucked young women. When Leonardo DiCaprio does it we all go 'Oh Leonardo aren't you a one' but when dear old Randy Andy does it he's a paedophile. Prince Andrew is not a paedophile. He's just a very naughty boy. Anyway this isn't about him. I just despair at the whole thing. The fact he had to come out and say he didn't remember that photograph of him with his arm round that girl, so embarrassing. 'Yeah I can't remember fucking her Emily Maitless' and poor old Emily has to play along with the whole charade. He was worse than Dominic. Not that Dominic has had sex with young women of course not that's not his thing at all, I just mean worse in terms of excuses. I think Andrew should have gone with the Dominic line of excuses 'Oh yes sorry I did have sex with that 17 year old, it was in Durham and I was just testing my cock.' I'm not making light of it, it's awful. But you know what, there's also something fairly awful in the knowledge that we won't be able to get up to any funny business in the future. Good Heavens some of those parties hosted by Alexander back in the day, I really can't repeat what I saw Mick Jagger and Joan Collins doing one night on the shores of the Lake Como. Or as dear old Joan calls it now - Lake Cummo! Oh dear God, maybe that night I grabbed the karaoke mic and sung 'Putin on the Ritz'. Maybe that's why he thinks I'm a cunt. No surely not, I was just off my tits on cocaine.

I need to play this careful however. Old Carole Cadwalladr is still on my dick (she'll be lucky!) and if I'm not involving Dominic I truly am going rogue. I know he wouldn't let me and this really would be the first time I've gone behind his back (so to speak). I feel terrible about doing so but what choice do I have? And in my experience getting away with things behind people's backs is really quite easy. As I've said many times - hide in plain sight. Remember that song from dear old Shaggy, 'It wasn't me.' That's always been my tactic. Remember when I was on *Have I Got News For You* and Hislop thought he had me by the bollocks by bringing up me helping to arrange beating up that journalist prick, remember? All I did was shake my head around and laughed and said 'Bibble bibble bibble' and the audience loved me. And they, to a man, thought Hislop was a potato-faced cunt, and they were right. I can swing this baby out whatever way I choose to. I have to remember something I sometimes forget in moments of crisis – I'm Boris fucking Johnson. I'm the fucking Prime Minister for fucks sake. I'm Boris fucking Prime Minister fucking Johnson. I am Bo-Jo. As a kid I said I was going to be 'King of the world' and now I am I should start acting more like a King. And the first thing a King needs is unlimited wonga, and then second maybe some Russian slaves. Maybe Olga D, I must text that little Russian violinist minx. That's what I like – sex and violins! With Alexander's help I will have all that and I shall be King of the world. And when you're King of the world you can do anything you like, anything! Yep, even have sex with 17 year old women. That's what I'll say if I shag Olga and she turns out to be 17 (she looks 17!) 'Erm, yes I did have sex with her Emily Maitless, of course I bloody had sex with her, whatya gonna do about it? I'm not Jeffrey Epstein. I'm King Boris Johnson, and I can do what the fuck I want.' God, I hope no one reads this diary. If they do, I'll have to kill myself. That will be a twist, I'll have been dead all along, just like Bruce Willis in *The Sixth Sense*. Ooh we've just won the Test Match. Up yours West India!

Wednesday July 29th 2020

Big news! So last night I was phoning Alexander and old sausage
fingers phones his son by mistake, dear old Evgeny. I think I
mentioned him, lovely chap and a great mate too. Looks like a young
Alfie Boe without the cheese-fest operatic bullshit and cringe double
act with Michael fucking Ball. Fuck a duck mate, bring back my glue
ear! Anyway, I get on with him and his dad equally well. His dad is
more of the hell raiser, party planner, Joan Collins thrower and his
son is more like me - the suave, sophisticated, owner of national
newspapers type. But still, a hoot all the same. And the best thing is I
know he likes me, he looks up to me, and surprisingly not many do.
Evgeny had a pet wolf and he named him Boris after me. The wolf
died as I recall, suddenly, and he doesn't like to talk about it. But he
likes to talk about loads of other stuff, including Russian's influence
in British politics. He's so honest. And he's a player, he once got off
with the least attractive one from the Spice Girls. He's a character.
In his office in Mayfair he's got a sculpture called 'Fuck Face', a child
with a penis for a nose. I joked when I saw it that it was like a spin-
off Pinocchio story, a child that when he lied his penis nose got erect.
He didn't laugh because I don't think he understood my point. But
most of all I like Evgeny because his sole purpose apart from fucking
pop stars is to improve the perceptions of Russians in this country,
and that is what I'm all about too, not the fucking pop stars bit
(joking, I'm sure I'll have a go on Olga D), the other bit. But what is
also very handy, is he is mates with Putin, or at least has access to the
man that calls me 'a cunt'.

So I opened with that, I hadn't talked with him for a while but I know
he likes the no nonsense approach so I just came out with it,
'Apparently there are Russians that want me dead, and Putin thinks
I'm a cunt, any idea why that would be?' He paused for a second,
probably stroked his gorgeous black beard (I'm imagining that it
wasn't a video call) and he said two words… 'Dominic Cummings'.
And he asked me the killer question, have you ever considered Russia
likes you Boris, but dislikes Mr Cummings? Shit a brick right? A bit
of a back story before I told you what I said. Dominic spent three

years in Russia in the mid 90's after Oxford. And I've never been able to get to the bottom of why. He's a bit fucking shady about it to be honest. End of last year dear old Emily Thornberry the Shadow Foreign Sex was asking about it and when I said at the time it was classified what I meant of course was I don't know, Dommers doesn't like to talk about those years very much. But I know he's been through the appropriate checks of course so as I've always said, people are allowed to have Russian friends just as they are allowed to fuck pop stars, as long as they're over 16. Make it 18 actually to avoid the bleaters. Anyway it was fully checked again last year, but then it struck me – it was checked by the head of the civil service – and who was that at the time? Mark Traitor Sedwill, the very man that told me of Putin's fairly low opinion of me, that I am a cunt. Anyway, I said to Evgeny, 'Why would they think Cummings is a cunt?' And that's when he came out with it – he said that Dominic had been helping Russia, all along, all the rumours about the elections and Brexit, Dominic Cummings was listening to Russia, just like I had done in my time as London Mayor. Now nothing wrong with that of course as I say, and Evgeny himself has been open about if they give the Conservative Party millions of pounds then they should bloody well have influence. But then the killer line from Evgeny – 'This is personal between Putin and Cummings, they were once friends, and now they've fallen out. That's what I've heard.' 'But why would he and Sedwill tell me that Putin actually hated me and wanted to kill me?' 'You'll have to ask him', he said, 'But I will say this, isn't Mr Cummings the master of diversion?'

And that was that, he said he knew nothing more. We then talked about girls and fox hunting for a bit and I said I'd meet up with him and his dad when all this bullshit calms down. And that's when he told me the truth – I had phoned the right number, Alexander just didn't want to talk to me, he wants no part of this. He's scared. He knew why I was calling and he's scared. Putin wants someone dead at the height of Government, and he doesn't know quite why. And he doesn't want to be caught in the cross fire. And that was it, Evgeny had to go, he said he was cooking dinner. Which is bullshit, he doesn't cook obviously. I imagined his penis becoming erect, if he had a penis for a nose and was Pinocchio and his penis got bigger every time he lied, I really thought that joke was self-explanatory. Clearer anyway than this fucking mess I now find myself in. Caught between a rock and a hard place. The rock of Putin's anger, and the hard place of my feelings for Dominic Cummings. I hope someone does read this now, it's turning into a real fucking page turner innit?

Thursday July 30th 2020

Every day just seems like the biggest day of my life right now, and I'm finding it increasingly hard to write this, so sorry if it's a bit rushed and shit, but you know what I say, if it's ok for our Covid strategy it's ok for this journal – lol. Number one in Europe baby! Number one excess deaths in the whole of Europe! More of that perhaps later but the man of the hour told me to say that represented a 'spectacular success' – I said that and the story kind of went away. I know right, it's like Jedi-mind shit. Anyway, the day started dreadfully of course as I didn't sleep a wink. Nothing to do with the latest nurses' protests as they yet again rather pathetically waddled on Downing Street demanding more money – they think I hear their pathetic squawks? I just stick my N.W.A. album on and drift off. I mean let me quickly deal with this one, the nurses are of course the very bedrock of our wonderful NHS, they are critical, but just because you're critical to something doesn't mean you deserve a pay rise. The guy or girl at McDonalds who cleans the bloody toilets is 'critical' to their operation, but I don't see that teenager demanding much more than free chips and a wanking off into the McFlurry machine at the end of the shift. And let's be honest, just for a second, whisper it quietly… nurses, God this is controversial but I told you I'm going to be honest – nurses generally do fuck all don't they? Have you ever been in a hospital? I have. What's the first thing you see when you go on a ward? I don't mean during Covid times when it's another dead pensioner being wheeled away (number one baby!) - I mean in normal times it's always a couple of nurses drinking tea and gassing about which doctor they fancy. Because I said it was those nurses that saved my life but obviously that was bullshit, obviously we all know it's the doctors that save your life when you're sick, not the nurses.

Thanking the nurses is just something you do isn't it? It's like when a top sportsman thanks the ground-staff and the cleaners and the ball boys and says 'Ooh I wouldn't have been able to do this without them, those ruddy bloody unsung heroes.' Don't make me laugh, a ball boy is not a hero, he's a boy picking up balls and giving them to the actual heroes. And that's what nurses are – ball boys, or of course in the case of nurses, ball girls.

Anyway this morning was the beginning of the fightback, not against Coronavirus that started weeks ago (number one baby!!), but against Cummings, and Sedwill, and whatever the fuck is going on here. I called Dominic at 7am this morning. I knew I'd catch him off-guard. He sometimes doesn't get into work until 2pm, he just swans in and flatly refuses to tell anyone where he's been. I sometimes thought about reporting him before I remembered I was Prime Minister and there was nothing even I could do. Dommers has become untouchable. Well today, I vowed at 7am, was the day that dear old Dominic would be touched. Not like that, I assumed. I woke him up of course. 'Boss!' he exclaimed gruffly, telling me the caller who was on the line. I said to him I had to see him today and I would not take no for an answer. He said 'no' and that threw me, but I drew on the strength I didn't actually know that I had, the strength of the Russian hammer and sickle hanging above my head, and I insisted, 'No I am definitely seeing you today, I am Prime Minister and I am definitely seeing you today, I swear on Wilfred's life.' I know one shouldn't go around wishing on one's baby son's life, and it came back immediately to bite me when Dominic told me he'd fucked off again to Durham for a few days to enjoy the beautiful weather and have a long weekend. I joked and said 'you'd better not tell your boss' and then I realised I was his boss and it made me angry. I think this is the first time I've been outwardly angry with him, blame my lack of sleep. 'Durham!' I exclaimed, 'Haven't you landed us in the shit enough times already going to Durham you fucking tit?' He hung up and I don't blame him. Don't call someone a 'fucking tit' - you instantly lose the argument. I took a moment, called him back and I was calmer, I said sorry but of course I was lying, he knows that. The Durham Police Chief came out today and said that Dominic had undermined lockdown, and loads of people were giving him as an excuse for breaking it. I told him that would happen, the fucking tit.

Anyway, so he said that's why I couldn't see him today, he was working from his third home. But again, I gathered strength from I don't know where. I pictured poor Wilfred crying (maybe helped by actual Wilfred actually crying in another room with Carrie) and saying he had to die, my baby boy had to die because I'd sworn on his life I would do something and then I didn't do it and that's how swearing on someone's life works, if you don't do the thing they actually die. So I said 'No no no no no,' I would be seeing Dominic today even if it meant me coming to Durham. I then looked at where Durham was on the map and I thought 'oh fuck', I was hoping just to get pissed today. So I compromised and said I'd meet him in York, I love York and it was the proposed bullshit place we were gonna plonk Parliament Mark II if you recall, and I could combine the trip with some bollocks about police numbers, and me and the Yorkshire Chief Constable dear old Lisa Winward did a bit of blow once. So yes, I said I'd see him in York and I wouldn't take no for an answer. Dominic said 'no' and as I hadn't sworn on my child's life for that one it gave me a get out and I said I'd come to Durham, secretly, after pretending the purpose of my trip was Yorkshire. Dominic again said no, and that his father hated me and thought I was a cunt. That angered me, and I said 'see you tonight' and I hung up. It felt good, then bad, then good again, and then normal, and then annoying that I had to go to fucking Yorkshire and meet the po-po. But my mood had stiffened, I would do anything now to get to the truth.

Oh the truth, that slipperiest of customers. So I found myself in Yorkshire just after lunchtime (I had ten sausage rolls) chatting shit about the first 4000 of our promised 20,000 new policemen had already been recruited. Of course, we've cut police numbers by 20,600 since 2010 with the sole purpose of saving money and then looking good when we recruit them again, but of course when we re-recruit we get those teenagers from McDonalds and the ball boys (and girls) instead of the experienced police heroes (and what do heroes cost? Money!) so it's a win win for everyone including terrorists who know they only have to get past the ball-boys to get to their prey. Not me of course, I'm guarded by 4 ex-SAS hunks, they're the fucking best. But I had to give them the slip tonight, and I drove myself to Durham. I know right, I sometimes just duck away in an inconspicuous 2007 Ford Fiesta. Imagine if I'd been stopped by the pigs. Oh fuck! 'I'm just testing my eye-sight'. Ha ha ha, imagine!

Anyway I arrived at about nine. It had just got dark, I pulled into the castle grounds where Dominic's meagre house is in the grounds of the castle, and suddenly, a dog runs toward the car, yapping and barking like one of those fucking nurses yesterday. It was Dominic's father, Robert. Angry little prick started shouting at me before he realised who it was. I wound down the window 'Hello Robert' I said with a big, cheesy grin. He then carried on shouting at me saying that he would 'call the police'. I couldn't help but laugh, if it was any of the spindly little ball-boys and shits I'd had to entertain this afternoon, I was hardly sweating up. I told him I was here to see Dominic, and he told me he'd go to get him. And this is where we are now. I'm waiting, in a car, in the dark, writing this, waiting to be allowed to see 'the boss'. It's fucking ludicrous. I wish I had my SAS guys here now, I've been waiting 10 minutes at least, we could storm that fucking cottage and shoot Robert through the head. Try calling the fuzz with a cap in your ass you fucking tit, and that's when 'fucking tit' wins the argument. As dear old Dr Dre once said 'fuck the po-lice' and 'fuck Dominic Cummings'. Not literally obviously, I've gone right off him.

Friday July 31st 2020

Funny how life works out isn't it? It was the hottest day of the year today, hottest that I can remember in the UK. Reminded me of all those wonderful times as a youth on holiday with my parents. We went to some wonderful places, my father used to joke that it was great to get out of 'this shit-hole country'. He was joshing obviously but I know what he means, however much you love this great country of ours, the second you land anywhere else we all scream as one 'thank fuck I'm not in Widnes any more'. You get me? 'I'm on a beach and it ain't freezing with homeless everywhere.' I used to long for the hot weather, now I can't take it. And particularly post-Covid. My aging body feels constantly like I played squash two days ago. I'm knackered. What I'm saying is things change, nothing is forever. People change, that's allowed, I'm allowed to evolve. I'm allowed rebirth.

DC was in his pyjamas last night. He said he'd been working but he had a wry smile on his face. An episode of *Star Trek* was on the television (you can take the man out of the stereotype!) and there was a half-bottle of Scotch on the nest of tables. 'I suppose I should get you a drink,' he mused. His father, Robert had fucked off some moments ago. Aggressive little tosser. He was shouting at me, terrible at the best of times but should be a criminal offence in this new normal… spit everywhere, saying the country was now 'up shit creek without a paddle'. I said 'you don't necessarily need a paddle to get out of shit creek'. And he asked me how else one would get out of shit-creek, and I hypothesised that depending on the flow of the shit you could just float out. He disagreed. 'OK I said, I'll get a paddle.' 'And you think you can make a paddle do you?' he spluttered, 'you've failed at everything else!' So unnecessarily mean. So I said, 'Well I'd hazard a guess I'll be better at making paddles than you, you shouty old twat.' I thought I'd shut him down but he then told me that after making oil rigs, he went briefly into the paddle-making business. I didn't believe him but Dominic backed him up and I later checked it all out on Wikipedia and indeed Robert Cummings did once make paddles. What are the chances that one would win a 'you can't make a paddle' argument so convincingly? Really fucking annoying.

Anyway, we were left alone in the cottage. It was warm and a dry wind blew through the open window in the lounge, teasing the leaves of Dominic's fake orchid. I asked him is that a real orchid? And he said no it was fake. And I said it looked real. He smiled and said 'and that my love is the secret of politics'. I didn't understand straight away but I laughed anyway, trying to break the tension. 'So why are you here?' He cut to the chase, handing me what looked like half a measure of Scotch. I pondered whether to pussy-foot around the issue, but I figured he knew full well I'd driven all the way to Durham, and you don't drive to Durham without a bloody good reason. So the chase is exactly where I cut to. I didn't tell him about Evgeny of course, I just said I was thinking of letting him go. Big right? I was nervous saying it, but I'm the big guy. I just said it, simply and with only one minor mistake, 'I'm afraid I will have to let you go please Dommers.'

He was quite calm at first and asked why, and I drew upon every single lying lesson I'd had at Eton and I told him that I planned on resigning myself, and I wanted to give him the option of resigning rather than being forced out of a job. His lip started to wobble a little, like Gazza in the 1990 World Cup Semi-final when he'd chopped that German in half. Dear old Dominic never shows that emotion, and I knew this time it wasn't fake, he believed me. This was the plan I'd hatched when I was driving to Durham. I trust Evgeny, and I trust his father, you don't get to be in the KGB if you can't be trusted. And I know Dominic is up to something, but there would be no way of finding out. No way that is, unless he was pushed to the edge, and realised that whatever he was doing was having serious repercussions on my will to go on. He said when did I want him to go, and I told him straight away. He immediately got angry, and he raised his voice a little, he had whisky on his breath. He said that we'd done everything together, we'd done the impossible, and now I was going to just ditch him. My plan was working, I knew he would react just like this, I know Dominic better than he knows his own father, because he quite likes his father when I know he is a cunt. And I'm no cunt, no matter what Sedwill, or Putin, or indeed Dominic Cummings thinks of me. I'm nobody's cunt. And then he dared me, he dared me to go just 24 hours without him by my side, feeding me lines, feeding me slogans. He told me that we had to roll back on our plans to open indoor entertainment today, and to explain the lockdown of Northern England, what was my plan? 'You don't have to worry matey, I've got a plan,' I lied. I've got it all sorted, I'd planned everything I was going to say tomorrow. And then he asked the killer question, 'So what's your slogan?' My lip now wobbled, like

Gary Lineker's after he saw Gazza's lip wobbling after he chopped that German in half.

I didn't have a slogan, but I haven't got where I am today by not thinking on my feet. So I looked down at Dominic's lizard-like hand and I said the word 'hand'. He laughed 'hand?' I looked up at his face scoffing at me and said 'is that it?' I said no of course not. I looked at his face and said 'face' and then looked at *Star Trek* on the television and said the word 'space'. 'That's it,' I said proudly. That's my slogan – 'hands, face, space'. 'What does it mean?' he laughed. 'Well obviously wash your hands, wash you face, or cover your face, you know,' I stumbled and…'. 'What?' he said, coming closer to me. 'You can't cope without me', he said, his deep red eyes reflecting an explosion on *Star Trek*. 'Yes I can', I lied. He took the glass out of my hand, and put it back on the nest of tables. He put his own glass down. 'You need me', he smouldered. 'You want me.'

Now, what happened next I will no doubt redact if this journal is ever released but just for completeness this is exactly what happened. First he winked, and then he teased his finger into his buttoned fly, and tugged out his semi-erect cock. He then started teasing the end betwixt his fingers until it was fully erect, it was small but incredibly hard, like a fat bullet. He then repeated 'you want me.' I'm not embarrassed but I was intoxicated, not by the whisky I'd only had a drop, and unless he'd roofied me I was fully compos mentis. I nodded, and with a certain inevitability, I fell on to my knees to the floor, as if pole-axed by Gazza in the 1990 World Cup semi-final. I want to make it crystal clear now if this is ever read, that I have never sucked a cock before, and may never suck a cock again, but it is something I will never forget. It lasted barely a minute but I heard pleasure from Dominic's mouth that I only dared to dream I may one day hear, and then after about fifty seconds I felt a difference, he went quiet as the cock grew larger and started to twitch in my mouth. He then said once more 'Do you need me?' And I stuck my thumb up. Not up him of course, just in the air. He then rose his hands in the air and, well, quite frankly what felt like a gallon of semen catapulted on to the back of my throat. I gagged but he reached down and grabbed my hair pulling my face in. He then shouted at the top of his voice 'I'm the King of the world! Dominic wins!'

His batter was all over me. All in my mouth and down my chin and on my shirt. I tried to smile but the taste was a bit dire really, load of gunky old spunk mess sticking to my teeth. I tried to make a joke – I said 'Dominic's Cummings'. But he didn't raise a smile. He just said 'never ever question that you need me again. Get out.' I said 'You don't mean that.' But he did, repeating for me to leave. I said 'What about the slogan?' And he said you've got one haven't you? 'Hands, face, space.' He laughed, maniacally and slammed the door in my spaff-spattered face.

I'll show him who's boss I thought. So today, I ignored his many messages, and went full steam ahead. I stood there proudly on that lectern, the taste of Dominic's gank still fresh in my mouth and I just repeated it as if it was grade-eight genius. 'Hands, face, space.' I tried to find the camera, I knew he'd be watching. I tried to find the camera and wink. This was to tell him I now had the upper hand. I can cope without him, sucking his cock to completion meant nothing to me. But that is of course yet another lie. Maybe it's time for the lying to cease now that I have sucked Dominic Cummings' penis.

And so I sit here in number ten, trying to cool down from the hottest day of the year and the hottest night of my life. My face and hands are still covered in Dominic's sperm and all the space in the world won't keep his face off my mind. To be honest, I can't even remember what my original plan was now in driving to Durham, it seems like a lifetime ago driving back from Durham with man-yoghurt still in my eyes unable to see, I wish I'd been able to do a short journey first to test my eyesight, it was really dangerous. But whatever I meant to happen, the result is the same, I am powerful now, I will do what no one expects me to do. And hear me and hear me well dear friends, if I have to suck every cock in this land to get to the truth, that is what I shall do.

RESUЯЯECTION

Saturday August 1ˢᵗ 2020

Pinch, punch, first of the month, no returns. Maybe we should make the no returns thing actual law. Making laws at the moment is a piece of piss. Everyone in Manchester has to stay in – a week later it's the law. I've seen a few cartoons actually today with various politicians, myself and Matty Hancock mainly throwing darts into 'spinning wheels of policies'. I have to say that's not so far away from the truth, as I've said before this whole thing is bloody difficult, it's very easy for you to say we're fucking it up - what do you do for a living? What was that? A dental nurse? Well, great, you my love spend your whole day sucking up shit and spittle from people's gobs and Matty Hancock told me the other day you need absolutely no training for that job, so do the opposite of what you don't tell your patients (because you ain't a dentist) and shut your mouths. And anyway, the current rules in the UK are very simple, in short…

In Greater Manchester, East Lancashire and parts of West Yorkshire different households are not allowed to meet in any setting. Unless you're in a support bubble with another household as that classes as one household, support bubbles obviously restricted to for example single adults living alone or with children under 18 bubbling with another family. You can't have 2 families bubbling, if you're not single you will need to split up with your partner and kill any kids over the age of 18 first, and once you form a bubble you can't switch and make another one. A bubble, as the name suggests, is for life. Same rules apply to Wales which makes it nice and easy, so people in Wales could form a bubble with a household in England and vice versa, which makes it nice and simples, however obviously Wales has different requirements in terms of bubbling so basically ignore everything I've just said. But good news is that I'm only talking about going round other people's houses, you can still meet your family and friends outdoors as much as you like, but only up to six people. And by outdoors I don't mean your garden. And obviously hands, face, space. Wash your hands and cover your face as soon as you come closer than 1m to people, you can take it off at 2m. Treat it as a little game. Oh and for those that think I'm racist, you can go to a mosque with your family but you must socially distance and wear a face covering, which you're probably doing anyway, lol! So, pretty self-explanatory so far – if you live in Greater Manchester, East Lancashire and parts of West Yorkshire you can't see your family in each other's houses unless you're bubbling but you can see them in a park. However, here's the great news, if you're all going on holiday together you can do that with absolutely zero restrictions, fill your flip-flops and enjoy a sangria on me! As Matty Hancock said the other day 'there are absolutely no restrictions on travel' apart from of course those countries where there are restrictions and those restrictions could come in immediately and without notice. Treat it again as a little game, but this time with the risk of being stuck somewhere and ending up bankrupt. But again the great news is that once you're abroad those countries don't give a flying fuck which part of the country you're from, they just want you to buy their patatas bravas (bad example, Spain is closed still I think, but you get my drift).

And to those asking why we're doing this, well just look at the statistics. In Wigan the cases of Coronavirus have shot up in a week from 4 cases per 100,000 to 8 cases per 100,000. And to those cretins that say 'that sounds like nothing', it clearly isn't nothing is it? Nothing would be nothing so shut the fuck up you moaning Northern bastards. And yes, comedy clubs are to remain closed (boo hoo for Frank Twat and his skits) because, morons, the risk of infection from one person talking and an audience laughing is far greater than a whole pub talking and laughing, so just go to the pub and make each other laugh, far better and from some of the comedy I've seen, far funnier. Your friends know your sense of humour, Frank Twat has to guess. And if you were getting married, sorry that's now cancelled. But as I say, go to the pub as much as you like, meet new people 'til the cows come home and have a giggle and forget all about it, even in Leicester from Monday. In the rest of England, well it's pretty much open season, fuck who you want. Hang on, only if you're bubbling. Fuck who you're bubbling with, so I hope you didn't choose your family as your bubble. Otherwise you've gotta keep your distance, so no fucking, maybe just masturbating in the same room in front of each other, from 2m, or closer if you both wear sex masks. Indoor meetings not recommended, so try to make mutual masturbation sessions outdoors, and you can do this with infinite different households, so terrific news for sex workers. In short, no gang bangs. And this also applies to anyone that has been shielding for 4 months, as of today you're free to fuck and drink like the rest of us. This is England I'm talking about. Scotland you can meet up with 15 people outdoors from 5 different households, but it's freezing up there so that's irrelevant, and eight people can meet up from three households indoors. Here in sunny England to remind you it's just 30 people from 2 households, in Northern Ireland 10 people from 4 households indoors and 30 people outdoors and in Wales 2 households can form one 'extended household'. Simple. Ps if you're not living with your partner you can now go round and have sex with them as much as you like, but again, no gang bangs. And I talked about pubs, that's just in England and Scotland, pubs only can open in Wales from Monday. I don't know what's happening in Ireland, but I assume there they've never closed. And finally, everyone should go back to work you lazy cunts.

Sorry, I'm pissed today, I need to black out sucking Dominic Cummings' cock on Thursday night. Normal diary service to be resumed on the morrow. And so my friends to bedfordshire, I'm just about to ask Carrie to, if you know what I mean, take the taste away. N night.

Sunday August 2ⁿᵈ 2020

As I've always said, all I've ever done is tried my best, that's all I've ever tried to do since University and for a few years after, since then I've tried my absolute best, and that goes for sucking Dominic Cummings' cock the other night. And when it's shoved back in your face it's particularly hard to swallow. Dominic called me today and made me feel dirty quite frankly. Old 'wandering hands' (…face, space) himself has been arrested for rape which we knew was about to hit of course and Dominic broke his text silence today and said 'I could have you arrested for the same thing.' I called him up to put a stop to this once and for all. 'What is that supposed to mean?' 'Well if you look at the footage back,' he said, 'it's not like I asked you to do that.' 'Footage?' I screamed. 'You know me,' he smarmed, 'I record every single conversation I have.' Now I knew that of course, Dominic records every single conversation he has, all private and personal conversations, those in pubs and restaurants or if someone came up to him in the street and asked him for directions or called him a 'ratty-faced fuck' he'd have it all on record ready to use against you, but I was obviously flabbergasted that he would record that most intimate of moments. 'Well I didn't know it was going to turn into that!' he shouted. Oh yes he did. The pyjamas, the whisky, the teasing out of the cock, it was a set-up, and a set-up that was now on permanent record in that grubby little traitor's hands. 'Don't worry', he slithered, 'I'm hardly going to sell it to the Sunday Times am I?' Well I don't know do I? I was panicking, can you imagine the headline? They'd definitely go with 'Bo-Job'. Utterly humiliating. He tried to reassure me again, 'We've done everything together and now we really have done everything together, it feels good.' Well it didn't feel good to me, I didn't even ejaculate, until much later. And then he said 'You can trust me boss, I've made sure that the news agenda was off you today as someone saw you in a service station at 3am on Thursday night with a jacket covered in spunk. You can't cope without me can you?' Do you know what - I actually can't, I knew it was stupid to stop off at the service station but I just had to get the taste of semen out of my mouth so I stopped off for some mints and a beer. I know I'm an idiot, but again, put yourself in my shoes – until you've sucked off Dominic Cummings and are driving back 7 hours with him still sloshing around in your mouth then you cannot comment.

Anyway, I relented and I'm not one to back down but I backed down and have just phoned Dommers back for a less heated exchange. And we got back to business. I may not trust him, I may now believe that he is the reason that Putin thinks I am a cunt but as a wise head once said 'Keep your friends close, but your enemies closer'. I think too there's probably something in the adage 'suck the cock of your enemy but don't entrust him with the footage'. Oh I don't know, things will be ok, for goodness sake they usually are. So, heavens I said to him look, we're in August now, I can't believe it, it's Brexit in 5 months now and we've done fuck all really towards that and I told him that I have done nothing personally for a week because I've been so worried about Russia. He said I know, 'I know, you called Evgeny.' You could have heard a novichok-soaked pin drop. I breathlessly replied 'how do you know?' And Dominic said 'I know everything.' I retorted snappily, there are things you don't know about me and Evgeny.' I was trying to make him jealous but it didn't wash. 'Evgeny cannot be trusted by the British Government.' I thought that was a little strong, and he flatly refused to expand, again calling it his 'sixth sense'. Dominic looks a bit like the boy out of *The Sixth Sense*. 'I see dead people… all the time at the moment!' Am I right?!'

Anyway Dommers quickly changed the subject but I hadn't in my own head – Evgeny is my friend and I trust him with my precious life, we have partied together several times and the drinks were always free - he's a top, top bloke. But the strange Mr Cummings said he had a plan to solve everything with Russia and get them on side with this Government once and for all. And it's this. Russia is preparing to start a mass vaccination campaign against Covid in October. I know this seems rather early doesn't it, but those Russians are bloody clever, and sneaky – from what I know of Russia they were probably working on a vaccine before the virus even hit the streets! That's how good and clever they are. Hang on, imagine that. If you could release a virus to a small community in say, China, and you were the only ones with a vaccination you'd make more money than the Spice Girls, TikTok and Pringles put together. Oh my God, is that even possible? Well yes of course it's possible, but it's also the exact plot of the film *Mission Impossible II*. In this film, a superior follow up if I may so to the slightly confusing first outing of the franchise, a biochemical expert (a Russian obviously, what are the chances?) has developed a biological epidemic and a remedy to make a load of dirty cash. And the virus? Chimera? Corona, Chimera. This is mental. And Cummings is he a goody or a baddy? You never know til the end of the film do you? And am I Tom Cruise? I mean in the past few days I have obviously acted like a bit of a homosexual hero. Oh goodness, I don't know what to believe.

But if I'm to believe Cummings, this cure for Corona is good to go in Moscow and this is the one to put our money into. 'What about the 90 million vaccines we bought from Oxford?' I said. 'Nothing is going to be ready until next year,' he replied, 'we have to act now.' So he's asked me tonight to fund 100 million vaccines by giving the Institute behind this new vaccine, the Gamaleya Institute 300 million pounds. So I'm sitting here tonight, having just tried to calm myself down by watching a funny little documentary on Indian arranged marriages in America on Netflix, with potentially the decision of my life. Dominic is telling me to do this, and is telling me that this, even more than the good-will gesture for the diplomats, will be enough to stop Putin thinking I'm a cunt. But who am I to believe? If I believe Evgeny then it is Cummings that Putin thinks is a cunt. And if I believe *Mission Impossible II* then it is the Russians who are the cunts and they have engineered Chimera virus to release the Chimera into the world and then become the richest Nation on the planet by forcing the world to buy the vaccine. What to do? I'm totally fucked for an answer. I think that film ended with Tom Cruise having a fight with the main baddy on a beach as I remember, imagine if this whole thing ends with me and Putin having a homo-erotic fisty-cuffs on Brighton beach, wouldn't that be the thing? Would be so exciting, and so risky as Putin is not in my bubble so we're not allowed to be within 2 metres of each other, as we live in separate households. I think that's the rule anyway.

Hang on, I've just received a text from Andrei Kelin, remember him, Russia's dodgy ambassador to the UK. It said 'Been getting Cozy with Cummings?' Oh. Shit. And Cozy with a capital C? The Cozy Bear – Russian Intelligence Services. Holy. Shit. That video of me sucking Dominic Cummings cock, is that in Russian hands? Is my mouth around his cock in Putin's hands? I panic, I dial Evgeny but he doesn't pick up. Even my Russian friend has deserted me. I'm going to go round there or something tomorrow, talk with Evgeny, he knows something clearly, why would he point the finger at Cummings? I've made my decision – I believe Evgeny, and I distrust Cummings. The man lies, he's got a track record of lying with virtually everything he's ever said. And I know that because I've repeated the exact same lies by his side every step of the way. But this is where we part ways my friend, if not literally as I must keep my enemies closer particularly if they have a video of me performing fellatio upon them. But metaphorically – Dominic is not my friend, Evgeny is my Comrade, and I will show him tomorrow. I know what I'll do. I'm gonna give Evgeny the best present I can give anyone. I'm going to appoint him to the House of fucking Lords.

That's great isn't it? Is it? I don't know any more. My poor head right now. Oh fuck. My head, just like Dominic Cumming's cock in my mouth, will self-destruct in 5 seconds.

Monday August 3rd 2020

Alright, this is getting weird now. I want out. What makes this whole thing all the more awful is that I'm just the figure-head, I'm not actually doing anything very much. And I can't even get away with anything any more, as dear old 'wandering hands' has proved you do that now you not only get called out you get arrested for Christ's sake, so I don't even get any of the benefits. I remember the times, every single occasion, where I would go round Evgeny's he would have a different fucked up thing to show me, whether it was flame-thrower, a huge gun, or just like a massive bean-bag or videos of foxes being killed by dogs. And please don't come down on me like a tonne of Dominic's ejaculate, foxes are vermin and a scourge on society, so watching them with a few beers being humanely and naturally destroyed by a pack of dogs is not cruelty, it is, as dear old Elton John once said, The Circle of Life. And that's me and Dominic right now isn't it? I'm Elton, and he's Bernie Taupin. It's so much better to be the puppet master isn't it? You're doing all the work, you're running the actual country but the tabloids aren't in your mush 24/7, and unless you drive to Durham to test your fucking eyesight they leave you alone. Taupin did everything Elton did and more besides probably, I've seen the film Rocketman, he fucked black models in tee-pees and kissed boys but he never gets any of the bad press. He's just the genius that wrote 'Your Song'. That's right, I'm the fucking puppet. And Dominic's the sculptor. I wish I was the sculptor. But then again, no, I do like being Prime Minister. It's so fucking cool. Chill Boris, chill.

Anyway, in short, I miss the old me, and the old Evgeny. Added to the content of what he said it's the way he said it, we don't have a laugh no more and it's upsetting. I said at the end, 'Shall we have a beer and watch one of those fox hunting videos?' and he shook his head and his lovely black beard and he said 'no Prime Minister'. I said 'Come on Evgeny old chap, I've just made you a member of the House of Lords'. And he said , 'Well now more than ever Prime Minister, my decision is the law.' I explained to him that's not really how our Constitution works and the House of Lords is there more in a checks and balances kind of role but he switched off. Just like he'd switched off the videos of the foxes being ripped apart. Fuck I miss them. We used to call it 'Jacked-up club'. I would nip over when his dad wasn't there and we would get 'jacked-up' with drinks, barbiturates and cocaine and it was just fucking cool, and particularly watching this shit with a Russian, who's dad is a member of the KGB. Fuck so exciting. You know what I mean right, I've mentioned this before but it's sexual isn't it, one is straddling a big horse, the purest of all God's beasts, you have that KGB style pleasure of moving as a unit and then you have the ultimate pay-off of watching as your enemy is torn to pieces like the scum that he or she (or they) is. Hang on I've just realised, I'm the Prime Minster now with a whopping majority and I can make anything law within days, I'm gonna bring back fox hunting. Freedom Comrades, freedom! And then let's get fox-hunting into the Olympics.

But before I repeal the Hunting act, I need to repeal the Hunting of Boris Johnson, and Evgeny offered me scant reassurance. That's what I mean, he was so cold. Not a beer or a decapitated scum fox in sight. It was like a fucking meeting, so boring. When I gave him a place in the House of Lords he just said 'thank you'. I said 'is that it?

What about a hug?' And he mumbled something about social distancing, the coward. 'I've had Covid you prick!! I'm immune!' I shouted. I shouldn't have called him a prick. Or at least I should have said Lord Prick. So anyway, I asked Evgeny first what he knows of the Cozy Bear. He laughed, like a shit Bond villain, and said I'd have to ask his father about that. I said, 'Your father isn't here Evgeny, can you just tell me yourself.' He said, 'my father is here, he just doesn't want to see you.' I shouted his name, I shouted 'Come down here now you coward! Call yourself a member of the KGB'. I lost my cool, I looked foolish and I calmed down. Evgeny told me they were nothing, playing around with tittle-tattle, he said it was much like a jumped-up Bullingdon Club, and told me as long as I'd done nothing like Trump pissing on prostitutes I should be fine. I tried to give nothing away, whilst thinking of course that sucking Dominic Cummings' cock if there were baskets of scandal would probably go into the same basket as Trump pissing on prostitutes. Or was it the other way around – did the prozzies piss on Potus? I can't remember now dash it, which would I prefer? Neither quite frankly. Anyway that's by the by. I then mentioned the 300 million Cummings was suggesting I give to the Gamaleya Institute. He looked genuinely surprised at that one, he walked away and came back, like he was considering an offer on Dragons Den.

Evgeny asked me if I knew who Nikolay Gamaleya was? I said I didn't, and that I don't read books. He said I didn't need to read any book, all I needed to know was that Nikolay was born in 1859 and he lived until 90 years old. The average life expectancy of someone born in Russia in 1859 was 40 years old. Process it. I did process it, but I didn't understand what his point was until he told me. 'What is the ultimate unspoken goal of all medical science Mr Johnson?' he said like a better Bond villain, 'eternal life.' Gamaleya's work was all about the search for cure, but more the search for eternal life. And let's face it, for someone born in 1859 he failed but he did fucking well. I'll be lucky to make 70 the way I eat at bedtime, or saying that 57 with this fatwa over my head. 'What do us billionaires want Mr Johnson when there is nothing more to buy?' 'Sex, titties?', I enquired. 'No Mr Johnson, eternal life.' And Evgeny told me that's why every single

Russian billionaire and indeed millionaire is giving money to this Institute – as they are close to finding the secret of eternal life, or at least living healthily until 150. And the drug they are working on is called 'Resurrection'. I mean this sounds fucking cool of course and I'm all for people trying to work stuff out, buy I wondered what it had to do with Corona, and Dominic, and my threat, and Putin thinking I was a cunt. He told me I was getting ahead of myself, and that he didn't really know. I said 'does your father know?' and he said 'he isn't here'. As a joke this time. That's the old Evgeny. But the new Evgeny made a swift return, and he said the following, I mean I'm paraphrasing as I don't record every conversation or blowjob I have like Dominic, actually maybe I should start doing that, but this is what he said...

'In all life there is good and there is evil. There is life, and there is death. And the good want to live forever and the evil want life to end. And so it will always be. Just because an Institute is close to discovering the secret of eternal life, there will be powerful forces working against that, who believe life and certainly eternal life is a terrible thing. The Russians are not the enemy Mr Johnson, *Mission Impossible II* is just a film, we Russians have enough money, but what we don't have, yet, is eternal life. To reach the bottom of this mystery Mr Johnson, you have to work out who is on the side of good, and who is on the side of evil. Who is on the side of Resurrection, and who is on the side of death.'

I know right, fucking deep. He assured me that he did not know who was on the side of death – he was on the side of eternal life and he had made the appropriate donations, what once was a fortune measured in billions was now just a few million as all his money had gone to the Institute, why wouldn't it? What was possibly left to spend money on in this life than trying to ensure there was another life, and another after that. Resurrection. In parting, Evgeny showed me a tweet, from dear old Sarah Vine, Michael Gove's wife, I'm looking at it right now – and it says...

'We all have to die sooner or later. If I get Covid and cop it, so be it. My time has come. I'll have a good life, better than most in this world at any rate. I certainly don't expect the entire nation to bankrupt itself to save my sorry ass.'

Evgeny stared at me, with those 'come to Moscow' eyes of his, and said, very softly, 'Now she, Mr Johnson, is a cunt. Someone that if offered the choice of the entire nation to bankrupt itself to save her sorry ass, she wouldn't take that option. Surely any sane person would take that option, any good person, any person who cares about the only thing that matters, and that surely is eternal life. Unless Mr Putin is right Mr Johnson, and you are indeed a cunt like her.'

I think I remembered all that quite well, and I hope I did because I imagine if this diary is ever read it's going to be one of the major plot developments. And also, I think I saw Evgeny's dad hiding behind the sofa on the way out. That's mental.

Tuesday August 4th 2020

That tweet from Sarah got me thinking about dear old Michael Gove. He gets a bad press does Michael, mainly because he's a Penfold-faced Machiavellian little shit. But aren't we all? We have all got good and evil sides to us. Good versus evil was of course foremost in my mind this morning as I headed down to Michael's house in Surry Heath this morning. My driver, dear old Eric, took me (ex SAS, depressed) and I'm now on my way back after what has thankfully been a slightly less traumatic day. I've realised today that old adage of 'keep your enemies closer' only works with someone like Michael. He's a clear enemy of mine in that he wants to be Prime Minister, that's all he's ever wanted, and as much as I try to tell him that it's a shit job that puts you in the firing line of 95% of the cunts on this planet he won't hear it and he won't rest until he has the top job. So with Michael his untrust-worthiness is clear – he doesn't want me dead, he isn't recording me sucking his cock (uurgh I'd never go there) and he isn't working for the Russians (as much as any of us aren't working for the Russians). He just wants to be Prime Minister bless him, and although he will never get the job because he's essentially completely unlikeable, he's a decent enough chap and I'd rather we are, to coin a phrase, both in the tent together shitting out. Anyway, in short, I would never say of course that I trust Michael but I trust that I can distrust Michael in a way that I understand. He's a decent man – he was adopted or something, he certainly didn't have the privileges I had. And we used to taunt him about that at Oxford and in the Bullingdon Club.

Anyway, I arrived at the house late morning and Sarah gave me an enormous hug. 'Wooah, social distancing I joked.' 'Oh you know us Boris we don't believe in all that shit.' She's straight talking that Sarah and I love her for it, and I've now completely forgiven her for stabbing me in the back after David resigned, I know she was only doing it because she loves her husband, and, as I've always joked to her, if you love Michael Gove then you must be mentally ill. I'm not joking about that in fact, imagine just for a moment how many Millennia would have to pass before you thought that Michael Gove was 'the one'. Jesus wept. Anyway, Sarah fixed me a beer and went on her way upstairs to write some more undiluted crap for the Daily Mail, but not before pointing out that my novel '72 Virgins' was on her bookshelf. 'Oh goodness,' I said. I'm a little embarrassed about that book now truth be told. It's about a tousled-haired hapless bicycle-riding MP, Roger Barlow (that I can reveal now is actually based on myself) and his plan to foil an assassination attempt on the US President. I made references to 'Islamic headcases' and 'Islamic nutcases', I said Arabs have 'hook noses' and 'slanty eyes' and I talked about 'pikeys' and 'half caste' and I said that the Jews controlled the media and were able to fiddle elections. All that was rollicking good fun and may I say so, incredibly good writing. What I'm slightly embarrassed about is that I depicted our hero 'Boris' Barlow as being a fraud with no real core values, ideals or beliefs. Looking back on that now with fresh eyes I think that was a bit self-critical, and I'm glad in later years I've given myself a break. Anyway, I guess I was pleased that Sarah had good taste anyway, and had me on the same shelf as books by dear old David Irving (wrongly dubbed 'The

Holocaust denier', as if he's never done anything else) and Adolf Hitler, so I'm in quite esteemed company.

I told Michael little of what had happened in the last few weeks, and I moved the conversation quickly on from Hitler and Michael's other favourites, Mussolini, Stalin and Thatcher to the concept of eternal life. Michael, although he didn't go to Eton, is a clever chap. Not 'Prime Minister clever' but 'book clever'. He's an avid reader. I asked him whether he had read my novel '72 virgins' and he said 'Yes Boris I enjoyed reading about your sex life'. Ha ha ha, he's got a wicked sense of humour has dear Govey. Anyway, the hot topic, eternal life. He pointed me to another of the books on his eclectic shelves, 'The Bell Curve', I can't remember by who, which claims that BAME people (I hate that expression) are less intelligent than Caucasians or whites (COW?) and that intelligence is what is separating society. Now obviously the first point is debatable, I know some very clever black people like Martin Luther King and Kris Akabussi but I hand on heart don't see the issue with the latter point, of course intelligence separates society. Those with higher intelligence want to mix with similarly good and clever people, and those with lower intelligence are happy to, so to speak, stay in the swamp. And Michael concurred, naturally, we are similarly intelligent. And then I asked him what this has to do with eternal life. And he made a frighteningly good point. Say you were offered a drug that would give you eternal life. Naturally that drug would be very expensive. So those that took the elixir of eternal life would be the richest in society and therefore in the main, scum lottery winners aside, the most intelligent people on the planet. So for Michael, he said that the greatest advantage of eternal life would not be so much about living forever; that he said could get a little bit tiresome (and I assume embarrassing if he lived forever and still never became Prime Minister) but more that it would eradicate the unintelligent. He smiled deliciously and put the book back on the shelves next to his Hitler, Mussolini, Thatcher and Boris Johnson books.

I'd never thought of that. But that it an added bonus isn't it? And come on now, please don't call the PC Brigade on me. What would the world lose if it lost the unintelligent? I'm not talking about wiping them out obviously, I mean over time. I'm often reminded of dear old Charles Darwin's theory of evolution, survival of the fittest and all that, well there's clearly been a spanner in those Darwinian works in recent times as the world has become more and more moronic. Come on, you only have to step outside your bubble and pop to any seaside town or West Yorkshire as I have done recently to know that you don't have to travel too far to bump into the real bottom-feeders in our society, those stupid people who offer little more to society than shouting on trains, being obnoxious in restaurants, buying chicken from chicken shops and queuing for shite at TK Maxx. If, and not instantaneously obviously in some mass moronocaust, but over a number of years these people were weaned out of society, what would we lose? We may lose arcades and ready meals and football but we would gain so much more - Shakespeare and Wagner, David Irving and Richard Osmond.

And this is now the seed planted into my head by Govey and now weaving its way to my brain – if someone ever did invent a drug to give eternal life, how would they stop the stupid people getting hold of it? Because they would surely want to. This sounds like another adventure for jolly old Roger Barlow MP – he's saved the President of the United Stated from the evil Lebanese Islamic nutcases and now he's saving the world from the equally evil dumb-as-fucks. But how would you prove you're clever enough to live? Not degree results, I got a second class degree just because I was pissing about. Lord this is a devilish conundrum, one requiring a man far cleverer than me, so I'm arriving back to Downing Street and will be straight back on the sauce once I give a socially distanced wave to my son. Obviously Dominic is on my mind today but I wanted to get through an entry without mentioning him really. I'm on Dominic detox. But of course I brought him up to Michael Gove and asked whether he trusted him. Michael replied, 'Well has he ever written a book? I think not. And that's all one needs to know.' I nodded sagely. Michael is very wise, and as he stood in front of his books by Hitler, Thatcher and myself I was fully confident that he would survive the thick as shit cut in any future world resurrection. I questioned myself actually, would I definitely make the cut?' So I've just asked my driver Eric, 'do you think I'm clever?' And dear old Eric thought for a second and replied, 'Well you're certainly more clever than me Prime Minister, I've been sat in this car for seven hours while you and Michael Gove got pissed.' So true. I would definitely survive Resurrection, and dear old brain-dead PTSD shell-shocked Eric would most definitely not. I feel much better now.

Wednesday August 5th 2020

That Beatrice Gove is a little feisty one isn't she? I saw her yesterday at her dad's and she came down and said something sarcy like 'Ooh it's the Covid Club'. She's had the 'Rona', we've all had it. I know she thinks I gave it to everyone and whilst this is probably true of most people in hospitals, I never go anywhere near her dad, he stinks of death. Anyway she mentioned TikTok, asking me whether I'll be banning it like Trump. I asked her why I should ban it. She said, 'Because it's Chinese'. I shouted up to her as she walked away, 'Racist' and she shouted back 'You can talk!' I shouted 'Fuck off!' but she didn't hear me. Anyway, saucy little minx that one, I'd say I fancy her but in some light her face looks like her father's, and I suppose she's seventeen, which no doubt makes her 'annoying'. On that note I must call that violinist, Olga D. She looks seventeen but is in her twenties, ideal. I'm just wondering how everlasting life would work, if there really was a drug. I asked Matty Hancock to put some feelers out but as usual I expect he'll do flop all. I mean, do you take the drug and are stuck at the age you are now, or do you get younger? Probably not the latter. I think I'd be happy as I am now, maybe a couple of years younger when I could pretty much pull any ass I wanted to. But I can't complain really, I guess the very best thing about being famous is that however bad I look, I always look like that very famous person Boris Johnson, and that's always tended to pay dividends in the fucking column. The only man I'd prefer to look like is Ian Botham, or actually I'd rather be Ian Botham – he's rugged, he's a hero, he gets somehow better with age and despite being a womaniser and a coke-head (ring any bells?!), he's universally loved. God I wish I was Ian Botham. I want him around more, so I've decided to give him a peerage like dear old Evgeny. I just hope to see him around the Commons and we can go for a few beers and watch the cricket together. Funny story actually - when he was walloping the Aussies in the 1981 Ashes, I was losing my virginity on the same day. The cricket was on in her kitchen. She said 'can I turn it off?' but I was worried that if I lost sight of Botham I'd lose my erection. It did the trick, and if I ever think I'm losing an erection now I'll always conjure up an image of Sir Ian to guide me safely through to the finish. And on that note, can we shut the fuck up about the peerages now please? Yes I gave one to my brother as well, Jesus, stop pretending you give a shit about irrelevant things, it's hardly like I've given one to Rolf fucking Harris.

And talking about misunderstood art lovers, dear old Evgeny has of course been on my mind all day, the cricket has been rained off for most of the day giving me time to plan my next move. And you know what I've been thinking, what would Sir Ian Botham do? When his back was against the wall (as was mine when I was losing my virginity) he just threw the bat as hard as he could, balls flying everywhere, no real skill or finesse (yes, all still like me losing my virginity) and he got the job done. Now is not the time to hide away, now is the time to swing my bat as hard as I can, and if I'm caught out then so be it I'll have a fucking good time until that happens. I have one chance, and I'm either going to grasp it or, alternatively, I'll be marked down as the worst Prime Minister in history - either way I've made my mark and made my father proud. So I decided to jot down why my back is against the wall, and work out, just like Ian Botham did, the size of the task ahead. So this is where we are – Sedwill has told me that Putin thinks I'm a cunt, and then subsequently told me the Russians want me dead. Dominic wanted me to let off those Russian Diplomats and then give this Institute thingy 300 million pounds, which purports to be close to finding the Corona cure but in actuality may be on to something far more incredible. And Evgeny has hinted that it's Cummings that Putin thinks is really a cunt and that Institute is close to finding the solution to eternal life. And I nearly forgot, I've sucked Dominic Cumming's penis and it's all on film. Fuck, I really regret the last one, however sweet it tasted at the time. But I'm gonna call his bluff and fuck him. Not literally of course, he's had his chance at the big dog. What would Botham do? He wouldn't have sucked the cock of the Aussie captain would he, unless he was coked-up in the bar afterwards or he was raising money for leukaemia. He'd have gone fuck it, and wielded his big bat. So this is what I'm going to do tonight.

I'm gonna call Cummings and tell him no, no to the 300 million pounds – thwack – six runs - if those filthy Russians want to come clean and tell us what they're up to then great, but until then, fuck 'em. Thwack, six more. We have the good old Oxford scientists looking for a cure for free, and I put my trust in them. And I know Dommers would never release the video of me sucking his penis, it's far too big a story and far too small a cock. Fuck him. Thwack, another massive six. And this is where I win the ashes – I'm gonna do a Dominic, I'm gonna start recording my conversations, starting with one tomorrow morning with Mr Cummings himself, and I'm gonna ask him straight up what his relationship is with Putin, what he knows and where this leaves us. Thwack – victory for England. Fuck the Aussies and fuck Cummings. I need to be less meek and more Churchillian, or as I prefer, more Bothamian. Fuck me I'm erect now, I'm as hard as the nails through Jesus' hands. And on that note, time for a line of white and then I'll do something that suggests I'm a nice guy whereas actually it's all about me looking better. I'll do a soundbite for the nine o'clock news about the explosion in Beirut. 'Oh what an awful tragedy, thoughts and prayers etc.' Whereas what I really mean is, fucking get in, a Government that was ready to store thousands of bags of ammonium nitrate next to a fireworks factory in the middle of the city – you've just done my job for me and made this Government seem competent. Beirut, I fucking salute you, you are the fucking bomb!

Thursday August 6th 2020

Sorry I regret that last sentence last night, I have no excuse but I was starting to get pissed, and since Covid I've gone real lightweight. The Beirut explosion was such an awful tragedy, the video is so, so shocking – totally unwatchable - I've been watching it on a loop all day. And the thing I can't get out of my head – I'm watching hundreds of people die over and over again. No amount of Resurrection is gonna save you from a big old ammonium nitrate bomb is it? And that's the thing isn't it, death will always find a way I guess, even with eternal life there will be death. Death is inevitable, even with eternal life. I mean eventually, you might live til you're about a thousand and then some idiot will start storing ammonium nitrate in a fucking warehouse down the road. 'How's that storage of ammonium nitrate business going Amal?' 'Oh very good Mr Johnson, we store 43 tonnes of it now next to the fireworks factory.' Fucking morons everywhere. That's what they need to cure, being stupid. There's no point finding the elixir of eternal life if you don't first find the cure for being fucking dumb.

Anyway, let's get to the point of today, I bottled phoning Dominic last night. Carrie wanted to watch the Indian arranged marriage thing on Netflix again and I've hardly seen her and the baby all week so I thought I better had do my duty and fall asleep next to them. That's another thing that would go straight away with eternal life innit, marriage. 'Boris, will you marry me, forever?' 'Erm, no thank you love, unfortunately forever now actually means forever, there's no fucking way I'm being with one woman for thousands of years, you must be off your head sunshine.' Anyway, I was in the garden with Dilyn this morning, nursing a sore head in the London sunshine, and working myself up into a Botham frenzy to call Dominic and tell him what for. And I couldn't do it, I'm just not Sir Ian am I, certainly not without a dab of white to grease the old wheels. But dear old Lady Luck was shining down on me again, as Dommers arrived too on a surprise visit - he doesn't tend to report in when it's hot weather. 'And to what do I owe this unexpected visit Mr Cummings?', I said jauntily. 'Well, we're only five months away from a no-deal Brexit boss I thought we had better start bouncing some ideas around.' There's the old Dommers, always the joker. But I knew straight away there was an agenda in addition to bantz. 'Alexander Lebedev tells me you paid his son a visit? I thought Russia wasn't invited to the party in the short term?' He thought he was catching me unawares, but I am Sir Ian Botham – 'And where did he tell you that from, from behind the fucking sofa?' I laughed heartily but Dilyn then did a shit and ruined the moment. It was startlingly clear that Dominic was worried, not about the shit but about the general shit. This was the time for the truth.

'Yes' I said, as Botham as I could muster, 'my great mate Evgeny Lebedev' told me…' Deep breath Boris, '…that he suspects that Putin thinks that YOU are a cunt, not me.' Dominic laughed, but I knew he was rattled – he put both his hands quickly through his wispy hair. 'Let's be honest for the first time in our lives Dommers,' I whispered, 'Jesus Christ man the other night you were cumming into my mouth… surely we have no secrets now?' 'What does cumming into your mouth change?' he countered. 'Surely everything dear Dominic,' I shone my beautiful eyes in his direction, reflecting the morning sun, the growing stench of shit adding to the tension. 'Tell me about Russia Dommers, I've sucked your cock until it exploded in my warm mouth, surely now you can tell me about Russia.' 'Well…' he stumbled, 'I can assure you Putin does not think that I am a cunt,' he struggled. 'Vlad was the one that persuaded me to come to Russia in the first place, you ask Evgeny's dad.' 'Can you not just tell me,' I said, wary of the fact that last time I went round their gaff, Alexander was hiding behind the sofa like a frightened tit. Thankfully he did, he was suddenly as panicked as I'd seen him ever since Kuenssberg was ripping him a new arsehole over the Durham eye-test drive bell-shit. And in an instant from consistently saying for years he had very little to do with Russia he wanted to prove that he was Putin's best mate. Dear old Alexander worked as a KGB spy based at the Russian embassy in London from the late eighties and made sure Dominic got out there in 1994, apparently on the bequest of Putin. 'Bell-shit' I said, 'Putin asked for you personally, bell-shit!' 'Bell-shit?' Dommers enquired. 'Oh yeah', I said, 'it's something I've started to do, I'm going to slightly change swear words, you know like Father Ted and "feck"'. 'Anyway stop stalling I said, you stalling cant!'. 'I'm not stalling' he protested, 'Putin was in charge of promoting international relations at the Mayor's Office in St Petersburg, so I was chosen through my University to fly out to Russia and learn more about how things operate over there,' he said, 'so Putin doesn't think I'm a cant, or a cunt, Boris, he very definitely thinks you are a cunt.' Be Botham Boris. 'How are you so sure?' I quizzed manly, 'have you actually met the geezer?' He said he hadn't, but I knew he was bell-shitting.

This is the official line of what he was up to in Russia in 1994 – he was working on an airline connecting Samara in southern Russia to Vienna. And it didn't go anywhere. Yeah mate, it's the classic, what do I do after University ting – do I go on a gap year? Do I take a high paying job with my underserved First in Ancient and Modern History, what do I do with my innate and pathological desire to change received views and bring down things that don't work? I know what I'll do, I'll go to work on an airline linking some Russian back-water with Vienna. Bell-shit my friend, pure unfiltered bell-shit. 'It's true,' he protested, 'my University professor Norman Stone set me up, they wanted someone clean with no past so I got the gig. But it was nothing under-hand, I did nothing but work for that airline!' I'd had enough of this crapola, so I went in for the kill. 'What do you think, Dommers, about eternal life?'

He quivered markedly, like his cock had done in my mouth just before ejaculation. 'Why do you ask?' he said. 'I'm just interested.' 'Bell-shit', smiled Dommers. I laughed, but stopped myself laughing quickly, the stench of dog poo really hitting the back of my throat now. 'I'm not going to tell you Mr Cummings' I teased, 'I just want to know your thoughts.' And my goodness, I had never seen Dominic so animated. 'I'll tell you what I think about that, absolutely boss, I'm against it as I've always been. It is the most dangerous thing you could ever do to his planet, to make humans live forever.' 'So that's not why you want me to give that Institute in Russia 300 million pounds?' 'What the fuck are you talking about boss?' he screamed,' that money is to cure Covid for fucks sake, what on Earth are you talking about, what have those dumb Russians been planting into your fat head? I want to cure Covid 19 boss, I want to cure the world of this terrible virus..' And then came the sentence that would change my world for eternity, '…But more than anything I want to rid the world of the one thing that nearly took the man I love.'

I know right, Dominic Cummings said he loved me. I mean letting me suck his penis was one thing, but he actually said that he loved me. And as soon as I said it, I knew that's all that I wanted, that's all I ever wanted. I instantly forgave him everything, and told him he could have the 300 million pounds, and anything else he wanted. I'm not Sir Ian Botham, I'm not a shit like him. I'm Boris Johnson, and I have a heart. All I've ever wanted to do is love. That's why I've had numerous wives and countless children. I'm not a cad, I just love to love. I love being Prime Minister, I love that we are a great country that does not store many tonnes of ammonium nitrate next to a fecking fireworks factory, and I love Mr Dominic Cummings. Shoot me. Even if you're a Russian assassin, shoot me. I don't care no more. And so I have asked Dominic to come round this evening when Carrie is in bed. He asked me what for? I smouldered, 'Round two…' I think he actually might come. I mean he turned his nose up slightly but that's because I was bagging up Dylin's big shit when I said it. But the stench of shit has gone my friends, and the sweet odour of hope now springs eternal. Eternal. Wherever you are, and whatever you're doing right now, just stop everything, close your eyes, and just imagine Dominic Cummings cumming into your mouth for eternity. I have just described heaven.

And heaven is where I've been all afternoon, I nipped to dear old Uxbridge and Ruislip Manor to pretend that I still cared about my constituency (the boss's idea!) and I even bought an on-brand book from a shop, 'Napoleon's Expedition to Russia. The Memoirs of General de Segur.' A remarkable memoir, much like this one is turning out to be, but I'm sure this one won't end up as 50p in some scum charity shop. And I see myself as a bit of a Napoleon – a myopic hero, described in the book as an 'aging rock-star on his farewell tour' – that's me all over isn't it? And Napoleon escaped a brush with death in Russia too. And that one campaign cost one million lives, we are nowhere near that with Covid, so it puts everything nicely into perspective. Maybe there will be a statue of me in Trafalgar Square one day, just like Napoleon, charismatic and brilliant, our imperial eye always on glory. And maybe this diary will be mentioned in the same breath as some of the great memoirs of the past. Napoleon's is one of the most striking and poignant descriptions of war ever written, and this one is most certainly an equally breath-taking and tear-jerking account of treachery at the very highest level. Plus in this one there's cock-sucking.

Friday August 7th 2020

He didn't come over. He said his wife was ill. I don't care, it's so fucking hot today in London, the last thing I want is Dominic's tiny penis spurting everywhere. Gross. I don't care. He said he really wanted to and I believe him, maybe over the weekend. I believe him now, I believe everything, it's fine. I'm so up and down at the moment, I guess we all are but I'm the worst because I'm the actual Prime Minister. So stressful sometimes. Jeez dear old Napoleon went through all those battles and ended up dying of a stomach ulcer - that's the thing isn't it, you can worry so much about an assassin's bullet, it's the worry that gets you before the bullet does. Anyway, I've instructed that the 300 million pounds is released to the Gamaleya Institute and I have a meeting set up with someone from there early next week I believe, so if I am to live forever then this is a very good first step I feel, and if I live forever well I can stop worrying about most things to be honest, there will certainly be plenty of time for blow-jobs. Hey, hum.

Dominic Cummings is really a remarkable man, truly old school, showing you don't have to go to Eton or be elected to be the most important person in Parliament apart from me. He's even got a kind of deputy. Imagine self-appointing yourself to be the most senior policy maker in the country and then appointing yourself a deputy?! Terrific stuff. His name is Ben Warner, lovely tousle-haired boy who works here at Downing Street. I work very hard on keeping it totally business… but I do like him, I see a lot of me in him, so to speak. Lovely young boy. He's our little cute geeky data scientist. I call him, affectionately, 'the gonk'. When we talk about 'Sage' it really is just Dominic and 'the gonk', Pat Val, Chris Shitty and a couple of other pricks, but I'd say it was Dommers that makes the policies based on what he thinks and what the gonk feeds him. Lovely boy, from a very clever family. His brother Marc also comes into the Sage meetings when he wants – he runs a company called Faculty that drove the Vote Leave Campaign. I know it's probably naughty but the digital technology minister dear old Theo Agnew has a £90,000 shareholding in Faculty, but it's doing very well by all accounts - Theo and Ben and Dommers told me to give it loads of contracts recently so they're all worth millions. That moaning old slag Rachel Reeves 'MP' said that it was 'contracts for contacts'. Who else are you gonna give contracts to my love? People you don't know?! That sounds like a plan you silly sod. And anyway, it's a very good company that does very good things – who predicted Vote Leave would win? Certainly not me! But dear old Ben can perform absolute wonders, he can feed you any bullshit direct to your mobile phone to make anyone do exactly what he wants, it's really very clever. It's all about the links you're fed in Facebook etc, frightening really. And it's Ben that really is behind our latest election triumph, I can offer him no higher praise than telling you he persuaded old mining communities to vote Conservative! Absolute genius. If turkeys had facebook they'd be voting for a Conservative Christmas every fucking year. Foxes would vote for Hunting. And nurses would vote for Covid. And The Guardian moan and moan about me giving one million pounds of contracts to my mates Ben and Marc, but their parent Group, The Scott Trust, also own shares in Faculty because they know how great it is so can everyone chill the fuck out please. It's not just 'who you know' and back scratching I can assure you, it's who you know who is clever and then you scratch each other's backs.

Anyway I mention dear old Ben because he spends a lot of time around Downing Street, he's here basically all the time, I guess it gives the illusion that Dominic is in work half the time when mostly he's back at his father's Durham castle trying to persuade him not to be so much of a social pariah cunt. Ben was on his lunch break today, he only takes 15 minutes because he's super keen bless him, so he was out in the garden and I made a point of sounding him out. It was a lovely hot day and he had his top off. I was going to take mine off too but I thought that was a little forward, and I still have work to do before I would become very confident in this kind of situation or for example at a Russian sex party. I sidled up behind him and said 'boo'. I always think of Hugh Grant in that Richard Curtis bellshit '*Love Actually*'. Have you seen that film? Don't. It paints a very unrealistic picture that one could literally dance around Downing Street. Downing Street is like an office block, a business, 24/7, people coming in and out, shoving their fat noses in. I have to lock several doors before I know it's safe to talk to someone let alone fuck them. Anyway I said 'boo' and did the Hugh Grant double wave thing. He was short tempered as always as he's always beavering away at some project of Dominic's, and said 'Urgh what do you want?' So I kneeled on the grass in front of him, submissively, talked to him about this and that, pretending to be interested in what he was doing now, which is getting everyone in the country thinking favourably about a 'no-deal Brexit'. 'Good luck with that, you fucking gonk!' I'm joking, as I say, if he wanted to, he'd make everyone believe they weren't fucked for eternity because them and their fat kids can get half price Nando's. He's a little genius. And I also know he has Dominic's ear at all times. I'm not jealous, he's far too young for Dommers. Anyway I just made it very clear that I liked Dominic. It worked in the playground and it worked at University and it still works here – if you want to get in anywhere, get in the ear of their best friend first. That's the ticket. Anyway I left him to it. But he had a parting shot for me. 'Heard you gave the Gamaleya Institute 300 million pounds Boss?' He calls me 'Boss', but it's just short for Boris, it's what the youth do. 'Yes they're doing thunderingly good work for Covid', I said. 'Really?' he said, sarcastically. I enquired what he meant but he wasn't forthcoming – he said that Faculty needed another 100 million of their own. I laughed and asked him what for. 'When this vaccine comes Boss, we need everyone to be persuaded to take it.' 'Surely they will take a vaccine' I said naively. Apparently only 30% of people take the flu vaccine, I know right, only about 70% of the over 65's, the very bastards which will of course croak it if they are infected. 'We need a major education programme,' said Ben, 'delivered straight to these morons' mobile phones'. So to cut a long story short, I'm giving them the 100 million pounds. That's how I roll - when you've got nothing bet big. The country is broke, no fucker will notice. We wasted £156 million on the wrong kind of face masks the other day because, naughty me again I hold my hands up, I gave the contract to a mate of mine dear old Andy Mills who said he could get masks and it turns out they had never made masks before and basically made play masks. Whoops. But again, who I ask you, is more trustworthy, your mates or people you've never met? Yes in this instance my mate wasted £156 million of tax payers money, but most of my mates wouldn't do that. So as I've tended to do in the past I'm one for believing that mistakes will never be repeated so there is no point learning anything from them. And you can argue all you like but I'm the fucking Prime Minister, what have you done?

And it's only hours later that I realise that most old fuckers don't have mobile phones, I really don't know how all this will work. But I trust Ben, and I trust Dominic. And I trust that my sweet words of affection will get back to him. Dommers still hasn't texted, but again I don't care, it was the hottest day in London for about 15 years today and right now one needs cool beers and plenty of them, and what one definitely does not need is molten hot semen shooting down my gob straight from the tap.

Saturday August 8th 2020

He still hasn't texted. Fuck Dominic Cummings and fuck this diary. I texted that Olga D to show him. I'll show him I thought, I'll fuck that violinist Olga D. She texted back straight away. She only fucking lives in Dubai, fucking hell. She said she'll be over in London in late August Covid-rules permitting. I said if that's the case I wont be adding Dubai to the banned list! She didn't text back either. For fuck's sake. Fuck Covid, fuck schools and fuck hope.

Sunday August 9th 2020

Sorry, I was in a bad place yesterday. That bad place is called Downing Street. Really is the worst street to live on when you're depressed. I can't go out unless I'm hidden in the boot of Eric's car, but really, lying down there, often in disguise, blacked-up or whatever,

I'm really on the lookout for a tad more dignity than that. It's so fucking hot. I'm sweating like Boris Johnson on the wrong end of a paternity test. Fuck being a new dad in this weather, I really don't know what I was thinking. Jesus I know people have it hard right now but you're not the fucking Prime Minister with a Covid hangover, an actual hangover and a new baby who doesn't realise he's rich enough yet to pipe the fuck down occasionally. I hope I get a fucking apology for these sleepless nights. So yes I didn't sleep last night but I'll sleep well in a minute, Dommers has just texted so all is ok. He kept it very business-like, just saying Ben had told him about the 100 million and thank you. I didn't text back, I probably won't, I'll leave it 36 hours or whatever. I mean tomorrow's Monday so he should really be in work, I don't know if he's still in Durham or whatever, I don't know where the fuck he is and I don't care but he really should get back to work soon as we need to get Brexit done. Once we get Covid done. And vaccine done. Fuck Dominic and these stupid sound bites. No, I'm sorry, let's not get angry again. You won't like me when I'm angry, if indeed you ever liked me.

Anyway, I'm glad I made that decision about Faculty, dear old Ben was telling me today amongst my screaming fucking mess of a son that one in six people currently won't take the vaccine when it's produced. I mean Jesus Christ the stupidity of the anti-vax brigade. Ooh we can't take the vaccination because we know that the Government are trying to inject us with trackers, yeah I heard that Bill Gates is injecting people with Microsoft Word, what a load of old baloney. Jesus these conspiracy theories are laughable – there was one the other week saying that Dominic's sister was running the NHS track and trace app and it turns out it was just someone else called Alice Cummings! For Christ's sake, I know Dominic's family and they wouldn't run anything as shit as the track and trace app, they are all either autistic or borderline psychopaths, probably as a result of taking too many vaccinations. So I'm sure Ben can sort out this small issue, I asked him how are you going to do it and he said 'need to know basis' which I thought was fucking cool, and he checked the company accounts and the one hundred million had been safely deposited so we had a good laugh about it and he said the drinks were on him, but he didn't then invite me out for a drink and just carried on downing the free drinks from, ironically, Downing Street. I wonder what Ian Botham is up to tonight. No I can't call him yet, don't wanna come across as desp where the Both is concerned.

I shouldn't drink tonight really but I guess it's too late for that I'm half-cut already but it's been another difficult week and next week isn't looking any easier. Looking forward to that conversation with this bod from the Gamaleya Institute tomorrow I'm not quite sure how I'm going to play it because I can't ask Dominic how I'm going to play it. I might text him again in a minute - that will probably get him into work, actually I'm going to do that. So bit of a nothing day really – I released £20 million for that Beirut balls-up if the press promised not to print anything about the 300 million for Gamaleya and 100 million for Faculty. I didn't really want to start paying for their monumental fuck-up – oh let's store Ammonium Nitrate next to a fireworks factory and expect BJ to get his cheque book out. Tits. But whatever, that's done and nothing much else has happened today as I just spent all day waiting for that text. Simon Cowell broke his back, either falling off his bike or under the weight of the shame of the irreparable damage he's done to the music industry in the last 15 years. And so I just put out a bit of shit about schools reopening saying it is a 'moral duty' and 'national priority'. I'm so lost without Dominic to be honest, I'm sure he wouldn't have let me say that I just felt I should tweet something really and I was thinking well I can't fucking wait to get this screaming child into some kind of care and so I thought about schools. I mean it would be great if kids go back but it's hardly the priority is it? Particularly primary schools – I'm sure the future of this country is going to be really badly affected if your little shitty 9-year old can't tell the difference between a rhombus and a quadrilateral. As we all know, no schooling matters until about 15 unless you go to Eton where you can make some great connections. Shoot me but 99% of where you get in life is about connections. Mark Zuckerberg is made out to be this genius but all he did was invented an app where you could judge if some college student's tits were better than her mates. If Mark Zuckerberg hadn't met those Winklevoss identical twins he'd be using that autistic ass right now to count fucking toothpicks from on the floor at a downtown Wendy's. It's all who you know, the schools could close for another year and as long as Eton and Oxford and maybe Cambridge stayed open, then the country would, let's face it, be absolutely fine. With the best will in the world the future saviour for the UK is currently not waiting to go back to school in fucking Wigan. But that's not the official line obviously, so I thought I'd put out the opposite of what I feel in a tweet. Always tends to work for me that – go with the opposite of what I think. I definitely didn't want another baby – oh I know let's put my unsheathed penis inside a vagina and ejaculate. What a moron. Goodnight, sleep better than my screaming fucking kid. I've got to text Dominic Cummings and then masturbate.

Monday August 10th 2020

I take it back saying yesterday that Downing Street was a bad place. You truly know you're in the pits of hell when you're at a final stop on a tube line. I mean I should know, I'm the MP for Uxbridge – fucking hell, why is it even on a tube line? The problem with being on a tube line is people assume it's London, people assume it's progressive, people assume it's civilisation when in fact the final stop on a tube line is the place where people are born, live and die in one physical place and in one metaphorical place – nowhere. And this morning I found myself in one of these God awful corners of hell, Upminster. Fucking Upminster. I seriously don't know why I'm doing this, I mean sure it makes my ejaculations twice as intense but fucking Upminster. And why am I here? To make the apparently controversial decision that the children of this country should stop playing MineCraft and get their lazy arses back into school – fuck me the bleating of parents and teachers 'oh it's a risk Boris, it's a risk'. Everything is a risk you stupid cunts. Putting on your socks in a risk. I've done myself more injuries putting on my socks in my life than I have cycling but I don't walk around bare foot. Because then people really would think I was Jesus. Dommers texted me this morning to brief me about the Gamaleya call, more on that in a second, but he also said I should hold my arms out more in photoshoots because it gives the suggestion of Jesus, and resurrection. I did that today. And more on Resurrection in a second, but really, particularly parents, shut the fuck up. The under 19's represent 0.8% of hospital admissions for Corona, only one or two children have died so get back to school for fuck's sake, not the children that have died all the other ones. It's never actually been a risk and it certainly isn't one now, and then you have the other half of the unwinnable debate saying 'Oh Boris why didn't you get them back to school earlier then?' Because it was a fucking risk alright? And I was lying half dead in a hospital being brought back to life by those 2 nurses – what was their names again this is so annoying? There was 2 of them, 1 of them was an immigrant. Don't get me started on immigrants. Anyway Dommers told me to start using the word 'moral' today, I said we have a 'moral duty to act' which went down quite well I thought. Confession - I don't actually know what 'moral' means. I mean I know it means 'right and correct', but what is 'right and correct'? People have been tweeting me all day saying it's our 'moral duty' to accept immigrants to the country. So maybe 'moral' is the word you use when rational arguments have all been lost. 'Meryl' was that her name, the nurse? She was Australian I think, or from New Zealand. She didn't swim over anyway I checked on that!

OK lets cover this quickly, I had an immigrant charity based in Folkestone up my bracket today saying what I said about immigrants today isn't very nice. What I said was this – immigrants crossing the channel in rubber dinghies is a 'very bad and stupid and dangerous and criminal thing to do'. My private English tutor at Eton would have pulled me up for one too many 'ands' there, but the flip side of that coin is he was buggering boys so I think that means he can shut his mouth and face and cake-hole. Again, please just have a think about this before you have a go at me – I'm stopping immigrants coming into this country. And there's always the same argument isn't there – immigrants bring a lot of skills into this country. Sure, true for the minority, as I say my nurses were immigrants. However I have a question for you, what percentage of immigrants who have come here on a fucking dinghy have contributed to our society? I'd hazard a guess at big fat zero. No doctors are coming here on a fucking dinghy are they, because they're clever enough to know the risks. And as the stupid British public will tell you, you should do nothing if there's any element of risk. It's the right-on brigade biting off their noses to spite their faces – ooh we really want more immigrants into the country – no you don't you lying pricks – you're just saying it because it makes you feel better – and that Folkestone charity banging on about that we accepted thousands of immigrants into the country in World War II, yeah we did love but this isn't a fucking War is it? They're coming here, yes I accept out of a War zone, but, look, I know what I'm trying to say and I know it's right and I know you know it's right so let's all shut the fuck up.

Shut up, because I have news. We have cured Corona virus!! Well Russia has. I always said those Russians were fucking brilliant. This afternoon I had a call not with any old prick at the Gamaleya but with Russia's Deputy Health Minister no less, Oleg Gridnev who has confirmed, drumroll please, that their vaccine 'Sputnik V' will be registered this Wednesday August 12th. Now apparently we must still be cautious as Sputnik V hasn't been fully tested and there isn't any data from any of the trials on Sputnik V at all but Oleg has said that thanks in part to the 300 million pounds I gave them (I joked that this was 'an arm and Oleg' but he didn't understand) – then Russia will indeed be the first country to register a vaccine for Covid-19, beating ourselves (sob!) and the US Project to deliver a vaccine 'Operation Warp Speed'. Rejoice and bow down to the great mother Russia. The vaccine is a joint effort between Gamaleya and the Russian Government, that's why I talked with Oleg and not who I'd planned to talk with, Alexander Gintsburg, director of Gamaleya. A damn shame really as I planned to sow some seeds about eternal life and Resurrection but I didn't think Oleg would be stupid enough to fall for any hints, those bastards give nothing away. I did try to chuck him a curve ball though - I said in my parting comments to him some minutes ago, 'I love you Russians, you give me a warm feeling inside like a Cozy Bear.' Oleg didn't understand and said 'pardon?' I repeated, 'You give me a warm feeling inside like a Cozy Bear'. He again said he didn't understand what I was saying, and I believe him as his English was fucking terrible.

Hang on, I have a call coming through. It's Andrei Kelin, one sec.

Fuck me, I'm in serious trouble. Fuck. More tomorrow, I've just blacked-up, I'm gonna hide out in the back of Eric's unmarked car and I'm off to a secret location. Wish me luck, fuck. Fucking Russians, block the borders, shit. Why did I listen to Cummings? Russia are the enemy they always have been always will be. Fuck I made Evgeny a member of the House of fucking Lords, I've just given them 300 million pounds. Fuck, the secret location is Dominic Cumming's house by the way if I'm killed en route. This is fucking awful, his wife will be there. Fuck. She will sense I have sucked her husband's penis. Holy fuck.

Tuesday August 11th 2020

It's dear old Mary I feel sorry for in all this you know. I really like Mary, I really like how her family own castles, how fucking cool is that? She's so lovely and her family own castles, I love them both dearly and I think they both love me, they named their son after me of course and I worked with Mary at the Spectator many moons ago. Never fancied her which is a strange thing to say for me, but if I was to ever fuck an aura it would be hers, she's so sweet, and that's why I feel sorry for her, she surely doesn't want to get roped into this mess. And a mess it is. I arrived late at Dominic's, I forgot to give him notice and he had company – traitor Sedwill. I mean I know Dominic and him have to work together but he's always around isn't he, like an atrociously bad smell. It was the best decision of my life to shunt him off in October and I can't wait for that day to spin around. But I guess it was good to have him here with his in-depth Russian knowledge. And as the night turned out, he wasn't the only one that knew quite a bit more about Russia than I thought. I'm talking about Dominic there by the way, obviously.

Anyway I guess I went in all guns blazing and said I wanted Putin on the phone. 'It's the middle of the night in Moscow', said Sedwill, showing his in-depth Russian knowledge that I just mentioned. 'I don't give a fuck if it's on the countdown to New Year's fucking Eve',

I barked, 'I want Putin on the phone right now.' Dominic gave me a bottle of Scotch to swig from to calm me down, he knows what I like that's for sure. So I told him what Kelin had said, that there was an immediate and present danger to my life because of what I'd said to Oleg Gridnev about 'Cozy Bear', if Russians have a trigger word then apparently that is it. I said to Dommers that the whole thing is ludicrous and could be sorted by a face to face meeting with me and Putin. 'No one is travelling anywhere like that,' said Sedwill, again, unhelpfully. 'My fucking father has just spent two weeks in Greece,' I shouted, waking dear old Mary up. She opened the upstairs bedroom door and shouted down, 'For fuck's sake people are trying to sleep up here' which no doubt woke their horrid kid, Alexander. Dommers encouraged another swig of whisky. I was getting through it quicker than I do prostitutes on a stag night. And then he whispered, in a reassuring but ultimately deathly tone, 'Don't forget Boris, that Putin thinks you're a cunt.' I don't know what it was but he must have felt sorry for me, he looked briefly at Sedwill who kind of gave him the nod, and Dommers said the fateful words that have unlocked a whole new section of this mystery – 'Well actually boss, I think it's me that Putin really thinks is a cunt.' With another nod from DC, Sedwill took his leave, picking up his car keys and his copy of The Daily Mail and The Sun and he was on his way. And then Dommers sat me down on the sofa and told me everything, well everything that he told me anyway.

Of course he hadn't been working on an airline to the middle of nowhere, he was brought in by Russia to work on their eternal life drug, Resurrection. That's right, they have been working on this fucking thing since the late 90's. I couldn't believe it. 'I can't believe it' I said, 'that's taken fucking ages.' Dominic never blinked, 'the Russians would work for eternity on a drug to give one eternity.' Very poetic I thought at the time, but on writing down it makes little sense, but I get his point. But Dommers and Putin fell out over Putin's plans. The whole thing a complete waste of time in his opinion, why on Earth would you want to live forever? Why would you want anyone to live forever? It makes no social or economic sense whatsoever. I've never seen Dominic so impassioned, even when he was ejaculating into my mouth. There was a rival plan, that he had backed, and that was cloning. Yes, cloning. 'Because cloning was (a) possible and (b) made far, far more sense to me as a concept,' said Dommers. Remember dear old Dolly the Sheep? That was 1996, that was why Dominic was sent out to Russia. He was given in-depth knowledge of what was going on at Edinburgh University at the time through Norman Stone at Oxford, and Putin had tried to change the concept to eternal life, but Dominic for three whole years stuck to his guns – for many reasons eternal life would never work and he would not help with UK resources to produce any research towards it. But the biggest reason for their falling out apparently – Dommers and Putin – Putin wanted to call his eternal life drug Resurrection, and Dommers, ever the pedant, said that a drug to give eternal life wouldn't give Resurrection, it's only by dying and coming back to life that one gets resurrection. And Dominic, the clever little fucker, had an ally in the unlikeliest of places – the Gamaleya Institute. They have secretly been working on research to take Dominic and Dolly the Sheep's initial work forward. Dominic's eyes lit up, a slightly lighter black, he said it was the best kept secret in medical science, not even Putin knows, and they planned to keep it that way. Putin has bet on the wrong horse, but in the background, more and more people have been betting on this horse that will surely win, and the horses name – Dolly the Sheep. Metaphorically. In actuality – Resurrection – the project is still code-named Resurrection. You die, and then you come back to life. Fucking cool. I want it.

I couldn't believe it. But then I thought about it a bit and I believed it. Dolly the Sheep was in 1996. If you Google 'cloning' like I just have for research purposes, then it just says 'nothing doing on that one'. Bell-shit! Of course it's bell-shit, they were cloning sheep a quarter of a century ago and they are close to cloning human life now. It's happening right now, in Gamaleya, aided by the good old United Kingdom, in the shape of Glaxo Smith Kline at Barnard Castle – that's why the sneaker fucker was in Durham. Fuck! 'You lying little cunt' I said in jest. He laughed, thinking he'd got away with it again. But he hadn't this time. At all. 'And because Putin thinks you're a cunt then I am a de facto cunt, that isn't fair!' I shouted. 'Calm down

Я

boss,' he smouldered. 'You need to calm down.' And he unzipped his flies and released his short fat cock again. He beckoned me on to it. I won't be as poetic about it as I was the first time because to be honest this one made me feel a bit dirty, and made me actually dirty, I still don't have my technique down his spunk literally went everywhere. But he was satisfied. I definitely was not, as he went to bed with Mary. 'When do I get mine sucked?' I offered up, lamely, as he went up the stairs. 'In good time, in good time the boss will get his willy sucked', he said smarmily. He's very clever, he said 'boss' there referring to himself. Cunt.

Anyway this morning I've been to Hereford on no fucking sleep, Dominic told me I had to go and take the heat off the 300 million for Gamaleya by announcing the exact same amount to the boring NHS. So I stood there like a prize turkey doing a selfie about this fucking hospital that no one gives two fucks about and now I feel filthy, I feel used and soiled to be honest, and now I'm not sure what is going on and who is control. And it's so fucking hot and I still have the taste of Dominic Cummings' cum in my mouth. I have to ask myself, would death be any worse than this? When does Boris get his cock sucked? I'm the Prime Minster for fuck's sake.

Wednesday August 12th 2020

Fuck it I'm going on the run. Dominic's idea but I would have done it anyway. I'm pissing off to Northern Ireland tomorrow and then fucking off to Scotland to lay low with Carrie for a bit, under the guise of a family camping trip or 'paternity holiday' (lol). Obviously we won't be scum camping I'll be staying in a top secret luxury cottage but yes that's what we're doing this weekend. My ex Petronella (her real name) has already been giving me grief after we leaked it to the press saying that this will 'finish off our relationship' and I 'cannot cook'. As I believe I texted when we were splitting up Petronella, go fuck yourself. You're hardly one to talk about relationships, you had an affair with a married man! (me of course) And when you did that you got me sacked, by all people Michael fucking Howard – the ultimate shame of it. I hate you Petronella and you're only jealous because you're 52 and Carrie is 32. Upgrade baby! 32 I know right? I can't believe I pulled her either! Well I totally can but you know what I mean, she worked for me and that usually works for me! But don't worry about Carrie, she has upgraded too – you know she used to go out with Harry Cole, the political editor of The Sun!! Ha ha ha! POLITICAL editor of The Sun! That's like being in charge of the truth at The Sunday Sport. What a wanker, and I have it on good authority, I have a larger penis than him. Dommers told me that. And I can cook actually Petronella, I just chose not to for you because you eat like a fucking donkey.

So yes, buggering off to Scotland for a long weekend. Won't be using the train there after what happened in Aberdeenshire this morning, terrible business. My twitter bod sent a tweet from my account saying 'my thoughts and prayers are with all those affected' which I thought was a nice touch. Obviously untrue, I've been thinking all day about Russian death threats and getting out of Dodge. Christ it comes to something when things have got so bad you consider going to fucking Scotland via Northern Ireland for your holiday. Where shall we go next year, maybe mother-fucking Wales? Fuck this pandemic, the last holiday I went on with Carrie was in the sparklingly stunning Caribbean, all paid for by dear old David Ross, boss of the Carphone Warehouse. Great phones at a great price. Awesome trip – all over New Year, cocktails, dancing and banging Carrie on the beach. And now look at me, looking around my bedroom earlier for three pairs of clean pants for a trip to fucking Scotland. The only good thing is I'm going to do a secret pop-in and have a chat with the boss at Glaxo at Barnard Castle on the way up, Dommers has hooked me up. I'm sure he's telling the truth about the cloning shit but good to check myself and see where they are, and of course get myself first in the queue. This is genuinely exciting of course, and a way out of all of this mess. Another chance at life. My goodness. We'd all like that of course but especially me. Because, well, despite being Prime Minister, I've really fucked this life up haven't I? I mean maybe not fucked it up, but how awesome to say leave another version of yourself copious notes about all the things they should and shouldn't do as they live your life again.

RESUЯЯECTION

Number one thing I'm going to leave as advice – don't get bloody married. What a fucking shit show that has created for me.

I married first in 1987, I was 23. Far, far too young looking back. Lasted 6 years (officially, lol!) and 12 days after that one ended, get this, I get married again!! What the fuck was I thinking? 12 days of freedom, that's all I gave myself. Was I being gas-lighted into it? The ridiculous thing is no, if I'd been gas-lighted or drugged into marriage I could have forgiven myself. 12 fucking days. We felt we had to get married of course because we had the little one on the way, but that's a load of bollocks as well isn't it? Who gives a fuck if you're married with a baby? Certainly not the baby. I mean yes there are tax breaks but that's hardly a concern for me isn't it?! Anyway I'm extremely proud that marriage lasted 25 years. I know right? A quarter of a century. Jesus! You'd get less for GBH of a journalist. But that's where I get the bad press unfairly I think as a womaniser, I repeat, that second marriage lasted 25 years. I mean yes Petronella and I did hook up a few years into it but we didn't have a baby together which I'm quite proud about (two terminated pregnancies) and then there was dear old Anna Fazackerly and Helen MacIntyre (I did have another child with her but I didn't want it I swear on its life). But all shitty tunnels eventually lead to the perfect blue sea and here I am with beautiful, young Carrie, who I've known (possibly in the biblical sense) since she was 20 and she worked for me, as have pretty much all my wives and girlfriends, I make a kind of point of that. But as I say, 25 years, pretty proud of that. Jesus, who am I kidding, I've royally fucked up haven't I? Just marauding around the land wielding my erection into any journalistic or Governmental employee that does so much as be civil to me, knocking most of them up, I'm a fucking disgrace. And you can quote me on that, as long as you then fuck me. But hey, if my future self is reading this, then let this be a lesson to you little Boris. Maybe they will give you these words of warning when you are 18 or possibly 16, but heed these words well little man, rubber up and do not under any circumstances get married, unless their father owns a castle. Lucky, lucky little fucker Dominic fucking Cummings. And don't make friends with Russians, or if you do, make sure they are very best friends. And don't go on *Have I Got*

News For You or if you do and Ian Hislop starts having a go at you, simply call him a 'snivelling little mole-faced cunt.' So many things I would do differently. I wonder whether Jesus thought the same way before his resurrection? 'I've fucked up, Judas is stuffing me up like a kipper - let me have my chance again.' That's me right now, a stuffed fucking kipper hanging on a fucking cross.

I'm sorry about this entry, it's got a little melancholy hasn't it? But what do you expect? This weekend I have chosen of my own volition to go on holiday in Scotland via Northern Ireland with a new born baby. Life doesn't get any lower than this. The only upside of Scotland is the Edinburgh Fringe has been cancelled this year. Last time I saw that many desperate people that would do anything for a chance they were crossing the Channel in a fucking dinghy, and just like the immigrants it's unbelievably stupid and if I have my way I'll make it illegal. And as I can literally make any law now you watch me – this time next year I'll make being a comedian and definitely being a juggler illegal. I hate the arts. Almost as much as I hate Scotland. Sorry I've dug myself into a bit of a hole here, I'm off for some cocaine. Up yours Delors!

Thursday August 13th 2020

I have to remind myself sometimes we are only six months to the end of the transition period – holy fuck! I hoped the Irish PM, Michael Martin, would have some bright ideas today but he had jack shit. Nice guy though, and the trip today did the trick of getting out of the heat, literally and metaphorically. It's fucking freezing every day in Ireland, and if I'm a moving target then the Russians aren't going to be able to shove a poisoned umbrella in my ass – win-win. As I was there last minute, I didn't really have a chance to do a proper briefing with Dommers as to what I would say explaining why I was there so I just went with the generic bullshit 'I look forward to developing our relationship in all sorts of ways – east-west, north-south, you name it.' I said 'you name it' obviously because when you're listing compass points you forget which ones you've already done, you try it, it's impossible. As impossible as Brexit – we are obviously just going to have a 'no deal' and it will just serve everyone right for voting for it, stupid cunts. You know what I mean, I realise it's the reason I'm here now but how much simpler would life have been if people hadn't voted for this stupidity? It's going to take about 20 years of sorting this shit out, if I'd known that back then I'd have sent in the other article I wrote backing Remain. I literally tossed a coin with Carrie. It came down Remain first as well and Carrie said 'best of three?' and I agreed because I was agreeing to everything as I was trying to fuck her some more. Anyway, funny to think Brexit is actually all Carrie's fault.

Anyway I didn't spend much time in Northern Ireland – most of the NI Executive table despise me as they think Brexit will fuck up trade with Europe and lead to years of recession, which it will of course, but as I say, it's not my fault it's Carrie's. And the coin's. Who could have predicted 2 heads on the trot? And I'm not talking about my sexual relationship with Dominic. I inevitably questioned today whether I am a gay man, and of course I'm not, I'm a notorious philanderer and plunderer of most of the young female journalists in British journalism and several Government colleagues. My dad sometimes jokes that I've seen more pussy that Andrew Lloyd Webber. The joke works on two levels there – the musical Cats and the fact that Randy Andy gets loads of young pussy. Anyway, as I say I was in and out like Lloyd Webber today, brief chat with the first Minister Arlene Foster (Foster, probably… the most boring woman in the world) and her Deputy Michelle O'Neill - hard-nosed bitches them two. I've had the growing impression for many years that women fall in to two direct camps when it comes to moi – they either fancy me and want to fuck me and then they fuck me, or they fucking hate me. And Arlene and Michelle are very much in the hate camp. I mentioned that I was looking forward to celebrating the Centennial of Northern Ireland's creation next year and sour-faced Michelle said 'there is nothing to celebrate'. Grumpy cow. I can't stand her. And I can't actually understand why she doesn't fancy me. Sometimes I wish I was gay, much easier I think. You know where you are with men. Kind of, I really don't know where I am with Dominic. Will things ever progress beyond mere sucking of his tiny fat cock? I could have never imagined at the start of this year I'd find myself in such a one-sided homosexual relationship. If it wasn't for the diversion from a Russian sword over my head I'd probably be fucking livid being someone's spunk bucket.

I phoned Evgeny on the way home and told him that Dommers had confirmed that Putin thought he was a cunt. He asked for the details but I called his bluff and said that he probably knows all the details already. He then called my bluff and said 'of course I know all the details.' I asked him why his dad hid behind the sofa rather than seeing me the other day. He called my bluff and said 'my dad wasn't hiding behind the sofa the other day' and he succeeded as I started to question whether I was seeing things, that now indeed does not sound very realistic. 'But', I said, 'he is undoubtedly avoiding my calls'. He confirmed this to be the case. If Putin does think I'm a cunt then he wouldn't want any of his agents associating with me. Evgeny doesn't give a shit about all that, he's a top lad. He asked me what being a member of the House of Lords entailed and I told him not to worry about it. I said treat it like another Maserati, it's there to show off about and it gets you pussy before you step out the door. He laughed a little but I sensed he didn't want to talk to me, maybe his dad was there hiding behind the sofa. But I did question one thing with him, whether he had heard anything about a rival project for Resurrection, the cloning project called, helpfully, 'Resurrection'. He said he had heard nothing of this, and raised a doubt in my head. 'I'm not paying many millions to give life to someone else,' he laughed, 'I want eternal life for myself, and I'm sure all my friends who have put money towards this would want that as well. When you have enough money, rule number one is you don't want anyone else to reap those rewards, you want it all for yourself, now. That is the beauty of eternal life, that is the beauty of Resurrection.'

You may think I remembered that last sentence well but I'm now recording every conversation I have, I told you I would. I recorded the audio of the last blowjob I gave to Dominic Cummings. I'm not sure what advantage that gives me really, I might just delete it, it's just a recording of one minute of slurping noises and then him screaming

'Dominic wins!'. Anyway the storage on this thing runs out in a day, I don't think anything is built really to record 24/7. Oh well, at least it makes this diary better and more accurate. That's what I'm going for here you see, 100% accuracy, 100% truth. And you want the truth, as I face another night packing for the long weekend in fucking Scotland, if Resurrection turns out to be as Evgeny says eternal life and not true cloning based resurrection then I don't think I'd take it even if offered. Dominic is right, of course he is. I think I've just reached the age where I see the end on the horizon, maybe it was seeing death straight in the eye when I had Corona, and you know what, it doesn't seem so bad. I'm knackered. I don't think I could put up with ten more years of this let alone eternity. Of course Dominic is right, imagine a world where everybody lived forever. Everyone instantly, overnight, would turn into the laziest fuckwits. What shall we do today? Nothing, I've literally got an eternity to put the washing on, or wash my balls. And I certainly don't want to take any risks, get into any bad relationship – imagine getting into a relationship with an arsehole or a cunt and you literally have to listen to their shit for eternity. Eternity, that's not just a long time, that is forever. And ever. No thank you. Let's hope Dominic is right about Dolly the Sheep. Although last thing for today, I'd better clean my teeth well before I go to Glaxo – imagine if they swab my mouth for DNA and there's still a bit of Dominic's spunk on my molars. I'll die all happy and I'll be resurrected as Dominic fucking Cummings. That would be like Jesus being resurrected as one of those other cunts that died on the crosses that day. 'Who the fuck are you?' The other thought I had just now is what ever happened to the real IRA, they've gone a bit quiet in recent years haven't they? Great name. 'Real IRA'. The IRA must have been livid. That's what I'll call myself if I ever get resurrected – 'Real Boris Johnson'. The next me will be the real me, without the mistakes, the drinking, the drugs, the fucking without a condom, the unwanted pregnancies, the arranging to have a journalist beaten up, the appearances on *Have I Got News For You*, the next me will be 'Real Boris Johnson'. What a guy he will be – all the privilege and none of the fuck ups. Imagine the pussy I'll get, I'm so fucking pumped for this now, Real Boris Johnson is gonna clean up!

RESUЯЯECTION

Friday August 14th 2020

Was back at number 10 today doing my final bit of packing for my weekend away in Scotland. Carrie had bought me a 5-in-1 scarf/headband/mask thing from Milletts and said it would be good for walks and going in and out of shops. I said that going for walks and going in and out of shops would be a security risk, I didn't mention Russia as I don't want to worry her, I said instead that Scottish people think I am a cunt and of course she believed me. I tell you who are cunts – children. For fuck's sake the moaning coming out today from some of them about their A-Level results. Dear old Gavin Williamson is a lovely chap and a great Education Secretary – he's a little Tim-nice-but-dim but I do believe in promoting people who aren't necessarily qualified if they are pleasant people and do their best. One of my teachers at Eton taught us that 80% of all success is turning up, so Gavin is at least 80% successful, when he turns up. And Gavin was educated in a comprehensive school, which is a tick in the box for the diversity quota - if he misses out on being a white, heterosexual male. Maybe he's bi-sexual who knows, bottom line is he's had a shit education and that's what you need in an Education Minister. And no prizes for guessing who was moaning about their A-Level results yesterday – comp kids and BAMEs. Gavin was worried bless him, comps and BAMEs crying all over the country but I told him not to worry and to completely ignore what Scotland had done, which was to base grades solely on predictions of grades from teachers. I mean for fuck's sake – teachers are going to have their favourites, that just wouldn't work. You're a 23 year old male teacher and there's a group of 18 year olds vying for the best grades – that just isn't going to work is it? A flash of eye-lash or an almost-formed tit and you're getting an A, grow the fuck up. I told Gavin to say that to the press but to use other words. He just said it was unfair and didn't mention Scottish school-girls' tits.

And they say the algorithm we use doesn't take into account whether BAMEs, free school meal kids, special needs kids are systematically disadvantaged. Well here we fucking go again with political correctness gone mental. Kids with free school meals are not getting

A's are they?! If you go to Eton it doesn't matter what your teacher thinks of you, you are getting into the best universities to do what you want. And say it quietly, BAME kids are… oh God look I don't want to say anything that gets me into trouble, I'll just say this, BAME kids are quicker on the running track than white kids. Ooh funny how I'm not in trouble for saying that. But when I point out the probable fact that statistically BAME kids are slower in the class room than white kids everyone calls me racist. Well I'm not racist as I've said before in this journal, some of my best Cabinet ministers are BAME, and some of the fucking worst ones! I had to be quite firm with Gavin today, he shits himself when it comes to the press because he's a Comp kid – Dommers gave us the slogan 'No U-turn, no change', again proving that he is a genius and the odd Comp kid can slip through the shitty net and strike gold. I asked him for another one for me and he told me to say the results were 'robust, good, dependable', which I thought was a slightly rubbish slogan, and proves that Dominic is still being arsy with me and I shall never suck his penis again. No U-turn, no change. If anything he should suck my penis, which I've been told by many women is robust, good, dependable. And you know what I say, 80% of sex is turning up.

Saturday August 15th 2020

We stopped off on the way up to Scotland as we had to do the VJ 75th anniversary thing in Staffordshire. I say had to, the buffet is always good at these things and I wasn't disappointed. These old timers love a cake don't they, they love a scone, clotted cream and a tray of nice sandwiches. And veterans are like the best bits at a buffet - I'm gonna really miss 'em when the last bits have gone. Hooked up with dirty old Prince Charles there of course. New series of *The Crown* starting up on Netflix and apart from Bradley Walsh's *The Chase* it's the one thing I never miss. I can't wait for them to skewer Charlie. Andrew has had it in the dick for his forgotten fucks with 17 year-olds, whilst people have conveniently forgotten that old filthy-pants Prince Charles was in his thirties when he hooked up with teenage Diana, and he got her engaged after 12 dates. The filthy sod. Just goes to show you that if you ponce around doing enough of these kinds of things that people quickly forget you are a sexual deviant. That's my plan anyway, 'always hide your deviance' my Eton headmaster often told us. For example in a letter to veterans today, I signed it and my signature looks like BJ with a cock and balls and if you turn it on its side it's actually a cartoon of me, naked, with a lob on. Makes me laugh every time, and hard most times.

Anyway that's really by the by today, the big news from today, and I have to keep this brief as I am on holiday in the arse end of Scottish nowhere, is that I indeed stopped off on the way up into the offices of GlaxoSmithKline at Barnard Castle. A huge success story is GSK, they did a 34 billion turnover in 2019 (no free school meals here!) and I was met by dear old Roger Connor, President of Global Vaccines, Cambridge graduate and all round good-egg. He's receding on top so my opening joke to him was 'clearly you haven't found the cure for baldness yet'. He didn't laugh and said he was quite self-conscious about his hair loss, but by the end of our meeting we were getting on and it was far less awkward. I think I can do no wrong really with Roger, we have put so much business their way and they give us so much cash (and a few drugs!) in return that in all honestly I could masturbate into one of his vaccines and he'd forgive me, and of course he was very, very grateful that we didn't sack Dominic. He actually told me at the time not to sack him and like a spunk-laced vaccine it's a bitter pill to swallow but I know that was for the best, and of course those roads all led me here today, to Barnard castle, but this time with perfect eye-sight and ready to see the future. And let me tell you, there is a bright future indeed. Roger confirmed that in addition to work on a Covid vaccine (yawn) they are indeed working on 'Resurrection', a drug to give eternal life through cloning. This of course is spectacularly exciting. He told me that it was top secret and not to write it down but of course they would be trialling this on the best of the best, and therefore he personally asked me whether I would like to be involved in the upcoming trials. I know right, so fucking exciting!! Of course I bit his dick off. I was like a whore on a Saturday. Over the next month, I, Alexander Johnson, will be one of the first humans to start taking this new drug, code-name Resurrection, along with having regular blood transfusions with the blood of younger, healthier men. This is to ready my body for the cloning process and to produce the best possible outcome. If it works I will then produce a baby just before I die and that will be brought up as Boris Johnson Mark II, or the 'real' Boris Johnson by parents of my choice. I will leave Boris Mark II videos explaining what he needs to do, but there is actually evidence to suggest I will remember my past life. Another 100 years baby!! And then another 100 years after that! That makes these few nights in fucking Scotland easier to take. What a waste of time. Everlasting life and no fucking WiFi, piss take.

Sunday August 16th 2020

I wonder how long I should serve as Prime Minister now. Again I'll keep it brief today as Carrie is on my back about working in my holidays and I certainly don't want her to discover evidence of this journal as it contains graphic descriptions of me sucking Dominic Cummings' penis. My security bods (particularly gorgeous four ex-squaddies) erected a tent in the garden of this cottage so I can go in there and write, sleep, and masturbate away from a crying fucking baby. But delicious possibilities open to me don't they – I could be Prime Minster for the next 40 years knowing I have another life coming. Let's face it Labour haven't got a sniff now for a generation unless we do something seriously fucked up to annoy every single young person, and with this majority I could conceivably vote through any election reform I like to make even more sure of my triumph next time and the time after that and the time after that. Just look at what dear old Alexander Lukashenko has done with Belarus – this genius has been president for 26 fucking years. 26 years! Makes Thatcher look like Vanilla Ice. And the way he's achieved his greatness? By repressing opponents of the regime - we can do that – and by making elections not free and fair – we have already proved at least twice that with Russian help we can do that. And things will only get better, get easier, as apps develop and people become more and more malleable. Who do people think of when they think of great leaders? Thatcher, Lukashenko, Alex Ferguson. What links them all – longevity. I shall be Prime Minster for the next 100 years.

Lukashenko is my new role model. I mean you think I'm a maverick shaking hands and spreading Corona round hospitals as the pandemic started, Lukashenko told his people that drinking vodka could prevent people catching it. Legend. And maybe he's right, since I got Corona I've drank like a Russian horse and I haven't caught it again, and Lukashenko caught it but it was asymptomatic. Vodka works! I mean it didn't work for Belarus, they have one of the highest per capita rates of infection in Europe, but not beating us of course. Still number one baby!!

Maybe vodka works after all, and today, the world's foreign leaders bleat and call him a cheat. Russia saying he's likely to resign, members of the European Parliament (whoever they are!) delivering a joint statement that they do not recognise Lukashenko as the president of Belarus (well who is then idiots?) and all the while he's going nowhere. He ain't going nowhere you chumps. Have you not learned yet? Nutters will not resign, nutters will not backdown – ooh Trump can't win, Cummings has to resign, Boris Johnson is a cunt with no morals – yeah nice try dick-head, see you in 100 years' time when I'm celebrating my Centennial as Prime Minister. What a guy Lukashenko is. And you always remember the good guys don't you? Your mates, the good eggs that support you. And I'll always remember the message dear old Alexander (great name again!) sent me congratulating me on our huge landslide last December…

"The Conservatives' best result in decades is a sign of public support for your work to consolidate the nation and your readiness to take responsibility for the most difficult political decisions. I look forward to fruitful cooperation with the new government of your country, which is one of the main trading and investment partners of Belarus in Europe".

Yes Alexander, my man, that is what I am about – fruitful cooperation with good people, til the end of time dear chap, for eternity!

RESUЯЯECTION

Monday August 17th 2020

Gavin Williamson – what a fucking waste of space. I had to make a dash to a different location today to get some WiFi to do a video conference with the prick. Turns out basically everyone is complaining about the A-Level results, and not just the Comps and the BAMEs and Gavin is terrified. He told me on this con-call that there were hundreds of angry students outside his Constituency Offices in South Staffordshite today… I look on the news later it's about 25 18-year olds. Yeah 25! Talk about con-call. It was really nothing – a load of Comp kids and no BAMEs with shitty home-made cardboard placards saying things like 'You're having a laugh, Gav'. Doesn't sound terrifying at all. He is having a laugh now. I employed him because he is incompetent yes, and it's just for diversity quotas yes, but I didn't think he'd be this fucking stupid. They protest, you ignore them. Thousands signed the petition over Dominic, hundreds of thousands – ignore. Ignore, ignore, ignore and literally after a few days there is another fuck-up bigger than the one we were all concerned about. That's rule number one in politics – there's always a bigger fuck-up round the corner. And I have to head to a conference room 10 miles away and risk a Russian snipers bullet because Private Pike has had a wobble. Private Pike we call him. Remember that cunt from *Dad's Army*? 'Don't tell them your name Pike' said the boss, and then they knew his name didn't they? What an idiot! And I know you shouldn't name the biggest loser in your Cabinet and for years it's been dear old Priti of course but now undoubtedly it's Gav. At least Priti doesn't listen to criticism, Gav demands an urgent con-call with me when I'm on fucking holiday. And the worst thing he could possibly ask for – he asked me for a U-turn. Dommers of course said no instantly – he said to me straight 'It's been barely 48 hours before we all said 'no U-turn, no change' over and over again on national television, you simply cannot U-turn on a 'No U-turn' slogan, that's impossible.

So I told Gavin no. But then something remarkable happened which has taken this holiday to an unexpected height of happiness. Gavin said that he couldn't cope with any more threats, even if they were

from 18-year old pricks with 'Trust Teachers' written on wet
cardboard banners…not after what happened with Russia. I asked
him what he meant and he told me that after the Salisbury poisonings
when he said that Russia should 'go away and shut up' – hilarious –
he received credible death threats from Russia and Putin which were
confirmed to him through his friend and mine, dear old Lubov
Chernukhin, who is the wife of a former Putin minister, and has given
millions to the Conservative party over the years bless her. And he
didn't want any of that again. He told me that when he had the
spokesperson of the Russian Defence ministry saying that he was
'intellectually impotent', then those protests questioning his
competence brought the terror right back, and he couldn't go through
with it again. So he couldn't resign and he begged me not to sack
him, he just wanted a U-turn and for it all to go away. Now this was
ludicrous of course, but when he mentioned Russian death threats I
saw my chance – use Gavin Williamson as a patsy. Yes! Gavin
Williamson is my Lee Harvey Oswald. Think about it, he has
confirmed that Putin already thinks he is a cunt. Bingo. And he is a
cunt, a thick cunt that angered Russia as Defence Secretary - this is
my chance to plant all the blame on to him. I will make sure Russia
thinks I am pro-everything they believe in, I have already given
money to Gamaleya and they must surely know through dear old
Evgeny, his elevation to the House of Lords, and all the other
Russian's whose dicks I have sucked (not literally but I would) that I
am not the enemy. If they need an enemy in this great Conservative
Government then it is not me, it is Cummings and it is Williamson.
And I shall distance myself from Cummings and I will make sure
every single criticism that we sometimes reluctantly have to send to
Russia comes straight from the gob of Mr Gavin Pike Williamson.

Brilliant eh, and I was such a sneaky cunt, I pulled it off brilliantly – I
know this because I record every conversation I have now and I've
just listened to it back – I said I would agree on a U-turn and I felt
terrible that he had got threats from Russia. But I made it crystal
clear - he had told Russia to 'shut up' once and if it comes to the
crunch he must do it again. He said that defeated the whole object of
his desire not to be in trouble with anyone, but I said cleverly that he

could feed his comments to the press as a 'senior Government source' but he didn't have to tell them his name. He said he didn't understand and I said, it's simple, 'Don't tell them your name Pike!' He laughed, but really didn't understand. I said he didn't have to understand, all I needed him to do was to act as my mouthpiece for Russian criticism and I would reverse the decision on A-Levels, I would indeed U-turn on the 'No U-turn'. He said he would do anything for me if I U-turned. And so earlier today, I green-lit the U-turn. And I green-lit my pathway to freedom. If I am to have eternal life, I certainly do not need a Russian death-threat hanging over me in the next life. Before I take my first pill, my first transfusion, I must deal with all the ills in my life. The first Russia, the second, Cummings. I stand here today back in my shitty Scottish outpost with a full and final declaration for the world – I need to cleanse all my ills before I step into eternity. And my first pronouncement – I, Alexander Boris Johnson, shall never suck Dominic Cumming's penis ever again. And that's a hill that I shall die on my friends, you can write that on your shitty placards, you can write it on my gravestone in 100 years' time baby - no U-turns, no change, no sucky sucky.

Tuesday August 18th 2020

Oh fuck, what a shit show. I'm trying to relax here in this very lovely cottage in the Highlands but every hour I have to do another fucking stupid clean up job, and today I have to defend the indefensible – Gavin 'retard Pike' Williamson. But worse I've just learned Dom Raab (yeah, where the fuck has he been?) has emerged from his fucking un-sanctioned sabbatical to call Alexander Lukashenko a 'fraud' and say that 'the UK does not accept the results.' Good job I asked for the WiFi to be upgraded here last night so I could watch the seniors snooker and the cricket this week. I called Dom up on Zoom for a dressing down. 'Who the fuck are you to say that UK does not accept the results you little prick!' I shouted. I love shouting at dear old Dom Raab into the little camera hole on my mac, he's unflappable but I am the one person that can make him flap. I go right up into his grill (on Zoom) and shout and spit all over him (metaphorically on Zoom), Corona or no Corona. 'Lukashenko is not a fraud!' I screamed at him, saliva everywhere, 'You're the fucking fraud'. And he is a fraud – runs for leader of the party and when he's knocked out early he backs me as leader. Ooh that's big of you Dominic you back-stabbing little cunt, like a boxer knocked out on the canvas reaching up with one bloodied finger and crying to the crowd – 'bet on that guy… I think the bigger guy who has just slammed me to the floor is gonna win'. Dick. And I told him if he doesn't start toeing the line and respect me as the boss I'm gonna kick the shit out of him. He laughed and said he was a black belt in karate. I laughed and said wait until you're one hundred and nearly dead and I'm reborn. He said 'what do you mean?' and I realised I had said too much, eternal life will only happen if I tell no one and don't write it down. But the question on my mind today as I pretended to Carrie to be interested in Scottish nature – who do I want with me on this eternal journey? Certainly not Carrie, no offence, but her use-by date will soon pass if it hasn't already. Not my children of course, so who?

Maybe I am destined just to never grow old, be reborn and fuck a series of young women who will grow older so I will have to stop fucking them and then fuck the next one. If that's my lot then so be it, I'll be the bigger man. And Raab isn't the bigger man, I'm exactly his height 175cm, he may look bigger but he's not bigger, I make sure of that with most Ministers. I'm like Tom Cruise with his co-stars. Same size or smaller. Cummings – same size as well. We'd have such a lovely kiss. Stay strong old man, stay strong. I've been lighting a fire a day in the field by my little tent, Carrie doesn't know why, I made some excuse today that I was pretending it was a birthday cake for my father (80 today, I forgot to call him!) – but in truth I had this idea I could burn away my homosexuality. Don't ask me to explain it I just thought I'd give it a try. And don't get me wrong – I'm not homophobic, some of my favourite Cabinet Ministers have to be gay, but it's just that it's going to be a whole lot easier from here on in if I'm not spending most waking hours thinking about cock. Burn brightly little fire, and as those ghost-like embers float into the air so let my homosexuality fade into the night.

Wednesday August 19th 2020

I tried to get hold of Vladimir Putin today on the blower. Reception is shit here in the Highlands obviously, most things are shit – food is shit, TV is shit, papers are shit, weather is shit - but enough is enough. I haven't talked with Putin since May now and I am certain that a quick two minute conversation would smooth everything over. I'd mention Gamaleya, Evgeny getting into the House of Lords, I'd say his dad could get in too if he wants (but being ex KGB may be trickier) and for added spice I'd tell him that the only Government minister that is now anti-Russia is Gavin Williamson and I'm trying to deal with it. Clever right? All went to shit though when Putin refused my call. Cunt. What is his fucking problem? At least with Lukashenko there's a swagger about his election fraud, a certain 'who gives a fuck'. Putin is like a little mole scurrying in and out of fraudulent holes but never popping his head up long enough to be whacked. So with all my old Russian mates avoiding me, I went for the last resort and called dear old Alexei Navalny. Now I'm not a huge fan of Alexei, while I agree with much of what he says I don't think you should go around necessarily telling the truth all the time like he does. He goes around calling Mr Putin's party a place of 'crooks and thieves' and while this may be true what benefit is it really shouting about it like that? It's a little gauche to be honest. It's a political party it's not a fucking monastery – of course there are going to be crooks and thieves, that is how things get done in this world I'm afraid. And I tell him straight when I talk to him, I say look at Lukashenko, or even Trump for that matter – the whole world knows they are frauds and won by fraudulent means but at the end of the day, no one cares quite enough. It's no good any more pointing out how someone else is a crook and a thief, it's up to you to be the biggest and best crook or thief out there and beat them the easy way.

Anyway, I asked Alexei whether I could hook him into Gavin Williamson, maybe hold an informal meeting with Gavin and tell him what he knows about Putin. He asked why Gavin Williamson as he said he knows he's a bit wet behind the ears, he's a bit of, in Alexei's words, a 'little prick'. I said Gavin, being anti-Russia himself, would be a useful ally for him. He said he didn't understand why I was calling him, and asked me did I support his opposition of Putin? And I made it clear that I think Putin is absolutely brilliant, a top bloke. Alexei then got very angry and said he knew I was up to something, which I was, so I tried to throw him off the track and mentioned something about stealing vaccines and the Gamaleya Institute. And that's when it got very interesting – Alexei said that he had heard the Gamaleya Institute was involved in some top secret work sanctioned by Putin, and he was flying into Moscow tomorrow to investigate. I asked him to keep me in touch and he said 'why should I? You are in bed with Putin.' And I came clean – I told him I wished I was, I have no relationship with Vladimir and I'd quite like one. I told him it was easy for him, on the outside looking in, it's very easy when you're on the outside to criticise and call everyone 'crooks'. He got very angry again and said it was never very easy to publicly question Putin, all he cares about is himself, all he cares about is ruling forever, and anyone that stands in the way of that would be eliminated. I said, 'what do you mean ruling forever?' And he said 'well, ruling for as long as he can.' And I asked again, 'But you said forever, what did you mean by forever?' He played dumb, but Alexei had made his fatal mistake, he had told me without telling me that he knew that Putin was involved in Resurrection, working with the Gamaleya Institute. I knew all this of course, and whether it's through Alexei, Evgeny or some other Russian crook, I'll make sure that Putin knows that I am on his side, and it's people like Williamson are the cunts. Alexei said that he had to go, and even being on the phone to me was a risk. 'Not everything is tapped,' I scoffed, 'dear Alexei this is not *Mission Impossible*.' And he said 'You think someone is not recording this conversation right now, you're a joke Prime Minister.' And he hung up. And he's the joke. No one is recording my conversations. I mean I am but that's not the point is it? I'm not going to kill myself am I? On the contrary, I'm going to live for fucking ever!

Anyway, maybe I should stop worrying about Russia. Alexei was right, this isn't *Mission Impossible* and that is screamingly obvious every time I tear my mind out of this whirlwind that is this Corona, Brexit, Cummings, Cummings' cock, Putin, Sedwill, Evgeny shit show. At the end of the day like now, I'm just a simple man with a much younger wife and a baby, and there's lots of jolly stuff on the telly, and I just have to bide my time before someone will give me a new life and then I can enjoy my childhood and decent fucking years again (I mean amazing fucking years when people realise I'm the human Dolly the Sheep) before almost certainly becoming Prime Minister again. I think I've got this under control now. Dominic called tonight to tell me that that York Parliament move thing we'd put in place to send the press down a blind alley had come to nothing so we need a new diversion for tomorrow. I told him he was worrying about nothing. He said that he was worrying about something – if the press don't have a blind alley they go up the alley leading to Parliament in London and discover that we are all crooks and thieves, 'just like you've been talking to Alexei about'. I knew he wanted me to bite the bait and ask him how he knew that I'd been talking with Alexei. But I didn't. I am strong now. I am Tom Cruise. This isn't *Mission Impossible* but I am Tom Cruise. And one thing Tom Cruise would never do is suck a man's cock. Even if the world depended on it. Now that would make a fun film.

Thursday August 20th 2020

Fuck! This is *Mission Impossible*! Alexei is dead! Pretty much. Oh fuck. I found out an hour ago, I've been literally rolling around in a tent in the garden of the cottage here ever since. It's what I do when I'm really stressed. I roll around on the floor like a worm. Fuck! This is real. He was on his way from Siberia to Moscow and I have scant details at this stage but it appears his tea was poisoned in an airport café in Tomsk on his way to Moscow. Fuck! I'm looking at my Coco Pops all weird now – maybe the milk is a little too chocolatey – I don't know, I'm looking at everyone with suspicion. Maybe Carrie is a spy, Christ if she is a spy she's damn good and in it for the long game. She could have poisoned me loads of times, I never cook or make any drinks. She sometimes even brushes my teeth.

Poisoned by a cup of tea. Idiot. Who has a cup of tea at an airport? Even if you haven't got a fatwa over your head why would you have a cup of tea at a fucking airport? Airport kettles are gross. Particularly in Siberia. Have you been? It's like Northern England but shitter, if you can imagine that. Shit-hole. Oh fuck. Breathe Boris, breathe. I'm replaying my conversation with Alexei yesterday, literally, I record every conversation we have now. He knew too much, that's what they always say in spy films isn't it, 'he knew too much'. And if he knew too much, where does that leave me? I know everything. Breathe Boris, breathe. If Putin was listening in then I said he was a 'great bloke' and I want to be his friend. Things are going to be ok. I'm flying home back to London (and drinking no tea on the way), blaming the locals here in Scotland for outing my position. Which they did but I don't give a fuck. I just want to live, forever, is that too much to ask?

While I think about it, the locals here are bloody annoying, so backward. It's like the opening scene of *Shaun of the Dead*. Zombies everywhere, bitten only by their addiction to cheap deep-fried food, shit television and alcopops. How does one even dream of connecting with these people? I mean don't get me wrong, they weren't aggressive or anything, no one called me a 'cunt' to my face which can happen really easily in Scotland, it's just people are so backward, so simple. It's like they don't know London exists. They've never been out for dinner. This cottage I've been staying in is a holiday cottage where for most of the year a family stays and there's just 4 knives, 4 forks and 4 spoons. No spares. There's no broom. The toaster is a two-slicer. There's no fucking television. I'm having to watch *The Chase* on my laptop. It's what Dominic said about eternal life, of course it's a terrible idea because there's a chance these window-lickers will take it and we will be saddled with these morons for eternity; at least over millions of years there's a chance of eliminating this scum. I don't know. Well I do know – of course it's a terrible idea but I want it. The things in life that are the most enjoyable are terrible ideas – whisky, cocaine, prostitutes, but it doesn't mean you don't want them and when you have them inside you, you just feel invincible.

That is what I must realise, I am invincible now. Come on Boris. They used to call me 'Teflon' because nothing sticks, but the analogy doesn't really work does it, nothing even touches me. What can't you touch? The sun I guess. I am the sun. I shine brightly, I give life to so many and at night you don't know where I am. Right, I'm flying back now. Quick leak to the press that we are going because of Scottish morons, but in reality we are going because of Russian killers. Not even Carrie knows why we're cutting this short, she's so angry with me. But I don't care too much about her, she worships me because I'm the sun. Where do I turn for help though? My instinct is Evgeny, my heart says Dommers but my mouth says no. Who knows most about Russia, who can I trust, who can get a message to Putin that I am on his side? I will work all this out on the flight home. 'Would you like some pretzels Mr Johnson?' Ha nice try sweet-cheese, you're gonna have to try harder than that to poison old twinkle-toes. The only thing going into my mouth from now on is stuff I've made myself, or Carrie has made as I trust her and don't make anything myself. That's it. Maybe Dominic's semen but that must be off-tap. I trust no one now. Not even my dog.

Friday August 21st 2020

I've got a trick that you might find handy. If you hate people so much for what they've done to you that you're feeling anxious, find one person to hate even more than all those people and that way you can direct all your anger towards one cunt. And that cunt, ladies and gentlemen, is Mr Kenny Cameron. I know people are blaming the SNP for revealing my holiday location but it was clearly Kenny Cameron, the cunt farmer whose land we were staying near at the weekend. He's gone to the press and said that it was his land that I pitched the tent in, and he was angry I'd done that. Yep you heard right, angry I'd pitched a tent in his fucking field. What is the problems with farmers? No wonder they have high suicide rates. So highly strung. 'Oh I know I own a million fucking acres but that tiny corner of those million acres, don't step on it or certainly pitch a tent on it or I'll blow your fucking head off before turning the gun on myself and my family and my dog.' Some of the things he's come out

with today, beggars belief. 'Usually if people want to go inside a
fenced area, they ask permission first, but I was not asked at all.'
Yeah Kenny that makes sense. 'Oh hi Kenny, I've trekked 3 miles to
your shitty farm house on the off chance you own these million acres,
would it be ok if I pitch a tent on the outermost corner of those acres
basically right next to the back garden of a house that you don't own,
is that ok you miserly little cunt?' Even though you don't really own
the land, no one 'owns land' and I'm the fucking Prime Minister.
Ooh – off to tell the Daily Mail where I am are you, you snivelling
little shite. And what's that Kenny? You have a problem with me
having a bonfire in the field? That Kenny was a bonfire specifically
designed to scare off homosexual thoughts. Now I bet you're a fan
Kenny aren't you, you backwards little prick. 'Mr Johnson is meant
to be leading the country and yet is not setting a great example.' Oh
Kenny, Kenny Kenny Kenny, I hate you. I hate you more than
everyone I've ever met and everyone I will ever meet. My hate for
you has concentrated all my hate into one person and it has totally
relaxed me. Thank you cunt Kenny.

Anyway, back to matters at hand. Alexei is in hospital with a coma. I
called Evgeny, I wanted to go round but for obvious reasons I need
to lay low for the weekend. Was just updating my kill list – remember
that? Sedwill, Cummings, Gove and now Kenny fucking Cameron.
Anyway, Evgeny was bullish as I thought he would be, he doesn't buy
into the Putin poisoning people line at all and thinks on the contrary
it's a Western hoax to discredit Russia – yes, he thinks the West are
behind these poisonings! The whole thing is fucked up. I said to
Evgeny 'Can I trust you?' over and over again and I just have to
believe him. So I told him I had been signed up for Resurrection
with GSK. They have left a message today and I am starting the
blood transfusions as early as next week. It didn't surprise him at all,
I expected more shock, I do think he knows everything. And I
suspect he is getting the same treatment as me, although he didn't let
on, as he shouldn't have done because I've been told this is a secret
and I can't tell anyone, or write it down. But fuck it, Dominic
Cummings has a video of me sucking his cock and that hasn't come
back to bite me yet. Hang on, that's Dominic on the phone now.

Oh fuck.

Saturday August 22nd 2020

I love Dominic Cummings and should not have betrayed him. I feel
like a terrible person. Politics (and life in general) is of course about
betraying as many people as possible to get to the top, but I do not
need to fall out with Dominic. I love him, and he loves me. He told
me again last night, he loves me, and I believe him now. Look, I
sucked his penis again until it popped in my mouth, but this time it
was totally what I wanted, and definitely what he wanted, he screamed
like a Beatles fan. Once I'd swallowed I looked up and said 'shut up
you'll wake the baby' and I laughed and a load of his spunk was spat
out on to my shirt and tie. I've thrown that tie out now, you can't
completely remove spunk from silk I am coming to realise, but I
don't care – I've thrown away one thing but I've found another again
– dear old Dominic.

He was angry last night, that's how all great sex starts. He was angry
that I had betrayed him, and as I say I feel terrible now. Roger
Connor, director at GSK, had told Dommers about my visit and my
plan with Resurrection and I couldn't have felt more silly. I should
have told him, I guess I just saw the chance to live forever and I
grabbed at it, without thinking of the people I'd hurt. That's me all
over isn't it? Maybe Putin was right all along, maybe I am a cunt. But
Dommers was the bigger man and forgave me, and then offered up
his penis for me so I could say sorry properly. Again he grabbed the
back of my head and forced it on to his cock because he was angry
but I totally understand, Dominic is my right hand man and I will do
anything for him because he loves me like no one else does. I'll do
anything for Dominic Cummings. Which is annoying as he wants to
move me out of Downing Street.

For months now he's been on at me to move the operation out of
Downing Street – I mean I agree in many ways, it's a fucking mess
here, nobody knows whose space is whose, Ben Warner is always just
around with a few of his mates changing everyone's social media so

that they don't think I'm a cunt, which I am. Dominic is obsessed
with The West Wing, I've never seen it myself, but it's all about
politics being glamorous, with lovely swanky offices and people
stomping around being all important. I've never seen it that way.
Politics is about facilitating life, not the other way round. I want to
have fun, and have power, I don't want to have to 'go into work'.
The whole joy of being Prime Minister is I can work from home, and
lounge around, and walk the dog, and suck the occasional dick in one
of Downing Street's grubby offices. I don't want to have to put a tie
on every day, as you've just heard I'm fast running out! So I've told
him I will think about this now but hopefully he'll forget about it. He
also wants another 800 million from me for his technology Projects
thing (that I don't really understand) but I really don't think we can
afford it. I don't know what is happening with Brexit but I was
passed a document earlier which I've only skim read and I've just lost
which is some tight arse at the Civil Service saying if a 'no deal' Brexit
and second Corona wave hits in Winter then the country is fucked.
Stating the fucking obvious there. But anyway, I don't know how
much money we have left and another 800 million for Dominic's pet
project seems a little too much to me. I suggested that we might be
running out of money and he said, 'Don't forget Boris, I have a video
of you sucking my penis.' I laughed and said that sounded like
blackmail, and he laughed too. We didn't really resolve that one.

Anyway the £800 million is in the manifesto so I guess we can do it,
but I'm not being blackmailed, I just now agree with him that we
should do it. Whatever it is, Dominic knows about it not me, can't
be bothered. It's all about 'high risk high reward' research into
technology that sounds fanciful. I said what kind of stuff, and he said
really not to worry about it, and if he told me what it was I wouldn't
want to back him. I insisted and said I'm not giving him 800 million
pounds if I don't know a little about what is planned. He laughed
arrogantly and asked me whether I had seen the film Face/Off. I
haven't. He told me to watch that and I'd have a better idea. So
patronising, I'm not gonna watch no film. Anyway I haven't got
round to watching it yet, I've been watching the cricket and the

snooker and Carrie has been watching her Indian dating shit on Netflix. I'll get round to it.

Today I've felt almost like this is the holiday I was wanting on holiday. Why does anyone want to get away? It's all stress, and tents, and cunt farmers. That's what I love about number 10 – so many little hiding places where you can have a nap, watch TV and suck a penis. I feel relaxed today dear diary, finally a weekend that feels like a weekend again. And I'm going to name this feeling, it's love. I am in love. I have that tingly feeling of a new relationship. And this has the added danger of being with a man that is potentially now going to try to blackmail me. I feel so alive.

Sunday August 23rd 2020

Well this is fairly bombshell news. My beloved Dominic needs emergency heart surgery, he's going in to have the procedure tomorrow. He Zoom called me from Chillingham Castle, dear old Mary's father's wonderful home. This is awful news. And I feel terrible again – I joked when I first saw him up in Chillingham again, 'have you given up work you lazy cunt?' I haven't actually seen him do any work for several weeks, but I can talk I suppose. And that's when he dropped the bombshell that he needed some quite complex surgery, and had I signed off the £800 million yet? Obviously I said that I would, I can hardly refuse him now he might die. He asked me if push came to shove whether I would donate any organs to him. I again misfired with a joke and said 'Well there's one organ I've been wanting to give you for weeks.' He wasn't in the mood for that – on the brink of open heart surgery is not the time to flirt, or not the ideal time anyway.

So there we have it, both myself and Dommers are going under the surgeon's knife tomorrow. Well I am having my first transfusion. I don't quite understand what I'm going in for – it's just a quick procedure in Harley Street to see if my blood is amenable to heavier stuff down the line – and that's to have the blood of a much younger man inside me to start building up my body for the use of

'Resurrection'. I don't quite understand it but I trust GSK with my lives. And what harm can getting a bit of young blood inside me, so to speak? I'm keeping that on the quiet obviously but Dommers has said that we will need to release to the press once he's had the procedure, obviously with a bit of bullshit to dress it up. But he won't be able to do much while he's convalescing. This is a huge blow, and despite the last 4 weeks or so since he's basically done nothing but cum in my mouth, I am going to miss his guiding hand, even if in recent weeks it has just been guiding my mouth towards his cock. I am a bit of a lost soul without him. Yes I have Carrie but she can't write a speech and give me a slogan, and it's nothing against her, she's a woman and I can't blame her for that. I just need him. He's the brain of this operation and I'm the heart. I would donate my heart to him if he needed it, as soppy as it sounds he already has my heart. God I'm getting upset now, I'm looking at a photo of him, and I'm putting my hand on his ratty little face. I really don't think I can cope without him. Oh dear diary, I must go and weep now. And drink enough alcohol to send me unconscious. Goodnight.

Monday August 24th 2020

I must say the GSK operation is very slick, I'd imagine this is what the KGB would do if they were running a service, ultra efficient. And just like the KGB I was picked up by a Russian today, part of the GSK team and was whisked off to this top secret location on Harley Street. I had to hide out and not tell my security detail. I didn't black-up though as I thought we were in enough shit without having race riots. It was all very clandestine and exciting. No one would tell me their names. Anyway I believe I gave some blood (like every good citizen should) and then I received the blood of a younger man. Simple stuff, and I'll be doing this every few days for the next two weeks before I start taking the Resurrection medicine to ready my body for the cloning procedure. Lovely stuff. And they've assigned me a personal trainer too as I've been told I need to lose a stone for these drugs to take hold, so they introduced me to a young chap dear old Harry Jameson, seems like a good sort. He said he'd previously worked with TV presenter Laura Whitmore. I said I only watch

Netflix and *The Chase*. He said 'oh'. Dominic had his heart procedure today too and he messaged me to say he was ok. I said 'Wonderful. You are wonderful' with a kiss, and he didn't reply. I imagine he's tired. Anyway I feel quite faint so I'm going to visit the land of nod now with maybe a quick stop-off first in the lay-by of self-pleasure.

Tuesday August 25th 2020

Fucking hell. I hate having to make decisions, I texted Dommers today and said 'hurry up and get the fuck better'. That's what people don't realise – this is my job, being Prime Minister. You have a job I assume? I know that's far less likely than it was a year ago but remember when you had a job, some days you are shit at it right, because you have loads of other stuff going on. I have death threats, blood transfusions, blackmail, eternal life and then dear old Matt Hancock called me on the Bat-phone today and said that I had to make a call on face-masks in schools if Covid kicks off. I told him, 'Didn't I make that call ages ago?' and he said yes I did, but it had to be revisited because of new thinking and what Nicola Sturgeon had done. What? Sorry? Are we fucking following her now? Jesus! I've made the decision! Why does anything have to change ever?! On a related note I've heard the BBC are going to drop the lyrics of Rule, Britannia! and Land of Hope and Glory, just because it bigs-up the might of the British Empire. This should be celebrated, if I had my way we would take over again the nations 'not so blest as thee'. Like Poland for example, they're weak. As I said in a news interview today there's so many apologists for what Great, and I underline <u>Great</u> Britain did in the past, riding rough-shod over countries, making slaves and pillaging treasure – as I said today on the telly 'it's time we stopped our cringing embarrassment about our history.' What is in history cannot be changed and I've said before cannot be learned from because it is history. What we have always done is what we should always do. In the same way that the BBC have taken off old episodes of supposedly racist sitcoms like *It Ain't Half Hot Mum* and *Til Death Do Us Part* and *The Black and White Minstrel Show*. If they weren't racist then, they aren't racist now. Things can't magically become racist can they? Fucking ludicrous.

Glad I got that off my chest. And I know what you'll be thinking, 'Oh you would say that you're a privileged, white male.' Well sorry about that, I can't change the colour of my face can I? Not without blacking-up anyway, and there's another thing that magically became racist overnight a few decades back. Ant and Dec blacked-up in a comedy sketch – it cannot be racist. I can't change the colour of my face, unless they develop that Face/Off technology. I watched the film today, was bullshit wasn't it? I fell asleep. But I've been googling Nicolas Cage and there's a great clip of him on *Wogan*, he comes on and does a shit somersault and is clearly off his head on cocaine. That's what I'm gonna do now, not the somersault bit – unless I get totally off my tits. I really don't think I've shaken this Corona, I feel like shit. I should have worn a mask. Certainly not gone around shaking Corona positive hospital patients. What the fuck was I thinking? I mean I've done some fucking stupid things in my life but what on Earth was I thinking? Maybe school kids should wear masks then, I'm gonna toss a coin like Carrie did remember for Brexit… There we go, kids have to wear masks now. Like that's gonna fucking work.

Wednesday August 26th 2020

Was looking on my Twitter today. I get my worker-bees to do the tricky ones where I have to express sympathy or some shit, but today I was having a fiddle myself. I've got 2.9 million followers which is annoying, I can't wait til I hit 3 million – that will get me jacked-up for sure. My worker-bods wanted to post something about Alexei, I was in two minds but they said something like 'oh that was bad wasn't it'. I told them to keep it light, I can't anger them Russians any more. So I was mainly just private messaging a few people I follow on there just for shits and gigs. I can imagine them just cracking on with their Wednesday, their phone buzzes and it's the Prime Minister getting bawdy. Cracks me up. I did Donald Trump first and just said 'Hi' and he came back a few minutes later with 'New number, who dis?' Very funny is the Donald. Also messaged Lord Sugar and Prue Leith from *Great British Bake Off* asking them when the new series are coming on – I love GBBO, there's always a nice bit of skirt on it. Mainly just boring MPs I have to follow, I mute all their accounts though. David Cameron was the first person I followed. He doesn't tweet much. He keeps his head down because everyone hates him. Funny how quick that turned isn't it?

I was looking at twitter as the press have been increasingly unkind recently. At least when someone calls me a cunt on Twitter I know they are probably poor. The Guardian was unbelievably rude yesterday. Dominic called me to joke about it but I didn't find it funny. They said the Conservatives are 'Johnson's head hosting Dominic Cumming's brain'. Dominic joked and said 'your head has certainly come in handy'. He laughed but I didn't. I'm more than just a head you know, Boris Johnson is more than fellatio. Dominic makes me feel second-rate and I asked him to apologise and he said he was recovering from heart surgery so he might not. I also told him to shut his father-in-law up, who immediately leaked to the press yesterday what I said about quitting in six months' time. He won't know but what I meant by that is as soon as this Resurrection lark is ready, maybe I want to tap out early if that's possible. Do I really want to spend the next 40 years doing this bullshit? Or shall I just crack on with the next life?

As I've said previously I love the power but this job is all flavours of shite at times. I was made to visit Castle Rock High School today in Leicestershire for example to ram home the message that these thick parents need to send their disgusting children back to school so they can get back and clean my fucking toilets or whatever hell they work in, and I was still pretty spaced out to be honest after my transfusion. I hate children, I don't why I've had so many. But they were pretty excited to see me. I felt a bit like The Beatles, young girls screaming at me, but I didn't have sex with any of them as they were under 16, which didn't stop The Beatles I'd imagine but I wouldn't be able to get away with that stuff as I'm bigger than The Beatles. Anyway I totally fucked the speech, I said (verbatim as I record everything)…

'And when you've been struggling with something in the classroom, like the supine stem of confiteor or nuclear fusion, or is Harry Potter sexist? Answer 'no' by the way? Is it politically acceptable to sing Rule Britannia? Yes.'

Total bollocks, like I'd picked words out of a crap-filled hat. I called Dominic straight after and said I needed him, he said he knew that but he was recovering from heart surgery so couldn't help me. But he was very interested in my transfusion, and wanted to know all about it, which shows he cares. I hope he comes back soon – I can cope with Brexit but not Dexit. His little laugh, his grunt as he cums in my mouth, I miss it all.

Thursday August 27th 2020

News came out about my personal trainer today in the Evening Standard, God you can't keep anything secret can you? I'm amazed that the Evening Standard or any of the other press haven't picked up on me having blood transfusions in preparation to take a drug to give me eternal life. I had another one today. There and back and the press aren't interested at all. I assume they think it's a Corona thing. There's rumours flying around that I'm struggling physically due to Corona, Dominic's dad spreading some shit about me being weak. Well he's a castle owning cunt and should shut up.

Anyway today I took part in a training session for MPs on sexual harassment and bullying. It was most informative, when it eventually worked. This young sort was setting up my Zoom in Downing Street and it kept failing, she's fit but she's fucking useless and I told her as much. Anyway, very good training session I learned a lot. I'm aware of course of the allegations against certain MPs, I'm pleased to say mostly retired and dead MPs, around sex allegations with children, but thankfully it didn't touch upon that hot potato. Old 'wandering hands' would have to attend of course, if he wasn't touching some hot potato. It was more about 'Valuing everyone' and I think is a really good thing for us to do. Well it's compulsory even for me so I have to do it, so it's something that I would never do normally but I now have to do. A little long I thought, 2 hours. How long does it take to say 'try to treat women like you would men, or at least like women you don't fancy.' I mean really, talk about over egging the cake. So yes, very good. The sexual harassment bit anyway, the bullying thing was a waste of time. Back in my day you were told what to do and if you didn't do it you'd be punished and made to feel small, and that never did me any harm. But I guess good to learn about how it felt being on the other side of the bullying. And to be honest I don't buy it. Sounds like a lot of people moaning about being told they have to do work that they don't want to do. I'm sorry, you work for me. This may sound cruel but as the saying goes 'if you're not sucking my dick you're cleaning up after'. As I say though, a good session, most informative.

Anyway, after the 2 hour sexual harassment session, I was a bit turned on. I guess an expected side-effect of talking about perving over young women. So... naughty me I thought I'd have another pop at Olga D, remember, the violinist. Anyway, fate finally gave me a break and she was over from Dubai doing some gigs in London at the weekend, so I invited her over. Carrie was away with family for the night. Well, a gentlemen never tells but I certainly did fuck her and my goodness she's amazing. So, so beautiful. She looks like a Russian doll, but thin, and there's not a smaller person inside her (well until I got in of course!). As I say a gentlemen never gives details but fuck me, my mind has been too on the cock recently and I've forgotten how good female flesh tastes. I mean young, female flesh. Nothing against Carrie but she's 32 now, which isn't that old of course but she's had a kid, which adds about 5 years on and does nothing for your tits and downstairs. Olga D on the other hand, is comfortably in her twenties, looks younger, and has spent all her life working her fingers on the violin, so she certainly know what she's doing with the old hands. She's incredible, working the C, and the A. I hope I was ok. I was very excited and just bounced around on top of her like an excited puppy and came within seconds, but I always feel like what I lack in finesse I make up for in being Prime Minister. She didn't stay the night – after that sexual harassment training earlier I didn't think it appropriate so I said 'apologies I think you'll need to scoot'. I kept it nice so it couldn't be classed as bullying. Anyway she didn't seem too upset as she said she would give me a ring next time she was in town. I said that would be lovely and of course not to tell anyone. I was quite insistent on that, without bullying her of course. She said she'd had a lovely time, and I hope she knows I had the same. Although I'm just watching the video back now, and I really was all over the place – I look like a hairy Octopus rolling around on a beautiful oyster – hands and legs everywhere. Oh well, that was terrific fun and just the heterosexual fill-up I needed to remind myself life isn't all about the D, it sometimes is about the Olga D.

Friday August 28th 2020

Sad news about Pret a Manger today. They've had to close 30 stores. I'd imagine because one corner of Euston Station is having building works. My joke there being that there's a billion fucking Pret a Mangers so who gives a fuck? Thousands to lose jobs! Yes, thousands of immigrants. I'm sorry I'm not sorry. The majority of the British public who voted in the EU referendum want us to stop accepting immigrants to the UK. I know the people that voted Brexit say that it wasn't all about immigration, but come on now, yes it was. Ask a person for another reason why they voted Brexit and they can't think of one, some jokingly say 'straight bananas' when what they mean is 'no Arabs'. I mean come on there isn't another reason, and it's fine. There isn't another good reason why we are doing this ridiculous waste of time, so let's just celebrate what's about to happen with immigration, let's embrace it. There will be less immigrants coming the UK. And I know people say oh our best doctors are immigrants – well firstly that's a lie most doctors who work privately are not immigrants and secondly let's face it, most immigrants are not landing on a beach in Whitstable and heading straight for Harley Street are they, no they are heading straight to one of those shitty flats near Dover station or straight into a Pret a Manger. I hate Pret a Manger, I despise everything about 'sandwich culture'. I've only been in a Pret once for a photo opportunity and they're all so fucking smiley all the time, I mean I know they had to smile because it was me and it was a photo opportunity but really, stop smiling all the time, it looks disingenuous. And there's millions of grumpy British unemployed who would love to have your jobs.

RESUЯЯECTION

I do worry about the unemployed, of course I do. We massage the figures we release to the public, I'd say most people are unemployed now. And most people that are employed sit around in their pants all day doing the odd Zoom call and doing fuck all. When did we become a country of lazy cunts? I blame New Labour myself, Thatcher was all about the City, and working hard (unless you were a miner), New Labour was too interested in Britpop and Oasis and Blur and forgot what makes this country great, which is millions of people willing to work their arses away for one holiday a year. 'Oh Sally if we work 10 hours a day for 360 days we too could afford that 10 day holiday on the Greek Isle of Saddos'. That is what this great country is built on, stupid compliant fuckers willing to dig in (not miners), and knuckle down, so they can have three days a year sitting on a beach drinking Sangria and eating pineapple from the beach version of Pret a Manger (immigrant selling over-priced fruit). Seriously, when I was in that Pret I picked up a small pot of mango, probably eight pieces of mango for £2.10 or something. I nearly dropped my cappuccino - these immigrants think we were born yesterday.

And I feel like I was born yesterday, these blood transfusions are clearly working. I feel younger and fitter than I've ever felt. I've banged Olga D and dear old Harry is doing wonders – he works me so hard – I even came twice yesterday, once with Olga and once the moment she had left. Nothing to do with Harry that one, I fear he's straight. I did that one over a girl on *Bake Off* (not in person obviously). There's something about *Bake Off* that makes me so horny, I call it 'Jack-off'. It's all the stuff rising and talk of 'soggy bottoms' gets me up like a flag pole. Anyway, what a turnaround. At the start of this journal I look back and I was tired, dreaming of a resurrection, and here I am nearly two months later actually on the pathway to true Resurrection. And today I have already begun the search for a partner who can share this journey with me. As I've said, it's not Carrie sadly. She may be the mother of my children but she's a tapper. I hate a tapper, I can't stand them for more than 5 minutes which is why (not the only reason of course) myself and Carrie now mainly are sleeping in separate beds. Another reason for that is she doesn't like me openly masturbating to the *Great British Bake Off*. It may well be Olga D but she's perhaps a bit Russian for my liking. I've been flicking through the old phone book and nothing crops up, I want a Katie Derham type but younger, that young girl off *Countdown* maybe. I'm not sure, I'll have a think. I have time now, I have all the time in the world. Which is more than I can say for the country – I am genuinely worried about it, no one is going back to work. I really didn't see this coming but I should have done – give millions of people the option of working from home and paying most of them 80% of their wages to do fuck all, of course people have got a taste for it. Damn it. I mean don't get me wrong, it is brilliant doing fuck all, it's the best thing in the world. But as Dommers warned me, if I am to live forever, do I want to be surrounded by these fucktards everywhere clogging up the system and smiling inanely at me in Pret a Manger? I need to focus. If I am to live forever the last thing I need is to be surrounded by poor people moaning at me. I will either rebuild this country and make it great again, or if that is too much like hard work I will disappear and live my next life in Spain. The beautiful irony of it. I'm gonna spend the next few years stopping people travelling here from Europe, and then I fuck off and live on a beach in Spain. Bring me that over-priced pineapple you stupid bitch!

Saturday August 29th 2020

I watched the football today. Liverpool versus Arsenal in the Charity Shield. Now I famously said 'I support all the London teams'. Dominic told me to say that and I think it's his one mistake – what a fucking ludicrous thing to make me say. 'I support all the London teams'. What, Millwall? I'm a Millwall supporter now am I? Why don't I join those skin-heads in South London and go down the beach trying to capsize boats of immigrants?! Actually, sounds like fun. But you know what I mean, I can't support all the London teams, that makes no sense. So can I make it clear in private that I support just the wealthy and progressive London teams, so Arsenal and Chelsea, and to a lesser extent Tottenham Hotspur but their ground is in quite a scummy area, and very ethnic - Corbyn would hate it! Anyway cut a racist story short, I was supporting Arsenal today and so was very pleased when a young Liverpool player, Rhian

134

Brewster, missed a penalty and allowed Arsenal to win. And there's a lesson here for everyone I think. Don't trust the young. Rhian Brewster is 20 and I don't wish to crucify him but he earns millions as a professional footballer and yet cannot hit the goal from 12 yards away. Let me make it quite clear – his penalty was not saved, he shot the ball against the crossbar, as I say missing the goal from a distance of 12 yards. Young people are fucking useless, and if you look at my twitter right now, all I am saying and I will say it until I am blue in the face (or red if I'm supporting Arsenal) – send your stupid kids back to school. I'll say it nicer than this on twitter, or my twitter-bods will, but, and I have many children so I come from a position of huge experience – you look at your children as gifted and wonderful because you love them. I am in a superbly privileged position of not being blinded by bias, because, and this may come a surprise to many, I don't actually love my children. I like most of them, but I love none of them. It was something else taught to us at Eton - do not love your own children. That way you can look at them dispassionately when the time is right, and the time is right, right now. Your children are not special, they are not gifted, and they are annoying when I try to run around the block or the park here and they consistently shout 'cunt' at me. You are the cunt kid, and get back to fucking school.

Anyway, the bad news is that Carrie walked in on me while I was watching a video of me fucking Olga D. I know right, schoolboy error. I was just watching it back - you know how you get those shivers of embarrassment and shame about something from your past, well I just had to look at it again. As I said at the time, she's so beautiful is young Olga, and I really think I fucked up. So I wanted to watch her one more time and maybe text her again and tell her I'll make up for it next session. Anyway I was about half way through the recording (which only lasts about 2 minutes) and Carrie creeps up behind me and asks me what I'm doing. I try to pass it off as a porn film but she said she would recognise that 'white cheating wobbly arse anywhere'. Yep, she was naturally miffed and I feel terrible. I mean she knew when she married me that with the smooth, rich Prime Ministerial Boris you do also get the white, cheating wobbly arse Boris but seeing it in front of her own eyes as she held the baby was not a good look. She's now saying she wants some time apart. Which is fine with me to be honest, the crying baby (and now her crying too) is doing my nut in. But obviously I feel terrible. That's the problem with cheating if the girl you are cheating with lives in fucking Dubai – you can't even call her up to make you feel better. I mean I did call her up and she did make me feel better but, I don't know, call it a conscience if you will but I'm feeling bad today. Who sneaks up on someone when they are watching porn? That's a rum do it really is. I know I shouldn't but I blame Carrie then for this mess. I guess it's what I was saying earlier, you really can't trust the young.

Sunday August 30ᵗʰ 2020

Well this is strange. Mark Sedwill popped round unannounced tonight. I was just having a snooze after drinking all day in the dog-house and I was woken up by Sedwill saying he really wanted to see me. I wanted to refuse but I couldn't, and I'm rather glad I didn't. Mark is an old friend and yes we fell out about not telling me that Putin thought I was a cunt but I feel we have bigger fish to fry now (which by the way would be British fish from the English channel, don't get me started, Brexit negotiations kicking off again). Anyway perhaps I over-reacted to dear old Mark, I guess he was just trying to shield me from the worst news, which I actually told him once was his actual job as head of the civil service. 'Hide the bad news from me' I do recall saying to him. So in short, all is forgiven. Anyway he was a little odd with me, and now I'm thinking about it after he's gone, a little scary - I feel like he fancies me.

I'm not sure. He helped himself to a stiff drink, and encouraged me to do the same. He asked me if I had heard anything from Russia. I didn't really know what to tell him so I just said 'bits and bobs' and hoped he wouldn't ask me what that meant. But he asked me what that meant. I said that the threat I felt had gone away. And he then nodded, but then kind of shook his head, and then nodded again and just said 'Well, yes.' And looked away. He then said he's really going to miss me. He leaves next week, we're announcing his replacement tomorrow, dear old Simon Case. So I thought maybe that was it, that he was leaving, but we had a meeting scheduled in the diary for tomorrow, so why did he want to come round this evening for a drink? I mean I know he can afford alcohol, we had to pay him off with hundreds of thousands of pounds. Anyway right at the end of the night after beating around the bush for an hour he said that he was going to miss me terribly, and he hoped I forgave him for everything. As I say, I guess I have forgiven him, but didn't want to tell him that (forgiveness being a sign of weakness) so I just said 'what is done is done'. I then said 'life's too short' and he looked me straight in the eye, shaking a little and said 'is it Boris, is life too short?'

I knew Dommers may have told him but I couldn't be done with the argument to be honest. Who cares about Sedwill now? He will die soon and I will live forever. Truly, those fights I cared about have now evaporated into the ever-lasting air I now breathe. So I just batted him off and told him it may be time to go. I needed a shit to be honest and hate going for a shit during a meeting (although I do one literally in the middle of every meeting). So he stood up and hugged me. I pulled back slightly and said 'I don't call that social distancing' and he stepped back and he said 'you're invincible Boris, whether you live on or not your legacy certainly will'. He then awkwardly nuzzled his lips into my neck, I think he tried to kiss me and then rushed for the doorway. He dropped his handkerchief on the way, it was a bit like Cinderella but I didn't want to chase after him as I needed a shit. I'll maybe go around the Kingdom tomorrow testing out everyone's noses seeing whose handkerchief has been dropped – actually it's not like Cinderella at all is it. But weird right? Anyway, job done, Sedwill has gone, that's an hour cleared in my diary for tomorrow and I've just had the shit of my life. I love being a bachelor again!

Monday August 31st 2020

Fuck Europe. I love Europe but this is getting frankly ridiculous. It's very, very complicated and I have to admit I don't understand any of it, but they won't let us have the fishing waters we want. Jesus. All

137

this mess over fish. It's sea off the coastline of the UK, of course they are our fish. If they wanted to swim close to fucking Germany then they would, but they don't – they are our fish, not German fish. I will not back down over these fish. I will go to war over these fish. I mean I won't actually go to war but World Wars have started over more trivial matters. Michel Barnier is a pernickety little prick isn't he? And he's thick – he says negotiations over the fishing waters are 'near the end of the road'. Fish don't swim in roads. But if they did they would swim in British roads and not German Autobahns. Anyway that's that, I really can't bear to think about Europe right now, it's still technically my Summer holidays and the sun is still peeking through the clouds. The EU top brass were accusing me today as having a 'wasted Summer'. Hardly mate, I've been on a holiday, started a new exciting homosexual relationship, come back from the dead and now am going to live forever. What have you done you froggy cunts?

Anyway, let's ignore that. It's Bank holiday Monday! Woo-hoo a day off!! All I did was have a very quick call with dear old Simon Case, traitor Sedwill's replacement. He's a lovely young chap is Simon, he's only 41, but I like him because he knows people, the top people, the people who matter in this country. And that's not the Russians, the dirty Russians (I'll still say that privately), I mean our Royal Family. Simon was William's Private Secretary, and by Secretary I don't mean as in what a woman would do, he was William's confidante, his right hand man, and who knows over time he may become mine as well, he may even become one of my best friends, I mean I'm paying him enough! And it's not just who he knows, Simon has also done a sterling job since May, in charge as he has been of improving our response to the coronavirus. Ha ha – joke! Only joking, he's clearly done a fucking awful job on that, fuck me it couldn't be any worse, but as I say, he's mates with the Royal family and that's good enough for me. I need a mate on the real inside, my relationship with the Queen has always been very formal, and I'd like to think I now have someone on hand to grab the crown off these people (so to speak) if the need ever arose. I don't know what the Queen thinks of me but I get the impression she doesn't like me, ever since I joked a bit

insensitively when I was first made Prime Minister. I went round the
Palace to formally accept the job and she said 'Well done Mr Johnson,
blondes clearly have more fun.' I was nervous, and I was trying to go
along with the unexpectedly informal line of banter. So I said…
(cringe)… 'try telling that to Princess Diana!' Ouch. I think ever
since then she's thought of me as a bit of a cunt. So, as I say, good to
have a friend on the inside. I did have Prince Andrew, but he's hiding
in Florida I think now, I heard he went to Tampa with the kids. Ha
ha ha – I've still got it!

Anyway the other reason Simon Case got the job is Dominic wanted
him to have it and I don't really know the man but that's the reason
why he's got it, so if it all goes tits up blame Dommers. I mean it
won't go tits up but you know what I mean, Simon won't really have
to do anything, certainly not since Dominic decided to split the role
so David Frost now does the security adviser bit. (not that David
Frost!!). Although that David Frost would probably have equal the
security experience that our David Frost has, which is none. So again,
I don't really understand why Dominic wanted him to have the job.
So again, blame him if it goes tits up. If you can get hold of him. I've
texted him seventeen times today with no response. My final message
to him was 'I know you're recovering from heart surgery but my heart
is hurting too.' He's read the message. Just hasn't responded. Oh
well, I don't care, I truly do not care. I'm a friend of a friend of
Prince William, how cool is that? And if you think it's not cool to
brag about having a chance to chat with Prince William, well try
telling that to Princess Diana! Seriously the Queen needs to grow a
fucking sense of humour the sour faced old bat.

Tuesday September 1ˢᵗ 2020

Another round of transfusions today, this one was a little longer, I
think I actually fell asleep, very relaxing knowing you are going to live
forever. All very nice but as I've said very stern and very Russian, I'd
say 'lighten up' to them but don't know the Russian for 'lighten up',
which I should do as I could tell Alexander Lebedev to lighten up, or
Putin. So grumpy all the time, so serious. I watched a private

screening of *Tenet* today at the House of Commons (I know, naughty us, dear old Michael Gove set up a little screening to celebrate the end of the Summer for all the Cabinet. I know we should have been doing Brexit negotiations but it's all got a little boring). *Tenet* was a superb film, loads of people got shot and the explosions were ace. It was all about people in the future being sent back to the past or something, I didn't really understand the plot. But it's exciting isn't it, the opportunities that are going to come up for me, now I am to live forever, or at least another 100 years. Imagine what they'll have invented in 100 years' time, I really don't need to worry about anything ever again do I? But that doesn't stop me worrying of course. Parliament was back today. Fucking hell.

Dear old Gavin Williamson, dear old Patsy, was taking the heat again for me today. He really is a lovely little puppy, he'll do anything I say, you have to respect a man like that. He stepped up to apologise for the A-Level and GCSE results fuck-up and his opposite number, Kate Green accused him of a 'summer of chaos'. Worked perfectly, the summer of chaos is now dear old Gavin's fault. Bingo. All we need to do now is for him to drop in that he hates Russia and I'm in the clear I reckon. Apparently 17% of parents are considering not sending their kids back to school. I know right, pricks. You've had 5 months at home with you awful child and you're seriously considering not having free child care 9-3 every day for them? You must either be rich or fucking stupid. As I said in Cabinet today, there is likely to be more of this wretched Covid to come, but your kid is not going to get it, kids do not get Covid, and I'm going to prove that soon enough by going into a school and doing a photo opp where I cuddle all of them. Actually that might be a bad idea for several reasons, I'll work on that.

Also there's talk of London dying, now this really worries me of course. No one is going back to work. I said at Parliament today that people were going back to work 'in huge numbers'. It was so great to get that message out there because it's clearly bullshit but no one challenged me on it so the message is still out there. I had a big smirk on my face watching the footage back on the BBC, maybe I'm not such a great liar after all, lying amuses me. I really do worry that London is dying. Without all these idiots going in there every day, doing their pointless jobs and office banter and flirting then whole industries are going to die off. I mean mainly dry-cleaners and Pret a Mangers so I'm not that worried, but still. I'm not sure what to do really, you can't force people to go back to work. I talked with Dominic today and he thinks you can. He said 'you can do anything you like Prime Minister, look at Belarus, there's an example of how we could really control the scum'. Yes I talked with lovely Dommers today, I haven't really been able to concentrate on much else really. He said the operation went well and he'll be back on his feet in the next few days. I asked whether he would accept a visitor and maybe I could suck his penis but he said no, Mary is hovering about by all accounts and he said following the operation he doesn't think he will be able to get hard. Oh well. Was so lovely to hear from him anyway. He was very, very interested in my transfusions again as well and exactly how they are going so I know he cares about me too. I have a warm feeling tonight that things are going to be ok. I mean ok for me, not ok for the country, oh dear God it's fucked. I really don't know what to do. So many fires, I really don't know which one to cover up next. I think I'll just let them burn out. I really don't think there's any chance of a deal on Brexit, they were trying to get through to me this morning apparently but I was watching *Tenet*. If only I could go back in time! LOL! Seriously though, this isn't my fault. It's theirs, and ultimately remember, Carrie's.

In more fun news I joined LinkedIn today. Dear old Ben and Faculty are just about to launch a load of shit on to people's social media so he said if people followed me there then we'd get the dumbfucks on twitter and Instagram and also the clever folk on LinkedIn, so in I've gone. Ben's set it up so people can message me and apparently we can more easily collect people's personal data and thoughts if they do that. I asked Ben what kind of messages were coming through and he laughed and said 'You don't want to know Boss'. I said 'I do want to know' and he said 'Well as of 3 minutes ago 27,500 people had messaged to call you a cunt'. I said 'I don't want to know'. Now I know too much, I'll have to be killed! Little does almost everyone know, I will never die. Dear old Dommers knows though, I'm now lying in bed thinking of him. He might not be able to get hard, so I'll get hard for the both of us.

Wednesday September 2nd 2020

Uurgh – back to work today. I'll soon get someone else to do Prime Minister's Questions (PMQs), I'll just have to change the name first to 'This week's annoying topics' (TWATS). And Twat in Chief, dear old Sir Keir Starmer going through the motions bless him, and on his birthday the poor, gel-haired little lamb. Still wanting more apologies about the GCSE and A-Level Results – Jesus, haven't you got the message yet Le Chiffre? It is Gavin Williamson's fault. It's all Gavin Williamson's fault – he fucked up as Education Minister it is all his fault. I was on holiday it was nothing to do with me. And Gavin Williamson also hates Russia. And he is responsible for every single Covid death. I haven't worked out a way to pin that one on him yet, but I will. And yes, the thorny issue of the Covid-19 Bereaved Families for Justice wanting to meet me. Oh God, this is so thorny. Look, you know me, I'm a good guy right, I've proved that time and again and written about it in this very journal. But look, come on, there's 1600 of them apparently. 1600 families in this group looking for answers. And their first answer they are looking for is to 'why don't I want to meet them?' I said in TWATS today that it is because they have 'litigation' against me and obviously that isn't true so for the record, here is the real answer, and believe me I'm in pain saying this, genuine pain. I just don't want to. Shoot me for telling the truth. I don't want to meet them. I'd rather watch the cricket. And this may seem harsh but me going to meet 1600 bereaved families or me watching the cricket is going to have exactly the same outcome for their poor loved ones, they are not coming back. However many times I attend a meeting in some shitty hotel with these people or however many wickets Jimmy Anderson takes there will be the same result I'm afraid, the dead will remain dead. And I'm sorry. And by that I don't mean I'm in any way responsible.

I'm sorry that people think that by meeting me it will make their situation better, when it simply will not. Dear old Dominic once said I was God, or at least Jesus, but alas I'm not. I have no powers to bring anyone back to life, apart from now myself through Resurrection. I wish to God that I could bring all your loved ones back through Resurrection but I simply can't. That just isn't possible. Well I'm guessing it's not possible, I haven't asked, but I'll ask at my next transfusion tomorrow but I'd imagine if they've been dead for weeks and/or cremated, you know what I mean, you can't revive ashes. As I say look it's awful, but it isn't my fault, really it isn't. I did my best. After as I say making a slight error in wandering around every hospital I could shaking hands with Covid patients and spreading the virus around the whole country I have done my absolute best to defeat this beastly thing, and me attending yet another meeting to explain what happened is not going to offer an explanation of what happened to anyone. As I said in July, and of course that's 2 months ago now, I am absolutely committed to a public and independent enquiry into this awful pandemic, but now just isn't the right time. We are still in the middle of the storm, and although in the middle of the storm nothing is now really happening and people aren't dying any more, this is not the right time as the storm may come back and we can't be having an enquiry until the storm is over. But I assure you, you will get your independent enquiry, when the storm is over and every single person that is going to die of Covid will have died from Covid. And that's my guarantee. After that final Covid death in a few years we will wait a bit to make sure that really was the last Covid death and then we will have that public enquiry. I promise, with crossed fingers of course one can never guarantee these things, but I promise. We promised on Grenfell and we delivered there, and we will deliver here too. Grenfell, God I haven't heard that word said in a while, I wonder what's happening with all that?

Anyway, enough of all this depressing stuff. I am going to live forever and I feel fucking wonderful. I'm full of positivity, hope and sexual energy. Of course I am still in the doghouse with regards to Carrie walking in on me fucking Olga D but I rather like it in this doghouse – she came back today but she's living on the other side of the house, so away from the screaming wife and baby life is great. I'm pumped, I feel like I'm permanently on a fox hunt it's wonderful. Dear old Rishi has launched his Kickstart Scheme today which he says is going to pretend to get hundreds of thousands of 16-24 year olds in work. It's so wonderful. Of course 16-24 year olds would be starting work anyway, so whatever we do it's going to appear like a success. It would be like ploughing 40 billion pounds into making sure it rains in the Autumn. Guaranteed success. Rishi's very clever. Maybe I should ask him for advice about all my issues. No actually, Rishi's too pure and happy, I'll leave him alone bless him. But I don't feel like I need much help at the moment, the thought of eternal life really does trump most other worries – the Russian fatwa, Dominic Cummings cumming in my mouth on video, they really are both far into the back of my head (so to speak). I'm just being very careful, learning from dear old Alexei, I must check back in with him. I've sent him a text but no reply, I think he's still half dead. So yes I'm not drinking tea in airports (obviously), I'm not drinking or eating anything unless it's been prepared by Carrie at the moment. I'm taking a packed lunch into work which I'm locking in my various desks and I'm spraying the box with disinfectant every time I see it – Donald would be proud. I'm staying at home a lot, I'm just controlling the threat against me. Yes I'm staying at home, I'm controlling the fatwa, and I'm saving lives (my own mainly). And I'm avoiding Andrei Kelin of course, and any other Russian. Evgeny left a message, and Olga D, but I'm not calling any of them back. I'm playing it British for a while. Kelin called to assure me that Navalny was not poisoned by the Russian state and I guess I have to believe him, but why else would you be taken off a plane after screaming in hideous pain on the floor for half an hour? Kelin is suggesting it was food poisoning. But what food I ask you makes you want to scream in pain for hours? And I can answer that one actually - Carrie's sandwiches. They taste like shit! And you don't need a public enquiry for that one! (God I hope she's not poisoning me, ha ha. I'm sure she's not). To extend the metaphor a tad further, she knows which side her bread is buttered, adultery or no adultery.

RESUЯЯECTION

Thursday September 3rd 2020

Oh, Mother Russia, my heart is torn. Have you been to Moscow?
It's a shit-hole. Russians drive like nutcases and they look at you like
you're a piece of shit if you can't speak Russian. And the food is shit.
It's all fatty, and it's freezing. It's basically Scotland. Like Scotland
but everyone either wants to be your best friend or wants to kill you.
It's Glasgow. And then there's the beauty of St Petersburg, the hope
of a glorious and great nation, and the endless cash of the oligarch.
I'm completely torn. I'm back from my latest transfusion and tests
and my Russian doctors and nurses and Russian drivers and security
staff are so lovely, they say little but they smile and are so subservient
to my every whim. I ask for water, they bring water. Today I wanted
Irn-Bru, they bought Irn-Bru. Really is a tremendous team. I'm
snuck out of Downing Street early morning and I'm in and out before
sun rise and I go straight back to bed and am up in time for *This
Morning*. Such a beautiful experience and if and when everyone has
the chance to be cloned I fully recommend it. On the minus side the
Russians definitely poisoned Alexei Navalny.

I telephoned dear old Roger Connor at GSK when I got back, fairly
flustered when this news was relayed to me. I needed reassurance. I
know I'm being silly but on the one hand I'm avoiding all cups of tea
in airports and I'm only eating and drinking anything that Carrie
makes me or produces from her own body, and then when I'm doing
these transfusions I'm trusting Russians to inject me with what they
like and they bring me opened Irn-Bru and I drink it. I surprise
myself sometimes with my own double-standards. But a quick word
with Roger and my mind was at rest. If you're going to trust anyone
then it surely has to be the President of Global Vaccines at
GlaxoSmithKline at Barnard Castle. He said the transfusions were
going well and next week they will take some cells from me for some
initial embryonic work on my bits and bobs, seeing if the Gods are
shining upon me and I indeed can be the new Dolly the Sheep. I'm
so fucking excited. I'm wondering who to tell. I'm texting Dommers
all the time (with little reply sadly) and I'm sure Evgeny knows but I
would love to tell someone. Maybe I should tell Carrie but I don't

want to worry her any more than she is already about me fucking Olga D. And as I've said previously I've decided that Carrie will not be my partner in the next life. She's a tapper. And I asked the doctor today if a tapper will always be a tapper in the next life and he didn't say 'no', and what I was looking for there was 'no' so I will definitely want to give the gift of a second life to another, if indeed that is the option. I mean I could try my luck with whoever is about when I'm 18 again, but how lovely would it be to bestow the chance of another life on someone I fancy in this life, who now is out of reach but would obviously be oh so grateful in the next life. My mind is running away, but luckily I now feel young enough to keep up! Unlike poor old Alexei, still not responding to my texts and now definitely poisoned by Putin with Novichok. According to the Germans. And I would trust Germans with my life.

So what to say on social media? The world and of course the Russians are waiting. For the first time I trusted Ben on this one – he's my social media expert and Dominic is away. I asked him to make it condemning, but vague, horrified, but unsurprised, disappointed but pleased. And I'm pleased with what he came up with… 'It's outrageous that a chemical weapon was used against Alexei Navalny'. Ben pointed out that outrageous while it could mean bad could also be taken to mean bold and unusual. It's often used in a sexual context isn't it that word – ooh she's outrageous – meaning she will get her tits out on the street in Newcastle. So clever old Ben. I also asked him to put in something about me, to let whoever that is reading know that I am aware of my death threat and I will not be bowed, so I added 'We have seen first-hand the deadly consequences of Novichok in the UK'. Some will take that to mean that stupid couple who picked up the perfume bottle and sprayed it on themselves, of course not, fuck them, I'm talking about me. And then the killer line 'The Russian Government must now explain what happened to Mr Navalny – we will work with international partners to ensure justice is done.' This was my direct plea to Putin – talk to me. Talk to me you beautiful man. I am your friend. You may be aware of what I am doing with GSK but I don't want to fight you. If you are to live forever then let me be reborn, and join you in eternity. I am not your rival, we are simply two great leaders on a slightly different path. Two great men, just like Dominic and I. And remember, when I watched him in the Rose Garden of Downing Street just a few months ago, explaining to the world's assembled press how he had driven the car to test his fucking eyesight, I thought I wanted nothing to do with this man. Cut to a few months down the line and what has happened? That's right, I have gladfully and gleefully sucked this man's penis thrice and swallowed a lot of his semen. What am I saying? I'm saying I guess that you never know where our relationship can end Mr Putin – and like every great journey starts with just one step, every beautiful relationship starts with a 'hello'. So call me, text me, WhatsApp me old friend, just don't fucking kill me.

Friday September 4th 2020

I HAVE TALKED WITH VLADIMIR PUTIN. I know I shouldn't be this excited as I am a famous world leader too but this is very, very exciting. And unbelievably Dominic set it up, all from his convalescing bed. I am so, so relieved I can't tell you. And all after the most boring of days. It started with an enforced visit to Solihull in the West Midlands. Now of course I wouldn't go to the Midlands unless I was forced. Stupid people without even the sense of entitlement or being downtrodden that you get from some of the thickos up North – people in the Midlands are just dumb aren't they? It's no wonder the accent is the symbol the world over for rank stupidity. Anyway, I was there and back as quick as I could, which ironically was rather slow as we went to visit and spread the word on the HS2 Interchange site. HS2 as you know will cut the journey time between London and here in the Midlands to just 38 minutes, so yes, in the far future, in just 38 minutes any North Londoner could be in a shit-hole. 38 minutes, which is quicker than getting to Streatham. So it gives people the option you see? 'Father, take me to the nearest shithole!' 'Well son, I could take you to Streatham or Kings Heath.' 'Kings Heath it is father! Are there real Kings there daddy?' 'No, but there are prostitutes.' You get the idea.

Anyway, so I'm on the way home and I'm texting Dominic and he's not responding, and suddenly he calls me. I try to make a joke about him never responding to any of my messages and he says 'shut the fuck up Boris, I've organised you a conversation with Vladimir Putin.' I say when? And he says now! And of course I say, 'Dommers I'm on the 3.15 into Euston, I'm in a public carriage!' Again he repeats 'shut the fuck up' and suddenly he puts me on hold and I'm talking with Mr Putin. He says 'Hello Prime Minister'. It is undoubtedly Vladimir. Unmistakeable. A camp Bond villain. I freeze, it's like when I was a kid I met Sir Jimmy Saville, one of the highlights of my life. He says he saw my tweet. I breathe sharply - I knew it, I knew it would reel him in. And then he whispers, softly, almost inaudibly over the sound of the prick train guard announcing about fucking masks. Putin says 'So Prime Minister, you say the Russian Government must now explain what happened to Mr Navalny. I do not think so.' I find strength from somewhere. I say, 'Well actually I think you bloody well should explain it, if you'd like to.' I'm asked by one of my people to keep my voice down – there's a family three tables away pretending to play Snakes and Ladders but apparently they are just marking it and listening in. 'No I would not like to,' he retorts, 'because the world will now forget about Alexei and any traitor of Russia.' I shuddered breathlessly and was about to ask him what he meant and then he lowered his voice even more and said 'We have the cure. Sputnik V has been found to be successful. We have the cure.' One of my lackies listening in point me to the Lancet reports and indeed what he is saying looks correct. And here comes the juicy bit – I congratulate him and he says it would not have been possible without the 300 million I gave to Gamaleya and I am now a friend of this vaccine and a friend of Russia! I'm beside myself, I say 'Thank you very much' and was about to double down and say 'Gavin Williamson thinks you're a cunt' but this was not the moment, this moment could not be ruined. He then laughed and made a joke which was lost in translation and reception, something about a whore's asshole, I laughed but as I say I didn't hear it, I've been listening to it back on the recording but I honestly don't get it, I just hear the words 'whore's asshole' but anyway, what I do hear is what he says to me in his final sentence, he says 'You are my good friend now Mr Johnson, but be careful, good friends can become bad enemies. Even a whore's asshole will give up if it is fucked one too many times.' He then hangs up. What. A. Guy. Fuck! I've already masturbated once about this and am almost ready to squeeze out some more. What a massive relief – it's like I'm constantly cumming right now. I've lived under this cloud for so many weeks and suddenly it is lifted by the man himself – I'm free. Wait until Evgeny and his dad hear about this. I'll tell him tomorrow, maybe we can get another party off the ground, invite Jagger and Joany Collins. Fuck I need to celebrate. I need to tell someone – I almost want to call Ian Hislop and shove it down his ratty throat. What you doing Ian? Rehearsing a new witty shitty joke that Shaun Pye has written for you? Well I'm mates with Vladimir Putin and I'm going to live forever you nasty cunt. Putin does not think I am a cunt, and while I toe the line I am completely off the hit list. I might call Botham!

Putin did make it clear however that I now had to do exactly what Dominic Cummings wants, I said I was already doing that, and he said the 800 million funds would need to be released more quickly to fund Dommers' secret technical project, and I of course bent over and gave him what the fuck he wanted. This guy has got Novichok and he is not scared on using it. What a guy. And he's my friend, and Dommers is talking to me again. He texted me tonight it just said 'well done xxxx'. There were four kisses. He texted me again straight after to say that they were just x's in place of my name 'Boss' in case his texts were being tracked. I said 'Nice of you to call me Boss' and he texted 'I didn't call you Boss, I was referring to myself. I am the Boss, I arranged this.' I said 'indeed' and asked him how he'd managed it but he just said he was too tired and we would talk over the weekend or next week. I am simply cock-a-hoop. I could do anything right now. I'm energised. Let's have some cocaine, let's get things done – let's get Brexit done. Seriously, get Michel Barnier on the blower right now – if I can make peace with Putin then Europe is gonna be a doddle. I've learned my lesson now – for years I've been listening to my Eton teachers – stand up for yourself Boris, make sure they all do what you want to do. But with other world leaders it's quite simple, let them do exactly what they want to do. And I will then have all I desire, they will just give me what I want for the mere fact of not standing in their way. Because at heart, we all want an easy life. And I want two, two easy lives, and then another after that, and again, and again. This is the first day of the rest of my lives.

And I hear you cry, 'you're just a puppet Boris'. Well I've just watched the 'Amarillo' video with dear old Peter Kay from 2005. Keith Harris and Orville the puppet, Bernie Clifton and his comedy ostrich, that prick off *Rainbow* with Sooty and Sweep – what links the three? The puppet masters are dead and the puppets live on. It's true. Because the puppet has no stress, no responsibilities… for the puppet life goes on, life is eternal. Because when the puppet gets tired, and the dirt has stuck, they just make another, identical, better model. 'Real Boris Johnson' is coming. Almost literally. And the puppet masters will die and I will live. I'm quite emotional now. Seeing Jimmy Saville in that video. He meant everything to me as a child, and I'd probably have to see him fucking those corpses to change my mind. What a day – and it's the fucking weekend tomorrow! Goodnight Comrades! xxxx

Saturday September 5th 2020

It was lovely and warm in London today. I was supposed to be doing some Brexit stuff but I thought, fuck it. You know when you think, fuck it. Well that was me today, fuck it. It's a Saturday. In no other job are you expected to work on a Saturday, apart from maybe Tesco, but I'm not 16, I'm 56. Funny how I don't mind mentioning my age now as I'm going to be zero in a few years again. I do hope the climate stays ok in the next life, it is getting warmer isn't it? I was really struggling when I was battling Corona, I used to love the sunshine but now I get hot and sticky walking Dyl round the garden. I can't even be bothered to pick up the dog poo any more, I just kick it into the bushes or squash it into the grass. I'm feeling a little grumpy today because, talking about the climate, I was woken up early today to be told that those hippies at Extinction Rebellion had chained themselves to the odd fence around printing presses around the country. I was like 'What has that got to do with me? I'm fucking sleeping here.' When anyone stands in for Dommers they don't know when to wake me – Dommers is the master of knowing when to wake me, virtually nothing is important enough to wake me up, or to interrupt me at all actually. I was once watching an episode of *The Chase* and Dommers interrupted me in the middle of the final Chase to tell me that Bruce Forsyth had died. 'Fucking hell man', I shouted, 'Do you think he might still be dead at the end of this episode of *The Chase*?' Dommers learned his lesson after that, even if my own dad or son died, just leave it two minutes. What's two minutes? If he's dead, he's dead.

Anyway, so yes, turns out about 100 swampies have chained themselves to railings and trees and their own sense of self-importance and stopped newspapers going out, protesting against the perceived lack of coverage in the press on climate change. What the fuck? Every one of them prints the weather? Every day! What more climate news do you need? It's getting warmer. Blazing hot Summer when I was nearly dead and now September 5th and it's tops-off weather in Downing Street, glorious! I realise it's important, as I say I don't want London to be like Palm Springs in my next life, but how much can papers print the same story? Well we're talking mainly about The Sun here and the rest of Murdoch's crappy papers so it's the same story every day in those rags, but you get my drift. Ooh who's on *Strictly Come Dancing* this year – let's make that front page news! Morons. There's a fucking global pandemic and we are hurtling towards a no-deal Brexit, and all the moronic British Public want to hear about is which D-List lesbian is doing the Pasodoble this year. On that note I noticed that dear old Jacqui Smith is doing it this year, that's awfully exciting, be a right old laugh. I have a lot of time for Jacqui, interesting fact actually I kind of broke my golden rule for her. She's a year older than me (and Labour of course) but we had a bit of a thing. Publicly we disagreed about lots of stuff, the banning of dear old Michael Savage from the UK being the main one (the thought of banning someone for being too right-wing now seems quite laughable doesn't it?) but when I found out she had submitted a claim for the rental of 2 porn films as part of her parliamentary expenses I thought – there's someone after my own heart, I wonder if she'll be after by dicky-wick. Can't remember what year it was, she was Home Secretary and I was Mayor of London so we obviously mixed in the same circles, and one night we were down Brick Lane having some cocktails and we ended up having a quick fuck round the back of some bins. Nothing special to be honest, but as I say, I have a lot of time for her, she's a great girl and from what I saw that night, she'll do well on *Strictly*, she can really grind her ass.

Anyway, where was I? Yes, as I say, annoying rather than something to wake me up over. I mean it affected The Telegraph but who cares if The fucking Sun is a few hours late? They'll be the same tits mate just hold off a few hours. So yes, the main news of today is I wasn't particularly planning to phone Evgeny but I thought I'd use this as an excuse to call him, make sure The Independent wasn't affected by the cunts. It wasn't thankfully, not that I read The Independent, I mean Jesus who would read The Independent, or the i or whatever shit he's branded it now. Anyway, of course I moved the conversation on to my discussion with Mr Putin, and that we were now best friends again and the threats against me had been lifted. He was very happy and told me to wait for a few seconds and his dad, Alexander came on. I joked 'Have you been hiding behind the sofa again?' but he wasn't in a particularly jokey mood. He was desperate to hear about Putin and shock news, it turns out he has been living in fear just like me, an apparent threat on his life. I'm stunned to be honest, I thought they were in bed together, or if not in bed together at least fucking against the bins, metaphorically. But no, apparently he has been just like me for months, hiding and not wanting to associate with any of Putin's supposed enemies. I said 'that will explain why you were hiding behind the sofa that day' and again he didn't laugh or make any comment. But what he did do is suggest drinks and a bit of a party. I mean that was on my mind but I never thought he'd suggest it to me. He said it would be like the old times, he'd invite some of the old celebs and we could maybe watch some foxes being fucked up, would be fun. So that's where I'm heading tonight. I told him to invite Jacqui Smith and he said 'who's that?' and I said she's the ex-Home Secretary, and he turned his nose up. I then mentioned she's a *Strictly Come Dancing* contestant and he got all excited, and even started clapping his hands and cheering, so I think she'll be there. Fuck, I must be good. I don't want to cheat on Dommers. In fact, what am I saying? I need to get back on the horse and make sure it's female.

So yes, apart from the odd drink with Dommers and the odd dabble with the old fellatio, this will be my first real night out since lockdown, I mean all-nighter, drugs and sex fuck-up like the old days. I mentioned it to one of my aides and she said I was technically breaking lock-down rules depending how many people were there. Fucking hell I can't wait for Dommers to come back. He is so perfect. He knows when to tell me to work and when to tell me to play. And he'd be telling me to play tonight. I've spent weeks in a ball of stress and now I need to let my hair down, and, if I play my cards right (as dead Brucie used to do), my penis up. And let's face it, if the press get wind of it and they get photos of me snorting cocaine out of Jacqui Smith's glitter ball, then I'll release all those cunts we arrested earlier today to block the Sunday papers coming out, and then just move the agenda on to the next major fuck up. So wish me luck dear readers, today I'm putting my trust in Vladimir Putin. A few days ago I wouldn't touch a cup of tea made my a Ruski, and now I'll probably let one of them piss in my mouth. What a turnaround. I love this country, I love Russia, and I love my life – can't wait for the next one. Spaceba!

Sunday September 6th 2020

Right, it's nearly 10pm on Sunday and I'm only just coming to. I have news but I need to get down on paper what happened if only to prove I've still got it. So the party last night was at Evgeny's country house, Stud House at Hampton Court. And he is a stud, and although he's about 20 years younger than me I think I more than held my own last night. Mick Jagger was there of course, and Joan Collins, plus dear old Keira Knightley (boring but still very young), Princess Eugenie and her arranged husband, Prince Andrew (awkward) and Sadiq Khan (you're not the police Sadiq, leave me alone). And Ed Miliband and Duncan from Blue. Let's deal with Joany Collins first, I mean fuck me she's 87 but she's still so fucking

153

hot, I think she must have taken some kind of Resurrection, and Mick Jagger the same (77 going on 17) – they were both acting like school kids and at one point fucked in front of all the celebs apart from Duncan from Blue who left horrified the little pussy. But who I was most surprised by was Prince Andrew. I mean he's 60 but you're as young as the woman you feel right?! LOL, he pulled an all-nighter too and left at about 5 in the morning to drive up to Balmoral. What a fucking legend that man is, a machine, and he is absolutely innocent until, inevitably, he is proven guilty. But I think he's a lesson for us all – until you are proven guilty, fucking party. And almost party more if you're accused of something, rightly or wrongly. The randomness of the justice system means you should get that partying out of your system while you're still free to fuck the streets, because you won't be fucking young girls in prison matey, on the contrary you will be the young girl and you'll feel what it's like to lose your virginity against your will. Still, until he is definitely proven guilty, top lad and we had a right laugh last night. At one point he was pretending to be in Pizza express in Woking and I was pretending to drive to Durham to test my eyesight. Top banter.

So the house, the house is fucking mental. This is the house I want in the next life. Jesus, Downing Street is so fucking pokey. Plants and light everywhere, and the whole gaff stinks of lilac. Which isn't as nasty as it sounds. Evgeny says the smell reminds him of Russia, I suggested the smell of blood would be more evocative of Russia, and I don't think he heard me as he didn't react at all. There's lovely animal skins and an art collection to rival The Tate – there's a Tracey Emin (who is shit) – a neon sign saying 'Go fuck yourself'. You can get these made to order from corner shops in Whitechapel. And an Antony Gormley. Jesus that man is obsessed with his own penis. Have you been to Crosby beach in Liverpool? Hundreds of 'lifelike' models of him naked with his cock out. I say 'lifelike' because if you are a male sculptor doing a cast of yourself, then your penis inside that mould would shrivel to the size of a penny chew. So obviously once you've cast yourself accurately you're going to add a bit to the cock. Obviously. More than a bit in Antony's case. And I know that because he was at the party too and at one point he started masturbating for the crowd. It wasn't that big erect so flaccid I'd be surprised if the morsel of clay had actually been able to take hold. He's a fucking liar basically. Good giggle though. He said to Andrew he'd do a sculpture of him after he commits suicide. I couldn't stop laughing at that. Randy Andy got kilned!!

But as the night went on then it took a darker turn. I should have taken Joany up on her offer but I didn't want Mick Jagger's sloppy seconds so I got stuck with Evgeny and his dad on the sofa sitting under the 'Go fuck yourself' neon. It added a strange pink hue to proceedings, looked like we were in a club in Ibiza. But the party was over as soon as they started talking. And do you know what, I think the whole party was about this, trying to get me off my tits so I would spill all the beans. And to be honest I think it worked, those crafty fucking Russians. I mean I did tell them everything. And now it does not make sense, and this is the worst time to try to make sense of it when you are trying to come round from a ten hour session. The first thing they told me is that Putin does not change his mind on his enemies. Dominic Cummings – enemy, me – enemy, Alexei – enemy. I told them that's not what Putin said and they challenged me, has Putin ever given me the impression of being the sort of guy to change his mind? I shook my head, I was too pissed to challenge anything, even when Michael Palin strolled past and showed me his anus. Evgeny just doesn't buy what I told him about Resurrection, he repeated that no one in their right mind would put their money into living again when there was the option of living forever. He was throwing loads of questions at me, where was the evidence this would work apart from Dolly The Sheep which was years ago? I didn't know. How could they be sure that the clone would grow up as you, nature versus nurture – unless you were brought up by your same parents in exactly the same way with the same experiences then you would be a completely different person. And even if they recorded your old self passing on advice to your younger self you would not be the same person, you would be a completely different person, so in effect the whole thing was completely pointless. Fuck, maybe it's because I'm still pissed and tripping but I can't work out an argument against what they were saying. Fuck.

And then they got darker still. They said it was Cozy Bear that had got to Alexei, and whatever Putin had said to me, there would be a reason why there was a threat on my life and now he is saying it has gone away. I did challenge that one – I talked with Putin, they didn't. Evgeny annoyingly said 'How did you know it was Putin?' I said that Dominic Cummings told me it was Putin. And then they said 'Do you trust Mr Cummings?' Alexander got very serious – the pink neon saying 'Go fuck yourself' reflecting in his eyes making him even more menacing. He repeated, 'Putin does not change his mind about people, and Cummings and Putin fell out about Resurrection many years ago, do you really think they have kissed and made up?' I was firm, I said that I trusted Dominic. And they told me to trust no one. They said for years they have been putting millions, most of their fortunes, into what they thought was the drug 'Resurrection', the one to give eternal life, or at least another 100 years. This was the drug they were promised and this is the drug that Putin has always been obsessed with, the very drug that he fell out with Dominic Cummings about all those years ago. Everything else is a smoke screen, they said, think about it, and I am trying to think about it right now – if there was a drug or the promise to give you another 100 years, why would you put your time and resources into anything else? The only thing you'd put your effort into is into smoke-screens, distractions, to take people off the greatest invention in our times. And, said Alexander, 'Dominic is the master of distraction'. I told them about his heart operation, and not being into work for weeks. 'Does that ring true?' said Evgeny, 'Mr Cummings is a workaholic'. They are right, things suddenly are not making any sense at all.

And Duncan from Blue stayed the night. I sucked his penis. I'm a fucking mess.

Monday September 7th 2020

Right. I don't give a fuck today. I've got toothache from the Mandy, I don't know who to trust anymore and everything is going to shit. I was asked to put out a statement on Brexit so in the absence of Mr Cummings I had to write it myself with the help of Duncan from

Blue. I know it's shit but I don't care any more, I said 'as we have said right from the start, a no-deal Brexit will be a good outcome for the UK. All Rise!' Everyone knows it's bullshit but I just don't have the strength to cover it up any more. I've instructed my aides and Ministers to now basically ignore the shysters from the EU and ignore the Withdrawal Agreement. I see the European Commission President Ursula von de Leyen has said we are like 'North Korea' for doing this. You'll see when we're like North Korea Miss von de 'Lying' when I line up the nukes on the beach in Dover. Fuck it. I'm ready to go to be honest. If this cloning thing is a reality then I'm ready to go before Christmas and start again – can you imagine what the next 18 years are going to be like? Pure unfiltered shite. But then it will be fine. So start again, have the next 18 years as a kid (nothing matters when you're a kid) and then come 2038 I reckon the dust of people's broken dreams will have blown over and it will be boom time again. Just don't bring up Real Boris Johnson in Ireland, the fears of a no-deal leading to a hard border in Ireland leading to violence is almost inevitable, and as I say, I'm out. I've tapped out. It was Carrie's fault for doing best of three on the coin toss, I am sorry, I am actually sorry ok and this is the first time I've ever said that. I'm sorry, I'm sorry for everything I've ever done and whoever is playing with me well you've won, and I'm on to the next life now. Good luck with everything, good luck securing those trade deals with the rest of the world, good luck with cricket, good luck with the second wave, I'm out of here.

But then again I'm not am I, I'm still fucking here. And expected to have the answers. There are no answers, I'm sorry. People lie, and if one too many people lie then we all just drown in a sea of bullshit. And being separated from Mr Cummings for so long I see through his bullshit. I am being played. If it wasn't for falling in love with him and sucking his penis I would surely see him for the two-faced, work-avoiding, snivelling little, unelected bullshitting slug that he is. And yes, these transfusions do not make any sense. The blood of a younger man, why am I not questioning more? I have my next round tomorrow when they are supposedly stepping things up and trying the new drugs on me, and I am not going, I will phone Dominic in a

minute and I will tell him that I am not going. I don't know, I really
want it to be true, if they are not what they say they are, then what are
they doing to me otherwise? I know they aren't poisoning me (if they
are they are making a right pig's ear of it!). On that note pleased to
hear that dear old Alexei is out of his coma and responding to basic
signals. Whatever Putin's up to he's fucking it up isn't he? And that's
the thing, I hate living in fear of this moron. He isn't a super villain.
He's got flaws like the rest of us. He goes to the toilet, he
masturbates, why should I live in fear of anyone? That's it, I've said it
before but I'm doing it now, I'm going to ring Ian Botham. He'll
know what to do. One sec.

Well there's good news and there's bad news. The good news is that
Sir Ian reminded me that although I feel at my lowest point I'm in a
very privileged position – I can do something about it. That's how he
felt in the '81 Ashes – all was lost, England 500/1 to win the test
match, but he was still there with a bat in his hand. And while you're
at the crease you always have a chance. And I'm at the crease right
now. And Botham said that my majority was like his strength at the
time – he was at his most powerful, physically, and I am at my most
powerful, metaphorically. I can do what I like, when I like, and that's
a very powerful position to be in, however perilous and precarious the
situation feels. Of course I know this, but it's damn good to be
reminded by the legend that is Sir Ian. I must remember that I am
powerful, I've just instructed the whips to force Conservative MPs to
vote against Labour's proposed Clause in the Fire Safety Bill which
would have put into law the recommendations of the Grenfell Inquiry
Phase 1. I'm powerful, I can do anything. We are having the Inquiry,
that does not mean we should necessarily implement any of the
recommendations. Power. I feel good now, I feel better. Dominic
texted asking me whether I'm all set for my transfusions tomorrow,
and I have a missed call from the cunt. Now it's my turn to have the
upper hand, it is my turn to make him sweat. I shall call him
tomorrow and demand a meeting, even over Zoom. I am Sir Ian, I
am in charge now.

The bad news is that Simon Case called me and said that the press had had information about an extra-marital affair. I laughed and said 'Jesus if those cunts want to print something from years ago then who gives a fuck?' He said it was from the last month. I had forgotten about Olga D. Fuck! But how would they know? They said they do not have any evidence it is just rumours and gossip at this stage. Has Olga told people? Carrie wouldn't, so has Olga? I've just texted her. I'm sure she wouldn't have done – I did as I recall tell her not to tell anyone in a very firm but totally non-threatening way. Fuck. Simon said he'd instruct another Super Injunction – I've got a few of those now! So should all be cool, I just checked the recording that I was watching so I've put that in the trash can now, all safely deleted. So, you know, fine, that will be fine. I've got too much to worry about to be honest, that will be fine.

OK, it's 9pm now and I'm just going to switch off and watch *Who Wants to be a Millionaire*. I love it. I don't know any of the answers but I enjoy watching the people sweat up over the chump change. I have 2 million pounds in the Bank. It feels so good, I often just look at my balance in the ATM. Makes me hard. Ooh there's a 19-year old politics student on it, it's like looking at a poor version of myself at 19. Uurgh he's a bit of a prick to be honest. I hope people don't see me as a bit of a prick. This prick is a know-it-all though so I don't think I'm viewed as that. People call me stupid I'm sure but at least I'm not hated for being too clever. There's nothing more annoying than being clever. Ah good, the toff doesn't know what a mimosa is – ha ha ha – he doesn't know about alcohol. What an awful cunt. He knows all about literature and nothing about cocktails. Virgin. Ha ha, so happy, I'm so cool actually. So rich, so powerful. Who wants to be a Millionaire? Moi. Who wants to be Prime Minister, moi. Who wants to cum? Wink wink. Duncan from Blue has gone by the way, I'm here on my own. I mean I'm off to masturbate. Goodnight.

Tuesday September 8th 2020

'The problem with Super Injunctions Prime Minister, is they do not stop cunts on Twitter'. If there's one thing I love about Dommers is that he's straight talking. He calls a spade a spade, which is racist but it's honest. And my goodness, what cunts there are in the world of Twitter – where 280 characters or less not so much sums up the word count restriction as a description of the entire platform. I did a quick search just now on 'Boris Johnson violinist' and someone that calls themselves 'Badgers Tadgers' (clearly not a character, rather I'd suggest, a cunt) writes 'Just look at @BorisJohnson morals and ask about the French violinist.' French?! Her name's Olga you thick cunt, does that sound French to you Badgers Tadgers? What's your real name you coward? Probably Alan or Mick. Anyway Dommers tried to calm me down but he couldn't, and as I made it very clear the majority of my anger anyway is directed towards him. I said that I had not gone to the transfusions today and I no longer believed the cloning story and I thought that the Russians were up to something, and without explicitly saying it I made Mr Cummings very well aware that I thought he knew more than he was letting on. And then he tried to scare me, which is never going to work. He said that just as I had got back on Putin's side, I risked angering him by dropping out of the Gamaleya Research Project at this early stage. I told him I don't give a fuck. And again he tried to scare me which is never going to work as I am basically Ian Botham by saying I was finally free of Russian threats did I really want them hanging over me again? And I said I don't give a fuck. And then he said the Press Injunction would break about Olga. So many people were naming me now on Twitter then it's only a matter of time before the French (it's always the fucking French) print something and then the British media would print their story and the Super Injunction means fuck all. And he said it may come tonight, Olga and myself could be named tonight in the European media. And did he want me to put a stop to all that? I mean, I am Ian Botham but fuck, he had me again. Of course I want him to put a stop to all that, I fucking need him. I'm flailing about without him and my marriage is now hanging by a thread. So I just said that he didn't scare me, but yes, I want his idea.

So we needed something to take the heat off for the Press, throw those hungry dogs a bone. So, as of 10pm tonight, we, and by 'we' I of course mean Dommers, has decided that we should take the country back into some form of lockdown. Numbers are going up slightly, mainly through young people gathering in stupid parties in the stupid Midlands. He said 'let's do something arbitrary like no groups of six people anywhere.' I said that sounded fucking ludicrous, we've just ended the 'eat out to help out' thing incentivising these morons to go out in groups and have spent the last two weeks encouraging and in some cases demanding that people go back to school and to work, and now we're going to reverse all that. And he said that was the beauty of it, it was so ludicrous that it would in an instant wipe every single other news story off the agenda. In the Government lying business it's called a 'News nuke'. It would buy us a week and by that time the Olga story would be dead in the water. The man Cummings is an awful liar but he's undoubtedly a genius. So as of ten o'clock tonight before the press started sharpening their 'Boris is fucking a violinist' pencils we announced to the media that this was coming and we said more detail was coming tomorrow. We haven't got any more detail of course but do not worry my little Covid sheep, I have slaves working throughout the night to put some meat on these brittle bones. And Ben is going to start flooding social media from tomorrow (a) telling everyone that this 6 person thing is a great thing and is going to save them (lol) and (b) starting the drip-drip on the vaccine compliance piece. And at the same time telling everyone how brilliant I am and a great giggle and basically who cares if I'm taking a violinist up the Stravinsky! Easy!

So that's tomorrow, but what of today? Have I given up on my dream of eternal life? Not a bit of it. But I have the upper hand now, I am back in control. GSK director Roger Connor has left a message asking me where I was today, and that message my friends was duly ignored. I am the Captain now. And with Dominic telling me what to do again and how to do it, I have never felt more in charge of my own destiny.

Wednesday September 9th 2020

An amazing day. I felt like the old Boris. Even if I am to do no more transfusions, I have the blood of a much younger man inside me, and a much younger woman (my angry, boring wife) and an even younger violinist on the end of four strings ready to pluck at any time - but at least not for the next week, be sensible Boris. But boy it's hard to be sensible when you're so fucking good. Did you see my PMQ's today? I was on fire. Ha ha, at one point a very flustered Le Chiffre (like a shit Bond villain who realised the poison hadn't quite worked) stumbled as he said 'Due to this Government's lack of incompetence' and then tried to correct himself about ten times saying 'lack of competence, lack of competence'. Alright Keir, sorry mate, we've all seen you step in the dog shit in your pristine white pumps it's no good now walking back over it saying 'I meant to do it, I meant to do it.' You have a severe lack of a lack of incompetence my friend. What a tit. Dear old Ben Warner is editing the answer to my final question in PMQ's now, ready to clip up for social media. It's very clever. Whatever Le Chiffre asks me I say 'don't worry about that shit' and then I move on with the scripted oven-ready clip for social media. They are getting thousands of views, and as no one reads the papers or watches TV any more, these clips are the only things that swing elections. Really very clever, and worth every penny of the 80 million pounds I gave the company the other week, or was it 100 million? Whatever it was, they are worth it.

So yes, busy day for me, announcing the Rule of Six thing. No gatherings of more than six people – that's my sex life fucked! Stop it Boris you're outrageous. But the main thing is it's done the job of silencing the violins! Not the Twitter cunts obviously but who is really trawling through Twitter truffling for shite? I had a quick look actually at Badgers Tadgers feed, maybe it's a Labour mole actually it's very anti-Conservative. Today he's moaning about us planning to break the law over the EU Withdrawal agreement. Fucking hell, as we told Parliament today we are just breaking the law in a 'very limited and specific way'. We are hardly Russia, they break International Law all the time. And they are still seen by many as a great country so it won't do us any harm in the long term. Seriously guys, I know we agreed to this last year but newsflash, that was before Covid. Covid changes everything! So what if we are set for a no-deal Brexit and this is going to cost the country hundreds of million pounds and cause chaos! Hello! We are in the middle of a crisis that

is costing us billions every day (and that's just the half price Nandos).
I announced something today (that I shouldn't have done, naughty
me, but I panicked) that if it came to fruition would cost 100 billion
pounds. I think we can forget about Brexit now. It's a no-deal, it's
going to cost us a fortune but a fraction of Corona and kill far fewer
people probably. And anyway, as Dominic made clear to me earlier
today, we don't need anyone else.

Yes, I relented and talked with him this afternoon, I just wanted to
hear him purr about my PMQ performance. He purred but was
mainly interested in the release of the 800 million pounds into his
secret tech project. I froze the assets overnight when I was fuming
with him. But I'm powerful now, and part of being powerful is giving
away that power to the less powerful who feel more powerful and are
then very grateful. In short, I am playing the long game here, but this
man WILL suck my cock. And he will do it against the backdrop of
an independent and Great Britain, free of the shackles of Europe and
with a world-leading technology, AI and genetic medicine industry
that just like me will be desired the world over but will only be made
available to the most attractive bidder. That's right folks – world-
leading technology, AI and genetic medicine. I don't really know
what he means by this but it sounds fucking cool. And he said this
morning something so great, so powerful. He said 'Boris, reach for
the stars'. I said that sounds like an old lyric from a pop song. He
replied 'yes it's S Club 7' and I said 'well with the rule of six they're
fucked now!' We laughed for ages. The old Dommers and me are
well and truly back. He then said something so great, so powerful.
He just said one word, 'moonshot'. I instantly loved that. I just
paused for a second and said 'what does that word mean?' And he
said 'Don't just reach for the stars Prime Minister, launch for the
moon. Moonshot.' I told him that sounded brilliant and can I use it?
He said 'of course you can use it my job is telling you what to say.'
And you know what's funny, I'd forgotten that. Because of our
falling out and him not having been into work for weeks I'd forgotten
that was his job. So I said to him, 'Dommers, I need you, do you
want your old job back?' and he said 'Boss, he never left'. I fucking
love that man. What an amazing day. I'm having some mates over

for a drink in a sec, a load of old Oxford chums who want to start up tech companies with all this cash we're about to hand out. And rest assured, there's 7 of them!! Fuck the po-lice.

Thursday September 10th 2020

Fucking hell it's called moonshot because it's ambitious. So much negativity in this country right now. The entire day has been people laying into me, and my useless fucking aides passing me messages about it. Guys, I don't need to know if people think I'm shit, don't you understand this, I do not care! Thank God that Dommers is coming back into work from tomorrow (although who works on a Friday right?!) – he's such a good barrier between me and the flak. He just sucks it all up and spits it out (if only!). Anyway, apart from the usual bleating about my Corona announcement - 'Ooh it's going to cost 100 billion pounds Boris, ooh there's no actual way of it working Boris', I think the biggest disappointment was Michel Barnier basically calling me a cunt (I've got previous mate) for the breaking International Law thing. I was in and out of the meetings because I was chatting to Olga D just to apologise for not being able to see her for a bit until all this dies down, so I was only catching the gist to be honest, dear old David Frost was doing the heavy lifting, but Michel was clearly if not calling me a cunt then he was definitely calling us liars. We are not liars, not in this case. Genuinely. When we signed that agreement is was in absolutely good faith, if truth be told I didn't really understand it that well, I skimmed it, we all skimmed it. One is allowed to change one's mind, that's the key. Michel, do you want to personally build a border down the Irish Sea? Do you? Well get to work my friend or just let us tweak this. I mean I say let us, we can do what we like. And people say do we think we are above the law? Well I certainly am, I'm the fucking Prime Minister.

Sorry, I'm just a tad miffed today. I can't turn on the TV or the radio without someone saying I'm a prick. And I had to talk to Roger about the transfusions, I'll come on to that. It comes back to doing my best, I'm genuinely doing my best here, I'm an ideas man. And the idea is a good one isn't it, everyone has like a pregnancy test thing but for Corona and they piss on it or whatever and they get a Corona result that morning and then that evening they can happily go to the theatre or the opera or even if they are mentally ill they could go to a comedy show. And people are just moaning 'Oh what happens if you get Corona on the way to the theatre?' Well fucking hell, what happens if you have sex between having the pregnancy test and getting the result? I did that once. I had a bit of a cheeky three night stand early doors when I was going out with Carrie and on our third date/fuck she said she was worried she might be pregnant. I have a stack of pregnancy tests here at Number 10 (literally hundreds) and so this dear old young girl, I forget her name, stood there crying in the toilets here on the top floor and pissing on to a pregnancy test. I don't know what it was but it really fucking turned me on. So literally in the minute between pissing on the stick and her getting the result I had fucked her. So, you know what I mean, anything can happen. And nothing will happen. She didn't have a baby for fuck's sake. I mean she was pregnant, but not from that one, from an earlier one, and of course I paid her good money for the abortion so everyone was happy. As I say, I'm a good person just doing my best.

So yes, I've just talked with Roger Connor at GSK and apologised for not coming into this week's transfusions. I didn't go into detail, but I asked for more assurances that what I was doing here was good and proper. He asked me what assurances did I need. And so I said well is anyone else undergoing this treatment, or am I the guinea pig? Is there someone else I can talk to about this who is going through the same thing? He tried to butter me up by saying I was the pioneer, who else in the UK would I suggest that they clone that would be better than me? I suggested dear old Diana Rigg who died today, why didn't they clone her just before she died? What a tremendous actress, I'd like to pay tribute to her now in fact, and what an idea to resurrect us both at the same time so in eighteen years I could fuck the young Dame Diana Rigg, just before she goes into the Bond film. Which wouldn't happen in the next life, but you know what I mean. I was full of questions as to how this would work, and he answered them all thoroughly with some big words, but then he had an out-there suggestion… why don't I ask Dominic to undergo this procedure with me? He is the one that facilitated this, he is the one that has been working on this with Russia since he left university, why doesn't he, like so many chemistry pioneers before him, test the drug out on himself first? History is overflowing with examples of inventors who tested out their inventions on themselves, and I realise Dommers didn't invent Resurrection but he was at the forefront of its inception. My favourite one of these stories is Franz Reichelt, we did lessons on him at Eton. A lovely chap, born in 1879, he was a tailor who invented the coat parachute. A pioneer. He climbed to the first deck of the Eiffel Tower and he had told the authorities he was going to test with a dummy, but no, Franz himself decided to take the reins (literally) of the coat parachute and jump from the first deck. A brilliant, brave man who stuck two fingers up to authority and believed in his invention. A huge lesson in early life that helped to shape me and my friends in our formative years. Of course on that first jump Franz plummeted to the ground and instantly died but that is by the by. You've got to be brave in this life, moonshot.

So in short, I said I will talk with Dominic, and if he is up for coming on this journey with me then I am back on board, and we can together grab an arm each of the coat parachute and jump into the unknown, knowing that, unlike Franz, if we do splat on to the floor we have the chance of eternal life. On that note, I did make it clear that I wanted zero publicity for this endeavour. With the amount of hatred in the world for me right now, the last thing I want to be if the country goes down the shitter is a small child. Imagine that, imagine the bullying I'd get? Didn't you used to be Boris Johnson? Didn't you fuck the country up ten years ago? If they don't kill me now, people will be after me then. It's like that old thing about going back in time to kill Hitler, people in this case would just be able to hang around for a bit and kill me as a baby in the second life. It doesn't bear thinking about. Then GSK would have to use the Boris mixture to make another one of me, and then I'd get killed again. Hundreds of babies would be killed and they'd all be me. Good heavens that's awful, I can't think about it. So I won't. Forgive me as I go now and forget about this difficult day by taking a bottle of non-Russian vodka and drinking myself into a black out. And I'll be raising a glass and indeed the whole bottle to Dame Diana Rigg. What a woman. My name's Johnson, Alexander Boris De Pfeffel Johnson, licence to kill. How do I kill? Through running around hospitals at the height of a global pandemic shaking everyone's hands and saying everything is going to be fine! Shaking, not stirred! I shouldn't joke.

Friday September 11ᵗʰ 2020

I was going to leave this blank, in respect of the loads who died on 9/11 in those attacks on America, but I have some very exciting news about Mr Cummings so I won't be doing that. But first up, yes, firstly I cannot believe it was 19 years ago now that those planes hit the World Trade Centre or those holograms were developed to make it look like they did, whatever story you believe the result was the same, fuck-loads dead. What I was especially proud about during lockdown is that even terrorists complied. March, April and May during lockdown, no terrorist attacks, restrictions lifted – terrorist attack, some nutter goes crazy stabbing people in a park. What the fuck were terrorists doing during lockdown? 'You must attack the infidels!' 'Sorry mate I'm shielding.' 'Get out there and kill!' 'How am I supposed to kill someone from a two metre distance? I'm staying in, I'm controlling the virus, and more than anything by not conducting acts of terrorism I'm saving lives.' 'Get out their son and explode your back-pack!' 'Yeah, sure and imagine my total embarrassment when I'm splattered all over a shopping centre, Matt Hancock comes along and says 'Cause of death – Covid 19''. Ha ha ha! Anyway, as I say, a very sad day. Along with being the best day ever, I'll explain in a sec.

But first, and most importantly, isn't Zoom shite? And I don't say that with any glee, I and several of my team have tried to get in touch with the owner Eric Yuan to chat tech and have a beer or a sake - but the word is, Mr Yuan thinks we are all pricks here at Conservative Towers. Well if that's the case mate, your product is shit. And moreover, I'm just putting it out there, Eric is from China yeah? China. The day after the WHO reported Corona in Wuhan, Zoom sent out a party invitation which said 'Mark your calendars for

Zoomtopia 2020!' I'm no conspiracy theorist but Eric Yuan is now worth 18 billion pounds. Seriously, can someone look into this fairly blatant Chinese treachery. And what's more as I say, the product is toss, keeps cutting out, glitching. Zoomtopia my ass. Zoom for improvement more like. I did a Zoom call today with about 250 MP's and it kept cutting out for ages. On about the 5th time of it cutting out I enquired to Ben 'You can't make a zoom work, let alone make the country believe something they shouldn't. Why the fuck have I given you 100 million pounds?' Ironically at that moment the Zoom call started working again and I had to explain to 250 MP's that I was joking and hadn't given Ben 100 million pounds. For fuck's sake that will probably turn a few more against the vote. Who should we worry about? Well obviously Ken Clarke, cunts like that. Dinosaur cunts that are stuck in the past that don't realise that I know there aren't just skeletons in their closets but skeletons of the most notorious paedophiles. Not saying Ken Clarke is a paedophile for any legal folk reading this, on the contrary I think he despises children like Thatcher did.

Anyway that's for next week, it's Friday night and I'm writing this after the most wonderful face to face meeting with Dominic Cummings, dear old Dommers. It feels like forever since I've seen him. He looked weak poor man, his skin almost translucent and his tongue was black (I later learned just through sucking liquorice sweets in convalescence). But my goodness what a powerhouse, and we of course all need him now more than ever. It was his idea obviously to be naughty and break the International Law thing (in a very limited and specific way) and I'm sure it will be him that stomps about the corridors of Parliament next week threatening to metaphorically smash a few faces in to get this Bill through. It was also his idea to make Mark Sedwill a Baron today, I knew nothing about that one, at his best Dommers really does do most of my work for me, he's terrific. He reminds me of Thatcher in many ways, I didn't meet her very many times but what struck me most about Margaret was an incredible sense of self-confidence, choosing the right moment to look you in the eye, and the almost total disregard for the feelings of others. Dommers really is cast from the same mould, a remarkable human being. And, quite remarkably, he has agreed to join me on my quest for Resurrection. I know right, I'm on cloud 9.

He assures me that he knows from his years of research and being there at the inception of this great project that it is now completely safe and now is the time to embark on civilization's last great quest, the quest for eternal life. So we've made a kind of pact, I joked that we should suck each other's dicks to make it concrete but he said he was too weak to give or receive a blow-job which is fair enough. But we have made a pact to undergo Resurrection when we mutually agree that the time is right, and we carry on with GSK's program together and move into a position where at any time we can flick the switch and move into the next life. It is real now. And we have agreed to something quite wonderful. When a family is found by GSK in the future to bring us both up as babies, we will be brought up as brothers in the same household. This really is tremendous and life-affirming news. Nothing else matters now - Dominic is my lover and now he is my brother. And there is no other. 9/11 will forever now not be known as the day that loads died, but instead the day that two survived, forever. And next year on the 20th anniversary of those awful planes crashing, I will, instead of crying, I will smile, I will laugh, rejoice, sing, drink and party. And then in the next life I will ensure that the message is passed on to baby Boris and his brother Dominic – never ever get unhappy on the anniversary of 9/11, always get drunk and celebrate, because 9/11 is when, just like those terrorists, you made certain of your eternal life. Forgive me dear reader, but holy Allah, let's roll!

Saturday September 12th 2020

I neglected to mention yesterday and I suppose I should as this shouldn't all be about me – dear old Liz Truss has secured a major trade deal with Japan, a phenomenal achievement orchestrated by Dommers of course but we made it look like Liz had done it to keep the women's libbers happy. An outstanding deal to boost trade with Japan to 15 billion pounds, which will increase our GDP by 0.07%. After 15 years. So that's a thing. Ha ha, of course it's not, it's nothing, but the headlines look good so it's brilliant news, and a great bargaining chip for next week's negotiations with the EU – give us what we want or we will sell crapanese to the Japanese. Come on! I'm sooo bored by these negotiations, and I don't even have to go to most of them. We've got about a month to strike a deal, and at the moment it's looking more likely that I'll get a 'husband of the year' from Hello Magazine. I noticed Mylene Class was in there this week showing off her wedding or some shit, proving that whilst you can be given Class as a surname, you don't necessarily have a massive amount of it. Something I don't have to worry about with the surname Johnson!

Anyway, a bit of a nothing day really. I just got pissed and watched Last Night of the Proms. And sung 'Land of Hope and Glory' very, very loud - so loud that dear old Rishi phoned me up on the Bat-phone from next door and told me to 'shut the fuck up'. Everyone that loves him, you should try living next to the mother fucker. Moaning twat. Anyway, my Johnson was certainly massive when dear old Katie Derham was ever on screen. I'm thinking - how can I persuade Katie Derham to join Dominic and I and be my life partner in the next life? Seems like a long shot, but I've pulled off bigger miracles before. Olga D and the like. When I turn on the charm it's very difficult for anyone to avoid being smothered in Boris' charm juice.

Anyway, the only other bit of good news is Evgeny called me up and invited me out to Italy on a grouse shoot tomorrow, near his gaff in Perugia. I said I should be swotting up for my Brexit debate on Monday and reading that Withdrawal Agreement, see what I missed first time, but fuck it I thought, you only live once (or some people do anyway), and I haven't been shooting with Evgeny for over a year, or to Italy in a while. So slap my wrists for jumping on a plane if you will, but I'm the fucking Prime Minister I'll do what I like. Evgeny's great, he really fucks up them birds, and if he sees a fox he shoots and kills that as well, and then we take them all back to his place and usually have a lovely barbecue and a few cheeky lines. I've got to be good though – as I say that debate is on Monday and I really need to be half awake, they are going to slaughter me. And if they catch me fucking off to Italy for the day they are going to baste me in my own Covid-resistant blood. But unlike the grouse, I have a massive majority so I could stick through a Bill to rename Parliament as 'Boris' house' and it would be passed, fuck me I'm powerful. Evgeny was worried about grouse shooting and hunting and shit being banned with this new Rule of Six shit coming in on Sunday, so I assured him that I'd get it added to the exemption list. That's right – work, school, and grouse shooting. And please don't come at me with your moaning – oh killing birds for sport is cruel. Actually, that's not true. If you are shot as a bird you die instantly I'd imagine and to make the shoot a success, a large amount of vermin creatures are poisoned and got rid of like stoats and weasels and golden eagles. So actually it's good for the environment. And it's good for the mental health. So many people worried about their mental health after lockdown – get out there in the Italian countryside and shoot some grouse through the fucking head. It makes you feel so damn good! And if you don't have £3000 handy to go on a grouse shoot then stay in school, and work harder. School, work, and grouse shooting – they are the exemptions to the Rule of Six and I couldn't be more proud. When that trade deal kicks in with Japan then I'll get them all over for some good old grouse shooting, apart from Eric Yuan of course, I mean he's Chinese but you get my point. He can Zoom it, the Covid-originating cunt.

Sunday September 13ᵗʰ 2020

There's nothing more disconcerting than two Russians with big fucking guns. Yes, I'm just back from quite a discombobulating day. So my driver, Eric, remember him, big fucker, ex-SAS, gets me out of Dodge unnoticed in the early morning in the back of the car. I hate early starts but when I know I'm off to kill some birds in Italy then it really puts a spring in my step. I join him in the plane in a very simple disguise (not blacked-up, just a beard) and Evgeny and his dad Alexander greet me in their place in Perugia, and we have a lovely breakfast served to me by their Russian slaves, and I know what you're thinking, what happened to your rule about only drinking tea from a cup made by Carrie? Well fuck it, if I can't trust an ex-member of the KGB and his son who can I trust?! And I'm still alive all these hours later so if it was Novichok'ed then it was a shit batch. Alive but as I say, a little perturbed.

So after breakfast we jump in a very exciting armoured vehicle with blacked out windows, I felt like Tom Cruise, as we made the fairly lengthy drive up to the grouse shoot on the outskirts of Perugia. Alexander joked that the 'Churchill' grounds near them back in the UK would be quite apt for me, I reminded him that Churchill, while a wonderful leader, was a terrible racist. He called whites the 'higher-grade race' and whilst that is probably true, great man, you don't say it in a fucking speech. So we arrive and everything seems normal, we are shooting birds and ringing their necks if they aren't quite dead and then Alexander comes out with it 'Would you like to be on the inner circle Prime Minister?' He stands there with a big gun, the glistening Italian sun behind him, framing him, as he repeats the question – would I like to be on the inner circle? I say 'What do you mean Alexander? I already am on the inner circle'. 'But would you like to be on the inner, inner circle?' he asks. I say that I already am, and he adds another 'inner' – you get the idea, before he gets angry and says 'Prime Minister, would you like to be in the inner circle of Russia, along with very few others?' I told them what I had told them the other day, that Putin was now my best mate again. And then Alexander said 'Putin is not in the inner, inner, inner, inner circle.' I told them I wasn't sure what they meant, and they were scaring me a little with their big guns. They said they were offering me the chance of a lifetime, and many lifetimes to come, if I was to accept the offer of joining the inner, inner, inner circle. I asked them to give me a hint. But of course they wouldn't. I thought for a second and thought, fuck it, why not, yes please, let me into the inner, inner, inner circle – this sounds like juicy gossip. But they didn't bite, and said they would need to be sure that I was committed to the cause, to even have a chance of getting into inner, inner, inner circle. I said 'Stop saying inner, inner, inner circle, it's embarrassing' and they said 'well what should we call it then?' and I said 'well the 3i circle' and they said 'that sounds perfect Prime Minister, would you like to be in the

3i circle?' To be honest by that stage I was bored and just wanted to return to killing birds, so that's what I did, and tried to forget about it. But then back at the villa, things took a dark turn indeed.

We were watching videos of killing foxes and shit, just like old times. And I made the silly mistake of bringing it up again, I was pissed by then of course. And I asked Alexander, 'so come on, tell me, what is the 3i circle?' And he said 'do you know what you'd need to do to get into the 3i circle?' Evgeny shouted 'no!' but his dad didn't listen to his increasingly desperate pleas as he reached behind a set of books on a shelf for a DVD. Evgeny then went deathly quiet as his father placed the disc in the machine and pressed play. What I saw was really quite horrific, and that is in the context of course of us spending the day killing animals and birds and then watching funny videos of killing animals and birds. The video was clearly shot by Alexander, and he was screaming at a younger Evgeny, 'don't you want to be in the inner circle boy?!' I joked to try to alleviate the terrible tension in the room 'don't you mean the 3i circle Alexander?' and he told me to 'shut the fuck up'. I just watched the video terrified, as Evgeny was crying. I have never seen Evgeny cry apart from crying with laughter when we killed animals. It was awful to watch as Evgeny said 'yes' and then Alexander said 'Well I've told you what you need to do a thousand times to be in the inner circle Evgeny, and that's kill the thing you love the most. Prove your commitment to the cause by killing the thing you love the most.' Fuck me right? I'd never seen Alexander talk like this, but here was the feared ex-KGB right in front of me. On video at least, in person next to me he just smiled, stroked a cat and drank Scotch.

But my eyes could only briefly be torn from the screen, even though I started to watch through increasing numbers of fingers and cushions as Alexander led Evgeny outside where his pet wolf, Boris, lay helpless in a cage. I screamed, 'No!' and Evgeny screamed 'No!' on the video, whilst in real life just sitting there shaking his head silently. And on the video, Alexander handed him the gun and shouted again 'Prove your commitment to the cause!' Evgeny again shouted 'no!' and then Alexander took a pause and said 'It's either the wolf or it's

173

the bear.' 'What bear?' I screamed, not on the video, in real life, I wasn't there in the video. He took the gun, and was crying, and then chillingly pointed the gun towards the sleeping wolf, and then away again, crying. I can only say it was like the end of the film *Seven*, I won't ruin the film but you know the bit at the end when Brad Pitt is looking at Gwyneth Paltrow's head in a box. Fucking terrifying, as was this, and although this was on film it was very much real life. And on the film Evgeny screamed and shot the wolf in the head over and over again. I screamed, Alexander said the word 'Yes!' on the video and I screamed more, and then when I started to see blood then natural instinct kicked in and I strangely started to enjoy it, and then I saw Evgeny's shaking, crying head in real life and I stopped enjoying it so much and was horrified again.

I just got up and said as calmly as I could muster with a racing heart 'Whatever your inner, inner, inner circle is Alexander, I want no part of it.' And I called my driver Eric to spin the hire car round and get ready for my exit. Alexander replied 'Don't you mean 3i circle?' and I told him to 'shut up'. I felt disgusted, what he had done to my friend Evgeny who was a mess in front of me, and yes I told him to shut up. I just told him straight, 'how could you force your son to shoot his beloved wolf?' And he said 'I don't force him – I told him to choose between his wolf and the bear.' 'I didn't realise you had a bear as well?' I blurted. But Evgeny just sat quietly for a few seconds, still shaking his head and then looked at me with true fear in his eyes. 'My father means Cozy Bear, Prime Minister, he wants you to join us in Cozy Bear.' My eyes popped out of their sockets, I heard the car pull up outside the villa and I just ran. I jumped in the car, clearly still shaking no doubt, and my driver Eric asked me 'was I ok?' I said yes and just asked him how he was. He replied 'Bored shitless I've been sitting out here for 12 hours doing nothing, just listening to the cricket.'

I didn't say another word all the way back to the Airport Travelodge, all the way through masturbating to hot Italian newsreaders, and all the way blacked-up on the early morning flight home, but all I could think was – Eric man, fuck, I want your job.

RESUЯЯECTION

Monday September 14ᵗʰ 2020

Ha ha ha! Keir Starmer has had to self-isolate. Pissed myself when I heard that. The only good news of an otherwise turbulent day as the Rule of Six kicks in and poor, stupid people around the country are handed £100 fines from self-appointed militia – ooh I feel great, just like Hitler. As for Cozy Bear, well, I'm of course intrigued. Intrigued enough to read something. Not in a book obviously I'm not a square, on dear old Wikipedia. So according to Wikipedia, and I believe this information is all checked and verified, Cozy Bear is a 'Russian hacker group' believed to be associated with one or more intelligence agencies in Russia. They are thought to have tried to hack the US Democratic Party in 2014 and 2016 and in July this year as I suspected they tried to steal data on Covid-19 vaccines. I mean to be honest that sounds all pretty dull. Do I want to be part of their gang? Not really. And if it means shooting the thing I love most then I would hesitate I'm afraid, I'm a good person, unless of course I could lie about what I love most (I'm a good liar remember?) and then just shoot my dad or Carrie and claim that I'm devastated. Worth thinking about. My dad particularly is an absolute nob jockey.

So, with all this swirling around my noggin, roll on tomorrow's joint transfusions with my beloved Dominic. In other news, as expected, the knives were out for our proposed Brexit Bill. Sajid Javid (who?), Tony Blair, John Major, David Cameron. Fucking hell, David Cameron is against it! Well it's dead in the water if that popular hero doesn't like it. Sorry, I'd imagine David Cameron's opinion carries slightly less weight in this country right now than Rosemary West's. There are two people with an equal number of secrets hidden under their patios. I'm not saying David Cameron has killed anyone, but let's face it we wouldn't be massively surprised if we eventually find out he has killed and killed again. And that goes for every single other Prime Minister that has come out against me. It would be like Milli Vanilli coming out against me – nice try guys but you are either discredited or dead. But the biggest surprise – Ed Miliband is back! I love that. With Kier-ona away sick, the world's biggest loser is back for another shot at the title. And boy did he put up a fight in

Parliament today, terrifying stuff. However sorry Ed my love, you're who you always wanted to be – you're David – but not Miliband, you're David as in 'and Goliath', and right now you're up against a giant, and there are no weapons on Earth available to bring me down. I'm arrow, boulder and bomb proof. So obviously the Bill was passed tonight. Obviously. What a waste of time. Sums up Ed Miliband's whole life. And what are you doing again Ed? Oh that's right – podcasts. The last bastion for the unsuccessful. 'Ooh I've got a pod.' You mean you've got a voice that no one wants to listen to and a computer and fuck all else to do? Well done, I'm sure you and your three listeners love it. I'll just get on with running the fucking country and getting Brexit Mark II - The Unlawful One done you prick.

I like Ed though, he's cute. He's just doing his job, only a tad too late after losing it. I couldn't help but smirk when he asked me 'Have you actually read the Agreement?' Ha ha. I mean as if. Of course I haven't read the Agreement, as I say I am not a square. I'm in charge of stuff, he wouldn't know because he never has been - I don't have time to read shit unless it's on Wikipedia. So I think he was asking me how this Bill that we are trying to put through will protect Northern Ireland from a food blockade. Look loser, I do not know! I am told to say things and I say them. One man cannot know everything. I am not superhuman, I am not like that teacher on *Who Wants to be a Millionaire* over the weekend who knew everything and won a million pounds. I wish I was him. I really do, imagine the pussy he must be getting, he'll be cleaning up. I'm one man, and I just try to do my best without reading. And it's done me fairly ok so far - I'm, ahem, the fucking Prime Minister. Back off readers, there's a do-er coming through.

And on that note, I'm never reading anything again – I just checked my entry under Wikipedia and it says Alexander Boris de Pfeffel Johnson is a British politician, author, wanker and former journalist... I know right, what sort of fucking vetting process does Wikipedia have if this kind of thing slips through the net? I'm not a <u>former</u> journalist – I'm a journalist, and still write regular stuff, mainly about me, for the Daily Telegraph, under a pseudonym of course. And yes I won't even mention the 'wanker' bit, I know those kind of things are taken down in seconds. I'll just refresh the page and say goodnight. Goodnight.

Three hours later and it's still there. There isn't even a fucking phone number! And I'm still a 'wanker'. Livid. And I've missed two calls from Alex Lebedev, and a text, again mentioning Cozy Bear. Jesus he's like some shit and scary late night call girl service, but instead of getting fucked I'm going to get fucked. No thank you. I'm happy with Dominic, and I'm happy with Resurrection. And if these guys have the truth, well if I'm going to have to kill to get it then I do not want it. I can't believe he killed his wolf, that is horrific. It must be something really worth knowing. Who could I convince them I love the most in this world? I've reached for my Death List – remember that? My goodness it's full of ideas – and who was top of the list, well it's funny looking back isn't it? Only one Dominic Mckenzie Cummings. My my my, I've folded that piece of paper and now it is going to stay with me at all times – just as a little reminder. I know more than anyone that things can change rapidly, and they can change again. I was watching my 1998 performance on *Have I Got News For You* just now, as I often do before bed, I watch it every couple of days, it drives me forward. I'd say about 40% of my motivation comes from trying to prove Ian Hislop wrong. I'm not a bumbling, useless moron mate as you paint me in your rag and on your shit comedy programme, I'm the fucking Prime Minister. If I could convince the Lebedevs I love Hislop then I'd kill Hislop in a second if I knew I would get away with it, I wouldn't even need the promise of being in the Cozy Bear gang. If I had my way I'd kill Hislop by force feeding him every bad word he's ever written about me, and then I'd arrange with Darius Guppy to have the shit kicked out of him, which would be a lot. That man is packed full of it. Anyway as I say, I'm a good person so want none of this. Sweet dreams.

Tuesday September 15th 2020

Still everyone moaning about Brexit today, change the record, we won. We will always win. But Brexit is not my concern today, as if it ever was. This is really fucking sneaky – it's been leaked to the press (half of which the Lebedev's own of course) by The Lebedev's obviously, who else, that I met Evgeny at his place '3 days into lockdown' on March 19th. Although lockdown didn't begin until March 23rd we've had to fess up (as there will be some snooper who has a photo of me going) that it was for a 'personal/social matter' – when in truth I remember it well, it was an absolutely cracking evening watching foxes being ripped apart. I can't believe we did that now, knowing what I know about poor old Evgeny and that lovely wolf, Boris. This is his dad's doing I know, Evgeny is a kind soul and his dad is a KGB shit. And I know this is just a warning. Of course he has lots of things on me (apart from a video of me sucking Dominic Cumming's penis) – it's just whether he is brave enough to use them. This is brinkmanship at the highest level. And my tactic for today is to ignore it like the Ostrich man I am and hope for the best, hope he will forget all about it. It's surprising how many times that happens – it's the most important thing to someone and then either they forget about it or they get killed.

Anyway I don't want anything to sour today, as today was rather wonderful. Dominic arrived early but not too early in a lovely pink shirt and dark suit, he looked every bit the first day at school. His shirt was unbuttoned at the wrists, and bless him he'd piled on the puppy fat during his convalescence – if I didn't know it was a heart issue I'd have guessed it was thyroid, he really did look chubby, but all the better for it I thought, he'd even piled on a few grams on to his face, and let's face it even his biggest admirer (which I surely must be) recognises his face looks like 1980s cartoon villain Skeletor. Well I feel like He-Man today, I feel wonderful. And Dommers makes me feel that way. My goodness the brain on this man is phenomenal. He arrived at Downing Street carrying a copy of a 1986 letter written by Bernard Schriever, a retired US air force general about the importance of modernising defence infrastructure - the suggestion he wanted out there is that Dominic believes that we should be spending more money on weapons and he's been on record before as to wanting to visit Ministry of Defence sites and carry out reviews of defence capabilities. All bullshit of course. Dominic does not give a fuck about the military, and neither do I. Like the threat to this country is really ballistic missiles and conventional weapons? The threat to this country is the war of words my friends, the war of information, the war of social media – Dominic always says that if World War Three does break out it will be on Twitter, and at most only 280 characters will die. Frighteningly witty, dreadfully clever.

Anyway, we caught up over breakfast, it really was like the old times. I was telling him all about my plans for the next life and he was just chatting away to Ben Warner about the social media strategies and the like, totally ignoring me but in a cute way, just completely back to work. And then we got to work with the transfusions. Dear old Roger Connor at GSK had organised early this morning to move the operation into Downing Street, which is so incredibly kind of him, meaning no more early morning trips blacked-up in the back of an Uber into Harley Street. Downing Street is massive, so we've converted one of the rooms on the top floor here into a bit of surgery, and my goodness Roger and his team have done a really terrific job. I now get to lie back next to Dominic and either watch television or listen to music. I wanted to watch *This Morning* with Pip and Holly, and Dominic wanted to listen to classical music, so we compromised and listened to my Russell Watson CD, who Dominic described as the '*This Morning* of Classical Music'. But I like it, and relationships are all about compromise. And today my friends, my relationship with Dominic has reached a new level, a level I could only have dreamed about before now. As you know, the procedure up to now has been a simple transfusion of a younger man's blood into my system in preparation for the cloning procedure so they can clone cells in their healthiest possible condition. Well today, there was a suggestion – Dominic being younger than me, when his blood is taken out then why not have that blood put into me? Initially it seemed mental but it very quickly made perfect sense – we are both blood type O and this way there is less blood wasted. And what I didn't say at the time but of course was almost my first thought – I now have Dominic Cummings' blood inside me. Like the blood brothers thing you do with your best mate at school – you cut your own palms and share blood – here was me, lying next to the man I love, and taking his blood into my body. It felt so fucking good. First his semen, then his semen again and again, and now his blood. What a wonderful day this has been.

After the transfusion, they explained that in two weeks' time on Thursday October 1st we would be moving forward with the next stage of the procedure, the cloning itself, where cells would be taken to create Boris and Dominic Mark II, the Real Boris Johnson and Dominic Cummings. And then two really quite wonderful developments. Firstly, I discussed with Roger Connor the question of who in the future would bring up little Boris and tiny Dominic, and he said there was an option for us both to bring them up as our own children. That way we could totally control the passing of information and the eventual telling our 'children' that they are indeed ourselves. This made perfect sense, and I'm surprised I hadn't thought of this previously. Of course, bring up myself to be the best me I can be. And Dommers can do the same. We can spend the next 20 years of our lives growing old together in the knowledge that we are nurturing the next versions of ourselves, not our children who will inherit what we have worked so hard for, but truly ourselves, people we can pass everything we have worked so hard for on to gladly and with open arms. So completely wonderful. And the only possible scenario where I would want another fucking baby. You cry Boris, you cry – it's music to my fucking ears! Oh you've done a shit in your nappy have you little man, boy that smells so damn good!

And the second development, Dominic allowed me to suck his penis again, fully to completion. It was again completely wonderful, and in many ways after being injected with his blood it was almost like drinking in myself, which I have always wanted to do. And when I went to brush my teeth afterwards I realised – it wasn't even lunchtime yet! What a morning! I had a little nap this afternoon as Dommers and Ben have been back to boring work, and I'm just letting all Brexit criticism and thoughts of Cozy Bear wash over me. It's been a crazy journey to this point, but I truly believe now that all these difficult roads have led to this wonderful point which is where I want to be - I am full of blood, and semen, but more than anything I am full of hope.

Wednesday September 16ᵗʰ 2020

So Evgeny has just called me, I think he wants to tell me about 'Cozy Bear', he was whispering, maybe his dad was upstairs. But he wants to tell me I think, I said just tell me, and he said 'I can't' but I know he wants to tell me. This is payback for making him a Lord. He loves being a Lord, and this is payback. I just need to bide my time. He asked me 'who do you love the most Boris?' and I said 'well if I'm being honest Evgeny, I love myself the most, and I'm not killing myself.' He laughed and said rather sinisterly 'Well I'm not certain any more that is such an awful option Prime Minister.' 'Nonsense' I said, I didn't tell him why but today I truly believe I have it all. I really do have it all – I'm Prime Minister, I have great friends and colleagues and a dog who loves me and a wife that hates me and a big telly and drink and a new baby. Yes the country is fucked but once this cloning is done I will rise again, I am truly blessed. Maybe there is a God, and maybe I actually am the new Jesus Christ. I feel that everyone hates me right now but with the right reinvention, resurrection, then I can come again. I had the craziest thought earlier today – maybe I should go on *Have I Got News For You* again. There's a pattern – I tend to do it at my lowest ebb, I watched the recording of me on it again this morning and what is remarkable is that everyone, not just cunt Hislop, but cunt Merton and cunt Deayton were all accusing me of conspiring to beat up a journalist with dear old Darius, the evidence was laid out bare and the whole audience as one collectively agreed that I was in fact a dangerous individual that would arrange to get someone beaten up or worse... which of course I am...All was lost, and then I bumbled something incomprehensible, smiled cheekily and said 'let's move on' and they as one applauded me! They fucking applauded me! I have to remind myself of this – I've got the magic fucking touch! People love me, they adore me, and I can get away with anything if I just get myself out there and say it with a shake of the head and a bumbling, ridiculous grin. I am Jesus, but better.

So I had a long chat with Ben Warner earlier today (well he gave me 7 minutes) and I got quite firm with him, asking him where all the millions had gone that I'd given them, why am I not feeling more loved. He said that they were releasing a social media bomb tomorrow. From tomorrow, everyone's feed will be blitzed with two main strands – take the bloody Coronavirus vaccine when it comes (very important of course, nothing is more important), but far more importantly, myself and the Conservative Government are great and Brexit is going to be ok. Ben told me to watch this new Netflix phenomenon this afternoon, it's called 'The Social Dilemma'. It sounded pretty boring but I guess anything is better than Carrie's reality shite, so I'm very pleased that Ben forced me to watch it. My goodness social media is frighteningly clever – everything that anyone does online is watched and our feed is manipulated around us to coercively control us until we are all just mere puppets in the conglomerate's evil machine. Brilliant! I don't use social media myself because I'm not a puppet and I'm not a cunt, as I say I get my twitter slaves to put out my tweets. It's not like I couldn't handle doing it myself, if I did it all myself I'd make all Donald Trump's tweets look like the worst ever Donald Trump tweets. It's simply because I really can't be bothered – I'm doing shit, not tweeting about doing shit. I'm drinking, eating, making love. I am socialising!   And I have no desire to be Mark Zuckerberg's play-thing thank you very much. I'm better than Zuckerberg – he's my bitch.

I'm nobody's bitch. Anyway, as I say Ben Warner told me to put a few things out today, the first was wishing happy birthday to my 'friend' Narendra Modi (Prime Minister Of India, don't really know her) because Ben wants me to show my caring, bedside manner side (and that's bedside manner, not 'on bed' manner!! – which people definitely wouldn't want to see on Twitter!!). Ha ha, there's more than 280 characters in my sex life! Ha ha, I would be brilliant on Twitter. And then yes, we've started the push to make people believe in the NHS again, and I've stuck something out about £150 million more to support the A&E capacity this Winter. Importantly Ben said we had to say we are to 'improve infection control ahead of winter'. All very clever that, it looks reassuring but it makes people panic inside – why do we need more capacity?? Why do we need to improve infection control? Saying it without saying it folks there's a second wave a coming and you and your dumb kids need to take this fucking vaccine if it ever materialises, you pliable cunts.

Ooh – Dommers has just called me, and the papers are starting to sniff around the Olga D story again. Good God, I've just looked on Twitter and there's hundreds of comments about me and Olga, 'Have you shagged her Boris?'... 'How's the Russian violinist, prick?' Well I'll tell you how the Russian violinist is shall I – she's young, she's hot and she's at my beck and call. How do you feel now, cunt? God I would love to put that out on Twitter. Trump gets away with it, why not me? 'Drink bleach you suggestible slags!' People are so stupid. Anyway, on that note Dommers said we need something else just to get us in the clear on this one and fill the papers with other guff, so he's suggested we go for a local lockdown in Newcastle and Durham. I said 'why there?' and he said the most wonderful thing – he said his family and his parents were there, and this would put a stop to him having to visit and he could stay here with me, focussing on our transfusions, focussing on our Resurrection. God I love him. And I hate Durham. I asked him to come over, and he said he was tired and didn't. Damn. I joked and said 'you should drive over to test whether you're tired' and he just said 'Goodnight boss'. I'm being silly I guess, but I'm almost certain when he said 'boss' he was referring to me. You make me blush sweet man, and sir, you'll always be the boss.

Thursday September 17th 2020

Sometimes I wish the day stopped at 6pm. If days stopped at 6pm I wouldn't have got into any trouble over the years, I wouldn't have had half the affairs, half the babies, half the planned GBH's. I'd be happier, healthier and wouldn't have had the phone call I've just had with Alexander Lebedev. Anyway, I don't want to make this all about him so let me tell you about the good progress we've made today, really jolly good progress. Dommers came round for our Thursday transfusion, we had a spot of lunch and a little game of Wiff Waff. I

let him win, he hates losing. The great thing about the transfusion is
not only am I receiving some of his beautiful young blood – I asked
him whether he'd like some of my blood and he quipped 'Your blood
is 90% proof!' – but we have time as we are laying back next to each
other to stare at the ceiling and come up with policies. The doctors
are all Russians but clever old Dommers speaks Russian of course so
now he can make them part of the conversation with us, translating
when he needs to. Now usually of course I'd make sure affairs of
State are more private than this, but these are medical conversations
involving Roger at GSK and his bods at Gamaleya so it really is the
perfect time to make difficult life and death policy decisions that
affect the whole country.

So, Sputnik V is ready, it's very exciting. The Russian vaccine for
Coronavirus. God it's so bloody thrilling. Sputnik V. I feel we are
on the edge of a new dawn here, a great discovery, a brave way
forward. But with every step forward there's a small bump in the
road, and the tiny bump here is that the boring old Lancet and other
yawn journals have investigated and found that the vaccine results so
far at best questionable and at worst fabricated. Jeez there's always
one party pooper isn't there? We're trying to save the world here
mother fuckers! Anyway, there are things that we can do. Vaccines
have to be licensed you see, unless we say as a Government 'Na, don't
worry about that'. So that's the plan, we will reassure the public via
clever old Ben that 'unlicensed' does not mean 'untested' – on the
contrary of course, it has had lots of tests as the Lancet says –
whether the results are questionable or fabricated it's still been tested.
And here's the clever bit, we can invoke an emergency power, I love
doing that – ultimately there's always a Get Out of Jail Free card –
and that would give the Government immunity from being sued in
the civil courts if someone dies as a result of an unlicensed vaccine.
Now as an extra layer of difficultly we are technically bound by EU
legislation until 31st December, but you know, as I've proved already
this week, fuck the EU. It really is nothing, everything we've ever
signed with them means nothing. Because there's always an
exception, always an 'emergency power', always 'specific and limited
circumstances' where we can look at what we signed up to and then

totally ignore it. There are still millions of people dying from this awful illness out there – I mean not in the UK I think it's around ten, but you know what I mean, it's still very, very dangerous and everyone must have their shot of the delicious Sputnik V. As I say, very exciting, and dear old Roger is very pleased with me. I'm a good patient and a very good boy.

Which is more than you can say for Alexander Lebedev. He called me this evening. I hate the way our relationship has worked out. We used to have such a good time, drinking and felating our way around Europe. And now it's all about bloody Cozy Bear. As scary as he makes it sound, I can't help being more relaxed about it now that little Boris will soon be on the way. On that note I phoned Carrie this morning as well, she's still mad with me about Olga of course and our marriage now seems irreparable – but I tried a last roll of the dice I said 'why don't we adopt a baby like Madonna or Angelina Jolie or Elton John?' – that's what couples do when they hit troubled waters. She told me to 'fuck off fatty'. So at least we're talking again. Anyway, Alexander started with an apology and said that he was over dramatic the other day, and I did not necessarily have to kill the person I love the most to be in the inner, inner, inner circle. He asked out of interest who was the person I loved the most and I came straight out with it, 'It's Dominic Cummings'. He sounded surprised, 'not your new born baby Prime Minister?'. I almost spat out my Scotch. So anyway I told him I would not be killing Dominic Cummings. And he said 'Why not? He's number one on your kill list?' I took a big intake of breath, 'How do you know about that?' I stumbled. 'Prime Minister, when you are deleting things on your laptop, you really should not just leave them in the trash folder. When you came round, the other day, you just left your laptop, lying around.' I was obviously incensed, what a fucking betrayal 'You went through my laptop? How dare you Alexander you unbelievable cunt!' 'No of course not Prime Minister, I'm a gentlemen, my son did.' 'Evgeny?' I shouted, 'Evgeny would never betray me like this!' 'Really?' said Alexander, 'in the way that you wouldn't have your closest colleagues and friends on your kill list... like Michael, Mark... Hislop?' 'Ian Hislop is not a...'. I stopped myself. Even when others would be panicked I can be calm. I had an idea. 'Yes… I love Ian Hislop, maybe more than Dominic Cummings, yes Ian Hislop, let's kill Ian Hislop and then tell me about Cozy Bear.' And that's when he came out with it, 'I do not believe you love Ian Hislop more than you love Dominic Cummings Prime Minister. I didn't see a video on your computer of you sucking Ian Hislop's cock.'

Oh good God. These Russians will get you in the end won't they? Alexander has seen the video of me pleasuring Dominic. That's it isn't it? I panicked for the first time in my life since Carrie said she was pregnant. I said 'so you have me where you want me, what do you need from me?' He said he would explain in person tomorrow. We are meeting in secret at 7pm tomorrow. Fucking hell, if only days would end at 6pm. If days ended at 6pm I'd probably be a teacher or something now, a geography teacher in a lovely little school in Middle England, with a beautiful but boring wife and a lovely young boy on the side, and instead I'm in the job I always wanted which turns out to be the worst job in the fucking world, embroiled in this fucking mess. Stay strong Boris old chap, you have the blood of younger men inside you giving you life. Care not of Cozy Bear and remember there's always more Scotch to send you to sleep. I love Dominic Cummings, he will see me through. I'm drifting off now. My dreams are my only escape these days. Kill Hislop, kill Hislop. In my dreams everything works out. I always live and Hislop always dies. And Mark Sedwill and DJ Nihal Arthanayke. I can't believe they hacked my laptop. Just when you think you have everything covered these clever Russian fuckers can watch something even when you've deleted it. Even if I deleted Hislop, dumb cunts of this country would still watch him on repeats. Take me to my dreams dear whisky my loving friend, where I am happy and Hislop is dead.

Friday September 18th 2020

So, I needed to go to Evgeny's place across town and I needed an excuse, so we popped into the Vaccines Manufacturing Innovation Centre constructions site near Oxford. I was pinning my hopes on Oxford as you know, tremendous bunch of people over there, but I

RESURECTION

didn't have the heart to tell them that the Russians have already found the cure, of course they have. The Russians have everything, and now they have me not knowing what the hell to do. I try to remain upbeat but today has just beaten me. The thing that people don't realise is – as Prime Minister I earn £150,000 per year. That is all. That's only just over £7000 a month after tax. I have 6 or 7 children. Many at University, new baby, a dog to feed - it's not fucking enough is it? I've had to give up all my other work. Eternal life is great of course but what I need right now is dollar. I've given millions away to various people over the last few weeks and what do I get? £150,000 a year. Dear old Gareth Bale is moving back to Spurs this weekend, and he will be earning at least £200,000 a week. My goodness the injustice of it all. I'm saving the fucking country and Gareth bloody Bale has spent the last few years sitting on a bench in Madrid. Takes the piss. And Gareth doesn't get anywhere near the grief I get. I get shit spoken about me on Twitter, my closest friends and colleagues turning against me like Lord Keen just because we want to break International Law, well Dommers does. I wish people would get back to hating Dominic and not hating me. It just isn't fair. And please, use all that in mitigating circumstances when you hear what comes next.

Evgeny and Alexander are very rich men, their house is massive, their telly is twice the size of mine. They have a lot of money. And a lot of influence, and a lot of friends, one of whom I assume was Putin. But no, they have assured me that Putin is not their friend and they have shown me direct evidence of that tonight, in the form of a text message exchange between them where Putin says to Alexander 'you're a cunt' and Alex says, 'No you're a cunt.' Maybe I shouldn't have been quite so worried about being bumped off. It seems like Putin has bigger enemies to fry. One of whom was dear old Alexei, still in a terrible state of course but thankfully up and standing poor lamb. And Alexander opened with that he was risking his life talking to me tonight, and assured me he wasn't usually a man who would 'hide behind the sofa'. Never has a man admitting to hiding behind the sofa been so threatening. I suddenly became very aware that I had no security around, no driver outside, nothing. Only Evgeny,

looking more nervous than me, was reassuring me. He looked like he
did when he was watching himself kill his own pet wolf, Boris. Was I
going to be next on the kill list? Clearly not yet, I'm still alive
obviously, I'm writing this – question is though, is it worth being alive
any more? I can barely afford a nanny and more than one cleaner.
Anyway, this isn't about how much I'm paid, but as I say it is pittance.
Here's the deal, they said that seeing what they saw on my laptop
changed everything. They had a good look through after I'd left – I
left my laptop in their house, I'm such a scatter-brain, particularly
when I'm pissed and have just watched someone murder his own pet.
Anyway, the fact that they now had a video of me sucking Dominic
Cummings' penis, along with a list of who I would like to kill, it kind
of worked in my favour as they said they had more than they needed
should I ever betray them. They took a copy of the fellatio video
obviously, they ain't stupid these ex KGB thugs. So they asked me,
with that in mind, would I like to be in Cozy Bear? They had me over
a Russian barrel, of course I said 'yes'.

Now, this is a few hours later and I'm yet to work out which way is
up and which is down any more, but they say that Cozy Bear are in
fact now in two distinct factions - the good guys, they were the bad
guys but now they're the good guys, they have splintered away from
The Bad Bears and what Putin really wants, what his plan is. And
that is apparently that they do have a drug, Resurrection, that gives
eternal life, and not just an extra 50 years, it stops the aging process
completely. They have tested this and it works, you can truly live
forever. And Putin is entering the final phase in his grand plan, it's
what I always said was the major problem if people could live forever,
how would you stop the morons, the idiots, the unattractive, the
Uxbridge scum, the shitty shop owners and their non-mask believing
sprogs, the cunt farm owners. Well it's quite simple said Alexander,
you kill everyone else in the whole world. 'How on Earth would you
get away with that?' I asked. And two words came back which sent a
chill to my very core… 'Sputnik V'. Sputnik V isn't the cure, it's the
disease, and it will be used upon everyone to end their lives as eternity
begins for the chosen ones. Putin, his Russian friends and anyone on
the inner, inner, inner circle. If I want to live forever and not die,

then I would have to be on the inner, inner, inner circle, knowing that 99% of the world would die.

I didn't know what to do, so I told them about Dommers, and what I was doing with him. Was that all a lie? He couldn't have been lying to me all this time. And they showed me a copy of my kill list – at number one – Dominic Cummings. They proved to me that I never really trusted this man right from the start, and his mantra – hide in plain sight. Has the real enemy been hiding in front of me all this time, with his trousers round his ankles forcing my grateful mouth around his cock? I didn't know what to say. But I believed Evgeny, I believed the pain and hurt in his eyes and he implored with me, 'Prime Minister, you have to believe us, everything my father says is true. Putin is the enemy and Dominic Cummings is in bed with Putin'. 'But you said to me the opposite Evgeny!', I shouted – 'a few weeks ago you and your father stood before me, or maybe Alexander you were hiding behind the sofa I can't remember, but whatever, you said that Putin thought Cummings was the cunt!' Evgeny looked at his father for permission to speak, and then he spoke, with all the hurt that I saw in poor Boris' eyes when that sad old wolf was shot in the back and then in the bollocks. Evgeny looked at me and said 'I'm sorry Prime Minster, we were in bed with Putin, we were lying to you, to throw you off the scent. We were planning to be in the inner, inner, inner circle. That is where all our money has gone for all these years, working towards this very moment. But now we have learned the depths of Putin's plan, to kill virtually everyone with Sputnik V. We can no longer with good heart be part of this, it needs to be stopped.' As you'll remember I record everything that people say, that was quite a long speech. I then asked Evgeny 'How do we stop it?' and my battery ran out on my recording device but I think he said something like 'Fuck knows.'

I'm back home now, and I guess I have this weekend to truly work out who I trust. I need to test Dominic, once and for all. But here's the issue, Evgeny on the way out tonight said 'Prime Minister, you must believe us.' And he handed me a package. I've just counted the package - £100,000. He just gave me £100,000 in a carrier bag. I've just literally shat myself with excitement. And on the added plus side, I can now finally afford a second fucking cleaner.

Saturday September 19th 2020

With everything that's going on, I have one question today, is everybody lying? I mean I'm lying all the time, I know that, for the greater good, but I didn't question that everyone else might have had the same idea. Who the fuck is telling the truth to me any more? Who can I actually trust? Maybe Olga D. Maybe just Botham. I don't know yes, maybe Botham, but this is not time to call Beefy again, he'll think I'm nuts. Maybe I am nuts. I tell you what I have got though, £100,000. In a fucking big envelope under my bed. Oh God do you know how good it feels not to have any money worries for a few weeks? It feels tremendous. I can pay my kids University stuff, get an extra slave or two, it's really top drawer. I've spent so long handing out contracts to friends of Dominic I have never before considered taking a piece myself, well good guy no longer, yes I've taken a bung - I'm the Big Sam of politics, I'm Stephen Lee, I'm John Higgins, Bruce Grobbelaar – every so often, people need a bit more cash, shoot me. And the other good thing is the cash has given me some head space, I no longer have to worry about where my next £100,000 is, as it's in an envelope under the bed, and I can now start forming a strategy. So here it is. If Dominic Cummings is indeed in league with Putin and plans to kill everyone in the whole world, then I have just one question, does he plan to kill me or save me? And there is one way of finding out – I convince Dominic that I am anti-vaccine. I convince him that there is no way I will take Sputnik V. Yes, that is what I will do. I have invited him over tonight for drinks and to watch the telly. There will be no funny business, I will keep my eyes on the prize – the truth.

And then – how do I save the world? God, it's so funny how things work out isn't it – this is not too dissimilar to the plot of '72 Virgins' - a tousled-haired hapless bicycle-riding MP and his plan to foil an assassination attempt on the US President. Well for US President now read British Prime Minister. And this is my chance to make amends – as I said I hated myself for depicting Roger 'Boris' Barlow as being a fraud with no core values, ideals or beliefs. I'm writing this story for Christ's sake, I mean my life, I'm writing my life, and then writing it down what happens in this diary. I will never read this diary back (I don't read books as you know) but my goodness it's taken a fork in the road from my primary intention, to chart this country's resurrection. God 'Resurrection' that's funny, that's taken on a whole new meaning now hasn't it? And that's the thing, I admit it, in terms of resurrection with a small r then we're a little bit fucked aren't we? Corona Virus cases on the rise, The Cock (Matty Hancock) telling me I'm going to have to go on the telly next week and announce another mini-lockdown. 'I don't want to do it Cocky, can't you do it?!' 'Prime Minister, this is fairly major, I'd suggest you do it.' 'I know I should do it but please please please, can you do it?' 'Prime Minister if you don't do this one you'll get so much abuse on twitter, people will suggest you're fucking that violinist again.' 'Good point Matt, thank you.' I'll have to do it then, and people will hate me all over again, everyone hates me. Maybe even Dominic.

And if it turns out Dominic is in bed with Putin, and trying to kill me, and the whole world apart from them and a few lucky Oligarchs, then what do I do? Or maybe Evgeny and Alexander are lying and it is them that are the baddies. God it's like we're nearing the end of a film or something, maybe the film version of '72 virgins' where the reader doesn't know who is good and who is bad. Whatever happens, I hope they make a film of this story, my story. I'm not sure whether they could legitimately call that '72 virgins', I'd have to count up, I mean it's fairly close - although that wouldn't really be the core subject matter of the book. And I think the ending of this book will all come down to this evening, and my testing of Mr Cummings. And by testing I do not mean sampling his man milk. Be strong Boris, this man could be the enemy, that could be the cock of Mother Russia herself. And I have to ask myself a very important question, would I suck Vladimir Putin's cock? No I would not, unless I was doing it purely for the rep. And let's be fair, that would make a fantastic ending to an after-dinner speech, if and when I get back on the circuit. Anyway, I need to get my Mark and Spencer Chicken Pie in the oven, I haven't really cooked a meal in about a year so I'm feeling unusually nervous. Not just about the pie of course, but this country, our resurrection, my Resurrection, and the fate of the entire world. God it really is very dramatic isn't it, it would make a blockbuster film. I miss writing books, I'm jolly good at them. Dear old Roger Barlow could be due for a comeback, potentially with less racial slurs and anti-Semitism. In fact, I have a brain wave – whatever happens with Dominic when he comes over in a minute I shall write the account of what happens (tomorrow's entry) as if this is a fictional account of what is happening to our hero, Roger Barlow MP. To make it clear when I am talking about Roger Barlow I am talking about me, Boris Johnson, and when I am talking about Dominic I shall call him Jones, but it's actually Dominic Cummings. Hope that's clear.

Although I'm focussing on the end of the world as we know it, this has suddenly made me all excited about showing off my writing prowess. You should read '72 virgins' it's very good. Don't read the Amazon reviews, full of fucking pricks and spastics. Alastair Ballantyne gives me one star and says it's 'rushed and sloppy' … 'Puerile drivel, offensive stereotypes and language (spastic, n****r, coon). A 12 year old (or even Bruce Dickinson) could do better. Simply embarrassing. Borisisms like "Christ on a Bike", "girly swat" and "bien je jamais" all make appearances. The quality of the writing was summed up for me by the editor not noticing the word "fart" had replaced "fact". Sloppy, simplistic nonsense.'

What a cunt. They all are. The people reviewing my book on Amazon can be summed up succinctly with the following phrase … '72 virgins'. Although there's far more than 72 of them. But they are all steaming shits, and that, my friends, is a fart.

Sunday September 20ᵗʰ 2020

Roger Barlow had made a delicious garlic chicken pie. He was in a state of sexual excitement looking at Jones' sweet face across the table, as they ate the pie. Jones was dressed in a white t-shirt and khaki V-neck sweater, typically scruffy for Jones but Roger liked it. And Jones had been around long enough in Roger's life to know that he liked it. And of course Roger had already sucked Jones' penis on more than one occasion. Roger talked with Jones about the pie and about nothing, but Roger's mind was wandering, and wondering why after spending years obsessing about the female form, he was now obsessing about Jones.

Roger mused to himself that he used to love breasts, and would form relationships with women based purely on how buxom they were. His first two wives were buxom, and his third wife is as buxom as all get out, and she is buxom and young which should make her totally fanciable, but since she's had the baby she is less buxom and more really annoying. So annoying it had clearly turned Roger kind of homosexual, so he just stared at Jones' beautiful face as he talked about himself, becoming more and more tipsy, struggling with the urge not to burp.

Jones finished his pie and said that it tasted 'very nice, very garlicy'. Roger Barlow downed his third glass of red wine, and took a deep breath, trying to maintain his poise and dignity. It was impossible to do this while burping.

'I am going to close down all Russian sources of Conservative Party funding with immediate effe-,'

As when scuba divers find a pocket of stale air in a sunken submarine, and the bubble rises to the surface in a distended globule, so the garlic vapours were released from Roger's stomach.

'Effect.'

They passed in a gaseous bolus through his oesophagus, and slid out invisibly through the barrier of his teeth. Jones was obviously taken aback.

'Why on Earth would you do that Boris?' said Jones.

'Because I do not trust the Russians. In one breath we are stopping immigrants with Brexit and in another we are constantly under their influence, under their terrifying spell – and that's what they are, filthy and dangerous immigrants.'

'I do not believe you,' said Jones, 'You've gone bonkers.'

Roger Barlow fully expected this disbelief, so had pre-planned his clever next move. He had dear old Lubov Chernukhin on speed dial, one of the Conservative Party's biggest donors, and so he sped dialled her on his phone, on speaker, next to the empty dish which had once been a comforting home to the garlicy pie.

Jones looked anxious. He knew full well that Lubov's husband, Vladimir, was secretly funded by a Russian Oligarch to the tune of $8million, and this Oligarch had very close ties to Vladimir Putin.

'Hello Lubov,' said Barlow confidently, now more certain that the garlic wind had subsided. 'I don't want you to fund the Conservative Party any more.'

'Why not?' said Lubov.

'Because I don't trust Russians, I don't trust any immigrants' said Roger, again confidently. He then hung up.

'What the fuck are you doing Boris', said Jones, 'are you drunk?'

Roger laughed. 'I've never been more sober, I've only had three glasses of wine and those pre-dinner shots.'

'What the fuck have you just done then?' Jones repeated, clearly flustered and less confident than Barlow, 'The Chernukhins are British Citizens, they aren't immigrants.'

'Well,' said Barlow, letting out the final surprising pop of garlic air, 'they still technically are immigrants, they weren't born here Dommers. And anyway, I don't trust anyone anymore, I don't trust anyone with links to Putin.'

This forced Jones noticeably back on his chair. He lifted both eyebrows and downed the remainder of his second glass of red wine.

'And what's that supposed to mean?' spluttered Dominic.

All roads had led to this moment. Roger Barlow was strong. He was strong and he was educated, he knew many big words. Maybe he wasn't a genuine akratic. Maybe it would be more accurate to say he had a Thanatos urge, which is a clever way of saying death wish. Of course it is easy to have a Thanatos urge when you also have the Eros instinct, life, the next life. But was the next life as Jones suggested it was a real possibility, or was he a duplicitous little cunt? All of that crossed Barlow's brilliant brain within a mere blink of an eye, raising of an eyebrow, downing of a wine.

Jones circled the table, and lay back on the soft cushions of the sofa, beckoning me towards him. He was a thousand times more delicious than anything I could find in the valleys of womankind. His arm gently lopped into my exposed stomach where it protruded out full of garlicy pie. Slowly he eased off his dirty trousers and he eased off my filthy pyjama bottoms, and he prepared himself to enjoy me in a way that he assured me was both decently spiritual and infinitely carnal. I bent over him as per his tacit instructions, bringing my cock and balls ever closer to his face, laughing low and praising him and dissolving all the onanistic wretchedness of our first lives and – Oh-oh, he thought. Carrie might hear, she's downstairs, I had better be careful and close the dining room door.

I found myself staring irresistibly at Jones, just ten feet or so away in his open shirt. I stared with the Wahhabi mixture of lust, terror and disgust at this portrait of sexually emancipated Western man. I glared at his thighs and he glared at my unambiguously exuberant bosom and yearned to punish me, punish my entire being, punish me for my criminal role in doubting him. And there was a part of me, a secret half-acknowledged corner of my soul that yearned for him on precisely those grounds.

It was above all that part of myself, that part that had been tempted, the part that collaborated with Russia and her values, that he wished to destroy. Oh, but he would purge himself, he would cleanse himself of the Russian taint. He responded to Jones' beckoning finger, and with sweating fingers he positioned his sizeable appendage into Jones' grateful mouth, and waited mere seconds for the life-changing moment when he could wash his soul in steep-down gulfs of liquid fire. Roger Barlow had lived many years for this moment. Here he was, barely fifty-six, and about to splatter his balls all over Jones' mouth's walls.

Deep in their retrospective unconsciousnesses, Jones and the Prime Minister lay on the soft sofa cushions, curled like twins awaiting their rebirth into a weird and unfair world.

Monday September 21st 2020

If my last entry was a bit too wordy for you, Dommers sucked my cock last night it was fucking incredible. I'm therefore going to give him the benefit of the doubt and ignore the Lebedev's. The only

slight worry bead, for both myself and Dommers (who stayed the
night by the way, a gentleman never tells…) is that in the newspapers
this morning two stories that could only have come from Evgeny and
his dad - Lubov Chernukhin and the shady Putin connection has
weirdly made the press today and more worryingly rumours of my
trip to Perugia a few weeks back – that can only be the Lebedev's –
no one else on that plane would have recognised me – I was bearded-
up (way there) and blacked-up (way back). This is them two, this is
the way those filthy immigrant Russians play ice hockey. So once and
for all I have sided with the right side. Fuck Cozy Bear. I don't need
the inner, inner, inner circle when I have Dominic's inner circle. I
have no doubts in my mind any more. My bollocks are empty and my
head is clear, if I do exactly what Dominic says then everything will be
fine and he will not release the video of me sucking his penis. And I
don't mean that to sound like a threat from Dommers because it's
really not meant to as I'm sure it wasn't really meant to sound like a
threat when he said it to me. As I say, he sucked my penis last night,
and in so doing passed any test I could have laid before him. We are
a team again now, and will be unbreakable in this and the next life.
Full steam ahead.

So first things first, Dommers and Ben Warner want another UK
wide-lockdown to take the heat off the Olga story again, in addition
to anything else we get up to before D-Day October 15th, and to get
everyone to take Sputnik V when it's ready, which makes perfect
sense. To think we only have just over 3 weeks before Brexit
deadline, and more importantly 3 weeks before the end of this diary.
I can't carry on, I'm exhausted. And it's about 80,000 words already I
don't want it turning into that brick of a Harry Potter book, and on
that note I do hope I've at least come across slightly less racist,
transphobic and reactionary than JK Rowling. I don't think I've said
'coon' once. Anyway, just 20 or so more entries. Gosh well it's been
dramatic enough so far, but I do hope we are heading towards an
exciting and unexpected conclusion. Which is more than I can say
for this bloody Covid thing. So boring. Chris Whitty give it a fucking
rest mate – the voice of doom was back today, 'Oh we might have
50,000 new daily cases of Covid by mid-October which could lead to

200 deaths a day by November.' Yeah and maybe that won't happen love, I know I've got my own shit going on but we don't want to scare people unnecessarily, I might actually go around a few hospitals later in the week, and give everyone a cuddle or at least shake their hands – and before you call the Covid police, don't forget I've had it, I'm immune. What were those bloody nurses names again? Doesn't matter, I mean I guess we do want to scare people which is what Ben and Dommers were saying earlier, and why we've raised the threat level to 4 (completely meaningless by the way), we need to scare everyone again into taking Sputnik V otherwise the scum won't bother, which makes perfect sense. I don't know, I've kind of checked out of this Covid thing since I had it to be honest. I even had to talk to Nicola Sturgeon earlier today – uurgh. We put out a statement straight afterwards saying that we had 'all agreed to act with a united approach, as much as possible' when in fact I meant to say 'Nicola Sturgeon will obviously make her own announcement and do her own thing, which will be almost indistinguishable from our thing but she likes to pretend every single thing is her idea and she knows best, when she doesn't even know best with regards to her own haircut.'

Anyway Dommers is staying over again tonight, it's really becoming quite lovely, I hate to think what Carrie thinks but she kind of checked out of this with the whole Olga D thing weeks ago. Shame. I must text Olga D. No, I mustn't sorry, I lose track. Anyway Dommers and I were planning our next life earlier tonight, well I was, Dommers seemed more interested in the footy. I think he has a Thanatos urge you know, which, again, is a clever way of saying death wish. I think he wants to start the next life sooner rather than later. He's just drifted off to sleep, I'm writing this with his head in my lap (not like that cheeky!) and as he was drifting away he was saying 'You're going to die boss, you're going to die.' That's an awful thing to say to yourself. But I guess that's what everyone is forgetting in all this mess, we are all going to die. Yes some of us will live again so that takes the edge off but it still doesn't take away from the fact that this life will eventually end, and maybe Dommers was right earlier, maybe we should check out of this life sooner rather than later.

Maybe before October 15th. Dommers quite specifically suggested the 10th October tonight. He said it had a 'ring to it'. 10th of the 10th 2020. 10.10.2020. I guess it has. And then he said we could rise again on the Sunday, just like Jesus. Two Jesus's. Two Jesi. He's a romantic little imp is Dommers, I look down at his face now resting on my crotch, his wispy hair and his funny, hairy little ear and do you know what I think, I think after all these years of sex and women and babies and marriages and drugs and crimes and promises and lies and Russian orgies, I have finally found happiness. I have a chum, I have a kindred spirit, I have someone I want to spend the rest of my life with, even if it is only until October 10th, and then we start a glorious new life together. Goodnight.

Update, he woke up and grumpily went home shouting 'No I'm not sleeping here Boris with your wife downstairs you stinking pig'. What I said still stands though, I love that man.

Tuesday September 22nd 2020

Dommers was so grumpy today, stomping around like a bear with a sore head, and not a Cozy Bear neither (more of that later). Yes it was a very busy day announcing the new lockdown to the nation (boo hoo) but I thought he would have been happier. I whispered to him as we lay next to each other for the transfusions this morning that yes, the 10th of the 10th did have a ring to it and he just kind of nodded as if he expected me to fall into his plans. I shall chastise him for that later I thought, you may tell me what to do and say and suck but I am still technically the boss. Oh well, that's why we work so well together – he's the bear with the sore head and I have the cream. So to speak. No cream today though sadly, only boring work, as we had to announce the nation the new plans for the Rona. I was down with everything Dommers suggested, he's a caring chap – work from home (oh-oh BANG BANG U-turn alert!) – if only my face mask covered my mouth, nose and ears I wouldn't be able to hear all the moaning bastards from the opposition benches – 'Oh we agree with what you're doing Boris but you should have done it 45 second earlier.' Shut the fuck up and watch the film *Sully* and realise what a hero I am you gob-shites. The 10pm closing time for pubs and restaurants I wasn't quite so sold on, not that I'm ever in pubs past 10pm these days sadly, I usually black out by about 7.30, but I wasn't certain on the science behind this, I asked quite legitimately at Cobra 'does the virus have a bed time?'. People laughed but it was a genuine question and apparently the virus does not have a bed time. So I repeated the question at Cobra, 'Why are we doing the 10pm curfew thing?' and everyone went silent and then Ben Warner piped up and said 'I'll talk to you later Prime Minister'. I said 'Ben! I didn't realise you were here, I thought we agreed you shouldn't really be in these Cobra meetings?' and he said 'Dominic invited me' and I thought 'fine'. Anyway caught up with Ben later when Gove reminded me to ask him and Ben said again 'I'll tell you later' and he winked and went on his way. Annoying. So I had to do Parliament, interviews with pricks and address the nation without actually knowing the reason why I was saying the 10pm thing, so every time I was asked I just had to come up with some bullshit, but of course I'm the world's leading expert on that.

Anyway, the real reason for the 10pm thing, Ben has finally just confirmed to me, is that he wants people in the house at around 1030 which gives them that 90 minutes at least of drunk scrolling. That's what clever people like Ben rely on to feed us the important messages of the day. When we're not drunk, we're more sensible – we look at the news and the weather. When we are shit faced, we go down rabbit holes, conspiracy theories, foxes being fucked up, I know I do. And that's a key time for someone like Ben to get his scare stories across to fight off those crazy anti-vaxxers. We can't have Fred Shit-for-Brains going to the pub and convincing everyone there not to have the vaccine – we need him to go home early and that's when Ben will blitz everyone's feed with scare stories of what will happen to them if they don't take this vaccine. In reality it's very little, an incredibly low chance of getting this wretched virus now but I absolutely agree that everyone should take Sputnik V, tested or not tested. I genuinely thought I was going to die in Spring this year, and it's easy to forget that, before eternal life was guaranteed, death was actually terrifying, and I want no one to go through what I've been through, apart from Ian Hislop. I see a new series is back of *Have I Got News For You*. I hope they're doing it in the studio and Hislop has a Covid positive guest next to him, who is told to laugh heartily at all his shit jokes about me, that have been written by Shaun Pye. Oh the irony Ian, to be killed by the spluttering, fawning and fake laughter that you have paid for, for the jokes you haven't written. What a tragic but fitting end you witless, gutless cunt.

Anyway, Evgeny called me just now and pleaded with me to join Cozy Bear and said that 99% of people on the planet would be killed. I said to him 'look mate, I know what's happened – it's after 10.30, you're pissed, and you've been going down internet rabbit holes looking for a story to scare you.' And he said 'No I have not Prime Minister, I am aware that the highest levels of the Russian Administration are working with countries and Parliaments around the world, including yours, for a mass vaccination programme which will be lethal to almost everyone in the world. This is an extinction level event Prime Minister which you are about to sanction for your people. I told him 'bullshit' and hung up. I then texted Dommers to tell him I was being a good boy and he said 'you are a good boy'. I then said we should go out to celebrate and Dommers rightly but rather boringly said 'Do you think on the day we announce pubs will have to close at 10pm, that it would be a very good look for the Prime Minister and his best mate to be propping up the bar at 11pm?' I almost choked with happiness at him saying 'best mate'. I was grinning from ear to ear - 'who gives a fuck whether it's a good look?' And he said 'I do Prime Minister. If this is the last three weeks of your administration then I want you to go out on a high.' It then utterly hit home… are we doing this? Are we really going to bow out of this world on the 10th of the 10th? This journal was supposed to be recording our resurrection, and instead I fear it has recorded our great country's demise, and my own death, and the death of my dearest friend, my 'best mate'. I was having second thoughts. 'Don't forget that video,' said Dommers, playfully. 'Shut up about that video Dominic', I countered angrily. 'OK Prime Minister, do you need me to come over and make you feel better?' 'Yes I do, thank you.'

So there we go, at the end of a harrowing day I'm about to get my penis sucked. And I'm going to film it. Two can play the bribe game Mr Cummings. I am the boss, and don't you forget it.

Wednesday September 23rd 2020

Right, so yes I got the video of Dommers sucking me, job done, but let's cut to the chase. Andrei (Navalny) called. He's in Germany and finally able to stand up, for now. He said he's survived but it wouldn't be long before they tried again. He was breathless. And, yes, what is slightly worrying is that he said exactly the same as the Lebedev's – that Putin is planning to kill 99% of people in the world or whoever he can persuade to take Sputnik V – and him knowing this was the reason that they tried to kill him. It explains why Alexander was so scared, why he wanted me to kill to get in Cozy Bear. Oh fuck. I just don't know what to believe now. But you know the weird thing, I had a google, hours later there's virtually no news of Alexei's recovery. And Alexei said something really quite worrying – he said everyone knows, everyone in power knows, that this is going to happen, that's why his recovery is being forgotten because it is meaningless. Those in power will survive, and everyone else will die. He said people in my own team know, people in my own team are Cozy Bear – virtually all of them – Cummings, Gove, Patrick Vallance. I know right, Pat Val? That cunt. He always hated me and maybe this is why, everyone around me is in the Cozy gang and I'm not. But if I'm not, is Dommers? Alexei said it was quite easy to see who was in Cozy Bear – who has given money to GSK or Gamaleya – I said I had – he said no, Dominic Cummings had. He then asked who owns shared in GSK – Patrick Vallance does. I was like 'bullshit' … and I've just checked out his sources – OMG he's right, Pat Val, the Chief Scientific Officer who has been advising us to take the vaccine when it's ready or before it's ready and we should be confident in Sputnik V, the vaccine developed by Russia and GSK – he owns £600,000 of shares in the fucker – oh my God they call me corrupt. Fuck me I'm earning nothing right now, even that dick Pat Val is earning more than me, so unfair.

I feel so isolated right now, Dommers is not answering my calls again and you'll think I'm stupid but I've just texted Olga D. I just said 'miss you' along with an aubergine emoji which if you don't know kind of means big purple erect throbbing penis. I think she's back in Saudi, maybe I just run away or something and be with Olga D, does she love me? I don't know. I even called dear old Rishi through the Bat phone and he said he was 'working on the financial measures to rescue the country' – boring right? I'm not cut out for this job, clearly, I think that saving the country is boring. But that's not me, I am a good person, yes I care about myself and I love having my willy sucked but if you look back at this whole diary in its totality, I would hope the reader will get a sense of a decent chap, a good person, and more than anything just someone that wants to be loved. I swear if someone loved me I would have done none of this – if my parents had loved me, if my dad had loved me rather than fucking off every 5 minutes to Greece and what have you, if my wives had loved me I would never have strayed, and I'm not blaming them, I don't blame anyone, I'm just saying don't blame me. To paraphrase dear old Richard Curtis in the excellent *Notting Hill*, I'm just a man, standing in front of a country, asking it to love me. Why does anyone do what I do? Because nobody loves them quite enough. I thought it was Dommers who would love me enough, maybe it still is. I thought it was Olga D that would love me enough… but really, people judge my sexual deviance but is it really as bad as some of the women that have been with me? I mean come off it, when the 20-something Olga D kneels down and sucks the married Prime Minister's willy, is she necessarily kneeling on the moral high ground? I don't know, I'm not judging. I just want a wife that loves me, that's all I want.

Of course I'm hard to love – I'm an easily distracted, philandering old borderline alcoholic that loves shitty ITV gameshows. I don't expect your sympathy. I have £100,000 in a box under my bed and I'm the fucking Prime Minister. But right now I feel very alone. I'm not ashamed to say I've had a glass to the wall this evening and was listening in on dear old Rishi's wife Akshata Murthy saying to Rishi that she loved him, I wish someone would say that to me. I mean Akshata would do, she's pretty fit that one. But I would never fuck

Rishi's wife, you may not believe me but I'm essentially a man of principle.

I'm looking out on the moon right now, and dreading tomorrow. It's the final transfusion before the cloning process begins. My God, with everything going on in the country and with my life and death and with the world's life and death, all I care about is my phone and Olga D texting me back. Richard Curtis was right, love actually is all you need. And yeah, Hugh Grant played the Prime Minister in that film and he was fucking a girl half his age and everyone applauded. Fuck me the British public are fickle and contradictory little cunts.

I'm trying to sleep but I can't – imagine if everyone knew something and you didn't. That's what I'm thinking right now. Putin, Dommers, Mark Sedwill, maybe they all know something and I don't. Why does Pat Val have £600,000 worth of shares in GSK? I've just phoned him and he's not picking up. The press aren't reporting on any of this shit. All they care about is hating on me, piling the shit on old Boris. Well fuck them, fuck Cozy Bear – if they are all part of it let's start smoking the little buggers out, I've just leaked to the press that Pat Val owns all those shares – get out of that one you snide little fuck-wit. Come on Boris, you can do this, if everyone is on one side and just you are on the other, then you can still win. You've proved that time and time and time again. You can still win young Boris, you can still prevail.

Olga D has just texted back. Three words. The three words I crave. 'Miss you too'. Not 'I love you'. She doesn't love me. Maybe when push comes to shove I don't deserve love, I don't deserve a second chance at life. What would Botham do? You know what, what would dear old Roger Barlow do? It was him against the world and he won, and if it is Boris Johnson against the world, maybe I can still prevail. I've just read a few passages of that book '72 virgins' for inspiration. Despite what my mates at The Telegraph said about it on the front cover, I'm really very, very sorry about this book, my God the writing is fucking atrocious. Glad I've made up for it in this one. 'Effortlessly brilliant page-turner' Daily Telegraph… where I worked, and got my mates there to say this. My goodness what a crooked little shitty life I've lead. They say before someone else loves you, you have to love yourself. I'm afraid I know everything I've done, so I've really fuck all chance of that. But there's still time, still time for, as I said at the end of my last book - 'the hero's welcome'. I could still be the hero. But time is fast running out.

Thursday September 24th 2020

So we've just had the final transfusion, I'm not sure how science works but if Dominic Cummings is trying to kill me well he'll be killing someone with all of his own blood inside him and most of his semen, so essentially he'll be killing himself. Dominic was very cold on me, I told him I'd been in touch with Alexei, he didn't blink. He just said 'don't trust him. He lies with every breath.' But that's exactly the quality that I look for in a comrade, that's why I loved Dominic. Loved, or love. I don't know. I just told him I was worried about what we were about to do. Again he seemed cold, and just said 'we are on the path now and we cannot get off.' And we didn't get off, I just wasn't in the mood. I told him I was leaving something behind, a book. It surprised him. 'You've been writing another book?!', he laughed, 'What is it, the sequel to 72 Virgins?' he laughed more heavily. 'What's it called? 73 Virgins? 15 slags?' Would someone that loved me belittle me like that? Olga D wouldn't do that. Her English isn't good enough. I told him I'd been writing a diary, telling everyone the truth of the last three months. It was my insurance policy if anything went wrong. He looked nervous, 'what do you mean if something goes wrong?' 'What do you mean Dominic?' I countered, 'we are planning to clone ourselves and be resurrected, anything can go wrong.' And I said I wasn't set on the idea of killing ourselves after this was done. That just doesn't seem right. He was more interested in the diary, asking me where I'd been writing it. I told him – on my laptop. He nearly choked on his milk. 'Your laptop?! Your fucking laptop?! Remind me what your password is again?!" I didn't tell him, you don't tell anyone your password, it's pussygalore (lower case). He shouted 'It's Pussy Galore'! 'This diary will already have been hacked you numb-skull,' he screamed, 'you leave that fucking laptop around more often than you do you own spunk.' He was angry, and flailing around, and in that last comment he was more than a little jealous. Maybe he knew about me and Olga D, he actually should know, that would show him. 'The Lebedevs will already have your diary!' he shouted, 'Do not trust those cunts, do not trust anyone.' And he stormed out.

Well he's right isn't he? Don't trust anyone. As I said, you have to trust yourself before you trust anyone else, and boy I'm a long, long way off that. I cannot be trusted. I was getting fit a few weeks ago, I haven't texted my personal trainer back in weeks. Every time I reach inside my pocket to call him I pull out another raisin and biscuit Yorkie. I just think fuck it, if I'm to die soon, who cares? My genes don't know I'm a fatty. Carrie hasn't talked to me for days, I miss her calling me 'fatty'. Again, I think all I have is dear old Rishi now. I know he doesn't really class me as a friend but he's not in Cozy Bear, I tell you that for nothing. He's too nice, and wealthy. He wouldn't fuck me over. He's doing a terrific job, in the Commons today delivering the good news to everyone with a viable job that they can get their wages topped up. And again, it's the fucking arts moaning. Moan, moan, fucking moan. And the worst thing about performers and actors moaning - fuck me can they project! What a fucking noise, they never shut up. So many actors and, excuse me while I choke on Yorkie, fucking comedians again moaning. I searched my Twitter just now and some nobody comedian called Nathan Cassidy has tweeted about me and Olga D. Well fuck you Nathan Cassidy I hope that you're crying in front of your 13 audience tomorrow at about 9.45 weeping about how I've stopped you telling your shit jokes after 10pm and why I've forced your tiny, shitty little audience to wear masks. Well let me tell you cunt, it's not the masks stopping them from laughing it's the fact that you're a dip-shit, who thinks 'telling jokes' will ever be a viable career, well it certainly won't be for you, you tweeting little cock-sucker. And if I could fit all that into 280 characters I'd reply to that fucking tweet. Anyway, sorry, dear me, I admit it I'm slightly rattled, ever so slightly vulnerable. It's very tricky to know which way to go when you don't know which way is danger, who is there to help you, and who wants you dead.

So I thought I'd give Evgeny a chance, I called him and asked him whether when they had my laptop the other day they also nabbed a copy of this diary. He said, 'Yes Prime Minister. And we've also got your death list. Dominic Cummings is number one and rightly so. Glad I wasn't on it.' He asked me to come over, I said I couldn't, as it was after 10pm. He said that rule only comes in tomorrow and I said I'd lost track of the rules. Oh fuck, Brexit, we've done nothing on that all week. No one is doing anything on Brexit. None of my useless fucking cabinet – do they know something that I don't know?

I don't know, but I know now that Evgeny is telling the truth. Next Wednesday we start the cloning process, and in nine months Boris Mark II shall be born unto this Earth. There's no way I'm bowing out on the 10th of the 10th. Dominic has lost his tiny mind. That clone is my child, that child is me. And I want to be there for him. Right now, I fear that he is my only friend. Apart from this lovely bottle of gin that I'm about to down with a generous side helping of hand sanitizer. Goodnight.

Friday September 25th 2020

I'm going to go into retreat this weekend, I'm going to take a few days off this diary. Maybe the Russians do have it now, I'm a bit terrified. I love Russia by the way, always have. I can't rush into anything too quickly now. Rushing into things has cost me so much in my life, and at least 4 of my 6 or 7 children. I bloody meditated today. I know right? What have I become? It felt really lovely actually, you just listen to calming music and actually after about 2 minutes I was fast asleep. I'm hanging out of my arse today. I tried to watch the new series of *Bake Off*, take my mind off things and that cunt Matt Lucas was taking the piss out of me, saying I couldn't make a decision. Well I've made a decision Matt, and that's for you lot never to work again, you entitled bunch of talentless pricks. And I don't call presenting *Bake Off* as work by the way – truly the last bastion of the dying comedian. At least if I did die tomorrow I can die with my head held high and I can say I rose to the top, I did exactly what I wanted to do. I lived, and I achieved. What I didn't do is go on telly and say 'On your marks, get set, bake' alongside a pathetic tweeted apology for blacking-up on Little Britain with EXACTLY the same wording as David Walliams. Don't think we all didn't notice that Matt because yes even me the busy as fuck Prime Minister noticed. However I do remember those sketches and they were very funny.

Anyway, forgive me, I'm going to take some Iowaska. Ayahuaska, however you spell it. I need to be knocked out for a few days, forget about all of this. We have a curfew of 10pm tonight and so just before 10pm I'm gonna take this mother fucker, it's always been there for an emergency. I'm told I will spend the next day or two hallucinating. Ben Warner gave it to me, him and his mates do it all the time. So I've told Ben I'm gonna take it and just be on the top floor here at Downing Street. He's going to keep an eye on me, make sure I don't go down too deep into a k-hole, or whatever the expression is. Anyway, so you might get some diary from me over the next few days, you might not. I'm gonna leave the laptop open so it might be a bit of fun see what I can come up with when I'm completely off my tits. I mean it worked wonders for Elton John. It's not just Made in England, let's face it everything else he's ever written when he's been off drugs has been shit. And he did a Post Office advert. Him, Matt Lucas, what's his name - Nathan Cassidy, they're all the fucking same – I'm sorry for a lot of professions that are going to the wall in this crisis – my journalist friends and the like, but performers and comedians can go hang, which most of them do anyway in sordid sex games gone wrong. I'll tell you something, if we are all about to die in some mass Russian murder, then let's hope to God they aren't saving any fucking performers. That's the last thing we need in the next life, the elite are saved to live on a cleaner, greener, more perfect planet, and the only entertainer saved is Matt fucking Lucas, doing the shittest Boris Johnson impression I've ever seen. Then again, if Matt Lucas is the only entertainer saved then at least they've killed off that cunt Hislop. Rejoice! This whole thing would have been worth it if Hislop has read out his last pre-written joke. I just checked on BBC iplayer, there have been 57 series of *Have I Got News for you*. 57! Am I hallucinating already? Fuck me.

It's like a great plague that has ridden of us of humour and humanity for a thousand years.

Anyway, see you on the other side, I'm off down the Io-well. Any reality is better than this one. I ask you, if they are planning to kill you dear reader, do you really care? It's got pretty fucking bad hasn't it? And I think you can see from this diary, none of it is my fault. But I'm sorry. And although I'm about to get completely off my face I'm not Elton John, and I can say sorry now. I'm sorry. I really am sorry.

Ha ha, fell for it. Of course I'm not sorry! I'm getting fucked, bye losers.

Saturday September 26th 2020

Elephants with toenails on their foreheads.

Sunday September 27th 2020

Elephants.

Monday September 28th 2020

Right, weird. They say on Iowaska it will get you closer to seeing the truth. Well, I'm really fucking close now. And sorry, I don't know why I mentioned elephants over the weekend, it got pretty strange. But I've just checked my twitter – good news, 3 million followers, finally! Bad news, there's a speech on there that I have absolutely no memory of delivering over the weekend. I've watched it back several times. My 'speech to the United Nations General Assembly' on Saturday. That was not me. I know me. I'm bumbling, I scrabble around for the point. This was too good. I'm using words I don't know the meaning of…. 'Zoonotic' – never fucking heard of it. I said things I don't believe 'I don't want to blame any country' … 'I don't want to points score'. And then there's giving £571 million to COVAX a global vaccine-sharing scheme to ensure that the accepted vaccine is distributed via the World Health Organisation to everyone in the world. I called the anti-vaxxers 'nut jobs' – I wouldn't do this, not in a speech to the United Nations, this is fucking ludicrous. It looks a bit like me, it sounds like me, but I'm telling you it was not me. I've just gone mental at Ben Warner and chucked him out – 'What have you done to me you cunt?!' I shouted at him. He acted like I had been taking drugs all weekend and was still hallucinating. 'I know you Ben, you can do anything you like, who has made you do this, who?! Who?!' It's Deep Fake isn't it? Ben showed this to me months ago – with Deep Fake you can do anything, you can make it look like Keanu Reeves is in Forrest Gump, which genuinely is hilarious but I stopped laughing so hard when he showed me Donald Trump announcing World War 3. I remember him showing me this and me shouting 'Fuck! He's launched the nukes' and Ben saying 'No, it's Deep Fake' and I repeated 'No Ben, he's just said it he's launched the nukes' and then Ben repeated it was Deep Fake and I finally got it. This is Deep Fake, I swear.

Fuck me, they've announced, well should that be I've announced that we're teaming up with the Gates Foundation! Good God we may as well team up with Prince Andrew and Ghislaine Maxwell for Save the fucking Children, I would never team up with that geek in a million years. What the fuck is going on? I called Evgeny. He is sure that they, whoever they are, Putin, Cozy Bear are now in the final stages of their plan, to develop this vaccine Sputnik V and make sure it is rolled out to virtually everyone in the world, and it will kill them. Fuck me I know I'm sounding like those nut-job ant-vaxxers but what would you believe? I sound like those twats who believe that Bill Gates is in charge of a global paedophile ring – that gonk couldn't pull an adult let alone a kid. But what am I supposed to think? I know one thing for sure – I did not do that speech. I didn't even know we were chairing the G7 next year. Whatever is being decided is being pushed through without my involvement. I called Dominic, he didn't pick up. I called Gove, he didn't pick up. I texted Olga D (unrelated to my panic but I really would like to fuck her again). She hasn't replied.

Oh fuck. I need to eat. I haven't eaten anything proper for days I

RESUЯЯECTION

don't think. When I came round there was half a bottle of full fat milk and ten Yorkie wrappers. I need to focus. I'm going to see Evgeny and Alexander tomorrow again and we are to formulate a plan to stop this mess. I want to live forever but I don't want to kill the world, I don't think. No I really don't think I do. I'm meeting them in a secret location, in a shitty hotel in Exeter. I go there to fuck girls sometimes. As in women, young women but women obviously. I once put a pin in a map and said to myself 'Where would no one expect me to fuck women?' The answer was a hotel in Exeter. So I've booked a room under my pseudonym 'Roger Barlow' and I'll be seeing the Lebedev's at 3pm tomorrow. My driver Eric is taking me straight from a trip to Exeter college we have set up as a diversion. Eric is very discrete. I think he's the one person I can trust now, apart from maybe Evgeny and Alexander. Why would they lie to me? They have so much money, if there's one person anyone should trust it's someone with lots and lots of money, they've no reason to lie. No that's a lie, I don't know.

I've just called Carrie as well, I need her. I really do, I need someone, maybe Olga D. No I need Carrie, I need my baby Wilfred, I haven't seen him for days now they've been with friends (no friends of mine of course). Who must he think his father is? I've abandoned him and maybe I deserve what's coming to me. No Boris, you are strong, don't forget you're the Prime Minister and never, ever forget you now have 3 million twitter followers! Fuck me I could never have dreamed of such a mountainous flock. I have such power, what should I tweet? It's Yom Kippur today Eric tells me, I'll tweet something about that, make myself look good. I didn't really know what it meant, Eric is Jewish and he says it's the day of atonement, the day where we are closest to our own souls. Maybe I am Jewish, that's what today has felt like indeed. 'For this day, He will forgive you, to purify you, that you have been cleansed from all your sins.' Fuck me, if only. But maybe that's what this is, maybe this is what I needed , to cleanse myself of all my sins. Forgive my sins, I am sorry. I love everyone, I really do love everyone. Even Ian Hislop. I love Ian Hislop if it means I am forgiven.

I've just tweeted 'I would like to extend my very best wishes to all Jews in the UK and across the world.'

First reply from 'FutureGhost'…. 'Government have lied about testing, death rate, cases, exams, economy, Brexit, track and trace, care homes, PPE, social distancing, breaking rules, faulty tests… why does anyone believe a word they say?' Well in the next few days I'm going to prove it to you dear 'FutureGhost', as I plan to save the world, I plan for atonement. I love everyone now, even you FutureGhost, even cunt Hislop.

Actually not Hislop, fuck him. Is he Jewish? Probably. Everyone else in the media is.

Tuesday September 29ᵗʰ 2020

Right, I fucked up the first part of Exeter today. My mind was everywhere, but mainly it was still on a come down from whatever Ben Warner fed me on Friday night to make sure I was out for the weekend while they plotted their devious Deep Fake plot. But look, come on now, I don't know what the fucking rules are any more. Even if I wasn't trying the save the world I would have lost track. So what did I say, I said that 6 people from different households could meet up in Newcastle and apparently that's wrong, but look, there are different rules for Scotland, Northern Ireland, Wales and within England virtually every town and city has a slightly different rule, am I really expected to know every single rule in every single place? You'd need the mind of Aristotle to keep up. And while I have such a mind, I haven't got the benefit of poncing around in Greece with basically no job (sounds like my father) I have a fairly big fucking job actually and that's saving civilization, so again, forgive me if I wasn't aware that 6 people from Newcastle could meet up in a pub, but yes, I misspoke (is that even a word?). And anyway yes from what I know of Newcastle it make eminent sense – I'd imagine when 6 people go to a pub in Newcastle at least 2 of them usually end up pregnant by the same dad, and the last thing we need in this country is more bloody babies. I mean even old Bozza have put the snake away for a few days, and if old Eros is on the fuck wagon then everyone else can be as well.

That's a good phrase actually as to where we are, 'on the fuck wagon'. We're fucked. I can confirm I have met Evgeny and Alexander in a hotel in Exeter and we are actually fucked. Look, this is where we are. The Russians want to roll out Sputnik V to virtually the whole world, who will be killed and the lucky elite who don't take it will be delivered a drug that will give them eternal life. Sorry if you're not sitting down reading this but that's the way it is. Actually, we spoke about this diary today. I said 'let's cut the bullshit guys, you've read the diary and what do we do about it?' They said 'well maybe you should stop sucking Dominic Cumming's penis' and I said 'No I don't mean that, and I have definitely sucked Dominic Cumming's penis for the last time if you must ask, I mean what do we do about this diary, getting out there into the public domain?' And they said that they wouldn't release it, I could trust them. And I do. But I said I'd left the laptop about loads, not just at their gaff, Ben Warner's on it all the time checking his Instagram (I don't buy that now actually he's got his own laptop) - I said that people would use this diary against me, to discredit me. So they had a genius idea, and this is actually the one good thing to come out of today. They said to release this diary to the public in the next few days before anyone else does. Sounds like a shit idea but give me a sec. They said release the diary but pretend it is a spoof diary, one written by one of those shit comedians that hate me so much and does their shit jokes about me. And I said 'Perfect, let's pin it on Hislop, let's say that cunt Ian Hislop wrote this.' And they said that wouldn't work as most of the diary was me calling Ian Hislop a cunt, unless I did a re-write. And I told them I didn't have the time or the inclination for a re-write, I'm not even reading it back to check for typos. So they told me to choose another shit comedian. So I said yes I would choose that cunt that sent the tweet about me the other day, I think his name is Nathan Cassidy. And they said have you mentioned him before in the diary and I said 'I can't remember' and they said 'Fine well as long as you don't put this conversation in the diary then that should be fine' and I said 'I'm not that fucking stupid' and we had a laugh and got back down to business.

And that business is the end of the fucking world. And this is
Alexander and Evgeny's plan - carry on as if everything is normal for
the rest of today and daytime tomorrow, and then tomorrow evening
we have the first planned extraction of my and Dominic's cells by the
Russians at Downing Street. I do that as if everything is normal. I
carry on doing exactly what everyone says to make it seem like I'm
being totally compliant. 'Sounds like a shit plan so far' I said.
However, here's the clever part - in the background, Alexander and
Evgeny will make contact with Andrei Navalny and others and collate
the evidence against Cozy Bear and their plans and then we will
schedule a live Government briefing for a week's time or whatever,
and without notice I will announce to the world what they plan to do.
The added advantage to that is if Putin then immediately kills me with
some fucked up perfume or whatever, there's a very slim chance that
this cloning thing was all for real and I get to be reborn anyway. I'm
playing the odds here. So all I need to do is act normal for a few days
– that's the easy part. But then once we have the evidence I'll need to
do the press conference of my life, and save the world. God I'm
getting hard just thinking about it, imagine me on that lectern,
imagine Chris Shitty and Pat Val's faces as I announce I am the
saviour of the world, what would they do? Chris Shitty would
probably chip and say something negative, 'Well Prime Minister you
say you're saving the world but we're all going to die anyway one day.'
Well how about shut the fuck up Chris, you depressing cunt. And
maybe let's be positive, who's to say that there isn't some truth in this
cloning business, why would they be putting all this effort into the
transfusions between me and Dominic and the procedure they're
doing tomorrow if it wasn't leading to anything? Is it really just a
cover for this bigger terrifying plot? I don't know any more, but
tomorrow, I will be sure. I am Roger Barlow, and tomorrow I start to
save the fucking world.

I say tomorrow because I'm knackered tonight, Eric has just dropped
me back. I complained to him before we parted that I was coming
back again to an empty house, he is obviously aware of the troubles

I've been having with Carrie. I've known Eric for such a long time and he genuinely cares about me. Because he's just my driver and has been for years and is on minimum wage, there's none of the duplicity that I see from others. Just like Joe, my cameraman, haven't seen him in a few weeks. Simple folk with simple jobs that just want to do their job and be happy. God I wish I was them. I mean not Eric, he just sits around in a car all day waiting for me, worst job in the world. But you know what I mean. Eric looked at me as we parted just now and said 'Is everything OK Prime Minister?' And I took a moment and I said 'Is everything ever ok?' And Eric said something really quite profound, he looked me in the eye and said, 'I was just asleep waiting for you Prime Minister, and everything is always ok when you're asleep is it not? And we spend so much time worrying about people dying when all that is, is a big sleep Prime Minister, the biggest sleep of all. And we know that when we are asleep it is always ok. So why do we spend our lives worrying about something that we know will be ok?' That made me feel much, much better. I laughed to Eric and said I might have those words written on my gravestone. He laughed back through his mask and said 'that would be expensive you'd be paying by the letter'... I took a moment and replied 'I wouldn't worry about that I'd be dead'. And as I closed the door on my dear friend Eric, I realised something very special indeed... death is ok. I'm ready.

Wednesday September 30th 2020

I want to live. Fuck I hope this cloning thing is actually happening now and Evgeny and Alexander are wrong, but I fear they are right. Dominic looks like he's acting, and he's no actor. I'm an actor, I was in school plays as a kid. I was a wonderful Zeus. And these Russian doctors look like they're acting too. I just hope they are doctors because they did a fairly invasive procedure today under a local anaesthetic, taking cells from various bits of our bodies. I was just looking at them as they were doing this, wondering... what the hell are you fuckers up to? The whole thing is now surreal. I can't even remember how this whole things started – oh yes I do, I went down on Dominic Cummings. Never again. That probably started Corona virus. As I say Dominic was cold but he was responsive to what I was saying, there would be no death on the 10th of the 10th (he said he was never up for that anyway, bullshit) and we stick around to bring up little Dommers and Boris Mark II. I tried to start a conversation with him about what he would call the baby, whether he would call it Dominic and I should call it Alexander. He joked and said yes maybe we should call them Alexander and Evgeny. I laughed but he didn't. I thought that was maybe because he was under local anaesthetic and having cells ripped out of his arsehole but I genuinely don't think he found it funny, and it was his joke. I told him that Alexander has assured me that this diary thing will be sorted, and I told him about the plan to release the diary under a different name. Again, he was dismissive. 'And what makes you think it will work?' he shouted, as best he could under anaesthetic. 'Because Evgeny and Alexander said.' I replied. 'Alexander said, Alexander said – that's what you should call your bloody baby isn't it boss, Alexander Said.' I kept quiet, and only ages later I remembered he was actually making a very clever joke. Dominic's only child is called Alexander Cedd. For real. He didn't look like he was joking at the time though, he looked fucking mental with me. All very odd.

Anyway, the doctors left and there was a moment of genuine awkwardness between us, like this was the end. When it should have been the beginning. Roger Connor of GSK had shaken my hand (naughty!) and had said just that 'Thank you gentlemen. Now is the start of the next chapter'. There is a final session pencilled into the diary for next Thursday if the cells taken this week do not 'bite' (don't ask me) but it's all bullshit anyway, this isn't the start of anything, when we were left alone in Downing Street it felt very much like the end. I had big plans with Dommers, and only some of them have been achieved. I mean it was a fairly main one, exit from the European Union, but neither of us imagined it was going to be this messy. There's rumours that the EU Commission is going to take us to court now for breaking the deal I signed to withdraw from the EU. Fine, take us to court, start the fucking troubles again in Ireland, I don't give a shit any more. All I care about is that the great plan I had with Dominic is now over. You know at the start of all this, many moons ago now, Dommers for a bit of a laugh got down a picture of John Major from the Downing Street staircase here and we had a ceremonial burning. Dommers said we should burn Thatcher as well but I suggested that would be like burning an image of the prophet Mohammed, in a dress. He then relented on his threat to burn that painting. But we burnt John Major alright. We had such a laugh that afternoon, reminiscing about all the great euro-sceptics of the past and the fact that John Major fucked Edwina Curry for four years. Legend. Stone cold legend, he really does not get the credit he deserves for that Curry nobbing. Class act. That was the start of our great journey together, and this was the end. And as I said goodbye to him at the front door, I looked up at the staircase, up at the hastily commissioned replacement of the painting of John Major, and I shed a tear. What's it all been for? What is any of this all for? I say I've been a good guy but I haven't really, I've been a self-serving little cunt. When I look back at my life whether that's next week or in 3000 years' time if this Resurrection shit is real, I know I'll have regrets. I knew right then – the only thing that would save me, is if I now save the entire planet. Resolve redoubled and squared.

Anyway in two bits of better news – firstly Pat Val and Chris Shitty are getting more backlash and I'm looking more like a hero in these press conferences, I'm actually starting to enjoy them now, bit of a respite from all this end of the world shit, I treat it a bit like a stand-up comedy gig without the laughs, which is like most stand-up comedy gigs. And secondly, Alexei Navalny is primed to do his own press conference tomorrow and Alexander has instructed him not to make any mention of Sputnik V. He's confident he will stick to the plan, I'm not so sure but Alexander has told him that if he doesn't there will be another load of Novichok heading his way. So we should be ok. I noticed on the BBC website today that they'd put up a video giving advice about if you're ever attacked with Novichok. They said things like 'wash your clothes' and 'wash your mobile phone'. Fuck me BBC, great advice. 'Carrie, I think Putin has finally got me, he's fucking Novichok'd me, I'm dying'. 'Don't worry Boris, strip off!' 'Yeah great now I'm dying on the floor and I'm in the fucking nude, pass me my phone I need to call the police.' 'Sorry Boris your phone is in the wash.' Piss take.

Thursday October 1ˢᵗ 2020

Alexei stuck to the plan which is great. Although he blamed Putin for poisoning him, he didn't mention Sputnik V. Putin's a right little tinker isn't he though – his spokesperson saying 'there is no evidence that Mr Navalny had been poisoned with a nerve agent.' Yeah mate apart from multiple doctors. I'm all for lying but when you get caught out you fess up don't you, I mean I don't but one generally does. Even my father did today, back from another jaunt to Greece and caught in a shop without a mask by some busy-body prick with a smart phone (which is everyone right?). Anyway father tells the press that these multiple visits are essential to 'Covid-proof' his holiday villa - ha ha ha! What a cunt! He's earning two and a half grand a week renting that gaff out and he does nothing to Covid-proof that place and the only time he actually cleans it is when he's banged some Grecian hooker on the marble floor – ouch! BUT – credit where credit is due, when he was caught without the mask he said that he wasn't '100% up to speed' on the new rules having been away for 3 weeks. I've just texted him and reminded him that masks in shops had been compulsory since 24ᵗʰ July and he texted back 'cock sucker'. No, no, he doesn't know about me and Dominic. No, surely not. I couldn't look my father in the eye any more if he knew that. Not that I see him ever, he's always in Greece, Covid-proofing his fucking bank balance and tan. Anyway, fuck my father, as I say, Alexei is on board so we are on track with this now.

And I've just come back from a meeting at Evgeny's office in Mayfair with him and his father, planning our strategy. D-Day is next Friday the 9ᵗʰ October when I will announce to the world what Putin's plan is. Alexander and Evgeny are to collate the evidence and I will have a run through of my speech with them next Thursday before announcing Vlad's horrific plan to the world the following day, live on BBC1. I said to Alexander, 'are you sure this won't unleash World War 3?' and he said, calm as fuck, 'Prime Minister, you are preventing

World War 3.' I trust him, I like him. Maybe after all this is through I might move to Russia, or at least move to Mayfair and get a lovely office like they've got. I'd get the same statue, remember the one, Fuck-face, a child with a penis for a nose. On the way out today, Evgeny showed me a few more things. Fuck-face is a Chapman Brothers work of art. Not only does the toddler have a penis for a nose but it also has an anus for a mouth. Great stuff, I hadn't noticed that, I was just looking at the boy's cock. (ha! Looking back there was a warning of things to cum). Anyway, he also has hanging in the hallway a suite of portrait paintings by the same artists – deformed aristocratic portraits from the 18th and 19th centuries – and it's called 'One Day You Will No Longer Be Loved.' God that hit me hard. I've spent my whole life on a desperate quest to be loved, and I fear that I've failed. I think only Eric my driver really loves me, and that's only because he's got PTSD and I pay him to be nice.

Evgeny then gave me a book from the Chapman Brothers, and it's called 'Bedtime Tales for Sleepless Nights'. One the very first page is the following…

Sticks and stones
Shall break thy bones
And words will
Surely hurt you
Eyeball and teeth
Shall be wrenched by grief
As nightmare comes
To shroud you.

God that really, really terrified me. Will I save the world? Or will my eyeball and teeth be wrenched by grief? Will the nightmare of all my past wrongs come to shroud me in my final moments on this Earth? Not a pretty thought. I couldn't even masturbate tonight.

RESUЯЯECTION

Friday October 2nd 2020

I was going to write about something else but fuck me I love the news, there's always something to take your mind off the end of the world isn't there? Trump has Covid. One more time for the cheap seats – Donald Trump has Covid. Well fuck a doodle doo. Who saw this plot twist coming? The big guy has the big C. Not that big C. He has the small c, he has the small c-19. Apparently. I texted him and said 'Sorry Don about catching the Rona, I hope you're up again quicker than that fucking wall!' And he texted back, 'wink-wink'. What does that mean? Is he making it up to win votes? Let me tell you, that won't work my friend. When I had it most people wanted me dead, such awful people in the world. People have a go at politicians for being awful people and when I got Covid millions wanted me dead. I don't want anyone to die. Apart from Hislop and the odd asylum seeker. Well I mean my goodness, I hope he's ok. And if he's making it all up, well good luck to the silly fucker. I saw him on the telly tonight in a suit looking quite healthy so maybe it is bullshit. But as I say, can't for the life of me work out why he'd make that up. People are dumb, and they're not gonna vote for you if they think you're gonna croak it. Although the other guy is 77 isn't he? It's like choosing between mouldy bread and rotting fruit, both will be fucking useless.

Anyway, that was a bit of levity to raise the mood today. I had a heart to heart with Carrie, she popped by number 10 with little Wilfred. Not so little any more, my goodness he's grown since I last saw him. Can't believe he's 5 months already, time flies when you only see someone once every few weeks. He looked a bit like my grandad Wilfred (who he was named after of course), always sucking on a pipe. My child wasn't sucking on a pipe, my grandad was. I mean my child was sucking on a dummy. I wouldn't let my child suck on a pipe. But you know, I also wouldn't stop him if he wanted to, let me be clear, he can do what he likes, he's his own man. God he's got my hair already, the crazy little shit. I hope he's alright. I fucked this one up too haven't I? Carrie just looked at me like one of my disappointed teachers and said 'The trouble with you Boris is you just can't stop getting your dick wet'. And she's right. I mean I just don't know what's wrong with me – it's not even that good any more, I can do it just as well myself most of the time, better more often than not. I know what I like, and not many of these young birds know what they're doing. It's a power thing obviously I get off on, and I hate myself for saying that. I should have controlled myself but I couldn't, it's so hard. I'm so powerful and women throw themselves at me. As I think dear old Chris Rock once said 'You're as faithful as your opportunities'. Now there was a comedian who spoke the truth, funny fucker as well. But I should have been stronger, I should have been better. I'll do better in the next life, if Boris Mark II shows any signs of going the same way as me I'll tell him I'll chop his dick off. Why am I even thinking about chopping my hypothetical child clone's dick off? It isn't happening is it? I don't know, I still really hope something comes out of the fire and it is. I want a second chance, if there's one person that needs a second chance it's me.

The ultimate question is, will everyone like me even if I save the world? Even that won't please some people. Literally, I'll save the world and some cunt from Uttoxeter will say, "I hate Boris Johnson, I was actually looking forward to dying.' Well kill yourself then pal, I've done my best here. Without me you'd all be dead. Putin isn't saving you is he you useless piece of shit. I mean who knows, he might save me. At least I have an O-level. I certainly wouldn't be taking Sputnik V, I'm not that stupid. I don't think many people are that stupid. Even Americans. Hang on, that's why Trump is pretending to have Corona isn't it – to convince the sceptical Americans to take Sputnik V. Oh fuck it all makes sense now. First Ben Warner and his Deep Fake, and now this. All over the world, Putin's fingers are working his puppets to take this bloody death potion, they all know, they're all in this, everyone is in this apart from me. I invited Ben Warner back to Downing Street tonight, I mean look, I've known him and his brother for years, they are generally good eggs and I just looked him in the eye over a beer tonight and said 'Man to man Ben, did you Deep Fake me?' I think he was going to lie but as I say, when you've been found out by an expert (in bullshitting) you've been found out. He said he was just looking after me, I'd been out for longer than he thought just barking like a dog and screaming the word 'elephants' over and over again and they needed me to put a speech out to get this vaccine out there. They've got to Ben as well. It's not his fault - he's young, he's a good kid. When I sack them next week along with most of my Cabinet I think I'll replace them all with ethnic minorities. I will you know. It's Black History Month this week. Yeah, right, I'm a good guy who understands black issues, in October.

Did you see my speech I stuck out on socials? It was very good. I was looking very presidential and talking about how black people have played an important part in our history and we don't ever thank them enough. I talked about a black guy throwing bombs back over the enemy lines in the first World War and then being a fire-fighter in the second World War, I talked passionately about the first black head teacher in this country and the abuse she got, and I talked about a nurse of the year last year, I forget her name, that did such sterling work to bring this nation back to health apart from the thousands who died. I announced I'd established a Commission on Race and Ethic Disparities 'to establish where inequality lies within our society and correct it.' Good right? And you know what's coming next? You got it! ... Ha ha ha, that was Deep Fake as well. Of course that wasn't me. I said to Ben, 'look you're damn good, how can I have a go at someone who is a fucking genius?' And we had a laugh and watched *Graham Norton* and then he left. But I will sack him, and I will replace him with an ethic minority. They're much cheaper.

Saturday October 3rd 2020

So, the Conservative Party Conference today. Online of course. First time I've masturbated during an opening speech! Well second time actually but that's for the next book! Dom Raab kicked it off, the duplicitous little cunt. I'm going to really enjoy this conference actually, as I no longer have to sit there pretending that I like any of these back-stabbing little shits. I can just sit at home with a beer and remember why I hate all of these conniving cunts. Raab is definitely in with Putin, we've never got on. When he said in his speech today that he considered me a friend I nearly choked on my Yorkie. I've made better friends with one-night stand prostitutes, and they didn't fuck me half as well as you have Dom. And then Gove came on and tried the same trick, I got Ben to take down the feed for a bit it was literally making me sick. I'm thinking of doing a spread-bet on who has shafted me the most. But you know what, the ones that are the true villains won't appear on this Conference Zoom shite this weekend, the real sneaky fucks get nowhere near the camera, and I talk of course of Mr Cummings and Mr Sedwill. I could easily forget if I didn't have such a brilliant mind, this whole thing started with Mark Sedwill, or should I say Baron Sedwill of Sherborne in the County of Dorset. How the fuck did that happen actually? Why do the people I hate the most get given the biggest honours? And it all comes back to Dommers.

Sedwill was at the house that day I went over to surprise Dominic - what were they doing? What were they cooking up? It is Sedwill that first mooted the idea that Putin thought I was a cunt, maybe there was no truth in that whatsoever. If the Lebedevs are correct, this whole thing has been a ruse to throw me, manipulate me, and knock me out for days so they can get a Deep Fake of me to announce that this vaccine should be taken by the world. It all started with Sedwill, I remember now, he was the one that started all this – Cozy Bear, everything. And I've never been able to get the way he said goodbye to me out of my head, remember? He talked to me with genuine affection, something I've only seen before from Dylin, and he's a dog. And he hugged me like Dyl, and nuzzled into my neck. And that nuzzle is now a niggle, that I need to scratch. He knows everything I think, and so tomorrow I shall surprise him. I'm off to Dorset. Sounds like an Enid Blyton novel, but it's anything but my friends - I'm going cunt hunting.

Sunday October 4th 2020

Mark Sedwill has a lovely little dimple on his chin. You don't see that very often any more, and it's a kind of trick of the mind isn't it? Because you think someone with a dimple on their chin, or on their cheeks, you think they can't be a cunt, but oh my God they can be. He opened the door and I was clearly the last person he expected to see. He had a significant tan but it suddenly turned white. 'Oh fuck' he said, 'what are you doing here?' 'I think you know why I'm here,' I said confidently, masking the fact I had no idea why I was there. 'Come in' he said nervously. I waved to dear old Eric sitting outside and in I went. After a little bit of small talk about how he hadn't tweeted for a month (he has apparently been 'too busy'… yeah right, with that tan) I cut to the chase.

'I know what's going on'. I went full bullshit. I can do this, I've trained for this moment. Sedwill will not believe I've travelled all the way to Dorset if I didn't know exactly what was going on. 'The game's up Mark,' I said, doubling down instantly, 'I know everything.' He took a moment, and poured himself a Scotch. His hands were shaking. 'Want a drink?' 'No thank you,' I lied. 'Is your wife around?' I asked, I really fancy his wife. 'What do you know Boris?' I smiled ruefully. 'What do you think I know?' This was going absolutely nowhere. I had to take a risk. 'Let's talk about Cozy Bear shall we?,' I said, instantly getting his full attention. 'You told me once that this was nothing more than a Russian Bullingdon Club, KGB and what have you popping their dicks into dead Breitovo pig's heads.' That's a Russian pig, I'd done my research, 'But it's far more than that isn't it Mark?'. I'll now just type out the exact conversation, from my recording of course, as this my friends, is everything.

'Why did you first tell me that Putin thought I was a cunt Mark?'
(that's me saying that)
'Erm, do you want the truth…?'
'Why do you think I've driven to Dorset today?'
'Didn't Eric drive?'
'Yes, of course.'
'How is he?'
'He's fine, a little depressed of course but that's…'

Oh God, this isn't working, there is too much chaff in this recording. He then went for a piss actually, but I reckon there was no urine he was just trying to calm himself. He was panting like a Covid-positive prozzy. 'The truth is Prime Minister that I wanted to warn you, I wanted to warn you of the Russian threat without I guess telling you the whole story, I figured that if I at least told you that Putin thought you were a cunt and there was a death threat against you then you would take more notice of Russia.' 'What?' I exclaimed, 'there was no death threat against me from Russia?' 'No Prime Minister, that was a lie and I'm sorry.' I shook my head, incredulous, totally discombobulated. 'Weeks I was shitting myself, weeks, actually shitting myself Mark, what the fuck?' 'I know Prime Minister, but I can assure you I did it with the very best intentions.' 'But why Mark, why would you do that to me?' He took another moment, but was suddenly calmer, more confident, more steely. 'Well Prime Minister, if you indeed know everything then you know why I couldn't tell you everything, I couldn't tell you the truth, I was in too deep.' Fuck, I suddenly remembered I knew nothing, or everything, I didn't know what I knew. I thought back to how Sedwill said goodbye to me that day at Number 10, I thought I'd go there next.

'Look Mark,' I said, 'I remember the very affectionate way you said goodbye to me a few weeks back. I thought if I'm honest that you were going to kiss me...' He took a moment and looked up at me and smiled, his tan now glistening as the afternoon sun pierced through the expensive, white wooden shutter-blinds, 'I guess I wanted to Prime Minister.' That made me feel good. I collected myself, this wasn't the time to start another homosexual relationship with someone that was trying to shaft me. 'Look Mark, you told me I was invincible, you said that whether or not I live on or not then my legacy certainly will'. 'Well remembered,' he chuckled. 'Well yes, I record every conversation I have Mark, I've been doing that for months.' 'Yes, and of course your diary.' He froze. 'Diary?' How do you know about my diary?' And that's when Dominic walked into the room.

So calm, so fucking calm. Like butter wouldn't melt. Full on psychopath. 'Enough' he said, 'enough'. 'The game's up,' he said. I was the one shaking now, but I quickly attempted to gather my shit. 'I said that to Sedwill, traitor Sedwill.' 'I'm not a traitor', protested Mark. Dommers told him to shut up, so aggressively. He was so scary. 'What do you know boss, what do you actually know?' 'Well glad you're still calling me boss,' I spat. He took a moment. 'I wasn't talking to you, you little cunt.' Yep, I've checked the recording back and that's what Dominic Cummins said to me, he called me a cunt. A little cunt. Just what I'd been told Putin thought I was, the whole thing was a lie, everything that man has ever said to me is a lie, every time he told me he loved me, every time his erect bullet-like squat, angry penis exploded in my mouth and he grabbed the back of my head and shouted 'Dominic wins' he was telling the truth. That was the truth, that was all that he wanted. If only that was the case, because he wanted my blood as well. And that's what he went for again. 'You've never been the boss to me!' he whispered, menacingly – I had to turn up the volume on the recording for this bit, it was so quiet, like a snake hissing after eating a rat. 'I've always been the boss, this whole charade is over Boris, me telling you what to do, and what to say, every moment of every day, it's tiring. It's tiring for me and I know it's tiring for you. You're out of your depth Boris, you know that. Time's up, the game is up.'

He looked like he was on the brink of telling me everything, so now I kind of regret what happened next, there are still a few doubts in my mind as to what is happening. But I guess this was no time for subtlety - I ran towards him, like I was a prop forward running towards one of those big rubber pads for tackle practice. And I floored the fucker, my fists flailing wildly into him. 'Not the face, not the face!' he screamed, like a little twat. 'Stop it!' screamed Sedwill, trying half-heartedly to pull me off (not like that). Well, what happened next I'm not proud of, but Eric was walking past the window on one of his little walks and he saw what was happening, so I guess using all of his SAS training combined with his depression and anxiety he launched a brick through the window and drop-kicked that cunt Dominic Cummings into the fireplace. Fuck, it felt so fucking good. He ended up in the fucking fire-place. Isn't that what happened to the wolf in Little Red Riding Hood, or maybe he got killed by an axe. In any case, fuck, I knew Eric had this in him but he went full beast mode, it was all over so quickly. The shattered glass still falling on to the floor, like perfect raindrops, falling like crystals to the earth.

'The game really is up' I said, like a fucking hero, as I was dragged backwards by Eric to the door. He flung the door open and was getting me out of there as quick as possible, but when we hit the outside I assured him I was ok, and we took a moment. And then I did something that if this ever gets made into a film, I want in the trailer. I took a few steps back to the doorway, Sedwill still shaking uncontrollably inside, Cummings laying contorted in the fire-place and I just said the immortal line, 'I'm the boss.' Yeah. Yes! That is my 'I'll be back' moment alright. I'm the boss, I'm the fucking boss. Always have been always will be. I'm back home now, the boss is back, and the boss is back to save the fucking world.

Monday October 5ᵗʰ 2020

I used the cover of watching the virtual Conference together to call my charges one by one to Downing Street today to say goodbye. It's my Conference speech tomorrow and then dress rehearsal Wednesday, and then Thursday I blow this mother-fucker of a plot to kill the world to smithereens. First up was Michael Gove. After a bit of small talk I told him that big things were going to happen this week, and if anything went wrong I'd want him to step up and become Prime Minister. He looked quite worried about me - he's a lovely guy at heart is Michael, and it's a quality that hardly anyone sees because he's never, ever shown anyone that quality. I just get a sense that it's there somewhere, a sixth sense. And like *The Sixth Sense*, as I've said before, maybe it will turn out at the end of this that I'm dead (which is the twist of that film, Bruce Willis was dead all along). He said 'why me Prime Minister?' And I was honest with him, I said that if something happened to me, someone would need to step into the breach, someone who spends every waking hour dreaming of being leader, someone who wouldn't be thrown by the challenge. He took that as a compliment. I said he'd be a wonderful leader of this Conservative Party, and a great temporary Prime Minister, until the country or the Party voted and he'd be swiftly ejected as he's about as popular and charismatic as cancer. I didn't say the last bit of course, these meetings were about being nice, about saying goodbye. I was even nice to dear old Priti, who when I suggested something bad might happen to me this week seemed to be elsewhere, and when I asked her what she was thinking she just said 'I was actually thinking whether the Loch Ness Monster exists'. She's a funny one that Priti, and I think genuinely retarded.

Dear old Oliver Dowden then cheered me up, bouncing in with his boundless energy and optimism, thinking I might have some good news for him for his portfolio of Culture and Sport. I told him what he knew already - 'if it was up to me I'd have all the pubs open 24/7 and all I'd do is sit there getting pissed and watching the cricket.' 'Well why don't we do that Prime Minister?' he pleaded. I love his naivety, it's so childlike, and I had to sadly pierce that bubble of positivity with truth like a parent shouting at her child that Father Christmas does not exist whilst simultaneously setting fire to all her presents. 'Oliver,' I said, 'you know how this works by now surely, I am just a figure-head, a puppet, we all are. We can't actually do what we want to do, we do what we are told to do.' He sensed I was talking about Cummings. 'But why do we do that Prime Minister?! We are the ones the public voted for, why don't we make the decisions?' 'Oh dear Oliver,' I smiled, 'It's that simplicity that the public love, it's that disregard to all the evidence that the public buy into, because they, like us, are essentially stupid. Don't take this the wrong way Olly, but all us politicians are the same at heart, we are in it for the glory, for the applause, for the theatre, we aren't in it for the hard work. That's why I relate to so much of what you've been asking for – more money for the Arts, more money for the Theatre, for actors. Because of course I myself am an actor, we politicians are all actors. And that is why I know that actors and comedians and the like are essentially useless, just like you and me, and the useless need to be told what to say and where to stand.' 'Comedians and some actors write their own material I think Prime Minister,' he countered. 'Indeed so,' I mused, 'but it does not mean that they are not, at their core, just useless cunts.' The truth is we need an army of people telling us what to do, and then we need the population to agree (in the main), we can do nothing in isolation and with that knowledge are hands are essentially tied, bound together by the strings worked by our puppet-master, which is the entire useless world, a world full of cunts. Olly looked down-hearted, like I'd set fire to his presents. 'But not all of us are useless Prime Minister, what about…'. He struggled to find the words. '…Sir Ian Botham.' I took a moment. 'Well there's always an exception young Oliver, there's always one hero.' Oliver took a big pause, a big sip of his Cherry Coke, 'I thought you were that hero,' he whimpered. I nodded sagely, 'well, old friend, you never know'. And with that he was gone.

Next up was Rishi who admitted he had been listening in to my conversation with Oliver. 'I agree' he said, ' we should say that all artists need to retrain'. He was just trying to do the right thing but he'd got the wrong end of the stick completely. I am just saying the way it is, the way life works, but it doesn't mean you shouldn't try, you shouldn't fight back, you shouldn't be the one standing up and being counted, winning those Ashes, saving the world. Rishi has far too much money to understand struggle of course, and to my knowledge he hasn't really fucked or taken drugs. You can't be a good leader if you haven't fucked or taken drugs, I think it was dear old Bill Clinton who told me that. But I had bigger battles to fight, so I said for him to do what he wishes, but I warned him that it would make him unpopular. 'We're not in this business to be popular,' he said, as if he actually meant it. 'Then why are you in this business?' I asked. He took several moments, 'do you know what Prime Minister, I'm not really sure.' Beautiful.

I had called Ian Botham to be next but he said he 'couldn't be fucked' (legend), Gavin Williamson also turned me down, I think Cummings has got to him too, telling him I was lining him up to be my shield if the Russians started shooting. If he had turned up I would have told him I'm sorry. I defy any general to go down without at least thinking about killing his own men instead of him first, it's what any great leader would have done. No regrets.

And then finally I summoned Ben Warner to my office, and this is the one I really enjoyed. I called his bluff. I told him that he had been duplicitous, he had been a scoundrel, and I knew exactly what he was up to. But keep your enemies closer right, so I set him a challenge. 'I believe that your sole focus young Benjamin over the last few weeks has not been on the social media strategy for Corona, it has not been about Facebook, or Twitter, or convincing the morons of this world to take the vaccine, I believe your sole purpose has been to Deep Fake me, to make it appear like it's me when it's not me.' He looked terrified the little lamb. 'Why do you say that Prime Minister?' Ah, de-dums. 'Because it's true Ben, isn't it?' He nodded, I had won. 'And I'll tell you why I know Benjy, because that speech was fucking incredible, that actually is one of the finest pieces of work anyone has ever done for me, or against me, you know what I mean.' He didn't know what I meant, he was utterly confused. But I was utterly clear. 'Whatever your motives Benjy, you have succeeded where I'd say almost all others have failed – everything this Government has tried it has essentially gone straight down the fucking toilet, but you are proof that if you throw enough shit rolled up in £50 notes, eventually some of it will stick. And this is a remarkable piece of work.' 'Thank you,' he said. I do look at him like a son, he may be part of Dommers' plot to get rid of me, he might be trying his best to kill me, but he's still my son. So I set him some homework. 'So Benjy, with that in mind, let's test this technology one more time shall we, I shan't be doing my Conference speech tomorrow...'. His eyebrows lifted. 'You will... you will make it look like it is me, but I shall be in my bed, masturbating.' He took a moment, and then smiled, 'Ok...'. And with that simple word 'ok' he knew he had in me an equal, a foe not to be fucked with, a foe that whilst he may be about to be killed, knows exactly who the killers will be and is still getting them to work all through the night because he's still the boss and they are all still just little vermin back-stabbing little cunts. All in all, a great day.

Tuesday October 6th 2020

God this week feels so huge now. Yes it may go to plan and yes I may indeed save the world but I'm not an idiot, I know these forces are powerful and against me and I realise the worst can happen. All it will take is one Russian bullet, one nutter outside Downing Street, one Novichok-laced pasty from Greggs at Heathrow. And if the worst does happen this week, my God I'm going to miss all this. I'm going to miss Dame P, Dame Politics. Despite what you might think of me, I'm essentially a nice guy, with a cracking sense of humour. Like that video before my virtual conference speech today, I did all that, so funny. We went into a chemist in Uxbridge and they said they'd been busier than ever and I said 'That's great news'. That would have got a good laugh at a normal Conference. Yeah we are in a global pandemic and the chemist is busier than ever! Ha ha! 'Yeah you say the country is struggling but the funeral directors, mortuaries and sales of coffins and shovels have never been better!' I did all that, wrote it all and filmed it with Joe when I was back in shitty Uxbridge a few weeks ago. I like watching myself, I'm a natural comedian, like a young Charlie Chaplin. I'm unlike most artists, I'm a natural. I don't have to think about it, I just entertain, I'm just good. And that's where dear old Rishi got it in the neck unfairly yesterday, when he simply said that struggling artists should look to retrain. And artists throughout the country started to bleat and protest 'oh The Beatles were once struggling artists' etc – oh Jesus for fuck's sake you know what Rishi was trying to say but couldn't say – when he said 'struggling' he was talking of course about the 'shit' artists, the ones with no hope, the talentless pricks clogging up most pubs, clubs, shopping centres, comedy clubs in the country. These no-hope, good for nothing talentless pricks who because they believe they are 'artists' then that's an excuse not to pick up a shovel and dig a fucking grave once in a while. Oh no, they'd prefer to do a play next to the grave or juggle the fucking ashes. Jesus. No one looked at The Beatles just before they became successful and said 'well they're shit'. We are talking about all the artists that everyone can see are shit and going nowhere, it is these people that should give up and retrain as wind-farm engineers, and I don't think any artist can argue with that. Or they might do but in the form of a musical at the Edinburgh Fringe in eight years' time where 32 people over the course of 28 nights will collectively sigh and applaud at the end because they have to instead of saying the truth which is 'you're doing this a protest against the problem but YOU are the fucking problem mate you over-privileged, entitled, talentless little gob-shites.'

Anyway, talking about great performers, I was of course interested to see what Ben Warner had come up with for my virtual Conference speech today at such short notice, and I have to say I begrudgingly accept that it did look and sound a lot like me. I mean I would have been much better, he didn't quite capture the twinkle in my eye but it is really fucking scary what Deep Fake can achieve. If I live another day after this week (and you'll know if I do dear reader based on how close this is to the end of the book – hopefully we are nowhere near the end) but I will surely utilise this terrific and terrifically scary technology to my advantage. I'd never have to do a boring old speech again. All I'd have to do is employ a lookalike to make the odd trip to Uxbridge to make people think I care and I could stay in bed all day watching the cricket and masturbating over what a good job I'm doing. I could masturbate while doing a 'live' speech to the nation. And that is exactly what I did today, after I got over some of the shit bits about what Ben had done. I mean first up he's made my hair look dreadful. I mean it's shit but it's not that shit. And the jokes weren't my kind of quality - saying I was too fat and that I had to 'search for the hero inside myself' hoping that that hero is considerably slimmer than myself. My comedy doesn't punch down, at fatties. I quite enjoyed... 'Touching elbows like a giant national version of the birdie dance'. That could have been a Cummings line, totally disregarding the tragedy of 50,000 people dying for a cheap gag about a dance that everyone left alive has now forgotten. And when I started to talk about Global warming and saving the planet it got a bit embarrassing... 'As the Saudi Arabia is to oil, the United Kingdom is to wind. We will build windmills that float on the sea, we will harvest the gusts.' Jesus help us, 'harvest the gusts'. So embarrassing. Although he got me saying that 'People can retrain to be a wind turbine repair man!' Ha ha, can you imagine all the 'struggling artists' listening to that – 'Nooooo Boris, noooooo! Don't make me take off these white gloves and my stage make-up and ask me to do anything fucking useful for once in my wasted fucking life.'

Anyway, all told, not too bad. I enjoyed it by the end, as I didn't write or deliver one word of that I thought I did pretty fucking well. I then checked back on the comments on 'my speech'. So depressing. Was about ten people commenting. Ten. One prick talking about how he can solve Global warming using fart gas from his own arsehole. One guy over and over again saying 'LET US BACK IN THE GROUNDS', yes in capital letters. That's all this jack-ass cares about. There was 'me' talking about building Britain back better, solving Global warming and what have you, and all the scum care about is farting and watching their fucking football team again. And that's why ultimately the heroes like me will never win. I stand by that actually, that would be the one thing about Putin's plan coming to fruition, that we'd get rid of the scum, the feckless, the stupid that have become a scourge on our society and a drain on the world's depleted resources, which thinking about it is the very reason that Putin is doing this, so, I don't know, looking at it another way what he's doing isn't so bad and does have good justification, but we can't just stand by and watch 99% of the planet be killed, can we? I mean I for one do not want to clear up the mess. So unless those struggling artists all buy shovels I'm going to stay on my path to save the planet like the Superman I am.

If only Carrie thought I was Superman. I'm not am I, I'm Lex Luthor, killing my inner Superman with the kryptonite that has always been my cock. I talked with her this evening. And I apologised for everything, and in front of her deleted Olga D's number from my phone (a symbolic gesture I have it written down in multiple places including my fuck-log, I haven't mentioned that, future book I guess…). Anyway, I told Carrie that something strange has happened over the last few weeks, I was told that it would happen one day and when it happens, it would rescue me. And I truly believe it has happened. I've lost my sexual appetite. Since Dommers last sprayed in my mouth I've lost the taste for it, I really have, and I feel suddenly free, free from the burden of my heavy balls and tingling cock that I could never control. My friends, the long walk to freedom from my own genitals is over.

RESUЯЯECTION

Wednesday October 7ᵗʰ 2020

I was checking the comments under 'my speech' where they had posted it on Facebook this morning just before PMQs, mostly scum repeating 'reopen the football grounds'. But there was one that caught my eye, replying to someone who said 'Sack Cummings'. 'Mr Brightside @imnotwealthy' counters… 'You know nothing about Cummings. He's just a side show. A distraction. A pantomime villain.' Yep, we all see why you're not @wealthy Mr Brightside, because you think that 'pantomime villains' exist at the height of Government. I'm sorry to tell you sir, but the only people that operate at the height of Government are real villains, very real villains indeed. Yes of course there are people working for the good, working for the betterment of the world, people like myself and to a certain extent Donald Trump, but then there of course the most awful people in the universe, people driven by a megalomaniacal brain to get money and power for themselves because they know they only have one life. That would have been the great benefit of Resurrection I guess, all these people, all these rotters, would have calmed the fuck down a bit. When you get to your late 30's, early 40's, you do start to realise that this one life is so very short indeed, and that knowledge in the wrong hands and in the wrong brains leads to the kind of psychopath like Putin or Cummings that will trample over their grandma, and worst still their dearest, most loyal friend to rise to the top. I'm upsetting myself now. All I wanted was to be loved, to be a friend. And now the hunted becomes the hunter, now is the time to kill Cummings. He always was number one on my hit list. Cummings, Sedwill, Putin, Hislop, they all die now. Apart from Hislop, shame. How could I implicate Hislop in my speech? Seriously, worth a thought. And that's what I've just finished doing, finalising my speech with Evgeny and Alexander.

We watched some fucked up videos round his Mayfair Office, just like the old days, the lads, jacked-up club. Alexander went to bed and it was just me and Evgeny. Reminded me of the time we watched the sun going down over Lake Como, before a couple of sorts went down on us. Great days, and they will return I'm sure of that now.

The evidence they have prepared is terrifying, and on Thursday I shall present this to the country. At 6pm we have scheduled a daily Conference but there will be no Pat Val, no Chris Shitty (well praise the Lord and hallelujah), instead I will go into the BBC and lay out to the nation and indeed to the world on the BBC 6 o'clock news the trail of evidence pointing to a Russian plot to kill almost the entire world. I have to hand it to the Lebedev's, they really have created the most wonderfully detailed package and condensed it all into a very simple PowerPoint Presentation and we will arrive in good time and they will arrange to get this locked and loaded and present this to the world. It's completely mind-blowing. I practiced my speech today and I really am quite humbled, I'm saving the Earth, just like dear old Roger Barlow I am saving planet Earth. And unlike David Attenborough who just sits around describing how the Earth is ending I'm getting up off my arse and doing something about it. And it all has the added bonus of moving Oxford back up to the number one in finding the real vaccine, of course it does, my friends it was always going to be Oxford University to find the cure for this, not some Russian criminals with pasts as dodgy as their cuisine and accents.

I really bonded with the chaps tonight, particularly Evgeny. Alexander was making sure I had everything right, constantly going over and over this speech, he was recording it and kept playing it back, checking, very, very thorough. Evgeny was more playful, and when his dad went for a well-earned rest Evgeny and I had a right old laugh like those lads in the hotel room before 9/11, and then quite a wonderful deep and meaningful… 'Why can't we all live as one Prime Minister?', he mused. 'Well there's a big question to ask someone who is coked up to his backside and just watched a fox being torn to pieces.' My reply to him was philosophical, I can't remember exactly what I said (I've stopped recording everything), I just mentioned something about 'foreign scum') but here's what I really think. And I'm very sorry to say this but I think a common theme of this book is the unquestionable recognition that people are stupid. And we have to recognise this if I am indeed to save you all and give you a second chance at life. You need to use this life now, and not just laze around watching *Love Island* and masturbating. I mean yes I love that too, but as you have got through all these words to this point, you have finally proved that you can achieve something, you can commit to something and deliver, even if that's just reading more than a fucking tweet and pretending you have achieved anything today . When Rishi talked of retraining, talked of not every job could be saved, let's be honest just for a second here. This is a great country but there are millions of fuck-wits inside her. When I save you tomorrow, recognise this is a second chance. Stop wasting this one life that you have. Stop moaning, stop having a go at me, and most importantly - stop watching *Have I Got News For You* - stop being a moron.

Love more and fuck less. I've told Carrie this evening that I am 100% committed to her forever. I've told her this just because I still may well die tomorrow, so I want to go out looking good. But if I survive, then I'm going to redouble my efforts to stay with her. (remember my trick from earlier on in the diary – redoubling nothing is nothing). Genius. Cummings may be a cunt who has nearly destroyed the world but my goodness it's not just his penis that has rubbed off on me, it's his bullshit skills as well. But I will be a changed man, I promised her that and I shall promise you the same dear reader. I am utterly fired up for this new dawn. When I save the world tomorrow it will be like a million ejaculations, it will be like the world ejaculating into my mouth, and I can't think of any better feeling. I wasn't going to mention this but if the truth be told I have just made love to my wife, and she has forgiven me. She forgave me so easily, she actually said she'd like to try for another baby. And you know what, I said 'why not.' If Boris cannot live on forever, then at least another 100 years through a fresh one I've just planted the seed for tonight. Olga D has just texted and I did not reply. Ok full transparency I've actually just replied, but I said I couldn't talk to her, I have a big day tomorrow. The biggest day. My defining moment. For Churchill the Second World War, for Thatcher - the Falklands, for David Cameron, the pig fuck, for John Major, the Edwina Curry nobbing and for Gordon Brown, who fucking knows, that argument with that silly old bag. But for me, the defining moment, of all of our lives comes tomorrow. I shall close my eyes and pray tonight, God, or at least Boris, help us all.

Thursday October 8th 2020

I'm shitting myself, and things aren't quite going to plan. I woke up early of course, hardly slept. I slept in the same bed as my wife for the first time in ages and I forgot how much she farts. Fucking disgusting. You don't get that from any man. Anyway, get this, Dominic has let himself in and gone upstairs with all those Russian doctors, as if the plan hasn't changed. Un-be-fucking-lievable. You have to admire the balls of the man (you don't - they look, smell and taste fucking awful). He just looked me straight in the eye and said 'it hadn't worked, and more cell extractions would be necessary.' What the fuck right?! Roger Connor was there again, all the doctors and nurses, all acting like nothing is happening, like I don't know what's going on. 'You don't know what's going on,' said Dommers. I just shook my head and let him carry on. I do know what's going on, and in a few hours I will be heading to the BBC for my speech. I have told Carrie to take young Wilfred out to the country for a few days, but to watch my speech tonight. I'm so glad we had last night, when I ejaculated inside her it was like falling in love all over again. As I came I think I screamed 'I'm so sorry' and I am. They say that's the only moment a man sees or speaks the truth, as he is cumming, I kind of know what they mean.

This really is quite unbelievable you know, Dommers and now fucking Sedwill are here, wandering about like they own the gaff. I know right, Sedwill! He hasn't even got a fucking job any more. I whispered to him 'Rishi has told you to retrain you cunt.' He looked ashamed. Of course there's nothing I can say to them out loud in front of the staff, it will blow my whole plan, but they are simply impervious to shame, still going about like they are in charge. Dommers telling everyone at a meeting this morning that next week will see more lockdown, more restrictions, and very soon the country will be fully locked down and primed to take the vaccine. He's not even trying to hide any more. 'Hide in plain sight' – that's what he always told me. And here he is, hiding, the devil amongst us, hiding by striding around Downing Street barking instructions, telling everyone what to do. Well he can't tell me what to do, I'm off to the BBC with Evgeny and Alexander and the Russians that I can trust, no time for this diary. All that remains for me to say is – wish me luck. The next time I write words here, it will be done. And I will either have saved the world, or ended mine. As dear old Vinnie Jones once said, it's been emotional.

OK, it's still not going quite to plan. I'm here at the BBC hiding in a toilet with my laptop. Evgeny and Alexander and the Russians have been talking with the BBC execs and I have been left to my own devices somewhat, it's 4pm and we are only 2 hours from D-day and it all seems a bit eerie and surreal here, sitting in this cubicle, hiding. Why am I hiding? Well, funny story and totally unrelated to what's going on, and a little bit fucked up but… you'll never guess who I bumped into twenty minutes ago… Paul Merton. He was just in the canteen here, and we exchanged a few pleasantries and banter (he's a bit of a grumpy cunt truth be told) and I asked him what he was doing and he said 'we're filming *Have I Got News For You* here tonight and they're just rehearsing in the next studio.' Oh my God right. So you can imagine my first instinct, 'is Hislop there?' And Paul said, 'yeah, of course.' You only get one chance in life sometimes right, so I asked whether I could go through with Paul to the studio, and of course he said yes. Well it caused quite the commotion and hubbub as you can imagine, a real frisson of excitement, I love a frisson, one senior exec who I half recognised said 'Ooh look what the cat dragged in.' Yeah great joke fuck face, you're still in the same job 20 years later. Anyway cut to the chase, I walk over to Hislop, sitting behind his little desk, revising his jokes that have been written down for him by Shaun Pye. He nearly choked on his Earl Grey. 'Well this is a surprise Prime Minister, hello,' he stumbled, 'are you looking to come on the programme again?' I took a moment, because I wanted to get this right. I had thought about this moment for the best part of a quarter of a century. I looked down on his balding pate and said to him, with complete and utter serenity, 'Ian, I despise you. You are everything that is bad with comedy, and indeed humanity. You are

RESUЯЯECTION

the reason, Ian, why the whole Government now hates the Arts and will soon end the Arts because it is full of silver-spoon fed, unfunny, untalented, unworthy cunt-spawn like you.' And I'll never forget what he said for as long as I live. He looked up at me, like the pathetic man he will always be and just said one word… 'Allegedly.' I then went in for the kill. And this is what I kind of regret now, I said to him 'That said, I've bought you a present, because sitting near you all those years ago and standing next to you now I remember, you stink, you stink of actual shit.' It's totally true, he does stink. I mean he reeks mainly of a complete lack of talent, but also just plain body odour. So I handed him a small bottle, something Evgeny gave me for later, to use only in emergency. Oh God, what have I done, it's aftershave, laced with Novichok. Oh God, I ran out of that studio, I think I've just killed Ian Hislop. And maybe the guy next to him, and as luck would have it that was DJ Nihal Arthanayake. Oh God, I'm panicking now. As I said a while back, I need to focus. I've killed Hislop and now I shall save the world. As Vinnie Jones once said, it's been emotional.

Right, well I'm sorry, I keep saying 'it's been emotional' and then nothing happens. I'm back at Downing Street and would you believe nothing has happened, nothing. Dommers is here. Sedwill, all the Russian doctors. I don't know what's going on now, Alexander and Evgeny said they'd called it off for today, we would try again tomorrow. But they didn't speak on the way back, they didn't speak at all, they looked scared. I'm scared. More tomorrow, I'm so fucking scared.

Friday October 9th 2020

Right, this is my last diary entry. Yep, quite a shock to me too. I shall do this entry and then I shall send off to the publishers as planned, saying that this has been written by the comedian Nathan Cassidy. I hope it works out for him. I really do. I've checked out some of his stuff online and it looks pretty good actually. I'd say he is as good as Chris Rock, perhaps better.

238

Well here goes, first things first, I didn't kill Ian Hislop. Perhaps the only regret of my life. He'll be on *Have I Got News For You* as normal this evening, shitting into the ears of the Great British public. But fortunately I won't be here. Well I will, but I won't.

Everyone was in one room last night – the doctors, Evgeny, Alexander, Dommers, Sedwill and they told me how it was. There are things you can no longer control. Evgeny and Alexander wanted to put this message out last night but the BBC would not allow it, they wouldn't allow something that they should never have even known about. I told Evgeny I could just stick it out on twitter and everyone laughed and just said I would look like a nutcase. A conspiracy nut-job. So I said, well what can we do? And they said nothing, Putin knows that I know and he will get to me, this is the end for me. If Putin really wants you dead, then that is the end. I tried to argue and said that his track record in Salisbury and with Alexei Navalny wasn't great - he was in essence, a really shit killer that never quite got it right and ended up just giving people horrible perfume or horrible cups of tea, and they laughed again and said they wouldn't make that mistake with me. So again, I said, what is the alternative?

Doctor Connor was there and he then took over. He assured me that the cloning was still a possibility. They had taken all the necessary cells and if I died then there was a good chance I would live on, with Dominic. I said I didn't want to live on with Dominic, he had betrayed me. Doctor Connor said 'how?' And I said nothing. To be honest I still wasn't sure. And Dommers turned to me, in front of everyone in the room, and said 'Boss, I love you, I haven't betrayed you, I've done all this for you boss.' I knew what he meant, the cunt, I think, I was confused. So confused, so scared. And I told the Doctor that I did not want to die, that was the main thing, was there any way that I could live on. And that's when Doctor Connor laid it out for me – he said for years GSK along with Russian assistance had been working on technology to totally replace someone but to keep them alive. I said, 'What like Ben Warner has been doing with Deep Fake?' Ben and his brother laughed but were half on their phones and not really listening. 'Yes', said Doctor Connor, 'but we have gone

one step further than that, we can replace you in real life.' 'How so?' I shuddered. It is a technique that has previously only existed in film Prime Minister, in fantasy…'. And that's when he said it… 'Have you seen the movie *Face/Off?*' 'Erm, yes, I think I have, Dominic told me to watch it… the one with John Travolta and…'. 'Nicolas Cage,' interjected Dommers. 'That's right.' 'Well someone could become you Prime Minister, for real. The operation would be done overnight and there is a healing process of course which takes time but in that interim period everything has been set up by Ben Warner to replace you, until such a time that you are replaced in real life. And that person will be you, and will face the sniper's bullet when that time comes, and you will live on.' I obviously thought they were taking the piss, and this was a prank. But then Carrie walked in. 'I think you should do it fatty'. How did she know? Why was she still calling me fatty? I've lost so much weight, I'm as thin now as…

And that's when I said, 'But who would willingly step into my shoes, to take that bullet for me?' And of course, Dommers… 'Me boss, I'll do it for you boss, I love you.' The doctors then told me that because of the transfusions and the mixing of the blood our bodies were now completely ready medically for the procedure to be carried out that evening. 'So Dominic Cummings becomes me, and I become who… Dommers?! No way, no fucking way… the one person in the world who is more loathed than me!' I shouted. 'But this is perfect boss don't you see, I would do this for you, the ultimate sacrifice.' 'No, no way' I spluttered. 'But we have shared so much boss, if you know what I mean…'. There it was – light as day – the balls of the man - the blackmail, the shit, the about to reveal that I have sucked that horrible cunt's filthy penis. 'There is an alternative Prime Minister', said Doctor Connor, 'you become….

'Me', he said.

'What?'

'Think about Prime Minister, just for a moment, this is what you have always wanted – respect of the community, retirement, and love of a

RESUЯRECTION

wife, and a daughter, who know nothing about this, and would just carry on loving you, you'd be so loved.'

Mark Sedwill. 'And you've always fancied my wife Boris.'

'So hang on, if I'm getting this straight. Dommers becomes me, I become Sedwill and Sedwill becomes…'

'Me,' said Dommers, said the boss.

At that moment, it all became clear. Every step, every twist and turn was always ending here, as the clock clicked forward to the 10th of the 10th, just like he told me. Watch that film he told me, there he was, hiding, as he always has done, and now as he always will, in plain sight.

I first turned to Alexander and Evgeny and asked them which bits were true, was anything true? Evgeny looked at me sheepishly and said, 'Prime Minister, you know how it is.' He looked at me then just like he looked at that wolf, I was dead.

And finally, one last word with Carrie. I shook my head and said , 'Really, you agreed to this?' And she looked down for a moment and looked back up at me and said something I will never, ever forget, for as long as I live as Mark Sedwill. She said 'You've always fancied Mark Sedwill's wife, now's your chance. Bit of fun isn't it, that's life isn't it for you Boris, just a bit of fun.'

I looked back at her, she knows me so well. And then I stared around the room. They all stared at me, waiting for the big speech, the big moment of defiance. But you want the truth, at that moment those nurses' names came back to me – Jenny and Luis – and call me a simple man but yes, I do really want to bang Sedwill's wife. So weighing that against having my face torn off and placed on Dominic Cumming's body, and his face torn off and put on Sedwill's and Sedwill's face torn off and put on mine, well it really was a no brainer. I'm joking of course, this is all a joke. Written by Nathan Cassidy.

But I will say one thing before I go, you may not believe me, but I did my best. I always did my very best. That's the only truth I've ever uttered. I did my best to make a difference, I did my best with this one chance I've had. My only regret - I was compliant, compliant to that one person I thought was my boss. He's not my boss, all of us are our own boss, to do as we please and crucially, to believe what we want, and not what we are told. I may have someone else's face by tomorrow, but I will always have my own mind. And I ask, how many of you can say the same?

Sunday October 11th 2020

Hey guys and gals. Resurrection day. You strapped in? Now the fun really starts! Yours forever and ever, the boss xxxx

RESUЯЯECTION

RESUЯЯECTION

FЯOM THE AUTHOЯ

Nathan Cassidy is an award-winning stand-up comedian and writer.

See his clips, live dates and more at www.nathancassidy.com

Also by Nathan Cassidy:

BOOKS

The Cure for the Common Cold
Believing in God
If… I Caused the Financial Crash of 2008

PLAYS

Double Murder
F-List Celebrity
The Cure for the Common Cold
Watch this. Love me. It's deep.

FILMS

I am Orig

MUSICALS

DIY-The Musical

PODCASTS

Psycomedy
Daily Notes

Twitter: @nathancassidy
Instagram: @thenathancassidy
Facebook: Nathan Cassidy Comedian

Printed in Great Britain
by Amazon

12901830R00140